A TR[illegible]
BEYOND
FULL

A TRUTH BEYOND FULL

ROSIE OLIVER

Elsewhen Press

A Truth Beyond Full

First published in Great Britain by Elsewhen Press, 2024
An imprint of Alnpete Limited

Elsewhen Press, PO Box 757, Dartford, Kent DA2 7TQ
www.elsewhen.press

British Library Cataloguing in Publication Data.
A catalogue record for this book is available from the British Library.

ISBN 978-1-915304-48-3 Print edition
ISBN 978-1-915304-58-2 eBook edition

Designed and formatted by Elsewhen Press

To my late husband, Chris Oliver, who encouraged me to write science fiction.

CHAPTER 1

Priest Kylone enjoys these grey Mirandan dawns. Nobody is around and the only noise is the susurration of the air system. He leans forward with elbows on the balcony's handrail and hands clasped in front to stare through the clear chapel wall at the cratered ice plain. Ghostly light streams are thrown over the surface's jagged horizon from the daylight creeping round on the planet's dark orb above him. His breathing deepens and slows, helping him to induce a trance-like state. It will lead to an inner peace that lets him survive the rest of the day, face those horrors of his past that refuse to be forgotten and wash out the pent-up anger, frustration and self-hate lingering from yesterday. Others have learnt to leave him alone at this time of day. Breathe in, out, in, out.

Muffled footsteps of someone climbing the stairs towards him. Their gait is familiar, the Archdeacon's. Breathe out, in. She stops beside him. Without turning, he says, "To what do I owe the honour of this visit so early in the morning?"

"It's time." Her clasped hands extend over the bannister in a similar position to his. "To expand the range of your duties."

His view shrinks from the plain onto the black of a crater slightly to the right. His breathing rate increases and his heart beats against his ribcage. "I'm happy plodding along here."

"I'm sure. But what will you do when you finish that crystal mosaic, in six-months' time, a year at the most?"

Kylone looks to the half complete mosaic to his right beyond the altar. Even with only some of the crystals able to reflect the darker shades of grey, the characteristic outline of the lower parts of Verona Rupes' sheer ice cliffs can be seen. The work has to be slow: the crystals have to be set exactly right to get them to change during Uranus' dusk crescent from clear, white and greys to what happens during the real valley's Greening. "Up to eighteen months. That work is tricky. After that?" He pauses. "Maybe extend my caretaker duties."

"How? Clean this chapel twice in the day instead of once? I'm sure we can find better things to do with your time."

His shoulders tense up as he turns to face her, a shadowy silhouette in the dimness. "You know I'm not able to…" He still cannot mention anything about working or even going down the mines without tears welling up in his eyes.

"I do. I'm not going to ask you to do something you can't cope with."

His shoulders stay taut. Whatever she has in mind, it will upset him. He waits.

"You've come a long way already. You may remember it as a long painful step by step haul through darkness, but your depression is all but cured."

"I—"

She holds up her hand to silence him. "It's time to move on to curing your phobia, your dread."

Kylone straightens up and grips onto the balustrade as if it is a safety line. Another fear, one he could not face up to these past ten years and still cannot speak of, surfaces to knot up his stomach and make him sweat in the cool air. "Our rules of obligation will lead to…"

"Like everyone else where you have your own need, you can assert an obligation on others."

"But I'm a priest."

"Yes, greater things are expected of us, but no, not to the complete ruination of any single priest, acolyte or volunteer. This includes you. It's why we train, and you have trained well. Otherwise, I would not have endorsed you as a priest."

He shakes his head. "You don't understand."

"Now that's an interesting word. What does it exactly mean? Does it mean clear thought that implies something about the real world? Could it be aligning emotionally with what you're concentrating on? Or might it even be part of your soul, pushing you to intuitively resonate with whatever?"

Kylone wonders what the answer could be. He smiles. "That old distraction trick."

"The fact that it worked should tell you something."

It does: his fear can be overcome. For now he lets the word, rockborne, slip through his mind. Just a slight drying of his mouth, but he can cope with that. He reminds himself he once was rockborne, able to read how the strata would continue on behind a rock-face. His hands tremble. He grips the handrail so tightly that his hands go numb.

He forces himself to look back over the plain onto the dawn's grey light streams. His focus falls on a distant ice hummock crowned in silver light. He compels his breathing to slow down.

What to him seems like unknown time later but can only judging by the progress of the dawn be a few minutes, he feels calm enough to let go of the handrail and looks at Archdeacon Ariadne. While the outlines of her face, lips and hair in a bun are distinct and much darker than her skin, the whites of her eyes gleam with reflected dawn-light. He catches a glint of milkiness in her pupils, but puts it down to an optical illusion.

She stares at him intently, then nods. "You've identified the new extended limits of subject areas you can deal with, haven't you?"

"Nice neutral way of putting it. Yes."

"Good. Can you talk to miners?"

"If they don't talk about my past."

"Then I have just the job for you. Miner Raoul Larsson is being given a hero's funeral. I want you to lead the service."

Even he, tucked away in this high up chapel, has heard about him. The hero had saved his fellow miners by holding open their escape route while their mine flooded with liquid oxygen, but at the cost of his own life. This is all he knows. He has deliberately not delved into more details to avoid triggering his depression. Now, thanks to the Archdeacon's shove, he realises he can. "It would be an honour, but I know nothing about the order of service."

"Neither did I when I took my first hero's funeral. You'll find it is steeped in tradition and very ritualistic, something that will appeal to your meticulous mind. Look up and memorise the details."

He nods and then frowns. "But–"

She waves her hand to quieten him. "The interaction with miners follows a script, except after the funeral toast. Even then, the choices are very limited. Just say the right phrases at the right times. Nothing more. Approach the funeral the way you work on that mosaic."

He glances at the grey crystals. They are brighter and more of them can be seen. The completed parts of the ice-cliffs have more detail, but are still shrouded in shadows. It is as if their enlightenment reflects his own, which nudges up his confidence.

"I was going to ask something else," Kylone says. "Why me? Why not a senior priest? I'm sure this is not just to help me out of my rut."

She stares out at the plain. "It's complicated."

"How?"

"By favouring a junior priest, I'm not showing any preference among the senior ones. The battle for my succession has started. You won't see anything in public. It's all whispers in dark corners. This will stop the secret in-fighting becoming an open brawl for now."

"That sounds like common sense. What else is there?"

"The widow, Alva Larsson, she's not a member of the congregation, yet his family is. Some seniors would not accept the commission because of her. You taking the service avoids the debate."

Kylone goes back to resting his elbows on the handrail and staring at the brighter and more subtly shaded ice plain. "Devious as ever. No wonder you ended up being Archdeacon."

She laughs. Her footsteps fade away down the stairs.

Patches of ice have turned bright. He has to squeeze his eyes shut against the glare. It is no use. His peace cannot be recaptured. He straightens up and walks along the balcony to his cubbyhole office to find out how to run a hero's funeral.

***

The shrink-wrapped body of Miner Raoul Larsson lies on top of the flat white ice in a five centimetre deep grave. He is dressed in his hero's charcoal-grey one-piece silk, gloves and ankle-high boots. On his right shoulder lies his hero's badge of honour, a diamond with four nested black-and-white chevrons holding a smaller black diamond, representative of Miranda's Inverness Coronae. His head, like all miners', is shaved and his eyes are closed. The only colour to be seen on his face is in his lips, which in the glow from Uranus above are grey-black.

His wife, Alva Larsson, a diminutive figure in her snug-fitting white spacesuit, stands at the head of the grave. She stares at the body, never lifting her head, only her tightly French-plaited black hair can be seen. One step behind her is a man with a similar colouring and bone structure, clearly a blood relative.

Kylone stands quietly at the foot of the grave holding a priest's staff and waits for the signal to begin the interment. He glances along the thirty-three mourners clustered in groups along one side. Gaps between them mean there is likely to be *arguments* among them, or inward-looking cliques. He is thankful for the ceremony's formality: it will prevent any public overspill.

The man steps forward and places his arm around Alva's waist to comfort her. He then looks up and nods at Kylone.

Kylone bows in response. "Dust to dust, void to void, ice to ice," he intones over the spacesuits' comms, steps to the clear side of the grave and bends the staff to form an L.

He positions its horizontal bar above Raoul's feet and

twists the knob at the staff's top. A fine spray of holy water spurts out from the level bar, some evaporating upwards and away in a thin white mist, the rest jetting downwards. He slowly skim-walks along the length of the grave to cover the body in a sheet of whitened ice. He reaches the side of Alva, straightens and locks his staff, bows to her and waits.

The mourners turn to Alva and also wait, standing up straight out of respect.

She stares at the covered grave, as if she were the one who was frozen in place.

Eventually, her blood relative steps back. "Come on, Sis. Let's get you back inside."

She does not budge. Her shoulders shake in time to the gentle sobs coming over the comms.

Kylone being next to her sees tears bulging their way out of her closed eyes slowly expanding into pools on her cheeks. He understands her pain from when he lost his fiancée and wants to comfort her. As the funeral priest, he is not allowed to. It has to be left to someone else. He discreetly looks away to make eye contact with her brother and flicks his eyes across to her.

Her brother nods slightly and hugs her shoulders. "There is nothing more you can do for him."

Her sobs become quieter and less frequent. She turns away from the grave and slowly walks down the smoothed ice path towards the shuttle, her feet dragging. Her brother walks close behind her.

Kylone watches the other mourners fall into line to follow them at a respectful distance and pace. As Alva turns towards the waiting shuttle she stops to look back. The procession halts. She shakes her head and continues on her way, but with her shoulders drooped and head bowed forward.

Kylone is the last to leave and the last through the shuttle's shimmering door, a plasma sheet that makes stepping through easy while stopping the shuttle's air escaping into the vacuum. The remote chance of power and hence door failure encourages him to keep his visor closed, like the others on board. He does a quick passenger headcount. They are all inside. He places his staff carefully in a locker above their heads and turns the door switch. Solid safety doors slide into place and, as one, all except Alva remove their helmets. Her brother nudges her. She too removes hers to reveal her large tear pools, which she wipes with a napkin taken from a holdall beside her seat. Her strained face is almost white against her black hair.

Even now, Kylone is not allowed to comfort her. "Are we all ready to go back?"

"Would you," she whispers and pauses to take a deep breath. "Would you fly us along the Heroes Path please, for Raoul's sake?"

A murmur of approval rises from most on board. The exception is a grey-haired older woman sitting across the aisle from the wife, glowering at her. She says nothing.

Whatever the right or wrong of the issue between the two women, Kylone is thankful it must remain silenced as part of the funeral etiquette. Nevertheless, he decides to keep an eye on them. He formally bows to the wife and then all the passengers. "I would deem it a privilege to do so, Wife Alva and esteemed bereaved."

Kylone takes the pilot's seat at the front of the cabin. After the safety checks, he dims the lights, gently lifts and flies forward. Across the wide pitted plain, a steel-grey slope juts up, diminishing to a point on both its left and right. On it, charcoal lines demarcating light grey triangles makes them look like a pair of partly unfolded fans meeting at their outer edges. They appear so small, yet he knows these fan blades are the tiers of the high cliffs of the Inverness Coronae.

He turns the shuttle again, to fly above the gently climbing ice-path. A dull pewter-grey cliff, the lowest and outermost one of the Arden Coronae, looms before him. At its foot and parallel to it are rows of ice graves, like that of Raoul's. The closer the graves are to the cliff, the greyer they are as they have had longer for space dust to fall on them.

He switches on the video. Most passengers will view it on upright screens on the backs of the seats. The front row will see it on tables pushed out before them. He could view it on his flight console, but chooses not to. He fears it will be too painful for him.

The video is a roll call of the names, heroic deeds and photos of each one of the Heroes buried here. The first and oldest is Helmut Schmidt, an ice-miner who torched into an ice-fault, which exploded on him from pressure of hidden gases, ripping his suit to shreds. That was over two centuries ago. Ever since, miners have been careful to measure fault stresses before lighting up their torch-lasers to slice into the ice.

Kylone mentally salutes most heroes. The few who used their rockborne gift to save others makes his eyes well up. He bites his lips to distract himself from his sadness and concentrates on flying the shuttle past the graves in synchronisation with the roll call, zigzagging it down the slope.

He turns the shuttle to face along the next to last row, where all twenty recent graves have the sheen of new ice. The oldest of these died less than fifteen years ago. He puts the greater number of accidents down to mining deeper in more difficult conditions. They have living wives, husbands, parents, children and siblings, who have gone through the process of losing someone special, just like Alva with Raoul, and him with his own fiancée, Selma. All the grief is swirling around in the hubs and tunnels. Yet, he has seen very few signs of it. The relatives and friends must be keeping it to themselves.

The realisation shocks him into numbness.

It is only three graves into the row when he realises he should be farther on. He gently accelerates the shuttle forward and concentrates on getting the timing right. The turn into the last row happens at last.

Kylone stops the shuttle at the 105th and newest grave. The voices of the different priests, many of them now dead themselves, fall silent as the roll call comes to an end. He must now add to the record. He wonders if people in the future will only focus on his words as an echo from the past, and not on him as a living breathing person.

"Miner Raoul Larsson," he pauses and wants to choke, "Iceborne." He continues with as much dignity as he can muster. "Your talent warned you of a liquid oxygen flood in time for you to hold the flood debris at bay, and enable your mining crew to get clear. But there was no escape for you. Hero, rest alongside your comrades in peace." He lets the shuttle linger as he darkens the portholes and screens, but leaves the front window clear.

The waiting silence lets him think back to Selma's funeral. She had a simple service in the miners' chapel, followed by interment in the new orchard tunnel. It was all over within an hour. He had needed to stay longer, to grieve more. But there was no chance. He wants to grieve all over again, to hide behind his own tear-pools. He closes his eyes, breathes deeply and slowly until he is quite some way into a trance, like Priest Patricianna taught him. Once calm enough, he opens his eyes and brightens the cabin lights behind him.

He flies the shuttle to the nearest hub, which is farther along the bottom of Arden cliff. He docks with the gate, stands, opens the door and waits.

The mourners leave the shuttle in dribs and drabs, colleagues and distant friends first, filing past Kylone as he acknowledges each in turn with a small bow. A woman stops in front of him with a frown of puzzlement. Signs of age disguise her so much that Kylone does not immediately recognise her: Helena Tyndale, Lenny to her friends, a scavenger on his old mining crew. Her eyes widen in astonishment. Finally, she nods and holds out her hand. He stares at it, disbelieving of the offer of friendship, especially after… He dare not think about it. They shake hands briefly and she walks through the gate.

He focuses on the other mourners as they leave the shuttle until only four are left: Alva, her brother, the white-haired woman who had not approved of the flypast and a younger brown-haired version of her. The young woman is up and about to step off the shuttle, but turns. "Mother, the others are waiting."

The white-haired lady stands to face Alva. "It's regrettable he had to do extra mining shifts to make ends meet, or he would not have been down there when the ice cracked open."

Alva jerks her head round to glare at her. "That's not true."

"Mother, please."

Rising tension and frustration is all around. Kylone has to intervene. "We all wish Miner Raoul Larsson was still alive."

The elderly woman blushes. "You'll have to forgive me, Priest, but a mother should not have to lose her son."

"A hero will never be forgotten." He bows as the mother rushes past him and her daughter out of the door.

The young woman hurries after her.

The brother gets up. "It is only her grief talking." He offers to help Alva out of her seat.

She bows her head and does not move.

She does nothing, her stasis imbuing stillness into all around her. Kylone knows the darkness of this mood too well, the hurt she needs to cringe away from, no matter how small, because she has reached her psyche's limit. If pushed over it, she must sink deeper to cut herself off from the rest of the world or go insane. He gives her as much time as he dares before intervening. "The mourning guests are waiting."

After a couple of seconds, she takes a deep breath and gets up without any help. Her brother stares at her as if asking *can you cope?* Her lips tightly sealed, she nods her head to indicate he should lead the way off the shuttle. He does exactly that.

Kylone follows a respectful few steps behind Alva out of the shuttle, through the short corridor with its safety doors open and into a room carved into the grey ice with bench seats round the walls.

A waitress in full black stands just inside the gate holding out a tray. On it is single remaining small ice-glass of firewater beside a small pile of black serviettes. Kylone picks the glass up with a serviette and waits for the mumbles to die down.

He lifts his glass. "Raise your glasses."

The mourners follow suit.

"Miner Raoul Larsson," he says in a clear voice.

The mourners chorus his words and drink their firewater in one gulp. Kylone is the last to do so. The liquid burns its way down his throat. One after another they throw their glasses onto the floor to shatter their ice.

Some mourners leave immediately, grinding down the ice-shards. Most go up to Alva to offer their condolences and help if she needs it. Some say the funeral has done Raoul proud. Finally there is only Alva and her brother left. Kylone retreats diplomatically back into the shuttle to retrieve his staff from the locker. He waits so they have chance to say whatever they need to. He hears footsteps scrunching ice fade away. When he returns only Alva remains.

"I did not realise you were still here," she says.

He gives the expected reply. "As a priest, I have a duty to ensure all mourners are given the necessary solace. That is why we are always last to leave."

"Of course," she says softly.

"I cannot help but notice you have been left without anyone to comfort you. You are welcome to stay at our Sanctuary, if it will help come to terms with your loss."

She hesitates. "I appreciate the offer, but no thank you."

"Our door will remain open to you for the next twelve weeks."

"I really ought to make my own way in the world."

Kylone bows his head. "As you wish, Widow Alva Larsson."

***

Kylone half sleepwalks in the near darkness of the corridor from his condo towards his place of peace on the balcony. Rapid tip-taps of slippered feet from someone in a hurry get louder. He pauses to rub his eyes to encourage the fug in his mind to vanish.

The running stops. "There you are, Priest Kylone," the familiar voice of Acolyte Thyone says.

Kylone drops his hands away. She stands in front of him, her white hair tied in a net and one-piece silk shining out of the dark. Her phosphorescent silk blatantly advertising wealth and presence repels him. This new fashion is one he will happily see the back of. At least she can be seen from some distance away in these dim tunnels.

"I'm glad to catch you," she continues. "Your counsel has been requested by a non-congregant." The last word is spat out as if poison.

Her nastiness is enough to sting him into being careful. "Who?"

"Widow Alva Larsson."

Dawn on the balcony pulls at him. "She didn't ask for sanctuary?"

"Why would she?"

"Sounds like bereavement counselling then. Priest Patricianna is better suited. Would you…" He notices her right hand move onto her hip into the akimbo position of exasperation. "Did she request me by name?"

"Why else would I leave reception?"

Today's bad start makes him so uneasy that he expects things to get worse. "Is she there?"

"Yes."

No other choice is left. "Would you be so good as to bring refreshments to counselling room three please?" He hates being prim and proper, but it is the only way to guarantee her help. She has a reputation for avoiding work that cannot be seen by other members of the priesthood, and being High Priest Diomedes' daughter, most times gets away with it.

"I would be honoured to be of assistance." She marches with hunched shoulders back along the corridor.

He follows until he has to turn left into another

corridor. Just before he opens the safety door to the well-lit reception, he composes himself into the calm authority of a priest, like he has been taught. Once inside, he checks who is behind the welcome desk running most of the length of the room to another safety door at the other end. Nobody.

Alva in a farm-worker's slate-grey silk is the only other person there, sitting on the farther of the two settees that are either side of a third door opposite the desk. She immediately stands. Dark circles under her eyes contrast with her tightened white face. Wisps of loosened black hair break up the strictness of her appearance. She elegantly bows. "Good morning, Priest Kylone. It is good of you to see me at such short notice. I would be grateful for some of your counsel."

He bows in return. "I am honoured you should ask me, Widow Alva Larsson. But may I recommend some of our other Priests who are more experienced than I in helping the bereaved."

"Thank you, but I do not seek counsel for bereavement. I have other concerns. If we could speak privately perhaps?"

The surprise of being consulted on unexpected matters almost makes him drop his priestly mask of understated kindliness. "Certainly. I have just now reserved a counselling room. Would that suit your needs?"

"Very much so."

"If you would care to come this way?" He goes to the other end of the welcome desk to open the safety door. Once he sees her coming towards him he turns to lead the way through the dimly lit corridor, through double doors into the back of the chapel and up the stairs onto the balcony. He glances up at the ceiling with its grey streams of light, but dares not look directly out through the clear wall to watch the dawn for fear of distraction.

The footsteps behind him stop. "It's beautiful," Alva says.

He twists round. She stands in the middle of a silver stream of light, staring at the ice plain. Her face and silk outshine the darkness around her. She is smiling. Her delicate features remind him of his lost love. Tears sting his eyes as he recalls how Selma outshone the other girls at a kaffeeklatsch when he walked through the Court Plaza. He needs to stop admiring Alva to prevent more tears. "I know. We could stay here to watch the planet's dawn if you wish to delay our discussion."

Her smile fades. "Maybe another time. I need to be at work by nine."

He nods, sad his new hope of watching the dawn has died. "Shall we?" He leads the way to the end of the balcony and opens the door to a small room with two armchairs on either side of a low table. A vacuum flask labelled 'hot water' beside a dish holding an assortment of fruit and herbal teabags and two cups is inviting.

As they settle and make their tea, raspberry leaf for her, peppermint for him, he says: "The offer of sanctuary is still open to you, if you wish to change your mind, and will be for the next ten weeks."

"Thank you, but I would rather not." She falls silent, her face becomes solemn as she looks down, apparently into nowhere, and turns her cup this way and that.

He waits for her to say more, but hears only her silence. "I can see something other than your grief is troubling you."

She stops handling her cup and looks up straight into his eyes. "It's about Raoul."

"You did everything you could for him. Rest assured, nobody could have done more." He knows these are standard phrases, but nevertheless hopes they will give her some comfort.

"Not quite everything."

Another surprise. "Oh?"

"Someone… someone suggested he died when he shouldn't have… sorry, this isn't coming out right."

"Take your time."

She presses her lips together.

"When did you start thinking something was wrong?"

"I can't really explain, not without breaking promises."

"Ah. How about stating the problem without explaining why you think it exists?"

She takes a sip of tea. "It's rather… dramatic, maybe even unbelievable."

His mind rushes through wild explanations: murder, cover-up for Chynoweth Mining Corp's crimes or sabotage by a rival mining company. These situations are very unlikely on Miranda, but possible, and he wants nothing to do with them. Yet he must deal with them if any turn out to be the case. Has to; they have all been included in the Priesthood's training. He hopes he will not fail her. He notices she has again fallen silent. "Use your own words."

She gulps. "I need the truth about why my husband died."

The unusual word is *why*, not the expected *how*. "You're not talking about the actual flood and subsequent cave-in here, are you?" He does not want to add the details of the horror: the disaster abruptly turned so violent that it threw sharp obsidian shards at Raoul fast enough to pierce his miners' spacesuit.

"No. About what caused them."

This conversation could lead to awkward subjects, ones he cannot face talking about – like being rockborne. But they have not reached there, yet. "Any one of a dozen natural phenomena could have led to that flood. Sometimes the reason might never be found."

"That's what they say. I'm talking about something else… they had a term for it at the dawn of the Space Age… the bigger picture."

"Contributory factors? The Coroner would have looked into that as a matter of routine. He found none."

"She, not he. I'm sure she did her best. Just… I keep thinking about all those new white graves in the Heroes Gallery. Why are there so many?"

"May their souls rest in peace. I'm still not sure what you're getting at here." He stares at her intensely looking for a clue, no matter how minute.

"The mining activity has been roughly at the same level

for nine generations or so. Nothing's changed, except the number of accidents and deaths. Why? It doesn't make any sense."

He is thankful her questions have avoided anything close to what he once was and can never be again. "There could be many reasons. An obvious one is the easy extractions would have been done first. Now they have to dig deeper into more difficult formations. It's bound to be more dangerous."

"That's not the way Raoul told it. He always said mining was as easy as in his grandfather's day. The techniques are certainly the same as they were over a century ago."

Kylone does his best to hide his surprise. He had never read up on Mirandan mining history; he had been too busy mining before his own personal disaster, and afterwards avoided the subject altogether.

"The number of miners is still roughly the same," she continues. "Yet there're more graves. I've really come to ask if the rules for acceptance into the Heroes Gallery have recently changed."

"No. Haven't for 219 years." He pauses to think of other possibilities, but cannot identify anything sensible. "Accidents are random events. Always have been. We could be having a run of bad luck at the moment. Or, the early days had a run of good luck."

"Too many coincidences for that. Isn't the Priesthood also our *Guardian of History*? Wouldn't you automatically be looking for such trends?"

This whole conversation has shifted from under his guidance. He eyes her up and down: she is determined, has good reasoning and is confident despite losing her husband. What is wrong is her wearing a farmhand's slate grey silk. "That's very perceptive of you."

She inhales sharply. "Maybe I stumbled across something."

He recalls her mother-in-law's comments. This could be guilt talking. He feels too out of his depth, even helpless, to unravel what is going on with her and has to act with the blandness psychoanalysts would instinctively use. "I'm sure our experts will have identified any correlations with other mining aspects by now."

"You would think so," she persists, "but they haven't proved it's a run of bad luck, have they?"

He knows the answer. Everybody at school is taught why, including Alva. The only way to prove a sequence of events is not random is to find out what the common cause of those events is. Occasionally those causes can be extremely hard to identify, which makes proving true randomness impossible. "Why have you really come to see us, I mean me?"

"I want to know *why* Raoul died."

"I don't see how—"

"I want you to do a trend analysis. It's too late for Raoul, but it may possibly save lives in the future."

This argument demands his attention. To act upon it could lead him down the dark paths he is still not ready for. If necessary, Priest Patricianna will help. She had done so when he had eventually investigated the causes of his own accident: bottom line, it had been unpredictable and nobody was to blame. "I can search our archives for any analysis our Priests may have undertaken, but our Guardians lock down results they're uncertain about. They don't want false facts to become embedded into societal values and doctrine. Takes at least three generations to correct and as for the damage some of them cause…"

"I want the truth not guesses, no matter how shrewd they are."

"Then I have no problem with looking into the matter, but I don't expect to find anything new." She has dragged him to this conclusion along a line of clear logic, even with its twists and turns into a strangeness he had not expected, much stranger than going forward on a path and ending up where you started.

An image flashes into his mind of the first gem he helped uncover: an eight-shaped milk-coloured strip with a twist in it. When he ran his finger over its glassy surface it eventually came back to the spot he started. Only violent volcanic processes could have formed such a one-dimensional shape, which had lain buried in the asteroid that had become part of Miranda. He had been the one to point to the mine-face's strange lines and striations to say there was something odd underneath it. His mining crew laughed at him because he was only an apprentice. However, their team captain, Meriel, gave him one of her classical quizzical looks and ordered them to take things real easy. They ended up getting the Moebius strip shaped gem out in perfect condition, which landed them with a good bonus. This was the first hint of him being rockborne, that strange ability to see behind a mine-face.

He suppresses anything to do with his ex-talent, fast.

"You really are far too smart for a farmhand. Why haven't you got a better job?"

She stares into the nearly empty cup in her hand. "I couldn't get one."

He lets his silence encourage more comment from her.

"Let's just say," she continues at last, "I'm known to lie out of habit."

"Really?" He narrows his eyes. "Those who persistently lie are trying to make life easier for themselves. None of what you have said today points to that. In fact you've refused sanctuary twice. No, you've been telling the truth. So were you a liar once?"

"Does it matter?"

"Not to me, but it may to you."

She slams her cup onto the table. "Let's just say I saw things others couldn't and leave it at that."

He has pushed her too far. "I understand your reluctance. Is there anything else I may offer help with?"

"No. No, thank you. I must go or I'll be late for work."

He stands and bows. "Of course. I hope I have been of service to you."

"I hope you will be. I can find my own way out." She stands to return the bow and leaves.

He stares at the now closed door and slumps back into

his armchair. Normally Mirandans are straightforward, with one, maybe two, traits that are the opposite of what they appear. That's what defines a person. But Alva has more: branded a liar while being honest; too smart for her farmhand job; refusing the help of sanctuary in their survivalist society; and should be in deep grief, yet carrying on as if she has lost a friend instead of a husband.

***

Kylone has spent a week of his spare time looking into Alva's problem, but not found anything unusual. He is thankful his normal routine of duties remains unchanged and finds their repetitiveness absorbing, like now.

Light streams into the chapel from a full day-lit Uranus with its awe-inspiring display of interlocking bands and vortices. He ignores it, instead concentrating on the grey trilliant-cut crystals laid out in a display drawer resting on his workbench. Of those closest to the desired mid-grey, he checks their exact colour against a shade card. Three are very close: one that is just a tinge lighter and a bit too small; one that is the right size, but a bit darker; and one that is exactly the right shade and size, but has a noticeable thread-like inclusion. None are satisfactory, but these are all that are available.

Holding it up to look through the inclusioned gem at the blank upper wall above the mosaic, he twists the gem round until the disfigurement is to the left. In its proposed place, the light will be refracted through the crystal without most of the congregation noticing it. Even if it does show up, it will make it look more like the natural cliffs of Verona Rupes he wants to portray. A grunt of satisfaction slips out.

"You the man to check in with about the electrics?" a voice says from behind.

Kylone places the crystal in the bottom right corner of the drawer and turns to the stranger. He is tall, clean-shaven and slender, black hair tied loosely behind. His ash grey silk and toolbox confirms his trade. "I didn't know an electrician had been called out. And you are?"

"Isaac Hawking. Part of the on-going wiring up of your fancy picture or lightshow or whatever it's going to be."

The column of lighting, to be pulled out from beside the mosaic and switched on to replicate the light of waning Uranus, will turn the crystals from grey into the Greening colours. Kylone hates artifice of any kind and morphs the look of disgust forming on his face to one of beaming serenity. "Does this mean you want the floor in front of the mosaic to work?"

"How else do you expect me to do the lining up?"

"Of what?"

"Sensors, lights, crystals and these fluoro-cords." He holds up a thread that twinkles silver as it moves. "Ah good, you've got sufficient ultra-violet in here. Let's see what the distribution's like." He walks round waving it and ends up immediately in front of Kylone. "Please get out of my way."

"But the mosaic isn't finished."

"Don't worry, I'll be back when it's done to do the finishing touches. What I need now is a decent cup of coffee and for you to hand me the tools when I ask for them."

"How would I know one tool from another?"

"You're Priest Kylone, aren't you?"

"Yes, but–"

"Then you'll do. Where's my damned coffee?"

The frozen moment of speechlessness finally melts. He prays his exasperation with the man will not show. "You'll get it after I've cleared this workbench for you." He tidies his tools into the lockers under the bench and returns the crystal drawer into its chest on wheels, beside the mosaic.

Hawking places his toolbox on the bench and goes over to pull out the lighting column. "Milk, no sugar."

Kylone snaps his head round to comment on his bad manners and stops, staring at his pigtail hanging freely down his back, ending in a weight at his waist. His miner's caution inwardly screams unnecessary risk: such a loose end can easily get caught up in machinery or snagged on some wiring. This man is so rash and reckless; any comments would go over his head. Yet he has survived on Miranda up to now. He must have a way of avoiding it getting caught up in other objects, though Kylone is at a loss to think how. He hunkers off in search of the coffee and camomile tea for himself to soothe his own nerves.

When he returns holding two steaming mugs, one side of the toolbox has had its drawers pulled out into a series of trays displaying tiny, labelled components held in by white memory foam. There are soldering lasers, screwdrivers, pliers, chisellers, cutters, plain hooks and tools he does not recognise of various sizes. The man sits cross-legged by the pulled out lighting column, peering into the vertical recess to adjust a component's position.

"Where do you want your coffee?"

Hawking places his tool on the floor, continues to peer into the recess and swings his arm around to hold out his hand for the mug. "And bring me hook size nine-point-five. It's labelled."

Kylone swaps the hook for his own tea and walks over to hand him the coffee and tool.

Several noisy gulps and a loud exhalation come before a: "I needed that." He waves the mug at the column. "This thing is a damned waste of time."

"You could say the same for the mosaic."

"Nah. That'll act as an insulator to keep the heat in, reduce slightly the amount of air required to fill the chapel and is good therapy for you." Another few swigs and the mug is offered back up.

Kylone hesitates before swapping the hook for the mug. "How do you know about me?"

He wriggles the hook end in the recess. "Apart from the smell of the camomile tea you mean?"

"That can only be considered circumstantial at best."

"Agreed. I hacked into your personal file. I need soldering laser number eight."

Shocked, he steps over to the workbench and drinks some tea to calm himself before returning to hand over the required tool. "Any other crimes you would care to admit to?"

He guffaws. "Cool response. But no, this is not a confessional." Zits of soldering can be heard.

"Why did you do it?"

"I'm particular about who I work with." He looks up. "I don't have the patience to explain things. I can't stand fools. And your blundering statistical analysis into the miners' mortality rates is the first interesting thing I've seen in months."

Only one man on Miranda who fits this kind of behaviour pattern: Dirk Schimmeratski, Chynoweth's Chief Compineer. He is known for being impossible to work with, getting the job done and being an all out bad-tempered recluse. The rest of what has been going on starts to make sense. "So you hacked your way into making an electrician's appointment under an alias just to see how dull I really am?"

"Yes!" He grins and stands up. "Here's the deal. Once a week, you help me with this naff job," he nods to the lighting column, "and I help you with your analysis. What do you say?"

"That you're acting like a spoilt little boy who wants to play with his toys."

"Whatever. So what's your answer?"

"I'm sure you'd have more fun working through the analysis done by our Guardians of History."

"That lot! They couldn't hide a fart in a cowshed."

"Huh?"

"They're data pushers stuck in a rut using the same methods over and over again, not thinkers. You, however, ask new questions, but don't yet know which tools to apply. Do we have an agreement?"

This is a first: hearing the work of the Guardians of History being trashed. "Are you sure? Of course you are, you've been hacking them as well."

Dirk lets out a growl. "You're testing my patience."

"I am honour bound to defend the Priesthood's services."

"Only when it's justifiable."

Kylone knows the Guardians of History use their analysis to discover historical trends, which they then extrapolate into the future. If they identify potential problems, they move to avoid them, usually by getting Mirandans to change their habits. "They do provide a unique service in improving our standard of living."

"Sure they do. And yes, what they come out with is valuable and all to the good. But they could do so much better."

"You have proof?"

"Give me strength."

"Of course, more hacking." Kylone nods. "I really ought to draw this to the Archdeacon's attention."

"No. Just answer my damn question."

Kylone stares straight into his eyes. "Let me get this straight. You want to help me do the miners' mortality analysis in return for my helping you with setting up the mosaic's lighting?"

"At last!"

"I have to report the results of our studies to the history analysts, which if you're right, might put me up against them."

"Forget it." Dirk snatches his coffee from Kylone's hand, gulps the rest of it down, strides over to the workbench and starts packing up his toolbox.

Kylone's mind hurtles to a different scene.

Meriel screams the same words down his suit comms as she pulls him back from digging into the avalanche. Lights on their spacesuits show the slope of ice boulders, gravel and powdery snow-sand. Its black crevices and holes beckon him to dive in to reach Selma and the rest of their missing crew buried underneath. They have to be alive. It is his reading of the rock-face that made them change direction. He has got it wrong, horribly so.

"They're gone," Meriel shouts.

"They can't be."

She yanks him away from the debris with a surprising strength and twists him round to face her. "Listen to me. It's not your fault."

Kylone snaps back to the now, just in time before the horror of what comes next. A deep feeling of guilt stays to nag that Meriel is wrong, it was his fault and he can only find forgiveness by preventing more deaths.

"I won't." He turns to Dirk. "I'm doing the analysis, with or without your help."

"Blundering idiot."

"I might not do it as well or as quickly, but my obligations to the people requires me to try to save lives. Even if you don't have a conscience, which I suspect is very likely, your citizen's responsibility requires you to help me out."

"Taken you long enough to throw that argument at me."

Kylone accepts the comment as his agreement. "One other thing."

"Oh? Conditions?"

"A helpful one."

Dirk puts his screwdriver slowly back down on the workbench and glowers at him across the distance. "Go on."

Kylone steps over to join him. "Widow Alva Larsson brought the main anomaly to my attention. I need to keep her updated on progress."

"A farmhand? A planting and picking job done mainly by… let's call them less capable people?"

The bluntness about such unfortunates shocks him, but it is reality by many Mirandan metrics. "She's got common sense and is far too intelligent for her job."

"Really? Then why hasn't she been promoted to farm manager?"

"I'm sure your hacking skills will be able to discover the reason."

Dirk places his hands palms down on the workbench and leans towards him. "Oh, now you want me to do some detective work for you as well?"

He cocks his head to one side. "No, just confirm whether she's telling me the truth."

"That'll cost you another coffee." He holds out his mug towards Kylone.

He inwardly smiles at the way Dirk accepts jobs and finishes his own tea. "I think I can manage that." He takes the mugs to the kitchen.

When he returns, drink in hand; Dirk is kneeling to peer into the bottom of the recess of the lighting column. Finally, he sits back on his heels and stares at the mosaic. Kylone smiles. Three crystals have turned from charcoal grey to green with a shade of cyan from Uranus' light tinting it.

"Yep, going to work," Dirk says. "Now where's that coffee."

Kylone hands him the mug.

"No camomile tea this time?"

"Didn't feel the need for it."

CHAPTER 2

Dirk sits opposite Kylone in counselling room three and takes a deep breath of vapour rising from the black coffee before sipping from his cup. "Hmmm. Damned good coffee. Pity your blackcurrant tea clashes with its aroma. Next time find a more suitable flavour. Vanilla or strawberry."

"You're a caffeine junkie," Kylone replies.

"Yep. It keeps me on form."

"And you'll die early."

"Yep, but I'll have had some real fun."

"As you? Or as your alter ego pretend electrician Isaac Hawking? Isn't it about time you stopped acting like a little boy?"

"Aw! You really are a spoilsport."

"You're as stubborn as a great spot in our planet's clouds."

"Finished your due diligence of priestly warnings?"

"For now."

"Good. Let's get down to serious stuff. I've found a bizarro in the mining data."

Kylone sits forward in his armchair. "Oh?"

"Before I show you my results, let me say I did an analysis all the way back to when Talfryn Chynoweth first discovered moisannite. I've included those miners who would've most likely been in the Heroes Gallery had it existed during the asteroid rover mining and early settlement phases of the moon's history."

Kylone like every Mirandan schoolchild is aware of Chynoweth's founding. Talfryn Chynoweth had been on the run from Oberon's police when he was forced to crash land on Miranda. He found an embedded asteroid of precious moissanite in a crater, which by serendipity let him figure out how he had been framed for murder. He and his twin, Aislinn, mined that asteroid only to discover it was far bigger than they thought, so called in their family and friends with their northern European culture and practicality to help. They ended up not only founding a colony, but also became rich enough to establish the Chynoweth Corporation.

Dirk opens the table's screen onto a graph framed by a full menu of symbols for further analysis. "There's been a steepening increase in the opening up of new deposits over the last seventeen years. That's the blue line. The light green line is the number of Heroes Gallery burials and the dark green is the number of serious accidents. As you can see they both show similar ups and downs, though slightly delayed, to the opening up of deposits."

Kylone studies the graph. "In other words, the main contributor to the rise and fall of deaths is the opening of new workings. What's the red line?"

"Overall mined ore volumes. Yep. Been the same for two hundred years now. Doesn't follow the trends of new workings or accidents."

"All that shows is recent new workings don't yield as much as the old. This would happen in any mining operation."

"There's enough history and experience to know what works best in such situations. Chynoweth should be slowing down the mining, upping the prices and investing in refining the mining tech for Mirandan conditions to get at unprofitable or inaccessible ores. It's not. This all points to them running our mining down."

Kylone's mind immediately hones in on their Mirandan mantra. Their survivalist society is reliant on all of its infrastructural elements. A single major disaster affecting any one of them will lead to their colony's breakdown. Escape to the neighbouring higher gravity moons would at best cripple people. Nor can the dust miners round Uranus accommodate more than a couple of hundred in their habitats. They are stuck on this moon.

"How long before they start shutting Miranda down?"

"Judging by the accident rate, they've started. The better question is how long have we got?"

"Are you ice-ghosting?"

Dirk's look turns even more serious.

"What proof have you got?" The priest can hear his desperation slip into his own voice.

"None, as yet. What bothers me is these changes in direction occurred soon after the Chynoweth family lost control of the corporation to a hostile bid."

"This off-moon financial practices and legal governances you're talking about?"

"Yep."

"That's way beyond my understanding."

"Not surprising. Miranda doesn't have the population to need such complicated resource control mechanisms."

The comment makes Kylone wonder what Dirk did for work before he came to Miranda. It adds to the Chief Compineer's enigma.

"I need your help," Dirk continues.

"Ice dust! What can I do to help you?" He emphasises the last word.

Dirk puckers his lips as if in thought. "You're not going to like this, but I don't know anyone else who can."

Nerves tighten Kylone's throat. He wants to shout 'no', but it is strangled off.

"Details matter," he continues, "and one detail is making a hell of a difference to my analysis. I need to delve into it, to understand what's driving it, what is producing this anomaly. I know your history and I hate asking this, but I've come to a point in my analysis where I need to understand the rockborne."

There it is.

His present need brutally demanding he fully resurrect his past from its deep burial in his soul, not ignore it or leave it hidden in the subliminal edge of his thoughts.

"How they work?" Dirk urgently goes on. "When do they succeed? And so on."

"I don't understand," Kylone croaks.

"My analysis shows the rockborne were successfully countering Chynoweth's rundown until," he pauses, "until about ten years ago, roughly the same time you had your…"

The missing word is accident. Kylone is thankful Dirk's being circumspect about the terror of his past. It still hurts deeply, but he can cope with this level of indirectness.

"Something happened then," Dirk continues. "What, how and why?"

Kylone's mouth dries. His hands shake. He must face up to his curse and silently prays that he can. "I'm not able to." Miranda's future expects him to save its lives, homes and society. Its demand has to be complied with, but he cannot. "I'm well out of practice as a rockborne. Nor have I kept contact with any of them… for obvious reasons."

"I understand."

Silence.

Kylone corrals his emotional stamina enough to carry on. "What I can say is this, Widow Alva Larsson–"

"Assistant Alva Larsson."

"Huh?"

"I employed her as my assistant." He chuckles. "She's survived two days much to the surprise of the other assistants at Chynoweth's HQ."

"More hacking?"

"Damn right."

Kylone shakes his head.

"Let's take your telling me off as said."

"One day…" How can he ever make a better man of Dirk? His heart is in the right place, just his methods are wrong. "Assistant Alva Larsson pointed out her late husband," he pauses, "an iceborne himself, believed that mining methods required similar effort and were as safe as in his grandfather's day as his. Does that help?"

"Only very indirectly. I need more about…"

Kylone suddenly knows what he really wants and laughs. "You want me to introduce you to another rockborne as Isaac Hawking, your friendly electrician who has an interest in how the talent works and would like all his questions answered."

"That'd do."

"Can't."

"Why not?"

"You've got to experience it to understand it. Words can't describe how we work. We talk among ourselves by hinting and hoping the other person catches on. As for talking to strangers, we don't." It has been eight years since he talked about being a miner. Not freely or specific, only generalities for now, which is as far as he can safely go. Nevertheless, his old life feels like a favourite well-worn silk that has been taken out of storage after a long time: comfortable, familiar with happy and painful memories, yet strangely alien.

"Looks like I'll be putting in an appearance at tonight's launch toast at the Kober Balyow. I might bump into a rockborne there."

"They wouldn't open up to you. Even among non-rockborne friends we are reluctant to talk, really for fear of being seen as freaks."

"Either you or me. Getting what I need without your help will just take longer." He pulls his plait forward and strokes it. "Well, what must be will be."

Kylone relaxes. "Where's the new find?"

"Level five, Carbo mine."

"Ah." Kylone has never worked there and knows very little about it. He looks away and down. His black sleeves with thin green wristbands are the standard uniform of a Priest, a reminder of his duty to help others. Letting Dirk go alone would be shirking that duty. He knows who the older more practical rockborne are. The difficult part would be to identify one willing to talk freely to Dirk. "I suppose I could do with a change of clothes. Let me see what I can do, but it's best I go on my own."

Dirk's eyes droop and the corners of his mouth turn down.

An insight strikes Kylone: Dirk's high intelligence makes him lonely and Alva's continuing presence will make him feel it more keenly. "Don't worry. I'll set you up a meeting with a rockborne if only to keep you from more hacking."

Dirk smiles.

Acolyte Thyone dressed in her formal white silk bursts into the room and glares at Kylone. She opens her mouth to speak as she looks past Dirk to gaze onto the screen.

Dirk swipes it closed.

Surprise flashes across her face. "I'm sorry for interrupting a counselling session."

Kylone wants to tell her off for not knocking first, but decides it can wait until they are alone. "This is just a friendly chat."

She looks Dirk up and down. "I hope he isn't charging us for this break."

Dirk's face darkens with anger. "I charge by the hour for time worked. Not for this." He lifts his mug and downs the rest of his coffee in one noisy gulp.

"I should think so too." She turns to Kylone. "Why're we employing an electrician when Priest Theseus is qualified and can do the job for free?"

"That wasn't my decision," Kylone replies through gritted teeth. "And it would be advisable to discuss such matters in house first."

"It's all right, Kylone. I'm sacking myself. Why do you put up with this idiot?" Dirk picks up his toolbox.

"How dare you," she says.

Kylone stands. "Enough, Thyone. What do you want?"

"The Archdeacon demands your presence immediately in the green office."

Dirk gets up. "You'd better hurry off to see her. I'll find my own way out."

"You're in real trouble," she tells Kylone.

Kylone forces a smile and bows slightly to Thyone. "Tell the Archdeacon I'll be along in a couple of minutes after I've apologised to my guest for your bad behaviour."

"The Archdeacon doesn't like to be kept waiting." She strides out of the room.

Once her footsteps are out of earshot, Dirk turns to him. "I'll message you."

"Sorry about this."

"Not your fault."

"And one other thing. Don't you dare hack Thyone."

"Aw! You're such a spoilsport."

Kylone narrows his eyes on him. "I mean it."

"Well, I suppose it would be a waste of my valuable time. Now run along to see your beloved Archdeacon, there's a good boy."

"One day…"

Kylone heads out along the balcony, down the stairs, through the doors and instead of turning left to reception, turns right along a curving corridor past doors on his left. He finally reaches a green door at the end and knocks gently on the panel to one side.

The door's plasma sheet shimmers before fading to nothing. The Archdeacon, her grey-streaked brown hair tied in a myrtle net, wears her official emerald silk and open-fronted coat. She sits in a high-back chair carved from one piece of translucent tea green silicara. She looks up, her face grim. "Come in, Kylone."

The lack of his title warns him to be very careful. As he steps in, he notices Thyone standing to attention just inside the door. "You asked to see me."

The Archdeacon looks him up and down while her left hand's third finger taps impatiently on the end of the armrest. "I have received a formal complaint about your activities."

"I am sorry to hear that. Did I do anything unsatisfactory at Miner Raoul Larsson's funeral?"

"Nothing, which is why this is so irritating."

Kylone prays this is a simple misunderstanding. "May I ask what am I supposed to have done wrong?"

"High Priest Diomedes has detected you sifting an awful lot of data on Mirandan mining activities, sufficient to do significant data analysis on them. Are you doing such analysis?"

"Yes, but–"

"No buts, Kylone. You know you should discuss these matters with our Guardians of History. Why haven't you?"

"I haven't come to meaningful conclusions yet."

"I see. Thyone tells me you've been sharing your results with the electrician fitting out the column light. Is that correct?"

"What? No, of course not."

"Then why was a graph on the table screen when I entered counselling room three just now?" Thyone asks, stepping forward.

"That was his analysis, not mine."

"You expect me to believe a mere electrician would have a sophisticated analytics tool on his account like that?" Thyone continues.

Kylone turns to face her. "It's the truth."

Only the tapping of a finger can be heard.

It sinks into Kylone this business could invoke a Truth Tribunal. The Priesthood has zero tolerance of liars within its ranks and the consequences for him, if found guilty, range from a public admonishment to being expelled from the Priesthood. The latter would mean being an outcast on Miranda.

"What is this electrician's name?" the Archdeacon asks.

"Isaac Hawking," Thyone replies, "That's the name on his invoices."

"Really?" the Archdeacon says. "It's rather old-fashioned. Is that the name you know him by, Kylone?"

The Truth Tribunal hangs over him like an axe about to behead him. This fear drives out his other fear: losing Dirk's friendship. "One of them."

"So he's the liar?" Thyone says.

"Not necessarily," the Archdeacon intervenes. "He could have a legitimate reason for using an alternative name. Kylone, what data did you give this…"

"Isaac Hawking," Thyone says.

"Man?" the Archdeacon says.

"The data I give him comes from Miranda's open net." Kylone replies. "I made it abundantly clear I would not access any locked analysis by the Guardians of History for him. He is happy with that."

"Thyone, is there any proof that locked data has been used?"

"Not according to High Priest Diomedes, but he wants assurance Kylone won't let something slip accidentally." Thyone's voice had a tiny tremble.

"I can understand his concern," the Archdeacon said. "But what he is asking for is vetting what Kylone gives to this Isaac…"

"Hawking."

"It would slow the information flow, would it not?"

"A price worth paying given what happened with similar incidents in the past." Thyone's tremble turns into a warble.

"Yes, I know that. Kylone, what is this Isaac looking into?"

The Archdeacon's scrutiny is uncomfortably deep and accurate. Kylone can no longer avoid openly acknowledged conflict with the Guardians of History. "Possible factors leading to accidents and fatalities in the mines."

The Archdeacon leans forward. "For what purpose?"

"He's looking for an explanation for the recent large increase of burials in the Heroes Gallery."

The Archdeacon stands up. "That's Guardians of History business."

A slight smile crosses Thyone's face.

"I agree, but until today, nothing has come out of his studies that the Guardians did not already know."

"And today?"

"An anomaly in the correlation between different sets of data on the graph Thyone saw. There is no reasonable obvious explanation and needs looking into. I have no idea whether the Guardians have already come across this."

"Are we talking about possibly saving lives here?"

"Yes."

"I see." The Archdeacon walks over to the window and stares out at the cratered plain, its ice reflecting the cyan light of Uranus hanging in the heavens above. At last she turns to face them both. "This is my decision. Given the aim of the work this Isaac whoever is doing, Priest Kylone will continue to assist him, but taking extra care not to pass on any locked-down analysis."

"Thank you." Kylone relaxes.

"But, High Priest Diomedes–"

The Archdeacon holds her hand up to silence her. "In return, Priest Kylone will pass on any results to the Guardians of History with any due caveats about what conclusions he and this Isaac are coming to at the first opportunity he is able to."

"The Guardians of History are already fully stretched with the work they're doing." Thyone's voice fades under the Archdeacon's glare.

"I'm sure they are, which is why they should welcome such valuable assistance. Are we clear?"

"Ye-yes, Archdeacon."

"Please inform High Priest Diomedes of my decision."

"Certainly, Archdeacon." She half runs, half stumbles out of the room.

"Thank you, Archdeacon." He turns to go wondering how he can get Dirk back on board, but finds the plasma door shutting in front of him.

"A word, Kylone."

He turns, scared of what she will say next.

"You have made enemies of the Guardians of History today. They will watch you meticulously, waiting for you to make a mistake. Don't make one. Is that understood?"

His throat feels constricted. "Re… ahem… regrettably so."

"Good. I hope the Chief Compineer can come to some useful conclusions."

Kylone frowns in confusion. "You knew who he was?"

"You just confirmed it. I had my suspicions when he used that ridiculous name. Let your admission be a lesson in how careful you must be from now on."

***

Too many years have passed since Kylone was last in Verona's only shopping street, the only one on the whole of Miranda devoted to luxury goods and entertainment. Nothing much has changed, including the overcrowding. Blue lighting fools him as usual into thinking the place is a bit wider and longer than it actually is. He painstakingly squeezes past window-shoppers selecting goods to view on the centimetre-thick holographs and shoulders his way through workers heading home or to their leisure spots. Nobody takes much notice of him: he is dressed in his old cream and sepia patterned silk to indicate he is here for serious relaxation.

He hurries into an alleyway. Its ceiling, walls and floor are painted in blotchy yellow-browns, reputedly to imitate a nineteenth century Cornish mine tunnel. Imitation Davy safety lamps shed so little light that the copper plasma door at the other end glows, with the silver words, 'Kober Balyow Open and Welcome.' The place name may translate from Cornish to a copper mine, but it is bar and restaurant in the evenings. As he walks towards it, the street noise fades into a merrier and livelier hubbub coming from beyond the door.

Light footsteps follow him into the alleyway. "Well, I'll be damned," a woman says from behind. "I never expected to see you back here."

He needs a moment to identify the voice: it has become raspier and deeper since he had heard it ten years ago. Their last meeting flashes through his mind: she tells him Selma was one of the lucky ones to die instantaneously; this gives him no comfort; some crew members must have died slowly, crushed by the weight of the avalanche and in pain. He prays they are all now at peace and for his inner calm to return. He puts on his priestly smile and turns. "Likewise, Meriel."

Her outline against the street's blue light shows up her sagging shoulders and her closely cropped chestnut hair has turned grey. Shock at her rapid ageing freezes him momentarily. That disaster must have taken more of a toll on her than he realised.

"It's good to see you again," he continues. "Want to join me for a drink?" He remembers the advice the Archdeacon gave to him on the balcony. "The only thing I ask is that we don't talk about the avalanche. Or my talent. I'm not up to it."

She shakes her head. "You really should stop blaming yourself. Others don't. I don't. But, as you wish, that is all I will say on both matters."

Kylone's muscles relax and his smile morphs from the priestly to the genuine. "Thank you. Shall we?"

"Absolutely."

The noise steps up as they pass through the door: laughter is staccato; chatter is clipped in short syllables; and glasses jangle. It is warm and smells of too much wine and beer. They stop to search for somewhere to sit.

A two-and-half-metre high central column with glowing shelves dominates the room. Every other shelf displays antique liquor bottles from Earth guarded by glass. Others are crammed with modern flasks of all shapes, sizes and colours. Evenly spaced spigots are fixed to a shoulder-high ledge.

A bar, comprising glittering counter and front, circles the column. A circular disk is both a roof to the bar and a platform used when required for entertainment and speakers. A metre high ring fence of the same material as the bar, except translucent, crowns the whole edifice. Two gangways exit on opposite sides of the platform, cross above the floor and cut into the Grand Circle, a large balcony sloping down from the wall. Above this is the Upper Circle, a smaller balcony sloping down at a greater angle from the room's roof as it curves in over the column.

They stroll past staircases to either side that curl up to the back of the Grand Circle and step down onto the first of five tiers that go round the room. Each tier is filled with semi-circular tables and settees facing the bar. Many are occupied with people chatting, giggling or glumly looking into their drinks. Waiters beetle between the bar and the tables with the barkeeps working hard to pour the drinks, and cover their glasses with plasma sheets to stop spilling that is too easy in Miranda's gravity.

The roominess without being inside a spacesuit is a rarity. Kylone wants to stretch, laugh and run. His ingrained discipline stops him. Instead, he luxuriates in this atmosphere of freedom.

"Whoever came up with the idea of using our Council chamber as a bar in the evenings was a genius," Meriel shouts to make herself heard.

"Agreed."

With the council being Miranda's parliament where the constituencies comprise work groups, they needed the huge space for when they have full meetings. Any High Priest, mining crew captain, farm manager, data controller keeping vital supplies flowing, or service provider making a major difference to society – such as doctors, head teachers and coroners – can sit on the council.

A waiter walks up to them. "Good evening patrons. A table for two?"

"Please," Kylone replies. "As quiet a one as you can manage."

"This way." He leads them down the tiers, a third of the way round the bar past the first tier tables labelled as reserved for the launch toast and up to the third tier at the back of the room.

It becomes quieter as they sit down on the alcoved settee. They order their drinks via the table menu.

"What's brought you here?" Meriel asks.

"Questions. Too many of them. Like why are there so many launch toasts these days?" He glances back at the first tier's reserved tables. Alva stands beside the launch party tables talking with a strong-looking blond miner. Kylone is thankful she has not noticed him.

"Lots of us ask the same question," Meriel says. "The ore seams aren't as long, wide or load-bearing these days. We're getting edgy about that lack of mining opportunities. That and…"

"And?"

"There's a general feeling that things have changed down the mines."

This supports Dirk's analysis, but she may have more insights. "Oh?"

"Little things that change so slowly that only people my age notice them. We've noticed children aren't saving up for their own place as quickly as my generation did. My youngest, Vince, is still at home. More are turning to the Priests for help. The congregations are gradually getting larger. At least you chose a good profession to go into. What else can I say? Life is just that bit tougher all round these days."

The wrinkles on her face may not be from rapid ageing, but continuous worry.

"How're you coping?"

"I get by as a scavie."

He is shocked at her fall in status and income. "Sorry to hear that."

"Don't be. There's no responsibility and it's easy work guiding the shovels to push the debris away."

"Even so."

"I still have an eye for useful scrapings. I pick up enough to sell for extra money to make me comfortable."

The slight quake in her voice suggests otherwise, but he has to take her word as truth. "If you ever need help, you know where to find me."

She smiles. "You always were the thoughtful one. The Priesthood seems to suit you."

"You stole my contract, Miner Cris," comes a slurred shout from the floor below.

The room falls silent.

A miner stands up from the table in front of the accuser; the same one Alva sits at. "I can assure you, Miner Torvald," Cris replies, "I won the contract fair and square within the published rules."

"By space and ice, you lie. You jumped the queue."

"I did not. I was called in."

Torvald turns to Alva. "Please excuse my interruption.

Business, you understand." He delivers a right hook towards the miner's chest.

Cris blocks it, but not the upward left fist, which punches his lower chest to throw him past the Grand Circle towards the roof. He swings his arms to reach out to a gangway as he floats down rather than drops thanks to the weak gravity.

Torvald on the recoil from his punch is thrown onto the settee beside Alva. He grabs the table's edge to stop himself from bouncing up again.

Alva pushes down on his shoulder to help him.

"Thank you," Torvald says before looking up at Cris. "Damn my brother."

"Brother?" Alva's voice peters out.

Cris lands in the centre on the gangway.

Kylone joins in the applause in appreciation of the manoeuvre. He sees Torvald also clapping, clearly a friendly dispute. There is no obligation to intervene and he hopes it will end there.

Two waiters from the bar head towards Torvald.

"If you'll pardon me," Torvald says to Alva while climbing onto the table.

The waiters start skim-running. Torvald jumps up to fly to his brother. Cris slips over the gangway's guardrail on the other side to drop down onto the floor. One waiter jumps to reach for Torvald's legs and misses, letting him catch the nearest guardrail and push on it to vault over the gangway.

A man two tables away from Alva dives at the waiter. "That's dangerous, you fool." He pushes the waiter to the ground. The second waiter diverts to help his colleague, but is tackled by a woman from behind.

The bar's plasma shutter switches on to hide the counter and all behind it, and to throw light into the room. Green arrows light up on the settee ends to show the way to the exits away from the fight.

"Please leave by the route shown by the green arrows," an auto-announcer booms repeatedly. Thuds, thumps and occasional screams muffle its words.

Kylone watches Alva half stand up and back from the fight in front of her table to search for a way out. She cannot escape. Fear creases her face. She sinks down to hide safe under the table, clearly not knowing what to expect or do next. Even in a fight like this, miners are safety conscious; it is others who will cause the damage.

Meriel tugs Kylone's arm. "Come on."

"You go. I have a responsibility." He looks over to Alva.

"Be careful. The lack of work has made these brawls nastier."

Her comment pushes him to get up, jump onto the settee in front, make his way against the thinning crowd to Alva's table, vaults over the settee and slides under the table to sit beside Alva. "Are you all right?"

"Err, yes. Yes, of course." She seems not quite with it. "Sorry, I didn't recognise you out of your priest's silk."

"Priests can be called anywhere." He folds his arms round his knees and looks out at the maelstrom of legs. "This should cool off in about twenty minutes. Best to let it blow over."

There is thud on the table above. A man rolls off onto the floor in front of them and continues rolling for several metres.

"Right."

The man struggles to his knees.

"He'll be fine, except for a few bruises tomorrow."

"How can you be so sure?"

He smiles. "I was a miner once."

A silent 'Ah' flashes across her face.

Cris bends down to look under the table, face gleaming with sweat, and notices Kylone. "You looking after her?"

"Yes, and I'm capable of doing so."

"Good, I owe you one, whoever you are." A hand snatches at his shoulder to pull him away.

Alva yelps.

"Don't worry. He's shown he can take care of himself."

"This isn't normal, is it? Raoul never mentioned fighting."

"It happens occasionally, when tensions are high. In a perverse way, it helps calm things down." His answer is for her reassurance. But his worry deepens. Meriel was right. A fight like this would only have broken out because people are feeling the greater strain. Nothing he can do about it now except wait it out.

He needs to distract her from the fight. "Did Raoul ever say anything about what he thought the future of mining on Miranda would be?"

"What a strange question to ask here."

"It takes your mind off this," he points to a group melee off to one side. "And passes the time while we wait."

"You're an odd man, Priest Kylone." She bites her lips. "I can't remember– wait, he did once say that if the ice keeps on getting more noisy at the current rate, he'd have to buy dampening pads for his hands. What does that mean?"

Kylone is puzzled. "You don't know much about mining, do you?"

"No, not really. What between me coming from a farming family and him not wanting to talk much about his work."

"That's typical of iceborne. Not their fault. They find it difficult to explain how they 'hear' through their fingertips. So they end up talking among themselves. It makes them appear cliquey, when it's really a limitation on what they can communicate to those who can't experience it. The noise in the ice is real."

Jealousy spikes through him. The rockborne talent has no such scientific evidence to back up their capability, only speculative theory. It would be hearsay and superstition if it were not for the successful results. But this is all behind him now. He will never be going down a mine to be able to use his own talent.

He continues, "It comes from natural effects like compressing micro-gas bubbles, scraping against rock and ice, and cracking under pressure."

"Oh." She pauses. "That kind of makes sense. Why is it getting noisier?"

"I'm not sure." Nobody has mentioned this in his hearing. Has he been that cut off from society? Or were the iceborne keeping this worry to themselves? He cannot believe the latter, as mining safety is involved. If the Guardians of History have come across it, then he can understand why they would keep their silence: to avoid spreading alarm and panic. But Chynoweth? Maybe they were listening to the icebornes' concerns on the quiet, and *this* was the cause of them limiting mining activity, except this doesn't make sense. They need work with all the miners and should therefore be open about the ices being noisier, even if only to keep the number of deaths down. Only one common sense explanation is left. "Sounds like Raoul was becoming more sensitive to the ice, which to him would sound like it was becoming noisier. It doesn't usually happen in someone of his age, but is not unheard of."

"Oh."

The bar's noise subsides to groans, clinking and clacking of glasses being tidied away and quiet hum and crackles of vacuums sweeping up broken glass and other debris. He pokes his head out from under the table. The fight is over; the waiters are clearing up; the injured are limping away. "I think it's safe to emerge." He crawls out and stands, dusting dirt off his silk.

Alva slides out and lets Kylone help her stand up. A woman leans on a man as they hobble up the tiers out of the room. About a dozen people, mainly farmers and support services staff judging by the fact their heads are unshaved, are slouched at tables scattered around the room, patiently waiting for the two people in medical green to get round to seeing them. A few people emerge from under the tables on the first tier and quickly leave.

The injured will welcome companionship to help them forget their pain. Their need is more immediate than his to find out more about Raoul's thoughts. He stares at one particularly pale woman. "I have work to do here."

"I can see that." Alva turns to a waitress passing them by with a tray full of glasses. "Can I help tidy up?"

The relief on the waitress's face is enough of an answer for Kylone to quickly step across to sit down beside the injured woman.

***

Kylone walks down the Archives' main tunnel with its curved walls and ceiling. Their deep pink colouring is from extra thick reinforcement to protect the precious records from the weight of Arden Coronae. It adds to his wariness. He is uptight about his imminent interview with the head Guardian of History, High Priest Diomedes. The official reason is to chronicle his viewpoint of events for the archives, not that he sees it will serve much purpose. But like all Mirandans, it is his duty to record history. It has been so ever since Miner Aretha Varoufakis used her personal diaries to successfully analyse where to find more moissanite ore. This started a vogue of diarising. When the Priesthood took over storing and analysing society's history, they changed their names to ancient Greek ones in honour of her heritage.

He reaches the closed plasma door to Record Office Five. He steps on its doormat, which immediately lights up blue.

"You're late," Diomedes barks over the intercom as the door fades open.

Kylone glances at his wristpad: only by thirty seconds. With the High Priest being so snappy and knowing their conversation will be recorded, he decides to soothe things down rather than answer back. "My apologies Guardian of History. I had not anticipated the long walk down to this Record Office."

"You'll know better next time."

Kylone dares to step inside. Diomedes dominates the room; his long white tied back hair and pointed beard contrasting with the black silk of the workday Priest's uniform and lively brown eyes. High cheekbones make his thin figure look gaunt. He sits in a standard high back green office chair at the utilitarian screen desk reading a report. Opposite the desk is a visitor's chair, comfortable enough to sit but not fall asleep on. The cuboid room's walls are lined with shelving full of silica-leafed books that form the ultimate information backups for computer failures.

Kylone waits by the chair.

"Sit, sit." The High Priest waves a hand vaguely towards the other side of his desk while continuing to read.

"Thank you." He perches on the chair's edge, alert for the next problem.

Diomedes sits back and eyes him up and down. "Taking a Hero's funeral is normally reserved for the High Priests. I hope the apparent favouritism our Archdeacon Ariadne had shown you hasn't gone to your head and you've overreached yourself as a consequence."

Kylone lets a small smile slip. "The Archdeacon told me she did not want to show favouritism among the High Priests with an election for her succession in the near future a distinct possibility."

"So our dear Archdeacon is playing by the rulebook, is she?" He strokes his beard. "Why are you here? More ridiculous results from Isaac Hawking?"

"No, something rather more serious and independent of his work."

"You call that work? He's playing you for a fool. Now if you could direct his work in a way that would stop wasting your time and be beneficial to us…"

It is a reasonable request, but he knows the Chief Compineer would never agree. His next words are chosen very carefully. "I would quite happily pass on any suggestions you may have to him, but he seems to have his own reasons for doing his analysis. Besides we have come to a quiet agreement. I help him pull off the publicly accessible data and he reduces the bill for installing the electrics for the Greening mosaic. We have had no complaints about the quality of his work, I might add." What he has said is the truth, but far from all of it. Inside, he squirms for not being up front and mentally slithers his guilt behind the shield of the Archdeacon's warning.

"Well, that's some benefit to the Priesthood. Even if it's highly unorthodox."

Kylone takes this as a light admonishment and bows his head accordingly.

"Why are you here?" Diomedes snaps with impatience.

Now is the time for his prepared speech. "I bumped into my old mining team captain, Meriel Hamblin and naturally, we had a lot to catch up on. She is now a scavie and complained about ore-bearing seams becoming smaller, with more having to be opened up. If this trend continues, there will come a time when poverty will make survival very difficult. Do you know of anything that will counter this decline into poverty? If so, I would like to go back to Meriel to reassure her. If not, then I would like to be advised as to how to deal with the congregation when they come to us for financial help and reassurance that things will be better in the future."

Diomedes sits very still, not even breathing, and his brown eyes turn hard and cold. "One woman's story does not make a trend."

"Looking for corroborative proof has been ingrained into me by our training. In this case, there has been a distinct increase in rate of launch toasts, yet the number of miners has decreased slightly over the past five years."

"There is both an art and discipline to identifying trends and causes. These two items you've given me as evidence could have very different and independent causes. Further work would be needed to identify the linking mechanism and its robustness."

Kylone's next words come out in more of a formal manner than he intended. "This is why I am bringing these aspects to the Guardians' attention. For them to investigate."

A brief smile flashes across Diomedes' lips. "An interesting potential correlation. One that is worthy of investigation. The short-term effects of both these aspects are economic, not life threatening, which makes it a tier two investigation. You can reassure your ex-captain we will look into it."

"Thank you for accepting this as worthy of the Guardians' attention. May I ask if you have any idea when such an analysis will be completed?"

Diomedes shrugs his shoulders. "We have far too many tier one cases to deal with, so I cannot give any promises. If Isaac Hawking would take some of our workload off our hands, then we could deal with your case sooner."

This proposal on directing the Chief Compineer's analysis takes Kylone by surprise. This is power politics in the raw: Diomedes wants control of Dirk's analysis. Kylone wants no part of the 'cut and thrust'. As a broken man who still keenly feels his fragility, he cannot risk doing battle with too powerful forces of people or environment. Yet he wonders if Diomedes is afraid of what Dirk might deduce. "As I said earlier, I wish I could help, but Isaac Hawking is his own man. I will, of course, make the suggestion to him, but I doubt he would follow it."

"A pity. I can only do what I have the resources to do. Is there anything else you wish to bring to my attention?"

Kylone feels he has been let off. "Just a very minor consequence."

"Oh?"

"This matter may have some bearing on Hero Miner Raoul Larsson's death. I am obliged by civil law to mention it to Coroner Sylvana Ventu. She undertook the original inquest." He carefully avoids mentioning she is the head Coroner on Miranda and has the responsibility for enacting and maintaining the Council laws in as practicable manner as possible. This includes allocating investigation and arrest powers beyond the Coroners to the most appropriate unbiased people. While her predecessor had given councillors the power of arrest in the absence of a Coroner or their directed appointee, she has jurisdictional precedence to reverse such decisions.

Anger flickers across Diomedes' face. "Do what you must." He turns his attention to his desk screen.

This is a dismissal, and a rude one at that. Kylone stands. "Thank you for your time, Guardian of History." He rushes out, his own anger driving him faster than normal, and heads through the tunnels upwards to Arden town located on the third cliff down.

The triangular plaza at the town's heart is a coffee shop bonanza, with chairs and tables hogging all the floor space except for the delineated pathways kept clear for pedestrians and supply carts. This contradiction of space and compactness generates a friendly bohemian culture where strangers readily talk to each other. Chatter and clatter of cups, coffee and tea aromas all demand Kylone's attention as he heads for the Coroners' Office, which is squeezed between the table-clothed patchwork cosiness of an English tearoom and the Italian coffee shop with its high round imitation marble tables.

Here is where he first met Selma. She had tripped and knocked his elbow that had sent his Americano splashing over Meriel, Robin and Raven, before grabbing the table to float back to standing on the floor. Selma had been so upset by her clumsiness that they had fussed over her until she had finally calmed down and joined them for some coffee. They had often laughed about the accident, until… no, now is not the time to wallow in those awful memories.

He steps through the plasma door into the Coroners' Office. One second there is the burble and the stench of busy people's body odours, breakfast food and drinks, the next near silent whirr of air fans and his nose tingling from dry dust. He faces a ceiling-to-floor screen projecting a pseudo-receptionist.

"Good morning," she says. "How may I help you?"

"I am Priest Kylone and would like to see Coroner Sylvana Ventu about her now closed inquest into Miner Raoul Larsson. Is she available?"

She produces a synthetic smile. "Just let me check her diary."

Kylone is taken aback. Normally these receptionists know exactly what the availability is of staff. Why is this computer simulation working so slowly?

"Coroner Sylvana will see you now, if this is convenient to you?"

"That's ideal. Where can I find her?"

"She is in office three, to your right round the corner."

"Thank you." He follows her directions to find the door open.

A female with short cropped black hair, wearing a dark charcoal silk with red neck and wrist bands, stands with her back to him watering a wall arrayed top to bottom with basket shelves of strawberries, lettuces, French beans, house leeks and aloe vera. Uranus' blue light shines out of a cord round the edge of the ceiling, which must lead to somewhere on the surface. She places her watering can on the only space of a waist-high shelf and turns with a welcoming smile. This relaxed friendliness hardly shaves anything off her aura of authority: the official red chain necklace with a black recording pendant that hangs down her chest is used to gather official evidence, take witness statements and to provide wi-fi links to the judicial AI to advise on the law. The pendant being black means it is off. "Come in, Priest Kylone. Take a seat." She gestures to the ersatz-leather settee and armchairs round a coffee table that is to one side of the room, facing a wall screen.

"Thank you for seeing me at such short notice." Kylone sits in one corner of the settee.

She takes the armchair next to him, leaning forward to rest her elbows on her legs and claps her hands to together. "What brings you here? Do I need switch my pendant on to formally record this conversation?"

Her efficiency contradicts the room's relaxing ambiance. He smiles and gets straight to the point. "I've come across evidence that may potentially affect your conclusions about the death of Hero Miner Raoul Larsson. It will need to be recorded."

She lifts her head slightly, the only sign that this is far from what she expected. After a second she presses her pendant with her thumb. It changes from black to a glowing red. "In the interests of truth, I will listen to what you have to say. Inquest of Hero Miner Raoul Larsson. New evidence from Priest Kylone who is the only person present in my office." She looks across to Kylone. "Please proceed."

He summarises the conversations he had with Meriel, Alva in Kober Balyow and High Priest Diomedes in the Archives, watching Sylvana's face going from intent concentration to frowning worry.

After a few seconds silence, she says: "The evidence you've given me is circumstantial, but nevertheless needs investigating. It has already placed you on a possible collision path with the Guardians of History and will almost certainly place you on another one with Chynoweth. If I follow through with my own inquiries, you might yourself become an outcast or worse. Are you prepared to take such consequences if I have to reveal you are behind the new evidence?"

There it is again: the fear he might break under the onslaught. He should say no. It is the safe choice. But when would the threats stop growing? Doing nothing is not an option.

"I'm a priest. We live by the truth. We prefer absolute truth, but in the absence of certainty, we know how to assess and deal with the unknowns, ifs and possibilities. Doubt and procrastination, no matter how small, are our enemies. Reducing them is part of our mission."

"Spoken like a true priest, but what about the human behind that priestly mask? Will you be able to cope?" She holds up her hand to stop him interrupting. "I was learning my job as an assistant to the Coroner that investigated your tragedy ten years ago. I know what happened to you. Would the man who has already had one massive nervous breakdown not more easily have a second under less exacting circumstances? Chynoweth's pressure can be all seven hells of ice rolled into one."

The response is out of the blue. "I'm intrigued. Why ask this and not about me possibly wanting to find excuses for my own mining accident?"

"You're doing your social duty, one that in many cases

will override personal needs. I can understand that in your case."

Kylone still does not how to answer her original question. "You've been assessing me?"

"Of course. Let me explain what I need to do next," she continues. "I have to ask those you had the conversations with to corroborate your story. It will lead me to ask other questions from other people. Sooner or later, the Guardians of History and Chynoweth will hear that you kick-started my investigation. How they react to you is out of my hands. So let me put my question another way. How far do you want me to take my investigation: up to the point where I can assure your reputation and your welfare; or are you willing to risk everything, and I mean everything, to get justice?"

"That's a stark choice."

"You're not the first to come to me with this issue. But until now, all have been miners or their dependents who cannot afford to go against Chynoweth…"

She does not need to finish her explanation. He is her first witness not reliant on Chynoweth for his survival. His choice is face up to them now with all its horrendous outcomes; or deal with the ever-increasing misery of the congregation; or the in-between of choosing the sufficient level of misery he thinks he can cope with. Decisions, easily made mistakes, living with himself all contend with each other. He wipes his bald head to chase the fuzziness and the lure of a comfortable existence away. He has to make up his mind. He struggles towards a decision, only to be caught in reviewing how he got here. "If I hadn't walked away from the mine face to check on some rock patterning back up the tunnel I would have been buried along with the others. I'm lucky to be alive. Priest Patricianna did her best to cure me of survivors' guilt, but I still feel it there in the background. I have learnt to live with it. One of its beneficial effects is pushing me to do the best I can with the extra life I have."

Sylvana stares at him and says nothing.

Decision time. His priestly training caution revolts

against this reckless and public course of action. His old self awakens inside: always smiling and easy to make friends with, but a calculating risk-taker, one who dares to do things the timid and careworn will not. The risks in his case are from others over whom he has no control. "If I don't stand up for what is right now, I will never be a true Priest. Go ahead; make your inquiries. I would take it as a courtesy if you would let me know when I can expect trouble heading my way."

Sylvana opens her mouth and then closes it. "Are you sure?"

"Yes." Kylone knows he has sealed his fate, whatever that may be.

She nods and straightens up. "Pendant, this interview with Priest Kylone is to be kept under lock and seal until I give permission for it to become public or Priest Kylone dies. Formally reopen the inquest into Hero Miner Raoul Larsson and let Widow Alva Larsson know I have done so without explanation. Arrange an interview with her."

"Interview under lock and seal and notification of Hero Miner Raoul Larsson's inquest becoming live again announced," the pendant's tenor voice announces.

"Is there anything else you wish to bring up with me?" Sylvana asks.

"No." Kylone stands. "We both have other things to do."

"This interview is now terminated."

The pendant changes from red back to black.

She rises to her feet and offers to shake hands. "You are a rare man. The Priesthood is lucky to have one of such principles as you. I won't pretend this will be easy. One word of advice: you may find strangers will want to help you. Take it."

"Thank you, and I will." Kylone accepts her handshake

***

After his peaceful time on the balcony, Kylone heads for the reception in Chynoweth's headquarters. The receptionist is dressed in the Corp's graphite grey silk with a standard thin stripe of black running down his left side from his neck, over his shoulder and down his arm to the wrist. Pressing a combination of points along it will make a holograph computer screen rise from his lower arm so he can check the firm's database any time anywhere. His brown hair is tightly tied into a plaited bun, his brown eyes look dull and bored, and his badge reads Assistant Jürgen.

He puts on a perfunctory smile. "How may I help you?"

"I have a meeting scheduled with Chief Compineer Dirk Schimmeratzski. Priest Kylone's the name."

A stunned look wipes away his smile. "He never makes appointments. With anyone."

"There's always a first time. May I suggest you check his diary?"

"Of course." His fingers fumble over his desk screen. His eyes move side-to-side reading something. His mouth trembles. "I don't believe it. There is an appointment for you."

"What the hell are you waiting for?" Dirk's voice comes out of the desk's speaker. "Escort him here and be quick about it."

Jürgen jerks and stares at the speaker.

Kylone clasps his hands in front of him, lifts his head and puts on a face of a Priest in rapture. His ploy of turning up on spec and letting Dirk backfill the appointment in his diary has worked. This whole incident confirms what he suspects: the Compineer has set a watcher AI on him. "If you would be so kind as to lead the way?"

He shoots off his seat and rushes down a corridor round to the right.

Kylone hurries after him, carefully retaining his rapture look, more for Dirk's benefit, should he be checking on his progress through the CCTV network.

He hears no footsteps, neither Jürgen's nor his own. The floor, walls and ceiling are that rare shade of beige of superionic coating. It counters pressure from anything it touches into silence, including footsteps and the surrounding ices' grating and bursting gas bubble noises. The lack of doors is like mine access tunnels. He starts to believe he is in one. Fear rises. Grief descends. He missteps and trips.

Jürgen continues round a corner, with a mirror reflecting his receding figure.

He hurries to catch up, inwardly cursing for his lapse into his horror memories. He needs a distraction. The new corridor has regular inset cuboid hollows, displaying holographs of the famous crystals Chynoweth has mined: Dark Light, the extraordinarily black hard shining cube; Arhans, the silver sphere that could be pressed into any shape only to resume its original perfection on release; and the most famous of all, Pasture Star, an emerald snowflake made of hexagons or what they call a hexaflake embedded in brown rock. The real gem is in the High Chapel above Verona Rupes and only displayed during the Greening ceremonies.

"Your first visit?" Jürgen asks, standing next to him.

"That obvious, is it?"

"The Star catches everyone like that, Priest Kylone. If you don't mind, the Chief Compineer is waiting." His nervousness cracks his voice.

"Of course." With reluctance, Kylone follows him down the rest of the corridor to a T-junction.

Rather than enter the corridor of solid double doors with plaques for the boardroom and meeting rooms, he takes the plainer one round a bend. They arrive at a plasma door, the only one on the outside of the bend. Jürgen's face turns steely as he presses the intercom. On hearing a click, he says: "Priest Kylone is here."

"About bloody time," Dirk yells back. The door's plasma fades. "Get your butt in here, Kylone, so I can give you a proper dressing down for your latest crazy antic."

"I'll leave you here." Jürgen's voice rises by half an octave. He dashes away.

Kylone steps into Dirk's realm. The wall to his left has

top-to-bottom shelves bulging with portables: anything from mini ear-computers, through strips of black that can produce a holographic screen, via flimsy rolled-up comp sheets, to laptops in fullerene-toughened cases for heavy-duty work in vacuum. Amazingly the room smells fresh as if the air has a little extra oxygen. Opposite is a desk abutting the farthest wall, at which Alva sits, keeping her head down and reading through files.

"Alva," Dirk yells. "Get Kylone some camomile tea. Make it very strong. A good five-minute soak. He's going to need it."

Alva gets up, smiles at Kylone and yells back: "How about a please?"

"Tea, now." Dirk's voice has a ring of determination.

Alva sits back down. "I'll enjoy overhearing your conversation."

"Grrr…" Dirk pauses. "Please."

Alva stands, passes Kylone and stops to turn round just in front of the door. "I'll make it ten minutes. That should give you more than enough time for your private conversation." She exits, closing the door behind her.

Kylone walks down a narrow, crooked aisle cluttered with various hub stations, flatbeds for holographs, screens in different sizes and definitions, and make-and-mend benches. He reaches a set of blue padded panels forming a cubbyhole in the far corner.

Dirk stands and glares at him. "If you so much as breathe a word how my assistant runs this place, I'll make your life a misery."

"Alva's that good?"

"She's the best I've had and, frankly, I don't want to lose her. Why does she hide her intelligence?"

"As I said before, that's for you to work out."

"Harrumph." He looks down and taps away at his desk screen. "I've read the transcripts of your conversations with Diomedes and Sylvana–"

"Read?"

"Reading's quicker than listening unless you're multi-tasking."

"Interesting insight."

"And wipe that smug look off your face. This is damned serious."

"I wouldn't be here otherwise. Diomedes certainly won't make progress in the near future and Coroner Sylvana has other cases to deal with. Yes, she'll get to the truth whatever it is eventually, but will it be in time?"

Dirk pulls his weighted pigtail round to the front and strokes it while his eyes look into the distance. His eyes lock onto Kylone's. "I need more background on mining. You know that. You're asking me to speed learn a vast subject involving a lot of individual experience in zero time. Even I can't do the impossible."

"I know I'm asking a lot, but I have no one else to turn to who can make a difference."

"You tickling my ego?"

Kylone chuckles. "You'd see straight through it if I were."

"Hah!" Dirk gives his plait one more stroke. "This Meriel, how good a miner is she?"

"A well respected mining ex-captain, though she only has the average miners' knowledge and skills. She relied on the people around her. Her skill was picking the best. If they got it wrong, she got it wrong."

"A people person then. Has she kept her connections?"

"I suspect so." He does not need to add that rockborne are very rare. This thought triggers the memory of the moment he told her to drill the left ore-bearing seam, and not the right. It had been a close decision. He shakes his head to chase it and the accompanying regret away. "Her advice will be only as good as she gets from others."

"Which will be better than average. Decisions by expert committee always are. I'll take her on as a sub-assistant to Alva for research purposes."

Kylone blinks at his brashness. There is in no doubt Dirk's hacking skills can manipulate her employment, but there is an overriding concern. "Won't that upset the Guardians of History?"

"Not the way I'm planning it."

Kylone waits for an explanation. When none is

forthcoming he says: "I need to know so I can help protect you from their undue interest."

Dirk gives his pigtail a couple of more loving strokes. "Only if they start causing problems, not before?"

"Agreed. I wouldn't want to be seen as having knowledge I shouldn't have."

"That's actually a good point." He swings his pigtail behind him. "I'll be getting Meriel to help on a study into effects of gravitational tides on Miranda. The excuse will be to ensure the infrastructure equipment will withstand any of its effects, double-checking Chynoweth's almost useless mining engineers. My underlying reason, if they push me to reveal something, is to take their impact away from the accident statistics. Of course the real reason is to pick her knowledge, or should I say gut feel about mining that no fools, statistics or extrapolative theories can properly explain."

"That's devious, but normal for you."

"I'll take that as a compliment."

"Wait. You're a techie through and through. What's this about relying on 'gut feel'?"

"Ooo! I've been caught out."

Kylone catches a hint of cynicism. "And? What's the answer?"

"You really want one?"

"I want the truth."

Dirk pauses. "All good techies, scientists and engineers rely on instinct. We have to get things done quickly. Turns out this instinct is good at warning us when we're going wrong, even when all the logic says we're right. That's all you're getting from me."

They stay silent.

"Another thing," Dirk finally adds. "If you tell anyone…"

"Gadgets around me will work in imaginative ways."

Dirk laughs. "That's one way of putting it."

"Wait a minute. Miranda is tidally locked with Uranus and always has the same side facing it. How can there be gravity changes?"

"You're forgetting the Sun, and the fact that Uranus' system has got a sideways tilt with respect to its orbital path. To be precise the planet's inclination is ninety-eight degrees. In simple terms, Miranda's orbit is perpendicular to the Sun's planetary disc. As our planet orbits the Sun, our moon cycles through permanent sunlight at the North Pole via equal day and nights at the equator to permanent sunlight at the South Pole, and back again. We're now approaching the point where the Sun is directly over our equator. We end up moving from directly between Uranus and the Sun to having the Sun behind Uranus. Consequently our dear little moon suffers greater variation in overall gravity, which means more warming. Of course this is rather simplistic in terms of orbital dynamics. Variations can and do occur because of the other moons gravity and a hundred other things that could add to the heating effects. As us engineers say, the devil's in the details. My research will look for details we missed like impact on the composition of mining tunnels. It would be rather timely and useful for our engineering."

"But we reached a similar situation in this planet's orbit, eighty-four years ago. Indeed it would have reached a similar configuration forty-two years ago. Safety engineers must have done some work on this effect then?"

"Of course they did. We've since built new tunnels and have a little better knowledge of Miranda's composition. A new evaluation will do no harm and might bring something to light that was previously missed. As a thorough job needs to be done, I'm really the only one who can do it."

Kylone groans. "You were doing so well without your egotism until now."

A rattle of cups comes from the other end of the room as Alva enters.

"No need to be that noisy. I can smell that camomile from here," Dirk says. "Wait. Where's my coffee?"

"Reckon with a Priest visiting you, you were going to need camomile." Alva walks towards the cubbyhole.

"Ice dust!"

A siren springs into life.

Fear grips Kylone.

The siren breaks to deliver the message: "All rescue miners report to Carbo Mine, level five hub with suits. Medical staff please remain on standby until contact or ingress is identified." The warble resumes.

With his face grim and full of concentration, Dirk's fingers dance across his desk screen. Images whizz on, off and to one side. After an interminable barrage of noise, Dirk rushes round the shelves gathering equipment into a rigid briefcase. "Alva, I'm going to need you to hand deliver this comms equipment to the rescue people." He looks back at Kylone. "Go with her. Make sure she isn't stopped from getting to Carbo five by anyone, even rescue miners. Time's short. We need this new comms link to the trapped miners up and running pronto. That understood?"

Kylone is about to object. Instead he hopes and prays his faith will see him through this.

Dirk picks out two earpieces from his desk and offers one to each. "Put these in your ears. Don't worry, I'll hear what you say as well as you hearing me."

Kylone and Alva take them and fix them in their ears. He notices hers is invisible to the world, which means his is also. Now is not the time to ask why.

"Go." Dirk says. "Both of you."

She grabs the briefcase and is slowed down by its inertia.

Kylone reaches out to catch it, but stops as soon as he sees she has coped.

"Come on." She rushes for the door.

Left with no choice, he follows, perhaps heading to what he fears most: going into the mines.

CHAPTER 3

The bitter stench of fear-tinged sweat hits Kylone's nostrils as he approaches the queue's backend to the registry for Level Five's hub out in the tunnel. Most have shaven heads and wear the heavy brown spacesuits of miners and scavies. Silent and grim-faced, they wait to be called to face whatever horror is in the mine.

Kylone puts on his priestly serene pose to lead Alva past them, making a hand blessing sign of an inverted 'v' with a bar across the top for those who bow their heads. A few, fellow miners of long ago, openly gawp or just nod their hello.

Lenny, near the front of the queue, gasps. "It must be bad."

"There is hope," Kylone replies before pressing onward to the registry's reception desk.

Strands of blonde hair have escaped from the chignon around the hassled face of the receptionist at the registry desk. On seeing Kylone, her blue eyes turn steely. "I'm sorry, we have no further requirements for a priest. If you would register your name, we'll contact you if we need your services."

"I'm here to help Assistant Alva deliver some comms kit sent by the Chief Compineer. I think you'll find we're expected."

A ripple of comments passes along the queue until it becomes a distant whisper.

The receptionist checks her screen and shakes her head. "There's nothing here. I'm sorry I can't let you through."

Kylone pauses for as long as he dares. "If you would be so kind as to make absolutely sure. The Chief Compineer said the kit was vital."

"It's done," Dirk's voice whispers in his ear from the comms chip. "Next time, just ask beforehand. I've got my hands full here."

This is a first: Dirk has slipped up, and therefore must be under real pressure. Kylone now understands why he was sent here: to remove any obstacles in getting the comms relay operating. He smiles kindly at the receptionist, which is really meant for Dirk to see through the CCTV as an acknowledgement of the message.

The receptionist presses her lips together, while fingering her screen. She blinks and frowns. "It seems I was mistaken. Please go on through to the control room where the Hubmaster is expecting you."

"And where," Dirk says with a smirk-tone in his voice, "your friendly High Priest Diomedes is giving his usual stupid advice."

"Thank you," Kylone replies, with more strain than he means to.

He leads Alva through the safety door beside the desk, a tunnel and another safety door into the hub. Noise shockwaves him: whirr of machinery, clanks and bangs of heavy equipment being moved and shouting. His nose curls at the niffier sweat: Chynoweth has been skimping on microbe cleaning again. Opposite, a crew of eight enter the hangar airlock with their ice-torchers, spare oxygen stacks, red-coloured explosive sticks for precision use in drill-holes and lighting kit. Two Corp greys replenish oxygen supplies and ice-torchers to the right of the airlock. Next along is an alcove where a nurse in a medic's green silk readies the sickbay, activating the headboard medical monitors and placing injectors with fresh medication in trays beside the beds. On the other side of the big airlock, four personnel airlocks wait expectantly for someone to step in. Farther on tiers of hanging spacesuits, mainly brown heavy-duty mining ones, are being checked manually by more greys. A woman beside the closest tier climbs out of her bespattered suit and shoves it into the cleaner.

He focuses on the hub's raised control room to his left, its silicara sheeting allowing a clear two-way view. Inside, another two greys concentrate on working the consoles facing the airlocks. A horseshoe table faces the back wall. Rising out of the floor in its centre is a holograph of blue pipework irregularly linking green nodules, which he assumes is the up-to-date map of Carbo mine. A red disk slices through the configuration to cut off a blue line ending in a green nodule from the rest of the mine. It marks the site of the accident.

Diomedes in priesthood black stands at one end of the table, next to a grey with a thick black stripe running down from her neck to her wrists. She is the Hubmaster.

Kylone, thankful his faith is powering him through this place, leads Alva into the control room through the door's plasma.

"...give you the names when I have them confirmed beyond a doubt," the Hubmaster finishes and turns to Kylone. "What do you want?"

High Priest Diomedes pivots round. "Priest Kylone? I thought you weren't supposed to come down to the mines?"

"Thank you for your concern, High Priest."

Dirk guffaws in his ear.

"I have recovered well enough," Kylone continues, "to be able to enter a hub. I was asked to escort Assistant Alva here with the vital comms kit."

"I didn't ask for any," the Hubmaster says.

"The Chief Compineer knows this," Alva pipes up. "He says you're unable to talk to the trapped miners because a shift in iron-base rock blocked the comms signal paths. Don't ask me what this means."

Diomedes straightens up.

"The Chief Compineer himself?" the Hubmaster asks as her face pales. "He only ever intervenes in situations doubtful of success."

"Which means he thinks they may be still alive," Kylone adds.

"He wants me to lay a wi-fi network of comp-sticks," Alva adds. "Don't ask me how it'll work, but he said that with the help of electromagnetic properties in some of the rock layers we could find a signal path through to them."

"You're not a miner," Kylone blurts out and wonders

why he feels so protective of her. "You'll need an escort."

"And you can't go with her down the mines," Diomedes adds.

"I certainly don't want to mount a second rescue operation," the Hubmaster says, "for either of you."

"The Chief Compineer told me I would by going along the stable Beta Reach that runs parallel but at a distance to the tunnel with the accident."

The Hubmaster glances at the holograph and nods. "That's true."

Even with this reassurance, Kylone senses danger and wants to stop Alva going. She, like every normal person aged over ten, would be competent at handling any type of spacesuit. Going into dimly lit rough-iced and hewn rock mines for the first time would be going into a claustrophobic unknown, which has caused mine sickness in a few unfortunates. "Take Lenny with you. She's experienced in dealing with difficult mines." He does not add she was the closest to his team's mining accident to survive.

"Absolutely not," Diomedes snaps. "We'll need all the miners we can get hold of when the big push comes, as experience with previous mine disasters has shown."

"We need that information now," the Hubmaster snaps. "Who's this Lenny?"

"Helena Tyndale. She's in the queue outside."

The Hubmaster catches her breath. "That settles it." She turns to the men on the consoles. "Joshua, call Helena Tyndale in from the queue. Special mission."

"Sir," one of them acknowledges.

"As the Guardian of History, I strongly object to this ridiculous scheme."

"I know this mine better than you do. Decision's made. Move on." The Hubmaster stares at Kylone. "I thought I recognised you. Good to see you back, rockborne, even if you can't go into the mines."

"Not by choice, I assure you."

"Get on with it," Dirk growls through the comms chip.

"If you'll excuse us," Kylone says, "I'd like to help Assistant Alva suit up."

"Go. The pair of you."

Both Kylone and Alva step towards the exit.

"One other thing," the Hubmaster says. "How do I get hold of the Chief Compineer?"

"You don't," Alva says. "Believe me, he'll get hold of you if it's important."

Kylone notices a slight shiver run through her, leaving him to wonder what has happened between her and Dirk. This is not the time to ask questions. "Come on," he leads the way to the suiting area.

A board above one of the brown spacesuits starts showing Alva's name, while its chest screen lights up and flashes greens through a start-up checklist. She steps over and pulls it off its hanger, and almost drops it. "I hadn't realised how heavy these suits are." She opens its front and starts climbing into its legs.

He holds up the top half behind her so that it does not pull her backwards to make it harder to suit up. Flashbacks of when he used to regularly do the same for Selma intrude on his consciousness, but he forces them away. He has a job to do; others need his help.

Lenny, helmet under arm, joins them. "They told me to report to you, Priest Kylone." The last words come out with an emphasis, as if to remind him he once was someone else.

Alva shrugs into the suit's shoulders. "I've never been down a mine before."

"Wise move," Lenny says. "Which tunnels?"

"Beta Reach and then some turn-offs," Alva replies.

Kylone almost says, "What turn-offs?" but bites his lips. Dirk trusted him to let Lenny go with Alva. It was time to trust his judgement in making sure Alva would stay safe. He glances round the hub. Everyone is getting on with their job. The Hubmaster and Diomedes have their backs turned to them, gesticulating at the holograph map. "We've both got hidden comms chips in our ears."

"That's illegal."

"The person at the other end has special license to do this at need and will keep private conversations officially unheard."

"Who is it?" Lenny says through gritted teeth.

"Chief Compineer Dirk Schimmeratski," Alva says. "I'm his Assistant, Alva Larsson, by the way." She holds out a gloved hand.

Lenny's eyes widen as she limply shakes Alva's hand. "What's the job?"

"Laying a comms relay to try to contact the trapped miners in tunnels to the side of the main rescue effort," Alva replies. "Dirk has worked out a possible route."

Kylone did not like the friendly way she said Dirk. "There are a couple of other things you both ought to know."

They both stared at him in silence.

"The Guardians may not be telling us everything they know about the mines. If you hear Dirk contradict them–"

"Take Dirk's advice," Alva says. "I get that. What's the other thing?"

Kylone stares at Alva. "I'm sorry, Alva. It's better if Lenny knows."

"Knows what?" Lenny pounces.

Alva presses her lips together for a few seconds. "If you trust her to say nothing, then I trust her."

"What the hell have I landed myself into here?" Lenny whispers urgently.

"Alva has a better rockborne ability than I ever had, maybe even better than Kieran Macleod ever was. Trouble is she doesn't know the significance of what she might see in the mine. She was never taught. She may ask you for help in interpreting the sight. Think you can do that?"

"Woo-hoo," Dirk sniggers into his ear. "So that's her little secret."

Kylone turns to Alva. "Don't worry, I'll deal with him, after he comes off his adrenalin high."

"Oh promises, promises," Dirk cackles.

"I always did want a long ponytail as a souvenir," Alva whispers.

"You wouldn't dare!" Dirk yelps.

Alva smiles sweetly.

"All right," Dirk continues, "I give in and have ordered the pair of you some camomile tea."

Kylone softly groans.

Lenny looks at Kylone. "What am I missing?"

"Nothing much. Just Dirk being Dirk." Alva fastens her suit up to the neck, and picks up the helmet and the case with the comms kit. "Shall we go?" she asks Lenny.

Startled, she breaks off her stare at Kylone. "The sooner this job's done, the quicker the rescue will be."

Lenny and Alva both enter a personnel airlock and the doors shut behind them. Kylone turns towards the hub entrance.

"Not so fast," Dirk whispers.

He stops and scratches behind his ear.

"I need you to stay put," Dirk continues. "Two reasons. Be on hand to stop Diomedes messing up the rescue. The second, if you're up to it, is to listen on Alva and Lenny. Lenny's not rockborne. You are. You might be able to interpret what Alva describes better than her. Do you think you can do the latter?"

He is momentarily dizzy as the blood drains from his face. His rockborne talent has been dormant for these last ten years. If only he had registered the fatal flaw in the rock seams then. He feels unreliable, and will question his own judgement.

But his fickle gift must be exhumed to help others in desperate need.

He calls deeper upon his faith to help him through this.

He heads for the spacesuits, scanning for one that is signed red, which means it is unsafe to be worn. There are two such, side by side at the very back. One has what he is looking for, an intact comms unit. He unlocks it from the helmet and hooks it round his ear. He turns to go the sickbay and almost bumps into Diomedes.

"I think it best you leave this hub," the High Priest says in a commanding voice.

"I will when I can escort Assistant Alva back to the Chief Compineer. I have a responsibility to fulfil."

"I'm overriding that duty. You are to leave now. The strain is clearly showing on you."

"I know. I'm already on my way to the sickbay." Kylone sidesteps him and marches past him.

The nurse takes one look at him as he enters and makes him sit in a quiet corner to his relief. She places a monitor patch on his wrist and looks at readouts on a handheld screen. "Looks like you've had too much excitement for one day."

"I've ordered another three boxes of camomile tea for you," Dirk whispers.

Kylone resents Dirk's comment; the camomile joke has worn too thin. He looks up at the grey-haired nurse. "Just some bad memories resurfacing."

She nods. "I guessed as much. I was in the sickbay ten years ago when they brought you in. You sit there, take your time and leave when you feel ready. Can I get you anything to drink?"

"Anything but camomile tea," Kylone ventures.

"Lemon balm?"

"That'll do nicely, thank you." He sits back, closes his eyes and listens in on the conversation between Alva, Lenny and Dirk via his earpiece and the comms unit from the defunct spacesuit.

***

"Same routine, switch the comp-stick on and fine-tune its back-relay to the previous comp-stick," Dirk says over the spacesuits' comms for the seventh time. Although he hides it well, Kylone picks out the undertone of boredom.

"Doing it now," Alva replies. A few seconds of silence pass. "It's linked successfully."

"Good. Set it up to maximum broadcast and try to talk to the trapped miners."

"I know this may sound silly," Alva says, "but how are you going to link into the miners' spacesuit comms?"

"An actual intelligent question."

"And?"

"Techno-complexity. Too long to explain."

Kylone sits up, alert to Dirk needing to hack. He guesses the miners have switched off whatever comms means Dirk wants to connect with, which will mean bypassing encryptions, sussing out passwords and cross-connecting systems that should operate independently for safety reasons. "It means that it's better you don't know."

"Oh." Alva replies, making it sound like she understands.

"What're you waiting for?" Dirk growls.

"It's on," Alva says.

"Can anyone hear me?" Lenny asks.

No response.

"Please, Miner Team Carbo Five-Fifteen, come in," Lenny says, urgency edging into her voice.

Nausea rises in Kylone. He should not be here in the hub's sickbay involved in another mining accident. The doctors had given him dire warnings of the consequences, like the next time he might not recover. His hand comes up to cover his mouth.

He has to stick with them.

"Carbo Five-Fifteen, please respond," Lenny tries again, desperation now blatant in her voice.

Kylone flashbacks to another sickbay. The final body bag they brought in could not hide the head at an impossible angle to the body and unbelievably twisted legs. He had read the label; Selma. He cannot remember what happened next.

"Have I gone mad?" a male voice comes over the link.

It sounds familiar to Kylone. His heart pounds in his chest with excitement.

"No, you haven't," Dirk quickly replies. "You're hearing us via your comp-stick. It was the only way we could get through to you. Keep it switched on."

"But it's switched off…" the voice says. "How? … Who are you?"

"The Chief Compineer," Dirk replies.

"Assistant Alva Larsson."

"Miner Lenny Tyndale. We need your status."

"Alva?" the voice says.

"That you Miner Cris?" she replies.

"Yes. Is this really happening?"

"We need your status," Lenny snaps.

"Hell, if I'm hallucinating, this is a good way to go." He laughs. "There was a cave-in about thirty metres back in our access tunnel. We fear a further breach. We've huddled together in an alcove about ten metres from the mine face to keep each other warm. There's one other thing."

Kylone does not like the way his voice turns sombre.

"Two of us were examining the tunnel wall at the cave-in. They're buried and the spacesuits' life signs do not register. For the record they are Miner Christina Welbrook and Scavie Michael Anderson."

"Sorry to hear that, but I need you to scan the site with your comp-stick," Dirk says.

Kylone lurches out of his chair for the nearby sink. He reaches it just in time to throw up. Words float past him. The nurse rushes over and holds him steady. He takes in deep breaths.

"I told you to leave," Diomedes says from behind.

In his weakened state, Kylone feels the full force of enmity behind that comment. He straightens up to face the High Priest. "You don't know all the facts." He barges past to head for the control room.

Footsteps hurry after him. "Go home."

Once through the plasma door, the Hubmaster, standing behind the two men at the consoles, turns to him. Her face registers shock. "What's wrong, Priest Kylone?"

"I couldn't stop him returning," Diomedes complains from behind.

"I regret to say, Hubmaster, that two of the trapped people are dead: Miner Christina Welbrook and Scavie Michael Anderson. They were beneath the cave-in."

"I see." The Hubmaster takes a deep breath. "How're the others?"

Dirk whispers in his ear. "Sending footage now."

"The Chief Compineer is sending pictures from Miner Cris Polhem's comp-stick of–"

The holograph in the control room trans-morphs into a miniature cavern with translucent floor walls and ceiling to allow them to look into it. Red edges around holes in the walls denote where Cris had not yet been able to take direct line of sight pictures, which pinpoints his position down the access tunnel's slope towards the cavern's mine face. What catches Kylone's eye is the pale blue flat floor at the mine face. The front edge of the boring machine has sunk into it. A streak of pale blue snakes its way back past the boring machine, past the line of wagons and on up to debris of the cave-in. Only that pale blue is not solid: it is liquid oxygen.

"Seven hells of ice." The Hubmaster turns to the consoles. "Tell the rescue team we've had new information. Stop torching the ice and work by hand or slow mechanical drills only. Tell the miners outside it's now a two-hour on, two hour off, shift system. Do it, now." This is enough to warn everyone about the liquid oxygen.

If it came into contact with any machinery with components rubbing fast enough, it would cause a spark that could lead to a fire.

The chances of the miners surviving their ordeal are miniscule. Kylone empathises with their cloud-storm of emotions they must be suffering: frustration at waiting without helping with their own rescue because they might make things worse; survivor's guilt at the loss of their teammates; wondering what they did wrong to cause the cave-in; fear and uncertainty of what will happen next. He swallows hard before he finds his voice. "Hubmaster, with your permission, I'd like to talk Miner Cris and his team through this crisis when you don't need to talk directly to them."

"Absolutely not," Diomedes pipes up. "Look at you. You're in no fit state."

"I'm one of the few people on this moon who really understands what they are going through." Kylone raises his voice slightly. "So is Lenny, but she has not had the counselling training. That makes me the best qualified here." It is the second time he has publicly challenged the

High Priest within such a short space of time: once can be forgiven as stupidity; twice means a formal review with perhaps consequences. He does not give a damn.

"I suggest you reconsider your intentions."

Before Kylone can say he will not, the Hubmaster intervenes. "Guardian of History we require your considered advice as soon as possible."

Diomedes acknowledges the call for help by bowing his head slightly and turning his face into the serene neutral mode. "What knowledge do you require of us?"

"This was supposed to be a dry mine." She points to the pale blue streak in the holograph. "Where the hell did that liquid oxygen come from? I want to know what possible routes it took from wherever to get into that access tunnel as I want to work out how to avoid that damned stuff, like yesterday."

"If you would send this information to our Archive library I will get our best analysts on the job."

"It's already sent," Dirk says from the comms on Joshua's control console.

Joshua jerks backwards in his seat. The Hubmaster snaps her head round to the console.

Diomedes glares at it. "Who're you?"

"The Chief Compineer doing some necessary hacking. High Priest, get your skates on and sort that analysis out. I've set up a direct confidential comms link for you from the doctor's office in the sickbay."

Kylone is hard-pressed not to let a snigger escape.

Diomedes glowers at him as he dashes out of the control room.

"If you need any help or are unable to continue," the Hubmaster says to Kylone, "let me know."

"Thank you."

"One more thing," Dirk adds. "I've sent all the spare comp-sticks I have your way. I want Alva and Lenny to lay them round the mine so I can measure where some solid ores are. It won't tell us where that liquid oxygen is, but it will tell us some places where it is definitely not."

An astonished look takes over the Hubmaster's face.

"Since when did the Chief Compineer know about mining?"

"I don't," Dirk says. "I'm a compineer and therefore by definition, curious. What do you expect when Kylone starts talking about the properties of crystals?"

Her eyes move to Kylone. "You know the Chief Compineer?"

Kylone closes his eyes, realising the Guardian of History can now easily find out about Dirk's disguise as Isaac Hawking. "Regrettably, yes."

"Six packets of lemon balm tea have been ordered for you." Dirks voice becomes serious. "If any one of you so much as mentions this little fact, I'll make your comms life hell."

Kylone snaps his eyes open. "Don't worry. He rarely carries out such threats for innocent mistakes or ineptitude."

"You take all the fun out of life."

Kylone smiles sweetly at the console. "If you would be so kind as to open a comms link with Miner Cris and the other trapped miners via my spacesuit's comms unit…"

"Seriously, it's variable and may cut out, but there you go."

Kylone sits down at the far end of the table away from the consoles. "Miner Cris," he says into his comms unit, "I'm Priest Kylone. You might have heard of me by my previous name, Miner Simon Redman." He swallows hard. It is a long time since he had referred to himself by his old name.

"I've never heard either of your…"

That does not make sense given how infamous his accident had become. Unless Cris *has* recognised him and his mining history; the miner is doing his Mirandan duty by trying, in his own way, to spare him remembering the long-ago horror and its accompanying emotions. In a way this is good news. Cris, in being helpful where he can be, is being realistic.

"I guess you've realised where you heard of me before."

"Are you sure you're up to this? I mean it could…"

"Bring back old memories?"

"Yes. Can't you call another priest in?"

"I can, and when the time is right, will. There are good reasons why it has to be me on hand at the moment."

"I don't like the sound of that." His voice rises by a couple of notes.

Kylone senses the man's panic. It is infectious and he has to take a second to push it away. The miner needs calming down. "I'm here as a personal counsellor to somebody who is essential for your rescue."

"You doubling up on duties?"

"No. But it gives me an insight as to what is going on, which I hope will end up helping you."

There is a pause before Cris replies. "What's going on?"

Kylone remembers his initial reactions to his own accident once it had dawned what was going on: what can I do to help, who else can I call on and what do I not know about? It was the last question that struck fear into him because he had to face the unknown and any horrors it hid. The nightmare became worse after that. His breathing quickens. He must not go there. His heart thumps in his ears. He pushes the memories back down into his mind. He has to for Cris's sake. He concentrates on choosing his words carefully, words that he would have wanted to hear then. "I think you can guess the answer, but I'll say it anyway. We're proceeding as fast and carefully as we can. We're working on removing the debris from the cave-in and taking new sensor readings to find out why the cave-in happened."

"That's what I expected." His voice is back down to his normal lower notes, but there is a slight tremble in the words. "I need to tell the others I'm in contact with you. So I'll be in comms private mode for a couple of minutes."

"Before you go, can you make sure the others are with you in the alcove?"

"They already are."

Kylone is glad of that. Companionship when facing

danger is an important boost to the people's welfare. The link goes silent.

Kylone wishes he had had his crewmates with him in those few early minutes after the accident ten years ago. The loneliness added to the uncertainty of what was going on. People were cramming his spacesuit's comms so much that it had turned into loud white noise. He added to it with his screaming for help. Suddenly Meriel shouted: "Stop talking, all of you." Dirk had not been on Miranda then to hack and control the comms into trying to create order out of chaos. If only he had arrived from Saturn a couple of months earlier, the outcome might have been a lot different. Kylone would not have gone in search for the deep truths of life; a search that he now suspects led him to joining the Priesthood.

"I'm back online," Cris says. "Everyone here is linked in on open comms to my spacesuit so they can hear what you say and vice versa."

"Good thinking," Kylone says and repeats what he said to Cris about their situation and gets them talking.

He concentrates so much on chatting with six miners to keep their morale up that he loses all sense of time. He notices the Hubmaster put a private comms unit to her ear. Her face slowly becomes grimmer.

"I understand," she replies into her microphone. She waves a hand across her microphone to signal all outward comms should be silenced.

It is bad news.

"I need to take a natural break," Kylone tells the miners and switches off his comms. "Am I talking to dead men?" he asks bluntly.

"The rescue team have hit a difficulty. They can't get to them in time. We might be able to get two of them out if…" She does not need to say the rest. The miners do not have enough oxygen to survive until the rescuers can get fresh oxygen stacks to them. It means four of them have to commit suicide now for two to live. Tradition dictates the two youngest would be given life: in this case Miners Elysia Sansum and Paul Johnson.

"Dirk," Kylone says loudly. "Did you get that?"

"Get what?" Dirk blurts out of the console.

The Hubmaster furrows her brows and glares at Kylone. The men check their consoles and look bewildered.

"They're out of oxygen," Kylone says.

"How can they be with all the liquid down there?"

"Let me rephrase that: they'll run out of oxygen stacks before the rescue team can get there."

"Give me half an hour."

"We don't have that time."

"Oh hell!"

Kylone closes his eyes. Scenes of his nightmare past flash through his mind more vivid than ever. He has to escape. He opens his eyes into the current nightmare. His hands tremble.

"I'll tell them," the Hubmaster says.

"Order the rescue team to stop digging. Now!" Dirk shouts.

"Why?"

"Long explanation. They're about to cause an even bigger cave-in."

"How the blazes can you know that?"

"Just do it."

The Hubmaster looks to Kylone.

He knows she is asking a silent question; is his judgement sound on mining issues? He, when dealing with serious matters, has never been wrong before.

But Dirk is working against the clock, having to take shortcuts in areas he must learn as he goes along. It means taking risks, but as a compineer he knows all about minimising risk. He is going against the course of action recommended by the Guardians of History, who have data-wise the weight of experience and years of long study behind them. They rely on the unsaid assumption of events repeating themselves in a predictable manner.

The question boils down to how much of the situation they are facing is new.

Kylone bites his lips while he mentally checks the Heroes Gallery for those involved in mining accidents with liquid oxygen. There have been very few, and only in the deeper mines. He glances at the holograph. The accident is mid-level. This accident really is a new type. The choice is obvious. He nods in reply.

The Hubmaster opens the comms link on the console. "Rescue team, you need a break." She checks at her watch. "In fact, it's only forty minutes until the next shift takes over. Why don't you make your way back to the hub?"

A comms light on the console switches from green to amber to indicate a private link. "Alvarez here. Does that mean there's no hope?"

"We've just been advised what we're doing is too dangerous to continue. We're working up a new plan."

"Will there really be a new one?"

"To be honest, I don't know."

"Ice dust! What the hell am I going to tell my sister? My niece is one of the trapped miners."

Kylone hears his dread, anger and frustration all too clearly. Smooth words of comfort so familiar in these situations will not be enough. "We're working on a way to buy them the necessary oxygen time."

"How? Putting them into a coma?" Desperation edges into his voice.

"Not a good idea if they have to move quickly," Kylone says, more for Dirk's benefit than Alvarez's.

"So what can you do?" His words are almost choked off with a sob.

"Just working a bloody miracle," Dirk intervenes. "Why does Chynoweth have to be such cheapskates with its equipment? When I write up my report of this, I'm going to damn well publish it."

Kylone relaxes a little. Dirk is back to his old grumbling flippant self, which means he has a solution to the trapped miners' oxygen problem.

"We've first call on the Corp's kit and we're using the best we can get access to," Alvarez replies.

"The Chief Compineer isn't talking about your kit, but what the trapped miners have," Kylone says.

There is a long silence. "That's quite a serious accusation he's making," the Hubmaster says.

Kylone feels coated in dampness. He had been honest and had not meant to get Dirk into trouble. The two are incompatible, but right now, those miners needed Dirk more than his honesty. "The Chief Compineer was talking under pressure. I'm sure when he realises his mistake he'll apologise."

The Hubmaster nods. "We're all under pressure. Understood."

"Done it," Dirk says. "I've got one of the miners breathing the liquid oxygen through a patched-in siphoning and regulating system to the suit. The others will be in about five minutes."

"What?" Alvarez says. "That's wonderful."

"Don't be so quick," Dirk replies. "I don't know how long this source will last, for various reasons. Time's still against us. The rock and ice have definitely shifted around them. We need a new map to identify a safe route to the miners. I can only do so much with Alva's comp-sticks. And have you got any reliable rockborne or iceborne with you?"

The Hubmaster looks to Joshua, whose hands quickly move over the console. He frowns. "No iceborne at all have come forward. As for the rockborne, only two B-raters."

Panic hits Kylone: the iceborne are very nervous and emotional, with an extra sense attuned to ice collapse and fast movements. Not even the least sensitive of them being here means the ice is shouting danger loud and clear. He prays for his own peace. What does not surprise him is the lack of rockborne. As soon as it was announced that it was a cave-in, the rockborne would know their talent could be of no help. They needed continuity in the rock to 'read it', which piles of debris would not have.

"Dave, order extra sensors from the Lacro mine," the

Hubmaster says. "Joshua, get the rockborne in and have them report direct to the Chief Compineer."

"Tell the rockborne to work in pairs each making their own assessment. If they agree on what they read, I'll use that," Dirk adds.

"That leaves one other deployable option."

"Nah!" Dirk says. "Don't even think about it."

The Hubmaster glances at the console in disbelief. "I mean Priest Kylone, if he can cope with it."

Sharp snapshots of past debris, claustrophobic spaces, absolute stillness, echoes of his own breathing in his spacesuit, the smell of his own sweat, the medics shouting at him, but not hearing their voices, the glow of reflected red lights from lit-up suit medical panels, the blood and the dead flick on one after another. Kylone's breathing quickens. He hears the thumping of his heart in his ears. He becomes dizzy. He stands to go to the sickbay.

Oblivion.

***

Kylone is restless to be out of the sickbay. A glance at his wristpad shows it is only two minutes since he last looked at it. The nurse continues to refuse to let him go saying she needs to be sure he won't have a relapse without help at hand. He is left wondering if something is seriously wrong with him, as it has now been twelve hours since he fainted. All he can do is wait and keep off the comms to those still working on the rescue.

He lies still with eyes closed and meditating his way to calmness on the gurney. The rosemary scent does not quite overpower those of disinfectant and human sweat. Muffled noises come from the hub: a rising and falling hum with the occasional snap of something crashing. There is brief increase and then reduction of both the smell and noise.

"What did I tell you?" the raspy voice of Priest Patricianna says.

He smiles. “To keep away from mines.”

“And how much do you think this antic of yours has set you back?”

“Best guess, about six months, but you’re the expert.”

“And you’ve got High Priest Diomedes calling for your retirement.”

His smile vanishes. “I’m certainly not ready for that.”

“I’m glad something can wipe that ridiculous smile off your face.”

He hears footsteps, a brief scrap and the whoomph of a seat taking some weight.

“I’m here to assess your fitness for priestly duties,” Patricianna adds.

“Can’t that wait until we return to the chapel?”

“Absolutely not. I need to know how to deal with Diomedes.”

Kylone sighs. “There’s only one way this will end: a Truth Tribunal. Mine.”

“Don’t joke,” she snaps.

He opens his eyes and turns his head. Her faded blue eyes are crowned by bushy white eyebrows and encircled with deep, fine wrinkles. “I’m not. The Archdeacon herself warned me not to challenge his authority, but that is exactly what I had to do to try to save those miners’ lives.” He nods towards the mine entrance. “Any news on them?”

Patricianna shakes her head. “Not yet, one way or the other.” She frowns. “They should’ve run out of air by now, so I fear the worst.”

“Give me another half an hour,” Dirk whispers in his ear.

“There was talk of only having enough oxygen between them for two to survive just before it got too much for me,” Kylone says aloud.

She narrows her eyes on him. “Is that what made you faint? It should have.”

“No. It was being asked to function as a rockborne.”

Her crinkled mouth opens slightly as if she does not know what to say next. “Something’s changed in you:

something very significant. I need to get to the bottom of it."

He inwardly groans at the thought of yet another intense consultation session. He finds the controls on the gurney, raises its back to sit up comfortably. "Let's get this over with."

"Interesting." She pauses. "Let's start with you telling me what happened from the moment you heard the alarm for this accident."

His mind flits back to the moment the siren sounded in Dirk's office, which he realises would raise a lot of questions. "There're counselling confidences involved."

"Tell me what you can without breaking those for now. Just give me an overall picture."

He knows all too well she can order him to break those confidences, this being an official consultation. He chooses his words carefully. "I was discussing matters with the Chief Compineer in his office when the siren sounded."

"Wait. Since when did you know the Chief Compineer?"

"Assistant Alva Larsson was there," the obvious implication is he was there to counsel her at her request. He does not counter the implicit suggestion. He dislikes the deception, but it is necessary.

"I see." She plays her fingers on her lips, a sure sign she is trying to come to a decision. Finally she lowers her hand onto the armrest. "Carry on."

He does, careful to leave out the business of the secret earpieces, the conversation he has when he was helping Alva suit up and any whispers that came through his earpiece. He reaches the point where the Hubmaster has switched off the outgoing comms on the consoles.

The screen opposite him is pulled aside. Alva, dressed in her Assistant's silk, holding two mugs of steaming drinks. "I was asked to bring you both some refreshment," she smiles. "Lemon Balm tea for the patient and Earl Grey for you, Priest."

Alva here out of her spacesuit means Dirk is confident

of saving the trapped miners. He beams a welcoming smile, though he is getting to hate the type of tea she has brought for him.

"Bless you, I'm afraid I don't know your name?" Patricianna stands to hold out her hand to accept her mug.

"Assistant Alva Larsson. I work for the Chief Compineer."

"Priest Kylone has just been telling me how helpful you've been." She takes a sip of her tea. "Lovely. Hm. Just how I like it."

"I try to do what I can." She steps up beside the gurney to hand him his tea with a big grin. "You're to drink it all up."

He accepts the mug and notices Patricianna's eyes flitting back and forth between him and Alva. "Thank you and the nurse for arranging this." The nurse in this case is Dirk who clearly wants to slow his conversation with Patricianna down.

"Nurse?" Patricianna asks.

"This tea is to help calm patients down." He wonders if his answer came out too quickly.

"Ah." Patricianna turns her attention to Alva. "Won't you be joining us?"

"Much as I would like to, Priest, I've had a long tiring day and need some sleep. If you'll excuse me." She steps out and places the screen back in its place.

Kylone watches her go, wishing she had stayed to help him distract Patricianna. He lets out a breath of exasperation. "Now where did I get to?"

She shakes her head. "No need to continue. I'm signing you off as fit for full priestly duties."

He is puzzled. "I don't understand."

"You will in time."

This confuses him even more. "If you say so."

"You'll see." She takes another sip. "I'd like to resume our weekly counselling sessions." She waves her mug in the air. "Just as a precaution."

"Against what?"

"The unforeseen."

When she is in this mood, Kylone knows she will not give a straight answer. Maybe, it is her revenge for him not being quite straightforward with her. Time to change the subject. "How's the supposedly non-existent politics for the Archdeacon's succession coming along?"

She laughs. "You've noticed."

"No, the Archdeacon told me."

"Let's leave it at there's a lot of time being wasted."

"Sounds to me you're enjoying the entertainment."

"Of course."

The screen swings aside again. Miner Cris grins ear to ear in his spacesuit covered in too many different types of muck. "Don't worry, I won't come in." He points to his suit. "Just wanted to say thank you to Miner Simon Redman, sorry," he shakes his head, "Priest Kylone for keeping us sane during those early hours. We are in your debt."

"I did what was necessary."

"Everyone got out?" Patricianna asks.

He nods. "Except for Miner Christina Welbrook and Scavie Michael Anderson caught in the initial cave-in."

"May their souls be peaceful," both priests intone.

"Looks like it's about to get very crowded in this sickbay. Fortunately nobody was seriously injured enough to need to be taken to intensive care. In fact." Cris glances back. "Thanks to Priest Kylone, we'll only need medication to avoid short-term depression, stress disorder and panic attacks, if at all."

Patricianna finishes off her tea. "They'll have one less to deal with here. I'm signing Priest Kylone off and sending him home. He has already done more than could be expected of him."

"Oh!" A look of disappointment crosses Cris's face. "I was hoping…"

"Would you accept my priestly services instead?"

Cris bows slightly. "Any comfort you can give me and the crew will be greatly appreciated."

***

After the stress of the previous day Kylone welcomes the restful task of laying out the Sacra ready for the Greening Ceremony, which is the most important of all the sacred rites. This natural phenomenon is the greatest of all lighting wonders in the Uranian system, its sheer size and moving beauty giving off a sense of awe and reverence. When the Priesthood developed to fulfil the spiritual and social development needs of Mirandans, it had to embody something unique to the moon. The Greening was the obvious choice. It became their lead icon.

Priest Patricianna probably had a hand in assigning him this duty here in the Sacristy, which feels more like a walk-in cupboard. He checks the priest's staff is full of the holiest of liquids – pure Argon stabilised below its boiling point of -186 degrees centigrade – before attaching the Pasture Star gem at the top and placing it on the side-bench, ready to be picked up.

The safety door opens a crack.

"Anyone here?" the familiar voice of the Archdeacon asks.

"I am." He expected someone to check up on him, this being his first time, but is surprised it is her.

In her official green she poses at her most serene with hands clasped in front.

"It is an honour to have you here. Please come in."

She enters, closing the door.

The room is now cramped. He carefully turns to unzip a black clothes bag that hangs to one side to reveal a glistening green robe, which the priest conducting the ceremony wears over their spacesuit. He reverently takes the bag off the hanger.

She runs her fingertip over the Pasture Star. "You know I've never been able to take the Greening Ceremony."

"Sorry to hear that. I gather its light show can be quite spectacular on occasions."

She grunts. "Epilepsy. Seems to be the curse of Archdeacons." She frowns. "Have you not seen the Greening?"

"No." He checks the folds of the cloak are just so. "I

was too busy in my younger days and now, well, I've not been that inclined."

"Then how do you check the mosaic is right?"

"Recorded pictures are better than relying on pure memory."

She bends over to view the readouts on the knob at the top of the staff. "The staff is in order." She attends to the cloak. "Do you want to know why I backed your mosaic? After all, there were other urgent tasks for the Priesthood."

Kylone loads oxygen tablets into a stack ready for any spacesuit. "I assumed you felt confident it was the most useful task I could complete, given my limitations."

She tilts her head. "You're right, but there is more." She strokes the shoulder of the cloak. "About one in a hundred of us cannot see the Greening without ill effect. I wanted them, and me, to have a chance to see some of its majesty, even if your mosaic can only show a small fraction of it."

"That's very kind of you."

"It was a means to an end: to get more visitors into the chapel, and from them more fervents." She scans the cloak. "This cloak looks fine."

Somebody gently knocks at the door.

Kylone checks the time. The priest taking the Greening Ceremony is not due for another five minutes.

The Archdeacon steps to one side. "Enter."

Alva opens the door. Her French plaits look super neat from a recent tidy-up; her make-up is too sharply delineated to have been worn long; and her grey silk is too smooth to have acquired wear and tear scratches and dullness. Above all else her rose perfume with an undertone of musk freshens the air.

Alva looks from Kylone to the Archdeacon. "Am I too early?"

"Goodness me, no," the Archdeacon smiles. "In fact your timing is impeccable. I've just finished my inspection here and found everything to be satisfactory."

He wonders why the Archdeacon is not being her

normal thorough self, but can say nothing in front of Alva. He tries to keep the surprise from his face.

"I still don't understand why you invited me to come along with you to the Greening Ceremony, though I am grateful for the opportunity."

He almost chokes.

Alva flashes a puzzled frown at him.

"Why should the Priesthood deny non-congregation members the chance to see one of our most beautiful sights?" the Archdeacon says. "No, after all you did down Carbo mine, consider this my personal thank you gift."

Alva breaks out into grin. "Then I'm happy to accept."

"The pleasure is all mine, I assure you."

High Priest Diomedes dressed in a black spacesuit, holding his helmet under his arm, approaches from behind Alva. His eyes lock onto Kylone.

The Archdeacon waves her hands in welcome. "Ah, punctual as always, High Priest Diomedes."

He bows his head towards her. "It is an honour to preside over this ceremony. Thank you for choosing me." He glances over the room. "Is this the first time Priest Kylone has done the preparation?"

A wicked smile cracks her face. "It is, but don't worry, I checked over the Sacra myself. I must say it's nice to see you two getting along so well."

Kylone now understands what the Archdeacon is really up to: checking that he and Diomedes can safely appear together in public when performing priestly duties. He silently commends her caution.

"Archdeacon Ariadne, may I have a word with you?" Diomedes pointedly looks at Kylone and Alva in turn. "Guardian of History business."

"If needs must." The Archdeacon's face drops into sadness and looks at Alva. "I'm so sorry. The responsibilities of office."

Alva smiles. "I quite understand."

"But," the Archdeacon turns to Kylone, "could you escort her in my stead?"

He had intended to return to work on the mosaic, but

that can be done later. "My task is done here and I would be happy to."

"That's settled. And thank you."

He takes his cue to sidle past the Archdeacon into the circular room with its smoothed grey walls, floor and ceiling, and seven doors, of which only the one to the Sacristy was open. He checks the title board of the second door to his left: 'Aerial Gallery – Verona Rupes', the way to the ceremony's viewpoint. Lights switch on as he opens the door. The whole tunnel has the usual translucent pink of reinforcement lining to keep the air inside and the ice in position outside. Behind it for the first metre is the typical brown of asteroid rock, and beyond, he makes out darker spots in the white frostiness, suggesting rocks embedded in ice. There is a small, yet noticeable drop in temperature to just on the edge of being comfortable for him. He glances at the cuffs on Alva's silk. They are thick and therefore meant for the cold. Her hands are clearly used for fiddly jobs such as picking small fruits and planting out seedlings, or more lately dealing with the Compineer's mechatronics. The important thing is they are the healthy pink of warmth. "If you would like to follow me?"

"If you'll excuse us," Alva says to the others.

"Of course." The Archdeacon flicks her hands to shoo them on.

After a couple of minutes' walk on an upward slope, they go through another door into an ellipsoid capsule, big enough to hold thirty people. Completely made out of transparent silicara, it is barely detectable by its sheens. The only concession to substantiality is a waist-high green guardrail around the capsule's girth.

The expanse without a cocooning spacesuit makes Kylone lightheaded. He will never get used to this type of environment, so takes time to check his feet are still on the floor, his head will not bump into the ceiling and his body remains upright with its sense of balance still functioning. "Follow what I do."

Taking hold of the rail and avoiding looking down into

the abyss, he lowers one foot to make contact with the clear floor, and then carefully places his other foot onto the invisible solidity. He forces himself to focus on the centre of the back wall, where the capsule adheres to the cliff's face of cut-through silver rock nodules in the ice. As his gaze turns towards the side of the capsule, the mottling dwindles to pure white. It then fades through translucency to transparency, letting in the dim blue light. Uranus' crescent, its horns sunk behind the cliff opposite, sits like an arch over a door into deep night. The vertical grey line of the planet's ring system seen edge on, is like a crack of an opening door that extends upwards into the star-field. The Sun's yellow disk shines from one side of the rings, close to the waning crescent.

He dares to lower his eyes onto the cliff. Its top-to-bottom facets gleam in shades of grey-blue to silver, darkening into the shadows further down. The valley floor, twenty kilometres under his feet, is speckled, with the edges of craters glinting reflected light. Although he cannot make them out at this distance, he knows the fervents are gathering on the valley floor, waiting for the Greening Ceremony.

The shushing of Alva's sliding feet along the floor rather than taking steps is a sure sign she is unused to walking floors she knows are there but cannot see, just like new miners finding their way through dim tunnels. Her hand, pale in this light, comes to rest on the guardrail close to his.

"It's so different from virtual reality, even the life-size one," Alva says.

"Even the most sophisticated immersive VR can't deliver every reality aspect. Processing limits and reality seeping through to the senses."

"Oh?"

"They miss out on exactly the right temperature, dryness of the air, changing air currents as people move round you, the tiny bit less gravity. Yes, you'll weigh a little less here, making you feel a little more euphoric than normal."

"That's a rather detailed statement."

Kylone chuckles. "Part of the Priesthood training. We're trained to observe the conditions around us and their impact on people."

"A shame really. You miss out on the ethereals like appreciating beauty and chasing the scent of mystery."

These are words that have long since lost their meaning to him, his appreciation destroyed by the brutality of his accident. All he has is ghost memories of appreciating life's intangible pleasures.

He turns to look at her, her pale features exaggerated in this darker room. There are too many aspects of her character to piece together into a coherent whole. He can only wait for more revelations, and hope that one of them condenses all his other knowledge into an easily understandable pattern.

She waves a hand over the panorama. "Look at all these subtle blues and greys. Isn't this a kind of balance of light and shade?"

He studies the cliffs, struggling to align with her description. "Nature, as we know it, fits into many different patterns. People are more attuned to some than others. This must be one to your liking."

"Is that your definition of beauty? Something unique to every person?"

"Not mine, but the scientific definition of beauty put into simple words."

"Let me guess. Part of your priestly training?"

"Yes."

The pull of an air current from behind them makes them both turn to face the opening door.

A mobile-chair carrying a white-haired lady hunched up in a blanket is guided in by a younger man with similar features, presumably her son. He pushes it to the best observing position and checks the lady is comfortable. She holds out a wavering hand towards Kylone.

He squeezes it gently in his big hands and waves the sign of blessing above her head. Her face is old, but her eyes sparkle like those of a little girl.

Others enter, in ones or twos. Kylone does his duty and blesses each one, until the gallery is about half full. Outside, beyond Alva, a promontory juts out into the valley. Fifteen metres below its top is an alcove with a carpet of small glistening crystals. How it had been gouged out of the ice like that is a Mirandan mystery the scientists still have to solve.

Staff in hand, Diomedes, wearing his black spacesuit and the artificially flowing green robe, climbs a manmade path from an alcove to the promontory's edge. He stands for a few minutes to let the robe slowly settle on his back and drop towards the ground behind him, and raises the staff to let the Pasture Star be seen from below by those with telescopes, binoculars or specially adapted helmet visors.

Kylone can only guess at the number of fervents down there. He has been told the numbers are usually around 750, a considerable number given the circumstances and way of life: about a tenth of the 150,000 population are non-fervents, a third will be on a work shift and about a fifth will be people like children and the infirm who cannot safely wear a spacesuit. Of the remainder, just over a third of Mirandans, many will be reluctant to pay the extra cost, feel duty-bound to help with the colony's survival or know they are too tired to trust themselves to be in vacuum. It is reassuring the Priesthood and the Greening are so popular, under such circumstances.

In silent stillness the planet's blue light reflected from the cliff walls opposite slowly wanes then changes at the cliff's top to a green-tinged silver. As the greening creeps down the cliff, the green strengthens at the top. Diomedes flicks his rod to spray the holy argon into the valley. Its sparkles float down in groups of blue, yellow and green glints. They will take twelve minutes to reach the valley floor, where the fervents will try to catch a droplet or two on their spacesuits. The green at the cliff's top intensifies further.

Alva catches her breath.

Kylone snaps his head round to look at her.

Her hands cover eyes. What can be seen of her face is scrunched up and her body is shaking. She slumps.

He catches her under her arms and gently lays her on the floor as the others move aside to give them room. The darkness beneath them is disconcerting.

"Here," the old woman says, holding out a folded blanket and a pillow. "They're my spares."

He quickly takes them. "Thank you."

He places the pillow under her head and lays the blanket loosely over her body. He checks her pulse in her neck. It is there. He holds his hand just under nose. She is breathing. These are all standard symptoms of an epileptic fit induced by the Greening. She will come out of it in her own time.

He half kneels beside her and watches intently for any sign of change. She looks at complete peace with her plump lips, perfectly arched eyebrows, long eyelashes and black hair outlining her smooth skin.

Behind him, the light moves from turquoise through green to a dim yellow. The Greening is finished. He sees legs move beside her towards the door and the bottom of the mobile-chair come up beside her.

"Will she be all right?" the old lady asks.

The words break his concentration and he looks up. "It's a severe fit in response to the Greening. No other causes."

"Oh, such a shame. Never be able to see something so wonderful."

He picks up the top two corners of the blanket to fold it back.

"No, you keep them until she is better. Her need is more than mine."

"Thank you. I'll make sure they get back to you. Sorry, I didn't catch your name?"

"Great-grandma Valerie Repton. Priest Patricianna's mother. Just give them to her. She'll get them back to me."

"Doubly thank you."

He watches her wheel her chair through the door,

followed by her son, and then goes back to studying Alva. They are alone.

A quiet groan escapes her lips and her head rolls to one side.

"It's all right, Alva. You're safe."

"What..." She opens her eyes. "What happened?"

"You blacked out. Although it's unusual, it has been known to happen. From what people who've experienced it have said, it's something to do with the light flicker from the Greening."

Her eyes roll from side to side. Then she shakes her head slowly. "No." She lifts herself up on her hands to sit up. Her green eyes widen as she shakes her head more vehemently. "Not flickering. More like a jumbled mess of lines and shapes. As soon as I tried to focus on one thing, another shape forced itself into my view. I know it sounds crazy, but it's the only way I can describe it."

Kylone glances at the cliffs opposite. They are like many other cliffs on Miranda. "Was it your ability to see through things playing tricks?"

She gulps. "It was and it wasn't."

He is confused and feels his brow crease tightly.

"Yes, I could see – no let's say register – the tunnelling behind the cliffs opposite, as you would see it in a holograph. But there was more, much more. I just couldn't make it out." She stares at the cliffs as if trying to bring back the memory. Finally she looks Kylone in the eyes. "Am I going mad?"

"I would say not, but I'm no psychiatrist. When Dirk thanked me for helping in the rescue, he mentioned he had to rely on what I call your rockborne talent. Did you use it extensively?"

She nods.

"Hm."

"What?"

"When the rockborne start using their talent, it becomes stronger until it reaches the individual's plateau. We've always assumed it's been about learning to understand what the rock structures mean."

"But that cliff opposite is pure ice. Virtually see through for me except for the haziness due to what might be dust. I saw that. Then I saw more. Much more. I can't explain it." She trembles.

He hugs her shoulders gently to comfort her. "I'm sure there's a sensible explanation. Just need to find out what."

She throws the blanket off her. "Let's get out of here."

He pulls his hands away, picks up and folds the blanket.

She stands. "And where in the seven hells of ice do I start looking for the cause?"

He picks up the pillow and also stands. "By checking what we know is still true first."

"And that is?"

"Have your eyesight checked out."

"That's stu… actually, that's not so stupid."

CHAPTER 4

Kylone watches the beauty of dawn slowly brightening the whole plain in cyan light from the balcony. He is at ease but not at full peace, more like being satisfied with the progress in his recovery from grief and certain of where he is going in life. Something still troubles him, though it is buried deep within his psyche. He still yearns for that inner peace he notices the most devoted of the Priesthood have and prays that one day he will achieve the transcendent state of being at one with himself.

A popping noise intrudes on his contemplation. His eyes focus towards where the noise came from: down to his right, beyond the chapel's seating, through the window at a jutting up crevice edge of one of the larger craters. Its sharp lines are blurred by scintillations of blue, green, white and silver, forming a tunnel of swirling lights going deep down into the crevice's ice.

An optical illusion. He pulls back his focus to the wall; a white splodge with spider-web thin scratches leading away from it above a downward graze. A larger than normal meteorite strike, but thankfully not big enough to bring the emergency shutters down. The fine lines are disappearing and the main graze and pit turn more translucent. The wall's internalised self-repair system, comprising see-through capillary tubes and nano-chip controls is doing its job of repairing the wall from outside inwards. He makes a mental note to replenish the window repair liquids after the graze has been fully repaired.

Time to attend to his chapel cleaning duties.

Familiar footsteps come up the stairs, the Archdeacon's. He has been expecting her summons or visit, and is glad it is a visit. There will be no formality. He settles down to watch the fading tunnel of swirling colours over the crater.

The footsteps halt beside him.

He continues to stare through the graze. "What can I do for you, Archdeacon?"

"I warned you to be careful of High Priest Diomedes."

"I took heed of it, until lives were at stake."

"That has not escaped my notice. However, he has asked for a panel review of your conduct of two separate events at the Carbo mine."

Although expected, it still comes as a shock. The added worry of possibly becoming moonless makes him inwardly cringe. "I'm not surprised."

"Well, I reviewed the recording of your conversation with him in Carbo Level 5 Hub's Control Room. I pointed out that another way to look at that conversation was that you were interpreting the Chief Compineer's words, not using your own. He then, very grudgingly I may add, dropped that charge."

He senses 'a but' coming, not that it really matters given his own decision. Nevertheless, he appreciates the Archdeacon being on his side – or, to be more precise, being on the side of justice and cautious progress. "Thank you."

"He then asked for a panel review of your refusing to leave the Level 5 Hub when ordered to, and how you came to volunteer supplying data to Isaac Hawking without letting him know."

"So he doesn't think I've given away any confidential Guardians of History data."

"He was reluctant to admit you had been most meticulous in that respect, but his argument is that if he had known earlier he would've been able to assist you both so as not to waste your time. I can't fault his reasoning on this one."

His mind flits back to when the Archdeacon had given her warning: she had then pointed to Isaac being really the Chief Compineer. She could have easily argued that if she had worked his secret identity out then, so could Diomedes. What is the Archdeacon up to? What can she, an astute politician, gain by keeping her silence? A review panel, yes and one that is likely to find him guilty at that. She would lose an ally for no good reason. She must believe he can win. How?

"You're very quiet," she comments.

"Thinking things through." He turns to look her in the eyes. "You're expecting me to call you as a witness to my panel review, so you can publicly show up how inept High Priest Diomedes has been, aren't you?"

Her mouth forms a small 'o' as she lets out an almost silent whistle. "Patricianna's right. You've changed, become more decisive and willing to…" Her eyes narrow.

"To take risks? That's what you were about to say, wasn't it?"

Her eyes waver before she nods.

"This business between me and High Priest Diomedes will not go away with my review panel. I am therefore exercising my right to call a full Truth Tribunal—"

She gasps.

"—which, and I checked our disciplinary regulations last night, I have a right to demand."

"I wouldn't recommend this course of action. For one thing, if you're found guilty, harsher penalties will be imposed."

"I know."

She hesitates. "What do you know that I don't?"

"Facts wise? Nothing. Otherwise I would've brought them to your attention."

A short nod of appreciation indicates she trusts him on this.

He continues, "Instinct wise? There is something very wrong with the way mining is being conducted. We need to find out what."

"How does going for a Truth Tribunal help that?"

"By highlighting the facts and suspicions in the public domain. Maybe someone will come forward with new information. I don't know. What I do know is that during the rescue High Priest Diomedes refused the chance to get more information, when he tried to stop Assistant Alva laying the comms relay. His excuse sounded at best inept, at worst false to me. I'm sure it did to the others, like the Hubmaster. It does beg the question why the Guardian of History would refuse new factual information?"

She turned her head to stare out across the plain. After a few seconds, "That does not give you a defence. It's a deflecting counter-attack, which the tribunal will see through immediately."

This is the first time she has given a combative political assessment in his hearing. Its bluntness shocks him. She is right. He would have to rely on her testimony, which would put him in her debt. Crystal trading, that's what this is; his loyalty for her protection.

He cannot accept such an offer. It could conflict him in the future. His first loyalty lies with the miners, their families and friends, and the safeguarding of Miranda's community. For without the mines, there will be no Miranda colony. This should be every priest's duty, even the Archdeacon's. There clearly is a power struggle of some sort between her and Diomedes, which can easily become the priority.

"I strongly recommend you go with a review panel," she interrupts his thoughts, with steeliness creeping into her voice.

This sounds like an order given to a wayward teenager with the usual 'or else' threat. There is only one she can deliver: an untruthful testimony saying she did not suspect Isaac Hawking was the Chief Compineer. This thought, so against what he had expected, takes seconds of stunned shock to sink in. It hurts the way it did when he first realised his parents were flawed. The disappointment is bitter.

He has no defence available. However, the very existence of this threat means someone is frightened that he might succeed. There is a way. He just has to find it. The only real question is will he find it in time?

He straightens up to face her in a formal stance. "Archdeacon, I appreciate your advice, but I must insist on a Truth Tribunal."

She turns her head to look into his eyes once more. "I can see there is no changing your mind. So be it."

"So be it," he formally acknowledges. "Now, if you'll excuse me, I still have a duty to clean this chapel." He does not give her a chance to say anything and marches past her towards the stairs.

***

Kylone hates travelling in mag-pods but, being in a hurry, puts up with the gradually increasing stuffiness of the ride. With a pod able to hold four people maximum, he finds the limited room for so long constraining. It is too much like the tunnel he, and others, dug as narrowly as possible to make the quickest progress to rescue his teammates. They went too quickly and he was working at the face when the second cave-in behind him happened, terrifying the hell out of him. He wants to forget those horror images, but cannot; he is on his way to meet Meriel. He fists his hands so tightly that his nails dig into his palms. The pain keeps him more focussed on preparing what to say to her.

The pod slows. "You are arriving at your destination, Dunsinane Regio Transit Hall," the mag-pod says. "Alight here for space and surface shuttles, and Dunsinane Farm and Rotunda." The same message streams along a panel above the door.

The red plasma door fades away. A rush of cool better oxygenated air enlivens Kylone to step out into the Hall, its floor, walls and ceiling a chequerboard of grey veneered ice and red plasma rectangles, exits for mag-pods. Behind him is the shushing warning of the door closing: it has either been ordered by another or is being placed in a local parking slot.

Three people head for the door marked for spaceships at the end of the hall. Judging by their rugged orange silks and thickened muscles they are freighter crew here to take a load of minerals and crystals off-moon. Like all off-mooners, they stay only long enough to conduct business and want to get away from the low gravity as soon as possible. Otherwise the hall is empty. Meriel has not arrived yet. He makes his way along a grey aisle, to the designated meeting zone that has several egresses to shuttles, cargo bays, emergency exits, the farm and living quarters in the Rotunda. He turns to wait.

The silence, the stillness, the seemingly being stuck in the eternal moment, lets doubt seep into him. Is he doing the right thing by demanding a Truth Tribunal? What can he do if he is found wanting? Keep on fighting for the miners and relying on their and other people's charity? That would only work for a short while, but maybe give him enough time to build the necessary muscles and bone structure to live on the other inhabited Uranian moons. The few space dust and gas mining habitats are very particular about who they employ, so he has to rule this option out. One of the moons it has to be, preferably Oberon. He makes an appointment that evening at the gym via his wristpad.

A floor square flashes amber and a translucent plasma sheath builds upwards, lifting the red rectangle from the floor to the ceiling. A pod is coming in. He appreciates the rarity of seeing through things, in this case through the sheath's near wall to the far one. Its closest vertical edges have a faint outer amber glow that deepens to a line of dark orange before fading into a steady carrot-orange hue.

A shadow rises from the floor inside the sheath, a mag-pod arriving. His mind's eye thinks of Meriel in her usual brown silk inside the pod facing him, staring up at the panel above the door. Surprisingly she wears a necklet. It is the first time he has ever thought of or seen her wearing jewellery. Its beads are the typical small craggy stones a scavie would pick out from the debris. It must his mind's symbol for her work. From the necklet, hangs a teardrop pendant of an intricate mosaic of Uranus with its main cloud pattern. That is also typical of scavenged material. The pod stops and its door fades.

Kylone watches a smiling Meriel step out of pod. She

wears the same pendant of Uranus he has just imagined. He blinks. The pendant is still there, unchanged: there is no denying it. The only possibility is his rockborne talent must have sensed it. That cannot be right: there was no continuation of rock layers. Just two blocks of air and a layer of vacuum between the plasma shielding and the pod's door. He rubs his eyes trying to get rid of that impression of the jewellery. But he is sure of his memory. He is forced to admit to himself what he does not want to: he has some of the capability of 'seeing through walls' that Alva has. He has to park this thought. More pressing matters must be dealt with.

Walking round a red rectangle, she approaches him. "I was surprised to get your call." Her smile disappears. "Is anything wrong?"

"Very. I need your help."

"With what?"

"I'm facing a Truth Tribunal."

"You? That's crazy."

"I hoped you would think that. I'd like you to be a character witness for me—"

"Of course, I will. But to be honest, I haven't seen much of you since…"

"Priest Patricianna will do the same for my time in the Priesthood."

"Then I'd be more than happy to. What's this about? What're the charges?"

"In order of occurrence, undermining the work of the Guardians of History, publicly challenging the tried and tested methods of the Guardians of History in a life-threatening situation without good reason, and wilfully disobeying a direct order from a High Priest also without good reason."

Meriel's face pales as she opens her mouth and then closes it. "By ice and dust, what the hell's been going on?"

"Do you remember our last conversation?"

"At the Kober Balyow about the lack of work? Sure I do…" Her eyes widen. She steps back. "Wait." She shakes her head. "Are the Guardians of History keeping us short of work?"

"What? No, at least I don't think so." Now she has suggested it, he begins to wonder if it might be true. For now he has to portray the best interpretation of their actions. "More a case of neglecting their duty to look into these things."

"That gets you a Truth Tribunal? How?"

The question penetrates to the nub of his issues. His soul feels naked in front of her. "Because… I'm a miner at heart, despite being a priest these past eight years. They haven't changed who I really am."

"Skid-brake. That's quite some statement to make. And the implications…" Her face goes through a kaleidoscope of looks from confusion via hope through disappointment to a final realisation and determination. "I think we need to have a long chat. Why don't we do it now in the comfort of my home?"

"But your home is way over in the Syracusa Sulcus."

"Not any more. It's here in the Rotunda."

He knew she had been struggling financially, but not that it had got this bad. Dunsinane Rotunda was the first Mirandan community to be built into the ice, using then-newly-developed pink coating as the perfect heat insulator to stop ice-melt outside. Its main part comprises a three-floored ring of condos surrounding a central flat agricultural area known as the Plain for items like beehives. The whole area's dome regulates the Uranian light, or in its absence uses artificial lighting, to mimic the light experienced in the twenty-four periods of New York. This lets the plants and insects keep to their natural circadian rhythm and Earth-seasons to maximise crop yields. During the Plain's night, light is diverted to a subsidiary neighbouring under-ice farm known as the Greenhouse, so that when the Rotunda has its summer, it has its winter, and vice versa. The whole complex allows year-round farming of various crops, which was designed to make it self-sufficient in food, energy and water. It was *the place* to live. Inevitably too many people moved there and turned it into overcrowded slums. It is now the ghetto of Miranda, where the poor and unhealthy drift to.

"I know what you're thinking," Meriel continues. "But I really feel comfortable here."

"Look, if you ever need any help…"

"I know where to come, thank you, but somehow I doubt that will ever be necessary."

This confuses him even more. "How can you say that when you're a scavie?"

She laughs. "Trust me on this. Come on, let's have some tea at my place." She strides towards the doorway marked for the Rotunda.

He follows her through a tunnel with bulkheads and safety doors closely spaced together until they pass through a blue plasma door into a corridor circling the Rotunda with the condos' doors and windows, and an occasional stairway up to the next level along its outer wall. Arched slit windows and a narrow doorway to the Plain to his left allow the planet's blue light through to form wide pools on a lawn of small leaved flowering plants, which he remembers are different types of thymes and ground-spreading rosemaries genetically engineered to produce medicines. A furrow in their middle suggests a well-trodden path. The air is scented with perfumes he does not recognise and muggy with high moisture content. He is sweating. Insects, more like fuzzy dark dots, flit here and zigzag there, making their way to, from and around the flowers on the herb lawn and erupting from a variety of plants in baskets covering any free wall-space. He finds their continual buzzing loud, more because he is not used to that noise than anything else. A dot-insect heads straight for his eyes. He, without thinking, bats it away.

"Good reaction," Meriel says. "Have you been here before?"

"No, my first time."

A flash of being impressed crosses her face. "In that case, I'll take you round rather than across the Plain. We've had some bad reactions from newcomers, not sure why. Unspoken rules about the corridor: use the single path and always go round with the condos to your left. If someone wants to pass you, step into a flat's doorway."

He catches onto why: they want to maximise the crop yields, including those from inside the corridor, to earn as much as they can, meagre though it will be. "Makes sense."

She leads the way.

He is careful to place his feet in her footsteps. As they pass the first door to the Plain he stops to look out. It is a patchwork of yellows, whites, pinks and mainly different shades of greens, even the walls opposite are covered in climbing plants. The only dark areas are the slits and doorways. The mass of colour is so rich and bright that his eyes start to ache. He turns his eyes away to find Meriel staring at him.

"It takes most first-timers like that. Wearing shades helps until they get used to it. For now try not to look out onto it."

"How do you people…" The burned image of the Plain forces its way into his mind. It is screaming something urgent and important at him, but he cannot pinpoint what. "…cope with it?"

"We have to survive. This semi-tunnelled corridor helps keep us in the shade." She turns smartly on her heel and marches onward.

He has touched a nerve, but has to concentrate to keep up. At the next doorway to the Plain, a thin woman with two children wait for them to pass, gawping as if they have never seen the black silk of a priest. The woman's grey silk is loose and shows up tears, a hand me down. The boys are dressed in collaged tunics made from silk rags, which allow for free growth. He instinctively signs a blessing for them, before hurrying to catch up with Meriel.

They are almost half round the corridor when she mechanically opens a condo's door and the inside lights automatically switch on. "What do you want to drink?"

He steps in. To his left below the window is a corner

settee hugging a table, both showing shiny spots from too much use. They face a kitchen bench with its cooker, sink and storage spaces. The right wall has four tall brown lockers, the doors with dents from too many mishaps. An archway between the lockers and the kitchen leading to a darkened hallway has a 'door' made of chains hanging from the ceiling, which are decorated with small badges of mosaics made from mining spoil. "Whatever you're having."

"Herbal tea it is. Take a seat."

He slides onto the settee and watches as she works away at the tea-making ceremony. "Do priests ever visit here?"

She snorts. "We're their forgotten."

"That can't be right."

"Look," she slams down an empty mug. "People here can't afford to give much in the way of goods, effort or time. They're the disabled who need aids to help them get slowly around, the people who can't do regular work because of intermittent unpredictable episodes of illness, the dying who've not been able to put enough money aside or collected enough favours to see them through the rest of their lives, those fleeing society because they've committed too many minor 'crimes'. Do you really believe the Priesthood think it's the best use of their time to deal with them? Hell no. They're so far down their list of priorities that nobody there gives a damn."

Stunned by her unusual vehemence, he does not know how to reply.

She finishes making the tea in silence and presents a mug of hot steaming tea of mint and other herbs he does not recognise before sitting down next to him, cupping her hands around her own mug. "Sorry about that, but the injustices and seeing the misery in others gets to me."

"And you see it every day living here," he adds diplomatically.

"Now you see why I don't do mining any more. I'd lose it."

"But equally the Priesthood should be helping here."

"No. Miranda lives on the edge of existence. We'd be a drain on the rest of you."

"But–"

"Don't give me that crap about duty to one another. This is realism."

"Surely–"

"Let's agree to differ."

Kylone smiles at once again hearing the calm voice of his old captain overcome her emotions. "Let's."

"And don't you dare bring any priests down here."

"Even if I wanted to, I doubt I can persuade other priests at the moment."

"Of course. Your Truth Tribunal. How in the nine hells of fire did you end up in that mess?"

He wonders the same thing. It started with Alva, but then Dirk intervened, and things got out of hand. Each important step had involved a confidence that could not be divulged without permission; he is treading along the thin ridge of conflicting secrets, which gives him very little freedom of choice. It also gives him another problem in the here and now. "I can only talk in general terms, not specifics. The obligation of confidences, you understand."

"That old excuse, but if it makes you comfortable… They say letting people just talk about their problems helps them make up their minds. So go ahead." She sips her tea.

He starts with a non-congregant talking to him about the increase in accidents, works through helping someone to do the accident analysis that puts him in conflict with the Guardians of History, asking the Coroner to reopen an inquest into a particular miner's accidental death, the added friction of what happened at Carbo Level 5 Hub, and ends on the argument with a senior person in the priesthood that leads directly to asking for the Truth Tribunal. "All I can do is wait for the analysis to kick up a conclusive result, but that may not happen in time. Hence the need to ask for character witnesses like you. I know it doesn't tackle the main issues, but I can't see what else I can do." He drinks the last of his second cup of tea.

“Can I make a couple of observations?” Her face is grim.

“Go ahead.”

“First, if the Truth Tribunal goes against you, you’ll be welcome here.”

He shakes his head. “After all the fuss I’ve kicked up, it’ll be off-moon exile, after a period of grace to wind up my affairs, but thank you for the offer.”

“Secondly, and please don’t take this the wrong way, you’ve been reacting precisely the way Mirandan society expects you to. Maybe you ought to consider breaking our unwritten ‘code of survival’.”

He cannot take that idea in. A person only breaks that if they think their new course of action increases the community’s chances. Which he realises is exactly what he has been trying to do. Will others accept this reasoning? He very much doubts it. If there are additional considerations he has not been aware of… “How?”

She pauses, biting her lips. “Get the miners as a large group to petition the Priesthood to do the analysis. The Guardians of History would have to take notice of that.”

He is about to say that they would not get the true answers as their techniques are based on too many simplifying assumptions, but stops; he was about to reveal the analyst is extremely good, and there are very few of them on Miranda. “It won’t work for reasons I can’t let on about.”

Meriel blinks and stares at him. “What the hell have you stirred up?”

Now that she has asked the question, he wonders too. Two separate issues, Chynoweth changing their Mirandan mining strategy to maximise short-term profit and the Guardians of History not doing the analysis expected of them, happening together. The failure of both is what is pushing him into his personal problems. What if they have a more direct connection? “I don’t know.”

“Well, if you’re not going to get that petition up and running, I am.”

“It still won’t work.”

"I'll take your word for it when it comes to the Guardians, but for a short space of time, it'll distract the miners from their struggles; it'll give them a cushion of hope to make their lives feel easier, maybe enough to make a real difference to a few of them."

"And when that hope disappears? You could end up making things worse. Delusion brings its own dangers."

"It's better than depression caused by feeling helpless," she snaps.

Another shock; has he really lost touch with the miners? It has been eight years since he became a full priest, after spending a year as an acolyte. Nine years to lose contact with the miners and miss out on the subtle build-up in changes and their camaraderie. Nine years to let the Priesthood mould him into one of their own. "I hadn't realised things had got that bad. Do what you feel is right."

"I will, but please," she grabs his arm on the table, "whatever you're up to, make it work. If you need our help, from any one of us, please, *please*, let us know."

He notices the deep-hurt in her old eyes. He puts his free hand over hers. "I'll do my best, but it'll take a miracle to succeed."

A bittersweet smile flickers on her face. "I know, but I have faith in you. You've grown as a person in ways I had not anticipated. Now, the sooner you sort this mess, the better. Take care of yourself."

It is his dismissal, yet her words hearten him. He stands. "You too." He leaves, remembering to turn left once out of the doorway and carefully keep to the furrow on the corridor.

An old man with a walking stick stands at the bottom of some stairs waiting for him to pass.

He automatically signs him a blessing.

"Long time since I had one of 'em," the man grins.

Kylone stops. "Do you want another?"

"Nah," he sniffs. "Brought me back memories. Good ones."

"I could get other priests to visit you regularly, if you want."

"No use. Too many people here been let down by you priests. They would get… not be welcome."

Kylone guesses what he would have said before he changed his mind. It is an unpleasant thought that priests are not liked here. "The same can be said of me."

"Yeah, but you came here of your own accord. Word spreads fast round here."

"So… I have Meriel's protection?"

"Nah! You don't need it."

"I don't understand."

The old man smiles showing his yellowed and missing teeth. "We know when someone's had to deal with real trouble. It changes 'em in small ways. Can't rightly explain it, except to say they're calmer in an odd way. You got that aura. And anybody who's had real trouble can see it in others. Like all of us here."

"Even the children?"

"Yeah, even 'em. They pick it up, don't know how, but they do."

"Then why can't I spot it in these people?"

"Yeah, we all say that to start with. You do, but you don't know it."

Kylone's mind flashes to Alva and her desperately hiding her ability to see behind solid walls. There has to be a reason for that, a very hurtful one, one that brought out his protective instincts. Why did she seek him out, rather than another more competent priest? This is the start of understanding what the man is trying to say. He needs more time to work on it. "Thank you for your insight."

"You're welcome, Priest."

Kylone signs him another blessing and walks back to an empty Transit Hall. He stands in the meeting zone, knowing he has a lot to process, especially that seeing through walls business, though insignificant by Alva's standards. He feels as if his psyche has been through a crucible and reshaped into something else. He is unsure of what.

His mind flits back to the patchwork Plain. Every

single bit of it is being utilised, its seeming physical chaos belies a well-ordered functionality. The use of that Plain is well organised. He can think of only one person who could go into such meticulous management: Meriel.

It dawns on him why she is a scavie: so she can have the spare time to help the people here. Typical Meriel.

A smile creeps onto his face.

***

Electric blue light from a full Uranus blazes through the chapel wall as Kylone unlocks and pulls out a drawer of crystals. A row of three vacant pockets, their cache of crystals missing – one of which he was hoping to mount into the mosaic.

He stares at the accusing emptiness trying to remember when he had last seen them: yesterday late morning, when he secured the drawer.

"What's wrong?" Priest Theseus has stopped examining the electronics in the pulled-out column of lighting.

"Three crystals are missing."

"You sure?"

"Absolutely. I locked them in here yesterday."

Priest Theseus, the replacement electrician for Dirk, comes to stand beside him with a screwdriver in his hand. "Has this ever happened before?"

"No." Kylone pushes the drawer in and locks it.

"Are you sure you haven't misplaced them? I mean… you are under a lot of pressure at the moment."

He turns to face Theseus. His short sandy hair and goatee beard glints with stay-spray, which makes his whole face more statue than human. The darkness of his brown eyes stands out against the paleness of his facial features, even his lips. What strikes Kylone most is the man's apparent age; mid-thirties, the same as his own. Yet, Theseus is calm, exuding contentment, the opposite of all the turmoil he feels.

"Yes," Kylone replies. "Whoever took them was

probably in a hurry and forgot to let me know. I'll check with reception, just in case." He pivots towards the door.

Theseus grabs his arm to stop him. "A lot of us are worried about you. As far as any of my friends can make out, you're... well... you're not going to survive the Truth Tribunal. If you need our help, just say so."

"Thank you. I don't want to get any of you in trouble as well. I..." What does he really need to say to take the worry out of Theseus' eyes?

"Yes?"

"I've done what I can for my defence. All I, no, *we*, can do is wait for the outcome in due course." Kylone marvels at himself for being so calm. If this had happened before his own mining accident he would have been dashing round, grasping at ore dust. Maybe the old man at Dunsinane had been right: having been through a life-threatening hell, he now does what he sensibly can to deal with his own problems and then moves on.

Theseus frowns. "You think you have a defence? Against the Guardian of History? Even when you disobeyed his direct order? What is it?"

"I would rather keep my own counsel, for reasons that will eventually become obvious."

Theseus' mouth momentarily drops. "You *do* have a defence. That'll be a first for High Priest Diomedes."

Kylone almost smiles at the minor demotion of the Guardian of History; he now knows Theseus, for whatever reason, is on his side. "Maybe. But right now, I'd like to see about those crystals."

"Go," Theseus nods towards the chapel's door.

Kylone strides down the aisle between the seats, through the door, turns left along the corridor and through into reception.

Nobody is around. He checks the bookings screen; interview room one has just started being used. The receptionist must be helping there.

He steps back to view the long tapestry behind the desk, a relic of the early years on Miranda when a wave of nostalgia took hold. A strip along its top shows the

Sun to the left and the planets with their major moons in the order of closest to farthest from it. Beneath each, are panels of scenes from where people lived, high rise grey New York, London's golden gothic Houses of Parliament, Kenya's yellow savannah, Brazil's green tropical rain forest, Switzerland's white mountains and glaciers, the Moon's Shackleton Crater chunky silver surface habitats and underground Mare Imbrium city, Mars' green and reddish-brown open-sky Melas Chasm with its air controlled by transparent nanobots, Callisto's sprawling dark grey city and Titan's red bubble domes. What they have in common is the continuance of Earth's way of life and values; they have the spare capacity, resource and luxury to do that. Here, on Miranda, every breath taken should be used to help stay alive, or keep another person alive. Even his crystal mosaic has that purpose: to give people a morale boost. It has an aura of the sadness of riches and a way of life lost forever on Miranda.

A glint on the Shackleton Crater panel pulls his attention onto a small cream square depicting a window and its beam of light falling on the regolith. What happened behind the real window over the years? Probably a lot of ordinariness punctuated by moments of high tension. His eye is drawn deeper into the window with its crisscrossing threads, and then on through the material's holes into darkness, only it is not nothingness. The holes allow fine light lines to hit the backboard to form a uniform speckled pattern.

"Everything all right, Priest Kylone?" Acolyte Thyone says from behind.

"Yes." He blinks hard to escape his trance. "I mean no," he turns.

"You sound confused, even out of your mind," she says with a hint of gloat.

"I mean I'm fine. Just want to find out if anyone left a message about taking some crystals from the chapel."

"Some gone missing?" she moves behind the desk to open her screen.

"Yes, three of them. I'm sure there must be a reasonable explanation, but I have to do due diligence."

"Of course," she smiles while reading her screen. "No," she shakes her head, "nothing here. I'll put an alert notice out now and let you know if I get a response."

"If you would be so kind."

She frowns and stares at him. "Are you sure you didn't put them down somewhere and forgot where you put them?"

"One hundred per cent."

She types away at her screen.

He looks back the Shackleton Crater panel and sees only the surface of the picture. The memory of seeing it unnerves him. Clearer, deeper and richer through a single material is one thing, but seeing continuously through the layers is entirely another. It is beyond the accepted definition of rockborne: the extrapolation from surface features. It is very different and far stranger. Is this a totally different talent? He does not think so: the first part, seeing through that first layer, is exactly what a rockborne does. This is the second time this type of thing has happened to him.

Another worry is that such a talent normally peaks at the age twenty-five. He is thirty-four. Why is it different for him?

Only one other person he knows of has had similar experiences. He needs to talk to Alva.

"Are you sure you're all right?" Thyone interrupts his thoughts.

"Yes. I was thinking about an aspect of my forthcoming Truth Tribunal."

"That explains your worried look."

"If you'll excuse me, I need to see to something," he hurries to leave.

***

Kylone steps out of the airlock beneath the chapel and scans the plain under the waning gibbous Uranus. He cannot see as far as he does from above. The shapes on the icescape are wider, shorter and darkened by shadowing. He imagines standing in his usual place on the balcony and turns to look in roughly the right direction to where he saw the strange glint through the meteorite's grazes. A streak of darkness below a risen chunk of grey ice next to a set of craggy ridges where the ice has been ruptured catches his eye. All these identifying marks correlate with his memory: it is the right crater.

"Where're we going?" Alva says over the suit comms joining him.

He holds his arm out straight to point to the crater. "The far edge of that crater."

She gets behind his arm. "It's in the middle of an ice waste. What could possibly be of interest there?"

"It gets me away from having to think about my troubles." He says this in case anyone is listening in to their conversation. It is the truth, but only part of it. Another part is fulfilling the mandatory requirement to walk the surface at least once a year: it gets Mirandans used to open space in case they need to come up here in an emergency. "Shall we go along this road and cut across the plain from the promontory?"

"Sounds good to me." She starts her skim-walk along the inner edge of the road, next to the cliff.

He focuses at the far edge of the crater, hoping for another glint, but it remains stubbornly light grey.

"Coming?" Alva says.

He turns right to find she is twenty metres ahead of him. "I was admiring the view." He catches her up.

In silence, they walk along the road. Nobody is in sight, which is expected. Most Mirandans consider the moon's surface a Solar radiation hazard area, only good for light harvesting, inspiration for artists and the faithful, dumping waste materials and graveyards. The danger precludes anything other than a few hours on the surface in a spacesuit. He checks his radiation badge; way down low.

They quickly reach the promontory and turn to their destination. The ice off-road could have gas bubbles and just a little bit of pressure, from a footstep, could break them. It will be slow going from here as they test each footfall; it would be so easy to sprain an ankle, or worse.

Kylone maps out a path that keeps to the local lowest level of ice to avoid slipping downwards. This brings the threat from dust accumulation that could hide crevices or allow your foot to sink into hidden depths. "You sure you still want to come with me?"

"I need a change from work. The Chief Compineer is giving me too much overtime."

He holds back his laugh, sure that Dirk will pick up on the comment. Then he realises this must be Alva's way of getting him to monitor their conversation, no matter what privacy level they are set to, her own extra safety net.

He slides one foot out onto the ice plain, pressing his toes downward to make sure it will be safe to stand. It is, but this close to the road that comes as no surprise. He puts his weight on that foot while he similarly slides the other one forward. "Want to follow in my footsteps for now?"

"You're the heavier of us two," she acknowledges.

They make slow steady progress. The ice around them gradually darkens as the planet wanes. White spots and streaks where meteorites have impacted on the ice to scour away the dust become more frequent as they leave the cliff behind. The low knolls are such unique shapes that he can make a mind map of their route, not that he will need it for the return walk with the cliff in front of them.

Three-quarters of the way to the crater, a light appears in the corner of the visor to indicate his comms have been switched to private mode.

"We've been quiet long enough for any eavesdroppers to think we'll continue in silence," Alva says. "What's all this about?"

"Sounds like some of the Chief Compineer's directness is rubbing off on you."

"Not really. I give as good as I get. Why're we here?"

"I saw a strange glint from the edge of the crater we're going to and would appreciate a second opinion."

"You mean you want me to use my special ability?"

"Please. You seem to be able to interpret what your talent shows you, as you demonstrated in the Carbo mine."

She pauses. "You're good at noticing and making sense of things around you. That's what I do with my beyond sight."

"I'm sure both Dirk and Lenny have noticed your 'rockborne' talent is always on tap and on the mark."

"Dirk, yes. Lenny, I don't think so. When she tried to persuade me to become a miner, she let slip that my damned good 'rockborne' performance was probably induced by being under pressure."

"That's true of a lot of rockborne, but not all." A worry nags at him: Lenny found Alva's talent too good and consistent to not believe other factors were at play. It is one step away from accusing her of seeing behind walls and therefore lying, which would lead to her being an outcast again. This needs to be prevented. She must be taught how to act more like a rockborne. That teacher has to be him. He does not want to be reminded of his talent turned curse, but there is no other choice. "For instance, my talent worked." He pauses. "Works by finding the pattern on the rock wall interesting. Don't ask what made the patterns interesting. I never fathomed that out."

He stops still. This is the first time he has talked about his talent since the accident without feeling the pain of loss or fear of the words kindling worse memories. It is about time, in fact, long past time for him to move on in life.

"What's wrong?" Alva asks.

"Nothing." He hesitates. "Nothing at all." He starts on his way again.

"What do you think caused this mysterious glint?"

"Most likely? A fluke set of conditions to produce a beam of light." He does not believe this, but it is the most rational explanation. "Other possibilities are a meteorite strike or there's a crystal inside the ice."

They reach the crater's edge and can see down into it. Roughly ninety metres in diameter and nearly circular, its sidewalls are more like facets than the usual curve, a sign of fracturing on impact. The floor is flat, markedly darker and as smooth as the sides, suggesting that the impact had been forceful enough to tear away a top layer of ice, but could not touch the layer beneath. It might explain the formation of the ridges to one side of the crater, the upper layer had nowhere else to go except to break up and squash together.

The far rim has no nicks, scratches or sharp crests that could have caused the original glint. Maybe the crater's shape was behind it, especially those facet edges. He considers this unlikely, as he would have noticed it at other times. This must have been a unique one-off event or... he hesitates to think about it... the start of something more permanent.

"Where do you want me to look?" Alva asks.

"Far side rim, just inside the crater. Suggest we circle round to make it look like we're going for a stroll."

"Kylone, please respond," Patricianna's voice comes over his comms.

He switches his comms to public while starting to slide-walk clockwise round the crater. "Hello Priest Patricianna," he says for Alva's benefit. "What can I do for you?"

"What in the seven hells of ice are you doing out there on the plain?"

"Getting my mandatory spacesuit hours in."

"Oh," the sound of surprise not being disguised. "Then why is Assistant Alva with you?"

"As a companion for safety reasons," Kylone says half-truthfully. He inwardly cringes, hoping she will not suspect his ulterior motive.

"You know you're not to do any counselling while you're facing a Truth Tribunal."

"I can assure you he hasn't," Alva intervenes. "I needed

some peace from the Chief Compineer and this is as about as far away as I can get from him. He is a hard taskmaster."

"So I have heard." Patricianna pauses. "A piece of advice, Kylone. Keep your comms open. It avoids questions of the awkward kind."

"As you wish."

"I would like you to meet me at six this evening for a long chat."

He knows an order when he hears it. "I presume you've checked my diary is free then."

"Of course I have," she says with a hint of frustration in her voice. "There's no need to show off your priestly serenity in front of Alva after the way you two worked together at Carbo."

"Then I would be happy to see you."

A click indicates Patricianna has cut the link.

Alva giggles. "Anyone would think she wants us to get closer together."

Surprise makes Kylone turn around. The type of smile on her face indicates she thinks it is a big joke. He is relieved; his life is already complicated enough and she must still be grieving for Raoul even though she does not show it. "Please excuse Priest Patricianna. She means well. She is doing her best to help me get over the loss of my fiancée, Selma, but I fear I may never be fully able to."

He tries to remember Selma's face, but finds the image is blurred, lacking in detail. It is as if she is finally fading out of his life. Maybe, just maybe, Patricianna is having some impact on him after all. He continues his slide-walk.

Once they reach the rearmost quarter segment of the crater rim, he ensures Alva sees him pointing down just inside the crater, then waving his hand to indicate the arc that needs covering. He says nothing, as their comms are open for all to hear, including Patricianna.

Alva nods. She stares long and hard at the first part of the arc while Kylone takes a couple of steps forward and waits. She takes a step forward keeping to the track of dusted off frosting he has made and does another long hard stare, while he moves another step further on. They continue repeating this duo dance until he sees a ten centimetre wide dark line beneath the grey ice that breaks through the crater wall between two facets. Unlike any crystal he has seen before, it certainly could channel light given a suitable light source. Where could that have come from? He goes down on one knee to stare to where it points; the left side of the chapel's clear wall, the position he saw the meteorite scratch.

He wipes away the ice dust from above the line to examine it more closely. The line's darkness comes from so deep down that he cannot see the bottom. He moves his head from side to side and sees an odd glint. There must be flat faces on parts of the inside walls of the line. "This block's very unusual. Have you ever seen anything like it before?" he points to it.

Alva looks as directed. She snaps her head away and her chest rises and falls as if she is breathing heavily.

Kylone is up and grabbing her shoulders to keep her steady. He switches their link to private. "You all right?"

Her breathing subsides. "It was weird. One second I was down there looking into a cave, with boulders to one end covered by gravel and dust, and the next… I can't really describe it, but my sight kind of expanded to see lots of different layers of ice and rock overlaid on each other and the occasional piece of mining equipment. I recognised Lenny next to the biggest machine away from a mine face. Am I going crazy?"

He could see the worry in her green eyes. "I don't think so. One way to be sure is to find out where Lenny is now."

"On it," Dirk interrupts their conversation. There are finger-taps in the background.

Now is not the time to tell off Dirk for listening into their private conversation. Kylone makes a mental note to discuss this bad habit with him later.

"Holy dust," Dirk says. "Lenny's near the ore processor

in Silcano Mine, hundred-twenty-five klicks in a straight line from where you are."

"What's happening to me?" Alva squirms.

Kylone glances at the line. "I don't know," his voice trembling. He is scared too, not only for her, but also for himself. "One thing we can do is to find out what material that line is made of. It might give us a clue as to what is going on. Fortunately I brought my sampling tools with me, so it'll only take half an hour to melt the ice and get a sample."

She bites her lips. "I can't look at it."

"I know." He checks his radiation badge. The bar has risen as expected. A quick mental calculation means they will with his digging out a line sample still have half an hour to spare. If digging out the sample takes longer, they will be tight for time. He cringes. "Best thing you can do is to make sure there's a safe path round the rest of the crater. Can you do that?"

She nods.

"Good. And don't glance this way, just in case," he reminds her.

While she starts her slide-walk, he digs out a torch laser from his sampling pack hanging from his belt and examines the ice around the line for the best way to melt it off. He glimpses the line's depth again and has to look away. That makes his mind up. He crouches down and aims his laser at the line in a shallow angle to avoid staring into the depth. He keeps his hand steady, concentrating its energy on the small area required to avoid wasting time. White gases crystallise as they spread out into thinness, some of it frosting his suit. He keeps moving to make sure he does not get iced into position.

He breaks through to the line's material, which he realises is transparent. The darkness is coming from further down, but the radiation does not let him have the time to explore why. Replacing his torch laser with a laser-edged knife, he cuts away at the line to break off three almost cube-like specimens and places them in the cold bag he had brought specially along. It will keep them safely frozen once they return to the warmth of airlock and tunnels. The hole left behind is neat and minimal. A grunt of satisfaction slips out: he has not lost some of his mining skills.

He looks up. Alva is waiting for him at the place where she has joined the path that leads back to the road. He starts his skate-walk to join her. "Alva, I'd like you to ask Meriel to arrange the sample analysis when you next see her at work in Chynoweth."

"Why her?" Dirk intervenes. "I can get you the best on Miranda there is."

"I know, which is why you're getting two samples. Don't be greedy about the third."

"But Meriel's currently only a scavie, even if I do temporarily employ her."

"I know that, but..." What did he actually know about her present life? Only what she allowed him to see at Dunsinane, and that was limited. She had acted as if she could call on others to make things happen. He is sure, even if he does not have proof, that she is the one who leads the organisation of the farming on the Plain, which is quite a feat. And yet he felt this is only part of what she can do.

A chuckle slips his lips. She had manipulated him to believe she is a helpless scavie until he was desperate enough to realise her true capability. She would have kept up her connections from her captaining days, which would include mineral experts she can call on for help.

"Let's just say," Kylone continues, "I have a sneaking suspicion."

Silence.

"Coming from anyone but you or Alva, I would take that as unjustified arrogance not worth ore dust. You sure do make my life interesting."

Alva laughs.

Kylone is relieved she is back to her behavioural norm he has come to know.

CHAPTER 5

Kylone paces restlessly outside the Maze, the place where the fervents gather before exiting to the Verona Rupes chasm for the Greening ceremony. The blue-white sheen of the ice wall penetrates through the pink layer to produce a pale lilac glow. Its supposed aura of comforting warmth does not benefit him. If anything he feels too hot. He stops to look at the old-fashioned deep green plasma door. They really should update it to a safer design, but the congregation are against it.

Meriel had asked to meet him and would not say what it was about. That she insisted on having it here, away from public scrutiny, means she does not want anyone to know about it. Only two days since he dug out the samples from the crater's edge, it is too early to expect analysis results from any of them, even hers. The only other explanation he can think of is she wants him to join the miners she is secretly banding together to revolt against Chynoweth. Yet it would be out of character for her. He is more confused than ever.

He searches for a distraction. A plaque to the side of the door is the only thing that demands any attention here.

The Maze
Opened February 9th 2147
Designed by Donna Stephenson using fractal mathematics to make sure the pressure from the 14 kilometres of ice above would be spread evenly into the ice below while giving space for people. This resulted in a maze with 128 small side rooms with a capacity to hold 512 people.

Once used for living quarters, now benefits the Greening fervents.

"Sorry to have kept you waiting," Meriel says, rushing down the tunnel towards him. She wears her clean miner's brown silk.

"I was early. No need to apologise." He frowns and wonders if his suspicions about why she wants this meeting are correct. "Has the Chief Compineer terminated your work for him?"

She comes to halt, looks down at her clothing and smiles. "I wish. The damned man keeps on interrupting with questions about mining, instead of letting me get on with his requested data searches. Had to tell him to extend my contract if he wanted me to complete my work. You should've heard his grumbles."

Kylone laughs: Dirk has been his usual self and manipulated her to stay longer without having to ask her to do so. "But the brown silk?"

"Yes, I still scavie in my spare time, what little I have of it. With that Chief Compineer demanding extra bits of work at random hours…"

Scavieing is the only mining task that people can choose their time to do it. Dirk must be working hard on his analysis to demand such varied hours from her. "Isn't the Chief Compineer paying you enough?"

"More than enough. But once you've been poor, you get addicted to making money when you can."

Kylone agrees: he has seen others go through the same mini life-arc.

She looks closer at him. "Why all the questions? It's not like you. You're…. defensive. I would say tense. What's got you into this state?"

"Not much gets past you, does it? It's just with everything that's going on…"

"Anything I don't know about?"

He has to reassure her. "If all this had happened a year ago, I would've been placed on auto-dosing tranquilisers. Now? I don't know what's happened to me, or why, but I'm coping better with things. Not sure what my limits are. I keep on surprising myself about what I can deal with."

"That's good," Meriel nods, her bald head glinting in

the light as if it had been shaved this morning. "That's very good."

"Why? Have you more bad news for me?"

"I'm not sure. It may be nothing." She hesitates. "There again you may see the significance of it I can't."

This really puzzles him.

"Shall we go and find somewhere quiet to sit?" she asks.

They go through the plasma door into the bluish light coming through the ice from outside. It takes a few moments for Kylone's eyes to adjust, and his nose to stop prickling with the air's dryness and freshness from the more than usual proportion of oxygen. It has been a week since the last Greening when this place would have been full and smelling of crowded humans.

The level floor suffers from shallow ruts where people have walked too often; the rest of the place is all curves, typical of when people first settled on Miranda. The bowing out of the walls in the semi-circular room does not follow a recognised geometrical shape. Instead it has a gradual steepening curve until the mid-height when it then curves inwards in a similar taller arc until it smoothly reaches an apex in the ceiling. He never understood the physics behind these shapes to distribute the pressure from the ice above. He is thankful they have withstood it since the day Chynoweth built it. Three exits are carved into the ice; their outlines are similar curves to the walls but shorter and ending in a point at their tops. The ice-light is a smidgen brighter to his left, which means to his right Verona Rupes is in shadow from Uranus outside.

"Light or dark side?" Meriel asks. "I brought a torch along."

"So have I. But let's make it light."

Meriel leads the way through the left exit and then turns mainly left, with an occasional right. Each exit has a black arrow dyed into the ice pointing back in the direction to the way out. She finally enters an alcove and sits on the ice bench against the far wall.

Kylone sits almost knee-to-knee next to her with a triangle of clear space for the bench between them. White breaths rhythmically push out, float and fade in front of them. Although his face and hands feel cool, his silk will keep him sufficiently warm for now. This is not a place to stay long in just a silk.

"How in seven hells of ice did people live here?" Meriel rubs her hands.

"It was far more crowded then." He did not need to add warmth of bodies and working devices raised the air's temperature. "What did you want to talk about?"

"It's about that rock sample Alva gave me."

He relaxes, glad it is not about joining a miners' revolutionary group.

"Why? What did you think it was about?" she asks.

"I…" He is not sure how to explain it without hurting her feelings. "I thought you might be putting some anti-Corp protest group together you wanted me to help out with."

Her laugh is a sharp bark. "You're in enough trouble without looking for more." She falls silent.

He has known her long enough to realise this could be bad news. "What do you really not want to tell me?"

"I can't be absolutely sure, but we uncovered a very similar rock seam the day before our accident. It was so out of place and seeing the sample brought it all back. It was in that alcove we were prepping for rock debris. Your interest in this sample worries me. It's as if you're still looking for an explanation for your accident to… to take the blame off your own shoulders. You were not at fault. Everyone says the same. You should stop this mental self-harm."

He cannot tell her why he wants to know more about the rock sample. Nor can he fully reassure her. It has taken him eight years to reach this level of acceptance, but as Patricianna warned him, he has no idea how much farther he has to go. He needs to sidestep her blatant plea. "The day before?"

"Yes."

"Around about the time we changed direction to work on another mine face?"

"Yes."

His mind flits back to when he stared at the mine face. The scavies with the roller cleaners had just swept away the last of the dust debris. An ice layer rests on top of the carmine face and floor that glistens with a scattering of crystals. They are shaving off the top of an embedded D-type asteroid for organic rich minerals for the farms. They have to dig carefully, because they are not sure of the asteroid's structure, which means drill a bit, check the face, drill a bit more. To the left is the white ice with all its entrapped small gas bubbles. On the other side the grey rock of chrondite asteroid that the other had been pulled towards, and finally iced to.

What is missing from this picture is any clear rock.

His talent had been pulled down towards an interesting crystal buried in the chrondite, which led to his fateful decision. His talent then had double vision, different from the precise duplication he had experienced with the seam out on the plain.

There is only one conclusion: the presence of that mineral bends the rockborne vision away from what is really there.

He switches his comms unit in his wristband on. "Dirk, you by any chance been keeping an ear on our conversation?"

"You're joking. We're low on lemon balm tea and I'm trying to source new supplies."

"Can you run an analysis for me?"

"No priestly telling me off? This must be serious. What do you need?"

Kylone ignores the look of utter astonishment on Meriel's face. "Correlate mining accidents with the rockborne changing the direction of the digging just beforehand."

"On it."

Meriel slumps back against the wall. "So my getting a job with the Chief Compineer was no accident?"

"He asked for a recommendation," Kylone replies.

"The data pulling and analysis of tidal gravity is all a front. For what?"

"Yes and no. He's doing due diligence on the tidal gravity, though he is pretty sure what the answer will be. He also wants someone on hand to answer his questions about what really happens down the mines. He'd have used me if it weren't for…"

"What's this all about, Simon?"

"Preventing more mining accidents."

"Why didn't he say so in the first place?"

"Three words. Guardians of History."

Meriel lets out a long hiss.

"I don't have a sufficient sample size to say it's definitely a trend," Dirk comes over the comms.

"Damn!" Kylone utters.

"But," Dirk continues. "If the ratio I've got at the moment is repeated in the required additional data, then we have a definite correlation."

He is not the cause of Selma's and his teammates' deaths. He has to mentally repeat this several times over for it to sink in. His guilt, which he realises he has been carrying all these years, should not be there. Emotionally he still feels it. He knows that given time that too will fade. He has to be patient.

"Damn it. I was sure the problem was in the ice," Dirk continues. "How could I have missed this?"

"Don't blame yourself for it," Kylone says.

"You're a fine one to talk. By all accounts, you've been doing exactly that… why in seven hells of ice haven't you gone into a mournful slush on me? What have I missed now?"

Kylone nods for Meriel to reply.

"That sample Kylone is asking us to analyse. I'm pretty sure I saw the same mineral uncovered just before his accident."

"You're not suggesting— no way I can run a correlation analysis— how would it affect people? By fire and ice this is too damned crazy—"

"Slow down, Dirk," Kylone says.

"What the hell are we dealing with here?" Dirk shouts.

"We need to warn the miners," Meriel shouts back. "Not next week, not tomorrow. Now!"

"How?" Dirk replies. "Nobody's going to believe us."

"They will if it comes from the Guardians of History."

"That useless waste of air. They poison the fertiliser they stand on…"

They listen while Dirk continues to swear at how useless they are.

"We've still got a problem," Dirk finally says.

"I can help," Meriel says.

"How?" Dirk asks.

"I still have a lot of contacts among the miners. All I need to do is spread the word that accidents are more likely to happen when rockborne unexpectedly change direction and they'll be far more careful, believe me."

"But you're only a scavie," Dirk says.

"So?"

Kylone eyes Meriel as he remembers the well-ordered plain at Dunsinane and her comment about organising the miners to get up a petition. He wonders just how much influence she does have among the miners, and whether there is a possible rebellion brewing. "She can do it, but it'll have to be on the quiet. I'm in enough trouble as it is."

"I can manage that," Meriel says.

Kylone decides he and the others are better off not knowing how. "That's settled. There's one more thing." He takes a deep breath. "Given what Dirk says about the statistics, we can be sure that something is affecting the rockborne's performance. I can no longer believe we have an innate ability to mentally extrapolate rock patterns, which is what the scientists say it is."

"Some believe," Dirk intervenes, "your brains might be processing to give you terahertz images, which can see through thin layers. But they couldn't prove that."

"I'll take your word for that. That rock sample interfering with our performance proves to me that we're registering something physical by… let's call it an unknown sense for now."

"You mean like Earth's pigeons can sense the magnetic field?"

"Yes, only something different."

Meriel bites her lips. Dirk drums his fingers for a few seconds. Kylone waits for them to find counter-arguments or say he is being stupid.

Dirk stops his drumming. "I don't even know where to begin. I'm no doctor."

"That's exactly what we need," Kylone says remembering his suggestion to Alva at the Aerial Gallery. "A damned good one."

"We've only got seventy-two doctors moon-wide," Meriel says. "That limits our options."

"Agreed, but not as badly as you think. I'll do the honours, shall I?" Dirk quietly laughs. "It's about time I annoyed the lovely lady again."

Kylone glances upwards to the ice ceiling at the thought of him doing some more hacking and judicious time management to fit appointments in. "One of these days."

"Ah, we're back to priestly lectures. I'll take that as a yes."

***

Kylone fidgets with his hands in the tunnel outside Doc Acheson's waiting room; he is running out of time to prepare for his Truth Tribunal. He keeps going over and over his arguments: good character witness from Patricianna and Meriel; how helpful he was at Carbo Mine from the rescued miners and the Hubmaster. Yes, he could call Dirk as a witness, but he would only be able to confirm which data sets Kylone had sent and the jurors already had those. And that is it. Objectively, even he would find himself guilty.

The analysis of the samples from the crater's edge turned out to be both the ortho and para types of water molecules and three silicon isotopes frozen into a crystalline structure. There was nothing to indicate how it could affect the rockborne.

What he needs is substantive verifiable results from Dirk's analysis. The Chief Compineer is doing his best, but has yet to find an analysis method that will generate firm enough conclusions.

Alva hurries into the tunnel, panting as if she had been running.

He stops fidgeting and smiles.

"Did I make it in time?" she asks, coming to a halt.

He glances at his wristpad. They have two minutes to spare. "Yes. Are you sure you want to go through with this?" He does not need to tell her the Truth Tribunal starts – and is likely to end – the day after tomorrow, and this may be their single opportunity.

"I want to know as much as you do, for my own sake."

They enter the small waiting area; an alcove with benches either side and a green plasma door in front with a booking panel to its right. Kylone taps in he has arrived and Alva follows suit. No sooner do they sit down than the door opens and a man with deep wrinkles from a long hard working life limps out of the surgery. "Good luck," he grimaces, "she's in a sorting out mood."

"And don't forget your physio exercises," Doc Acheson shouts through the door.

The man throws a look of dismay in the Doc's direction. "See what I mean." He limps onward into the tunnel.

"Next," the Doc shouts.

He notices Alva biting her lips. "She's not as bad as she sounds."

"Of course I'm not. Now get your butt in here, Kylone."

"Or maybe she is," he goes through the doorway and turns left into the surgery. Alva's footsteps follow behind. The door pings shut.

Doc Acheson rapidly swivels her chair round, throwing up her mass of red hair. The desk beside her has an unlit holographic flatbed, greyed-out keyboard, slotted-in black legal stone, a touchscreen medi-pad sitting at the corner and four blood sampler machines in a row at its back. The wall above them is an irregular pattern of coloured shiny rectangles.

As her hair drops slowly down into its crinkled chaos, she glares at Kylone then Alva. "Before you settle down, I don't like appointments from patients who have not asked to be on my patient list, especially when they somehow break the confidentiality safeguards. How did you do it?" Her green eyes laser into Kylone's. "In fact, if you weren't a priest, I'd have chucked you both out without seeing you."

Each Mirandan is taught to control fury for safety reasons and to subsequently let off steam in the gym or other physical activities. Kylone recognises this type of anger as a controlled outburst to prevent future repeats of what they have done. "I… we…" he pointed to Alva and himself, "have very little choice. We need the best and were told you're it."

"You haven't answered my question?" she growls.

"We had help," Alva says, "from an expert."

"Who?" Acheson snaps.

Alva cringes under her gaze. "My boss, the Chief Compineer."

"Well, you tell him that if he ever does something like that again, I'll make sure I'll under-dose his meds next time to make him even more erratic than his intolerable normal self."

"What the…" Alva whispers.

Kylone laughs. "I should've realised he would register with the best available doctor." He straightens his face. "Seriously, we need your help. If you can't, then I suspect no other medic can. And we're short on time. At least I am."

The Doc sits back, seemingly partially satisfied with the response. "Which brings me to the second problem. I don't do multiple consultations except for members of the same household or those with legal rights to sit in. Do you fit either of these descriptions?"

"No," Alva sits on the chair beside the desk.

"We're here about a common problem," Kylone remains standing. "One where you'll need to examine both of us."

"Why do you say it's common?"

"Same symptoms," Alva replies.

"Then you can see me individually."

"Except you'll find it hard to believe if only one of us showed up," Kylone adds.

"Since when did you become a medical expert?"

"I haven't. Which is why we decided to see you together. So you could get a truer scope of the issue."

Doc stiffens up in her seat and turns to Alva. "Did Priest Kylone in any way coerce you into this?"

"I need the answers as much as he does."

"And I'm currently barred from any counselling activity by order of the Priesthood."

She drums her fingers on the desk's flatbed. At last she takes a deep breath and fingers her legal-stone. It turns red. "Priest Kylone and Assistant Alva Larsson are both in my surgery now and wish to have a joint consultation with me. Are you Assistant Alva Larsson willing to have your confidential medical records discussed in front of Priest Kylone?"

"Yes."

"Can you confirm that your agreement is free from any blackmail, bribery or other form of coercion?"

"I can."

Doc takes him through the same questions, to which he gives the same answers. He pulls out the chair from beside Alva's and sits opposite the Doc.

"Legal," the Doc continues, "Please put these statements under lock and key unless they are required for legitimate legal purposes."

"The statements have been put under lock and key unless required for legal purposes."

She touches the stone again. It goes black. "Now which one of you wants to go first?"

"I will," he says and goes on to tell her about his rockborne experiences.

Alva then talks about her seeing-behind-walls experiences, how they continue even now, though she has learnt to tell nobody about them.

During their descriptions, Doc Acheson slowly relaxes and at the end has her lips on two steepled forefingers pointing up from folded hands. "Interesting. What do you want from me?"

"We want to know if there is a physical difference in our eyes or brain that could explain what we're experiencing," Alva replies, "or is there something weird in the way our brains process what we're seeing."

Doc eyes Kylone. "When's your Truth Tribunal again?"

"I didn't say," he chortles at the information exercise. "It's the day after tomorrow."

"And you think I might find something to help you with your defence?"

"I'd be surprised, but I might be exiled immediately after the tribunal and then the opportunity would be missed."

"Good job the Chief Compineer arranged for you to be my last patients today," she does a few taps on her keyboard. A blue twenty-five by fifteen centimetre rectangle in the wall pushes out and rotates horizontally to show a dark lens surrounded by a pleated green sleeve inside a black cavity. "If you would hold still."

The instrument extends out on an arm, places itself over Kylone's right eye, and extends sleeve from the box's edges to touch his skin and block out any extraneous light. He sees three dots, red, blue and green swirl round in the lens in a synchronised dance, while doing his best not to blink too much.

"Yep, that's a good reading," Doc says.

The instrument moves to his other eye and does the same. Then it is Alva's turn.

Kylone watches the whole process in silence. He notices tiny brown flecks on Alva's green irises, a detail he had previously missed. There are hints of crows' feet and smile lines round her mouth. Short wisps of her hair take away the strictness of her French plaits and her skin's rosiness is greater than at Raoul's funeral and their first meeting in the chapel. She is well on the way to recovering from the loss of her husband, something he has helped with and hopes for her sake she can continue on her own. He is left with a puzzle. She should still be in deep grief for Raoul, yet clearly is not. It suggests her marriage was not the normal close relationship experienced by most couples. Was it a marriage of convenience, or was their relationship in the process of breaking up; does she have more resilience than most, or is it something else entirely?

The instrument moves away from Alva's second eye scan and tucks itself back into its slot. Doc works the screen, tapping the keyboard, viewing the cross-sectional scans and reading graphs. Her movements become quicker and the muscles on her face tighten.

Kylone waits for her to come to her conclusions.

"What have you found?" Alva asks.

"Not sure," the Doc mutters, working away.

She has discovered an oddity, and with her comparing the same view of four eyes, looks like it is common to him and Alva.

They may have a physiological clue as to what makes a rockborne. If it turns out to be true, then Chynoweth can scan for those who can have this talent. This would lead to a societal shift, but he can only guess at what and by how much.

Doc swipes the desk clean and pushes back her chair to turn to them. Worry on her face warns him she is struggling with her conclusions. "Before I say anything can I check something?"

Kylone nods.

"Sure." Alva replies.

Doc points to Kylone. "You developed into one of the stronger rockborne in your time?"

Kylone wonders where this is going to lead. "Yes." He frowns. He has deliberately avoided using his talent ever since the accident. Has he become stronger since? "Not sure about now."

The Doc nods and turns to Alva. "From your description of how your 'beyond sight' works, would it be true to say you would've made an extremely good rockborne had you been given the chance?"

"Given what she did during the recent Carbo Five mining accident," Kylone intervenes, "I'm certain of it."

"Better than you?"

"I would say so."

"Interesting. That aligns with what I found on the scans. You've both got slightly thicker retinas than other people, Alva's more so than Kylone's," she nods at each of them in turn. "But it's not a normal thickening from the usual causes. It's difficult to detect, but from what I can make out, it's a separate extremely thin translucent layer with thickened spots shaped like the rods and cones a normal person has in their retina. I really do need a whole load of more tests, with nonstandard kit, make that newly developed instrumentation specifically engineered for the task, to work out what's going on here."

"I don't understand," hurt coming out in Alva's voice. "Why hasn't this been spotted by the medics before?"

"When did you first start seeing behind walls?" Doc asks.

"When I was about ten."

"And you, Kylone, when did you think you might be rockborne?"

"Only when I went into the mines, at seventeen, but if I'm the weaker of us two," he points to Alva and himself, "I'm more likely to not notice the onset."

"Agreed. It means you both developed that extra retinal layer after your last statutory medical when you were eight. Of course I'm assuming that neither of you have been to any medic for a thorough eye examination since. Am I right?"

"Yes," Alva says.

"Don't think so," Kylone says, unsure of what the doctors looked for after his accident. His mind races on. He wants to blurt out many more questions one after the other in quick succession, but does not know which to start with. Doc's revelations have changed the perspective. He no longer feels like a normal Mirandan with an unusual life arc, but someone on the edge of society wanting to be with the in-crowd.

A soft sob escapes Alva.

"We all need time to absorb this," Doc says gently.

"No, that's not it. It's a relief. I know it's not me being stupid or insane," Alva replies, "except I still can't say anything."

"That's why I say we all need time, you and Kylone more than me."

"And even if I do say something," Alva continues, "then people like my mother-in-law will still trash me, call me a liar and worse."

"There will always be people who refuse to believe things they can't experience. They're in the minority. But there are enough of them to make trouble when it shouldn't exist."

Kylone notes the Doc has taken on a counselling role, not the type Patricianna doles out, but a gentler, more soothing, more on the patient's side role. Empathy is the Doc's real strength, on top of being good at diagnosis, which is not that difficult with all the computers and sensors she has.

"We can't say anything about Alva in public," he says, "but us rockborne…" He mulls over the use of 'us'. He admits to belonging to a club that sets him apart from many others. "We… they work openly without people feeling threatened by them."

"Before you race ahead," Doc says, "I need another rockborne test subject who's willing to go public. Any idea who?"

He cannot identify a candidate. He wonders if Alva's fear is silently shared by all rockborne. What else has he missed? "I need to think about it."

"We all do," Doc says. "But you have more urgent matters to deal with."

"I've done all the preparation I can, but you're right in a sense. I could do with going over my case," he stands. "Alva, are you going to be all right?"

"I'll make sure she is," Doc says. "Now go."

He does exactly that.

***

Kylone settles a small grey crystal into the tacky gunge at eye-height. He concentrates on very gently pushing one edge of the crystal in to get its light refraction angle exactly right.

"There you are," Patricianna's voice carries from the back of the chapel. "I've been looking everywhere for you." Her footsteps become louder.

His finger slips to knock the crystal askew. He snatches it off the mosaic and places it clean side down on the corner of the bench beside him. He forces a smile and turns. "I'm sorry I switched off my comms, but I wanted to get this done before tomorrow," he waves his hand back towards the panel, "in peace and quiet."

She halts on the other side of the bench and glowers big-eyed at him. "I've booked counselling room two for us."

"I appreciate your forethought, but I doubt that will be necessary."

Her eyes widen further and her lips thin.

"I presume this is about your testimony tomorrow," he continues, "As whatever you're going to say will be in public tomorrow, I'm sure we can deal with it here."

She opens her mouth to say something, closes it and frowns for a few seconds. "Your logic is impeccable. And it's the fastest I've ever seen you function like this. You're still improving. Which is why I'm so angry."

This comment is so out of the blue. "About what?"

"Your appointment with Doc Acheson and Assistant Alva Larsson yesterday."

"Huh?" Nobody saw them go into the surgery together: the old man was well down the tunnel by then. He left it alone. "How did you find out?"

"So it's true?"

"Yes. Who told you?"

"High Priest Diomedes. That's not what bothers me–"

"Wait. How did he find out?"

"No idea. What worries me is your irresponsibility."

He is flummoxed.

She carries on. "Whose crazy idea was it for you two to arrange having a child after you're exiled?"

His hands are placed on the bench to help keep him upright. He feels a small shake go through his body. A glint from the crystal attracts his attention as it falls. He is too slow to catch and ends up picking it up from the floor. It gives him time to get over the shock. His anger builds.

He places the crystal back on the table and looks her in the eye. "That is the silliest thing I've ever heard."

Her head jerks back as if avoiding a swipe. "Then what the hell did you go to see Doc Acheson about?"

His thoughts jumble and tumble through consciousness: doctor consultations are private; keeping her seeing behind walls secret to avoid further ridicule; the physical evidence that her talent is better than any rockborne's cannot be released or even talked about without her permission or the Doc's; how did Diomedes find out about this appointment; and so it went on for far too long.

His comms on his wristpad buzzes, despite being switched off. It snaps him out of the confusion. He stares at it as it buzzes again. Only one person can get through like that, Dirk. He opens it. "Make it quick. I'm in the middle of something."

"Did you feel that little tremor just now?"

"Huh?" Of course, that must be what caused to crystal to slide off the bench. "Yeah. What about it?"

"A moonquake, from normal shrinkage. Need your consultative help. Same deal as before."

He is thankful this event is explainable by the natural process of heat loss leading to the tectonic shifting of the underground ice blocks and layers. This has nothing to do with extra mining accidents or the effects of the type of rock he had discovered at the plain's crater. It is a relatively ordinary situation that requires a routine response from someone other than him. “Can’t Lenny do it?”

Dirk pauses before replying. “She’s one of the pair of miners who’ve fallen down a newly opened chasm. They’re alive, but we need to find the route for the rescuers to climb down. It’s narrow and there’s ice down there, so no drones.”

His head drops and he leans more heavily on the bench, relieved this incident is not taking his mind back to his nightmares. Exact timing of moonquakes can never be predicted, but strategic monitoring of the pressure build-up along certain fault lines normally gives ample warning. This must be a rarity, one they had no hint was going to happen.

He owes Lenny for helping him learn mining, trying to rescue Selma even though it turned out to be useless and looking after Alva at his request. She is more like a caring aunt than a friend.

“By the looks of Priest Kylone, I don’t think he will be able to help you, whoever you are,” Patricianna says.

“Damn it, woman, I wouldn’t be asking if I had any choice,” Dirk replies.

“It’s Priest Patricianna to you.”

“Go and take a jump off the cliff at Verona Rupes. Kylone?”

“How dare you wish for my death. You need to be taught some manners.” Patricianna looks to Kylone. “Who is this idiot?”

Kylone thumps a fist on the bench. “Stop it, the pair of you. I need a private comms link. Any chance of that?”

“Counselling room 2 available now,” Dirk replies. “I’ve block-booked it on your system for the next eight hours.”

“You can’t do this,” Patricianna says.

“On my way,” Kylone says.

“You can’t give counselling advice, to anyone.”

“This is a necessity.”

“What the–” Patricianna splutters.

Kylone continues. “And no sending of itching powder

through the ventilation system to Priest Patricianna's quarters. That understood."

"Hey, that's an idea," Dirk says.

"Absolutely not. Or any other such silly prank."

"You're such a spoilsport." The link switches off.

"Who the hell was that idiot?" Patricianna asks.

He stops short of saying 'Chief Compineer'. "You wouldn't believe me if I told the truth." He half-runs through the chapel, leaps up the stairs three at a time, and marches to counselling room two.

Even before he sits down in the room he opens the comms link and activates the holo-plate built into the table, which remains stubbornly blank. He puts a call through to Alva.

Nothing. She must be on her way to wherever.

"Dirk, you listening?" he says out loud.

"Yep."

"Where's the problem and who's in charge of that mine?"

"Carbo. Level 7. Hubmaster knows fully what you and Alva did during last accident, so is friendly. Copy from Hubmaster's current map on his plate coming your way."

Seven makes Kylone wince. Mapping below there will be broad brush. The quake will make it out of date. The Hubmaster is sure to be trying to build a better map now, but sonics, radar and gravimeters have limitations. That leaves Alva's behind the walls sight as the only option.

"When will Alva get to site?"

"Forty-five minutes. Assisted travel priority."

"Good. That'll give me a chance to talk to Lenny."

The holo-plate switches to a kinked pink line with an occasional purple bulge in it. That is the mine tunnel, where the bulges are now debris-filled spaces, having had their ores dug out. Below is a large flashing red smudge. Dirk must have done his comms tracking magic to identify the approximate position of Lenny and her companion. Spread out between the line and smudge are a few curving sheets to denote the boundaries between different layers of ice and rock.

A blue cross on the tunnel marks Lenny's last known

position before the quake. No routes are marked between the cross and the red smudge, which is the first thing the Hubmaster would have done. This must be the pre moonquake set up. He wonders which parts and by how much those layers have shifted, while putting a call through to Lenny.

"Good to hear from you, Kylone," Lenny says.

"How're you bearing up?"

Lenny chuckles. "You know me."

Patricianna strides into the room and stops dead on seeing the map.

"Sure do, Lenny, which is why I think we can do what I'm about to suggest." He waves his hand to indicate a chair opposite. "I now have Priest Patricianna with me who is much better at counselling than I am. If you feel you need to have a break or just need to unwind a little, I'm sure she'll be happy to help out."

Patricianna gawps at him while standing for a few seconds, fumbling round to the vacant chair and slumping down on it.

"When you're busy elsewhere, I'd welcome a chat with her about girly things. What do you need from me?"

"I should warn you, Kylone is not allowed to counsel," Patricianna says.

"Oh shush," Lenny says. "We're old friends. If anyone can get us out of this mess, he will."

"But he's…"

"Damaged?" Lenny finished for her. "His experience took its toll, yes. But he's the stronger for it. He knows his limits, and when to hand over. If he has to, you can guarantee he'll tell you the way forward. As Meriel puts it, in a strange way, he's reliable."

This is new to Kylone. It gives him some confidence, something he has been lacking for these past years.

"Seven hells of ice. How did I miss it?" Patricianna says quietly.

Kylone ignores her. "Lenny, much as I appreciate your praises, we need to get you out of there sooner rather than later."

"We can talk another time, over a beer in Kober Balyow?"

"Sounds good to me. Now, I'm going to need you to remember the details of your fall using all three vacuum senses, sight, gravity and touch. Don't worry if the memory isn't continuous. We can use what you say as recognisable waypoints."

He pulls a stylus from its slot on the table and cuts away chunks from the holograph either side of a column containing the blue cross and the red smudge. A quick shove moves it to one side of the plate. He puts up a duplicate next to it, the one he is going to work on to identify the differences from the pre moonquake set up.

"I'll help out if I may?" Patricianna says.

He knows she is better at this than him and is thankful for the offer, but the sudden change in tone surprises him.

Lenny hesitates a few seconds. "Thank you, both," emphasising the last word. "This might just work for all of us." There is a slight emphasis on 'all'.

Kylone gets her hidden message. Lenny knows Alva is on her way, but will not say anything to Patricianna about what she thinks of as an exceptional rockborne talent.

"What worries me," Lenny continues, "is that a gap opened for us to fall through and then may have closed again afterwards. In which case…"

"Let's establish the facts first," Patricianna cuts her off.

"One step at a time," Kylone says. "First of all can you confirm where you were when the quake happened?"

"Eighty-five metres in from safety pod seven, tango. We were examining how the ice stuck to the rock. We needed a new debris dump and were considering melting the ice to get the space."

"That's a good start." That fits in with it being the classic weak spot for tectonic movements and is where the blue cross is marked on the holograph. "Looking which way?"

"Had the mine face to my right as I was looking at the ice."

"Good. Tell me what you noticed about the hole opening up."

Silence.

"When did you first notice something strange happening?" Patricianna intervenes.

"This is going to sound crazy, but I thought I momentarily felt heavier before the ice broke up."

"Actually that gives us a rough direction of where the main movement was taking place."

"You're right, but I'm not sure."

"Details like that," Patricianna says, "can build up into a picture. We can then discard the ones you're unsure of that don't fall into line with the others. Please keep on giving us those glimpses."

Kylone smiles. She had told him the same many years ago. It had worked on him then, and he is sure it will work on Lenny now. "Moving on. What changed in the ice?"

***

He runs out of questions for Lenny and compares the before and after moonquake holographs. New fault lines had developed between the trapped miners and the hub, and natural pressure pushed up the Mirandan segment they had been standing on. Rock and ice cavities had changed their shape under the extra or reduced pressure. A chain reaction of one movement forcing another had created a hole in space and time that they had fallen into. From Lenny's descriptions he is sure that chasm divided into smaller chasms as she went deeper. These branches will add to the problems of the searchers. The end result is Kylone is far from sure how the layers are now configured.

The miners had initially been tipped sideways into a hole. Most of the rest of the quake they had tried to slide along the ice and rock to reduce the rate of descent. That had not been enough to stop them falling, even in the low Mirandan gravity. Occasionally they dropped into the void out of reach of the chasm's walls. They tried to grab protuberances along the way, but they were too smooth to hold onto. Yet, it seemed a disturbingly long time for them to hit the bottom.

Lenny, the more experienced miner, had managed to keep her eyes open for a lot of the fall. When she could not, it had been really scary. Patricianna got her over those moments as quickly as she could. They were left with three gaps in the description; ones that Alva's looking beyond walls ability could fill.

"Kylone," Alva's voice comes over the comms. "I'm out of the hub airlock. Where do you want me to start?"

He rubs his hands over his face and checks the holograph. "Working on that now. Priest Patricianna is with me."

"I… I can't," Alva says, her voice trembling, "not with her online."

"Priest Kylone cannot counsel you," Patricianna says, "and given his impending tribunal, it would be best if there is a witness to what is being said between you two."

Silence.

Kylone has no idea how to break this impasse.

"Would another priest do?" Patricianna says at last.

"Alva has difficulties in dealing with authority figures," Kylone says. "That includes any priest."

"She doesn't seem to have problems with you," Patricianna retorts.

"That's because he understands," Lenny intervenes.

"Understands what?" Patricianna asks.

More silence. They are losing precious time. A way out of this impasse must be found fast.

He is unsure of what Lenny is referring to. He wants to think it is the grief of losing a partner, but fears she might have latched onto Alva having the ability to sense beyond the extrapolated patterning that the rockborne do.

This is guesswork. He has to deal with facts. Lenny knows Alva is definitely a strong rockborne. He told her this. The most likely explanation for her words is that he understands Alva's talent because he was once one. Correction; he still is.

The admission hits him hard right in the deepest depths of his torso. He wants to double up and cry out against his prison of the past. He dare not. He does not know how he holds himself together, but he clings to the idea he must protect Alva and save the miners.

While explaining Alva is rockborne would satisfy Patricianna here and now, her analytical mind would chew away at the issue, always coming back to it and looking at it from another angle. She is not one to give up that easily. Worse, it would take only one slip from Alva for Patricianna to ask why her rockborne talent was never recognised as such, or how her talent is far better than normal. Alva would panic and her talent might go into stasis, unable to do even the minimal of seeing just beneath the surface.

"I'm sorry," Kylone says to Patricianna, "but lives are at stake here. I'm going to have to ask you to leave."

Patricianna's face pales. "This will count heavily against you in your tribunal."

"I am aware. Now please." He holds out his hand to point to the door.

"Don't worry, Priest Patricianna," Lenny says. "I can be witness to the follow-on conversation."

Patricianna stands. "True, but sometimes counselling can be subtle, and you might miss the nuances."

Lenny laughs. "Kylone nuanced? That'll be a first."

Patricianna frowns puzzlement.

He understands her reaction. She is so used to looking under the surface for strategic motivations, minor inconsistencies and subconscious influences that she can no longer take things at face value. Under her guidance, he has developed similar traits, but he is not so far gone as to forget his past simplistic innocence. He feels sorry for her. "Go. We'll sort this out later." He has no idea how, only hope.

"Find me when you've finished here." She shakes her head and leaves, carefully closing the door behind her.

He feels a floating sensation as if released from a great weight. "She's left the room."

Alva breathes out heavily. "That's a relief. Thank you. I'll be with the rescuers in a couple of minutes. Where do you want me to concentrate first?"

Kylone checks the holograph zooming in on different parts. The top of the holograph originally sent by the Hubmaster has had details added. He must have got the rescue miners to do a survey there. The strata where the tunnel still exists are lower than those opposite across the chasm that has opened up. It means one side has definitely been subsided from the other. There is also a noticeable squashing of the ice layer below the floor's rock layer, probably due to liquefying under the extra pressure and the squeezing out of the locked in gas bubbles. The liquid could easily have seeped away through tiny cracks or narrow gaps.

He squirms. Liquid could have easily become trapped during the movement. It might be under pressure from the ice and rock above and also possibly due to expansion from warming up. If they release it in their trying to get to the trapped miners, it could mean more tectonic shifts. The rescuers need to know where any liquid pockets are.

There are likely to be aftershocks, not as bad as the main quake, but with added uncertainty of the stability of the adjusted strata they could cause a bigger disaster. He wants Alva out of there, and the rescuers and trapped miners.

"Are you able to differentiate between solid ice and liquid?" he asks.

"I've never tried it before," Alva replies.

"Let me ask this another way. What do you see when you see beyond walls?"

"Shapes, colours, some vague idea of distance. That's it. Identification of what I see comes from what I'm familiar with."

He is not surprised by the quickness of her reply. She has had a lot of time to think about what her talent can do. It is enough for what he needs. "There has been a squashing of at least one layer on the opposite side of the chasm, which probably disrupted the smooth shaping of that layer. Identifying those abrupt changes will help with Dirk's analysis, which I'm sure he's already doing."

"You bet I am," Dirk intervenes.

Alva groans. "So you want me to search for sudden changes in the depths of ice and rock strata. Anything else?"

"Sheets between strata that are slightly thicker than what you'd see as normal between the layers. They are likely to have what look like irregular shaped blisters. These will be thin sheets of liquid due to pressure between the layers. There's one other thing to look out for. Possible single pockets with no connection to any sheet. This may be where liquid has drained out between layers so that one layer sinks down to rest on top of another trapping the remaining liquid."

"Got that," Alva says. "Now where do I look? I'm just behind the rescue team, keeping out of their way."

"If you are facing where the mine face would have been before the moonquake, Lenny's about five degrees up from the viewing straight down from where you are, and about thirty degree clockwise from your left."

"Any idea of distance?"

"Difficult to judge from the holograph."

"Certainly no longer than fourteen hundred," Dirk adds, "but could be only down to twelve hundred metres."

Kylone winces. That was a long way to fall.

"I'll only see her as a pinpoint from here," Alva says.

"You don't have to see her, just find a possible route that goes that way. The closer we can get easily the better. Can you find some sort of marker for that direction?"

"Hold on."

"Don't forget to concentrate on the rock," Kylone says. It will make her look like a rockborne and therefore questions will be less likely.

"Ahead of you on that."

Of course she is. She has had a lot of practice at hiding her talent. Why is he so nervous for her? He resettles in his chair to get more comfortable. His edginess does not abate.

"I have a marker," Alva says. "What next?"

"Can you see..." This is the blind leading the sighted. He should not be telling her what to do, only she does not have any mining experience. He must dig into his memories, to work out for her what she should concentrate on and why. These are buried very deep in his mind, under the shield of deliberate forgetting to avoid the pain of his accident. That threat has now gone. Instead, he worries about how reliable his memory will be and there is no time for checking things out. He must hope he gets it right. "Can you see the gap that forms the top of the chasm through the rock and ice in front of you?"

"Hold on a second."

He falls silent to let her concentrate, and checks his holograph again. More crinkliness is added to the lines between lower layers a little way down into the chasm. The rescue team must be dropping down a camera on a line to map the new layout. There will be no need to ask Alva for descriptions there. It is further down where Lenny had her eyes closed that needs the details filled in. Would Alva be able to see them that far away?

He rubs his chin. It's her lack of judging distance that will hamper them. But there is one measurement they know.

"Got it," Alva says.

"Can you see the line attached to the camera that goes vertically from the edge part way down the chasm?"

"Yes."

"They'll know how much line they've let out. I'll get them to send you an automatic readout of that."

"What do I do in the meantime?"

"Find the deepest spot you can in the chasm, which is roughly in the same direction from where you're standing as your marker. They may be dropping the camera line off to one side of it into the wrong branching down of the chasm. If they do, direct them to the one that will get closest to Lenny. I'll get them to accept your directions by order of the hubmaster on the grounds you've got the equivalent of rockborne capability, courtesy of Dirk. On the way down check for the blisters I mentioned earlier close to the chasm branch. We want to identify where the rescuers are not allowed to dig."

"Got you."

He has stated the obvious precaution again. He really must be nervous, but is too busy to take time out for a relaxation exercise. The worry eating him is others will realise Alva can see that camera line through vacuum, a real giveaway she is more than rockborne. "Dirk, you still listening in."

"Course I am. What d'you need?"

"I'm going to get the hub to send me that camera line depth. Can you relay it on to Alva without letting others know?"

"Will do."

"Alva, I'll be on open link for a few minutes."

"Right."

"Dirk, hack me through to the Hubmaster."

"Done."

"Sorry to interrupt, Hubmaster. Priest Kylone here. Judging by the changes being made to my holograph the Chief Compineer has been sending over to me, you've got a camera line going down the chasm. Is that correct?"

"Good to hear you're helping out. Yes, you're right."

First, he has to get a cover story for what Alva is doing. "Can you send me an automatic camera depth update so I know the fidelity of what I'm looking at here?"

"Absolutely. Whatever you need. How is it looking from your end?"

"Working hard to help identify a way through for you with Alva's assistance."

"Great. Any help you both can give is appreciated. We're not making much sense of what's gone on in the ice and rock."

"Could I also ask that if Alva gives the rescue team directions, they be followed immediately?"

"Because of what she is sensing with her talent?"

Dirk must have told him about Alva's capability – and, given the shortage of time to get things done, probably threatened him with all sorts of nasty pranks. This is not the time to speculate on something that can be dealt with later. "Exactly."

"Of course, providing they don't override safety considerations."

"They won't."

"I'll let them know, but keep me aware."

"Will do. I've been talking to Lenny and put together my best estimate holograph from what she noticed during her fall. Use with care, but it might give you a clue."

"That would be welcome."

A flicker of his holograph meant Dirk had done the send for him.

"I'll keep you posted as and when."

Alva yelps.

Kylone drops the link to the Hubmaster. "What is it?"

"We've got a problem. Two in fact."

His heart races. He dreads the thought that the gap through which Lenny and her companion fell is now closed. "Describe them to me," he says in as calm a voice as he can manage.

"The camera line is heading down a dead closed-off end. It needs to be brought up by about fifteen metres and moved by about two metres to the right before it will drop down into the deeper pit, where we'll come across a second problem."

"Let's deal with this one first. Is there a continuous rock between where you are and that dead end?"

"Yes."

"Good. Exactly what rockborne can deal with. What are the unique characteristics of that dead end? Ones we can definitely identify for the camera to be going down it?"

"There's a small bunch of silver cubes jutting out to our right. But you'll need a description for the branching." She pauses. "Take the branch with the wider brown rock. They'll know what I mean when they see it."

"I'll order them to pull up and over on your behalf," Dirk says. "You deal with the second problem."

Kylone wishes Dirk would not interrupt them like this, but it will save time. "What's the second problem?"

"The main pit divides into three pits at its bottom. At this distance I cannot make out which of the three can lead down to Lenny."

He checks the holograph again. A steep diagonally inclined rock stratum about half way down to the trapped miners could easily be a shale-like layer. Chunks of it could have simply slipped down in the moonquake ahead of Lenny falling through one of them. It is a guess, but it fits in with Lenny's description. "Any of them could lead to miners. I have no indication at this end. Are they all approximately aligned with your marker?"

She hesitates. "Yes. That camera line could easily go down the wrong one."

One crucial question remains unanswered. "Let's note the problem for now. Did you notice any of those blisters I mentioned earlier?"

"Yes, but they are some distance from the chasm walls. The rescuers are unlikely to go anywhere near them with their digging."

"Makes sense. Any liquid close to the chasm was likely to have poured into it or evaporated." One danger less. Relief is short-lived; there is more to do. "Alva, you've done all you can with guiding the line, you might as well go back to the hub. You've at least saved the rescuers some time."

Line, correction, lines are the answer. Kylone knows what to do.

"You sure?"

"Not a hundred percent. But as good as."

"I'll stick around the hub, just in case."

He does not want her to risk more than she has done, but has no time to waste in arguing. "Understood. I need to talk to the Hubmaster privately." He finds his link switches over to him.

"…if you weren't the Chief Compineer, I would think you're nuts," the Hubmaster says.

"I've pulled in Priest Kylone to this link," Dirk says.

"Thanks. Hubmaster, any chance of getting two more camera lines down the fault?"

"Yes, but what's the point?"

"The rockborne has noticed the fault narrows into three different pits. She was unable to identify which is the correct one that will get through to the trapped miners. They may all do, but I wouldn't like to place a bet on that."

"I'll get those extra lines down there."

"One other thing," Kylone says. "I might be able to match it to what Lenny's told me, and my model here. If we identify the right pit sooner…" He knows the others can mentally finish the sentence for him with various reasons.

"Will do," the Hubmaster replies. "But what about your Truth Tribunal tomorrow?"

"This is more important," Kylone says firmly.

"As you wish." He breaks the link.

"It could be a long few hours," Dirk says.

"I owe Lenny."

"I've ordered you some supper."

"Not more lemon balm tea?"

"No. Some decent coffee this time. I'd better get back to prioritising rescue supplies."

Kylone sits back to close his eyes and take a few seconds to relax. He is sure they will now get to them in time. But things can, and do go wrong, which is why he wants to stick around.

He opens his eyes to look over the holograph. That first camera must be close to reaching Lenny's second gap in her knowledge.

"Kylone," Lenny says through the comms.

His body jolts a little. He had forgotten Lenny was still on line. "You've been quiet." These words sound foolish even to him.

She chuckles. "I know when to keep out of the way."

Sensible, ever practical Lenny; nothing seems to faze her. Yet there was an edge in her voice that made Kylone frown. "Only too well. What can I do for you?"

"Tut, tut. You know you're not allowed to counsel."

"I'm up for friendly chat with an old friend."

"More like another run through of what I saw when I fell?"

"That as well."

"Before we get started," she pauses. "Come and see me in sickbay when this is over."

He sits up straight. He has made a mistake, a bad one. Others would not have picked it up, but Lenny knows him too well.

She is giving him a chance to talk it over in private.

CHAPTER 6

Kylone drags his feet into the sickbay. The quiet unsaid urgency in Lenny's voice had forced him down here at this late hour. The hub is in semi-darkness, all the mining staff having gone home. Mandatory downtime after a rescue to give Chynoweth a chance to assess what is best to do next in the mine itself. He heads towards the only normal light where a nurse is reading his desk-screen.

The young man looks up and smiles. "Priest Kylone?"

"Yes."

"Miner Helena Tyndale is in cubicle two and expecting you."

"Is she all right?"

"We're keeping her here for observation. Just a precaution."

Kylone knows this is all the nurse will tell him. Being kept in like this is very rare in these days of quick accident diagnoses and remedies. It suggests there are some serious concerns about her health. Monitoring for concussion is a possible explanation, but he cannot understand how she could have banged her head so hard inside her helmet. He fears she has a worse injury. "Is there any topic of conversation I should avoid?"

The nurse shakes his head, his stone-encrusted hoop earrings scintillating in the light. "Go on through."

He gently knocks on the side panel of Lenny's cubicle and pokes his head round the curtain. "May I join you?"

Lenny is sitting in bed with the support of an almost upright backrest, pushing a reading screen on its semi-automated arm back into the wall behind her. She wears a standard grey-patterned white hospital gown and is covered up to her waist by a green sheet, made of the usual silk that keeps body temperatures just right. "Good to see a friendly face. Come on in." She waves her hand towards a chair.

"How're things?" Kylone settles in the armchair that is so comfortable he could fall asleep.

"Frustrating." She hesitates. "And boring. I just want to go home."

"I'm sure they wouldn't keep you in without good reason."

"That mad doctor has done so many tests that I'm sure she's looking for a medical problem in us to up her fees."

"The Council medics would take a dim view of that."

"In the meantime she'll be cashing it in. If she does one more test on my eyes, I'm going to scream."

Kylone sits upright. "Eyes?"

"Oh don't look so worried. My eyesight's fine."

"Would this by any chance be Doc Acheson? The one with red hair?"

"How in the seven hells of ice did you know?"

He is grateful the Doc is prioritising her spare time on finding out how the rockborne talent and Alva's beyond sight work. However, he does not want her doing this research on other people without their informed consent. This would require explanations and breaking the doctor-patient confidentiality. He can understand her dilemma. "I recently switched doctors to her. My first visit was a barrage of eye tests. But they say she has a good reputation. According to someone who should know, the best on Miranda. You're lucky you got her."

"How weird."

Weird is not the word he would use. Conniving is a better one. Doc must be getting data on normal people to compare with his and Alva's tests.

"Did she also take your DNA readout?" Lenny continues.

He reviews his visit at her surgery. "Don't think so. She did quite a few tests. Not sure what they were all for."

"One of those. Anyway, I didn't ask you here to talk about medical matters."

"What then?"

Lenny presses her lips together in thoughtful mode for a moment. "Alva Larsson. What exactly is your relationship with her?"

"Not you as well." He rests his head his hand on the upheld forearm from the chair's armrest. "It's bad enough Priest Patricianna having romantic notions about us."

"Are you?"

"Am I what?"

"Falling in love with her?"

He did not know what to say for a few stunned seconds. "Of course not."

"Then what?" Lenny's hands move palm outwards to add weight to the question.

"She needed help. I am… was a priest at the time of asking. So I helped as best I could."

"I forgot. She recently lost her husband, didn't she?"

"That's not what she asked help for."

"Wait." Her eyes move round as if searching for something in the distance. "Did she ask you to investigate why her husband died?"

"I'm not at liberty to discuss this."

"I'll take that as a yes. She's the cause of the mess you're in, isn't she?"

Kylone thinks about it. "Yes and no. Yes, she was a link in the chain of events. No, she is not the direct cause." He is, for letting himself be talked into helping the Chief Compineer in the way he did and calling for his Truth Tribunal when he should not have.

"You really don't have any feelings for her?"

There is that question again. He leans forward, puts his elbows on his knees, clasps his hands together and looks her straight in the eye. "Absolutely not." He wonders if he is deluding himself. Could he be falling in love with Alva? It is not the same as with Selma. There was an immediate attraction between them. With Alva, it is more like companionship, driven together by having a common cause.

"Good. Then you won't take what I say the wrong way." She pauses. "Alva is a rockborne talent. You and the Chief Compineer said so. She demonstrated it very effectively when you got me to accompany her on that rescue. A strong one too. But tell me, how can she differentiate between ice layers? She must have done so to read that deep. They're not extrapolations of patterns on rock faces, which you rockborne claim to be able to do. Nor is the ghosting of rocks, assuming there is ice where rock isn't seen. Far from it. While I think about it, how could she notice the strata across the vacuum of the chasm? And how in the nine hells of dust could she see the camera line?"

Blood drains from his head. Her speech confirmed his worst fears. His mistake has been noticed. He needs time to think and to be sure. "Why do you say that?"

"You forgot to switch me out of your conversations with Alva, the Chief Compineer and the Hubmaster. What she was describing was far more than a rockborne talent can do. What is she?"

These words confirm the worst. He has betrayed Alva's trust, and in doing so demonstrated he cannot trust himself to do the right thing. His immediate issue is to minimise the damage he has done. This is the least he can do. "I… we don't know. What we do know is that she has proved in most instances reliable. There are some things that fuzz her… talent for want of a better word. We're working to find out exactly what, but until we do, she knows the warning signs and so can back off."

"Do you know what miners can do with such a talent?"

He shakes his head. "It won't work. You saw how she reacted to Priest Patricianna, didn't you?" Her silence lets him continue. "She just closes down when any figure of authority is present."

"What about the Chief Compineer?"

"He may be her boss, but they are more like friends." A pang of jealousy flashes through him.

"And you? Aren't you a figure of authority too?"

"I showed her kindness when we first met, when I had no need to."

"Hell dust. There must be a way we access her talent."

"I'm doing the best I can." He wishes he could limit his own recklessness. "Please don't tell anyone. If and when she finds out, it will inhibit her even further. This might stop her assisting the rescues."

She briefly closes her eyes and breathes out heavily. "What if she gets it wrong?"

"It's why the Chief Compineer does spot checks on her descriptions with other data where he can." He suspects Dirk has a second reason, trying to work out exactly what her talent is. It will be more like a puzzle to him.

"That's sensible." She curls her lips inwards. "All right, you have my word that I'll keep quiet when it comes to normal mining operations. But if there's another accident where we don't know enough about the ice and rock configuration, then I'll ask for her help. Discreetly if possible."

This is the best he can hope for from Lenny. Nevertheless, Alva has an increased risk of exposure, the kind that might lead to her being hated by society once more. "Thanks, Lenny. I mean that. Was there anything else you wanted to discuss?"

"No." She looks away with pouting lips and droopy eyelids, clearly dissatisfied with their conversation.

"If you'll excuse me, I've got a rather busy day tomorrow." He stands.

She nods his dismissal, but keeps looking away.

He has failed her as well. Everything he does seems to turn out wrong. Nobody is really happy with him, despite trying to do his best. Nothing he can do here for now. He makes his way out of the mining hub and along the tunnel to the mag-pod station. His wrist-pad buzzes with an incoming important message.

"What now?" he mutters as he pulls up a holograph page to read it.

Doc Acheson has arranged another appointment at her surgery for him later the next evening to have his DNA read after his Truth Tribunal is likely to have finished for the day. He automatically accepts it, too tired to otherwise react, more like numb. He closes down his wrist-pad and calls for a mag-pod. Why is he so tired?

The Archdeacon had warned him not to make any more mistakes. He has done exactly that in letting Lenny listen in on their conversation. And he did it without realising at the time. How many more serious mistakes will he make like this? Or worse? He yawns as he gets into the mag-pod that has just arrived and directs it to the bottom of the stairs that climb up the chapel.

His next mistake may be fatal. Someone might die because he has made the wrong decision about why there have been more accidents and fatalities. Can he live with such a consequence? The answer is a definite no. He has already failed Alva, though that was not life threatening, just potentially destroying her way of life. It is a warning of his tendency to make mistakes. While he just looked after the chapel and was making the mosaic, he could always correct them. Now the stakes are higher and the consequences likely to be permanent. It is not so much a balance of risks, but a balance of penalties. He knows what he must do. His eyes close. He relaxes. The lack of acceleration and fresher oxygenated air rushing into the pod means he has arrived at his destination.

***

The evening light from waning Uranus tinges the glow of the strip lighting in the chapel. Kylone, standing on a low raised platform with a chair behind him, can see past the makeshift bench the Convener, High Priest Skiron, sits at, through the chapel's wall. The corona beyond the plain massively out-glow the shadowed plain to give the impression of two floating deep blue unfolding fans, outer edges together. This beautiful sight has no power to alleviate his depression. He may be innocent of the accusations or have acceptable mitigations, but he is guilty of failure.

High Priest Xuthus, the last of the three jurors sitting in a line with their backs to the altar, rises and walks across the empty floor-space. His bald head glints in the light as he stops by the witness stand. His grey eyes outshine all his face except for the glistening bulb of his nose. He stands akimbo, looks at the audience and then at Kylone.

This is the juror he fears is the most likely to force him

to say something he does not want to. Xuthus had previously been a Coroner. During his time there he had gained a reputation of being thorough in his investigations, having a phenomenal understanding of the law and the Council's wishes, and the ability to be quick at thinking complicated matters through.

"I'm going to be blunt," Xuthus starts. "If this were a civil court, you would be found guilty of the charges based on the evidence we have seen so far. Would you agree with this statement?"

Kylone does not want to voice the answer; it will have finality to it, he cannot escape his doom. "Regrettably, yes."

Xuthus cocks his head to one side. "Regrettably?"

"I have no wish to be here in this situation."

"Quite. So why are we here? I mean you could have avoided all this," he waves his hand round to indicate the courtroom, "by accepting a formal review of two of the three accusations."

It is one of the questions Kylone had been expecting and he is surprised it has come down to the last juror to ask it. "Because… at the time I thought it would help to save miners' lives."

"How?"

"By encouraging further analysis and getting the results I expected to see."

"You expected to see? Isn't that rather presumptuous?"

Kylone can feel the animosity coming from Xuthus. In fact he can see it in the faces of the priests in the audience scattered in the front three rows. The empty chairs behind them act like an echo chamber for that hatred, its focus coming from High Priest Diomedes' and his daughter, Thyone. "The evidence I have helped uncover so far is circumstantial and hearsay among the miners. It is worth investigating."

"So we have already heard. We have also heard from High Priest Diomedes here," he points to him sitting in the front row, "that they investigate these matters in the priority of usefulness and urgency in the limited resources they have. In fact he even asked you to help out with the resources, which you refused. So I ask you, why did you think you and this Engineer Isaac Hawking could do better than our Guardians of History?"

Kylone expected this question too and has a very carefully worded answer prepared. "Sometimes an independent investigation can look at an issue differently and throw new light on the problem. If not, it independently confirms the answers already obtained, which adds a little more weight to them."

Xuthus narrows his eyes on him. "That's a well thought out answer, one which even the Guardians of History would find praiseworthy. But with our limited resources don't you think you might have been at best mistaken, and at worst arrogantly selfish?"

"The only selfishness on my part is that having survived a fatal mining accident, I don't want others to go through what I did. Sometimes those killed in a mining accident are the lucky ones. The survivors can go through hell afterwards, physically and mentally."

"Ah… now we might be getting to the motive behind some of your actions. Would you admit this was a possible motive for disobeying High Priest Diomedes' order to leave Level 5 Hub during the rescue operation of Miner Cris Polhem and his crew?"

"It could be. It certainly contributed to the reason why I stayed."

"Doesn't that go against the way we priests should behave?"

"On a personal level, or a societal one?"

Xuthus' eyes widen. "This is the first time in your testimony I've heard you fight back. You really care about the miners." He looks to one side while pursing his lips. "Let me go back to my previous question. Why are we here? No," he pauses. "Let me put a different question. Have we heard the truth from you today?"

"Yes."

"Have we heard the whole truth?"

"That is for you to judge."

"Explain your answer."

"There may be factors I have not mentioned which you and the other judges would consider relevant, as you have just demonstrated. To you, the way I went about my investigation may in retrospect appear selfish. At the time I made some of those decisions, I had, like the Guardians of History, limited resources at my disposal that left me very few choices."

Xuthus stares at Kylone for a few seconds before turning to Skiron. "I judge Defendant Kylone here to have demonstrated that he has his full faculties and is therefore fully capable of defending himself in this Truth Tribunal."

The statement takes Kylone by surprise. What worries him is the omission of his title of Priest in such a formal statement. It is as if Xuthus has pre-judged him, which is unacceptable for any priest.

"Thank you High Priest Xuthus for your consideration," Skiron formally replies.

"But I'm not finished yet," Xuthus says and turns back to Kylone. "Why have you not called Assistant Alva Larsson to be a defence witness? After all, she did start you on this whole chain of events."

"Nobody disputes or has questions about her role in this. What would she add to your considerations?"

"So you're saying she is not here to save us all time?"

"Effectively, yes."

"Can the same be said of this Isaac Hawking?"

Kylone wonders where this line of questioning is going. He can only go along with it to see where the High Priest is taking this. "Yes, for now. He has not told me of any significant new analysis results that I have not informed the Guardians of History about."

"And if he had?"

"The Guardians of History would be informed at soon as it is practically possible. These are my instructions from the Archdeacon."

"What I find interesting is your use of the word significant. Have there been some tentative results with work still in progress?"

"Yes, but that is what they are, tentative. They have insufficient data behind them. In fact, there is very little data to back the conclusions. Certainly not yet worth bringing to the attention of the Guardians of History."

"Your assessment?"

"No, the… engineer's."

Xuthus frowns. "You've done the basic course in what the Guardians of History accept as relevant data, haven't you?"

"Yes, which helps me to judge what to pass on."

"And yet you let this engineer judge. Is that really the case?"

Xuthus is getting close to unravelling Dirk's identity. He scans the audience. Still no sign of the Archdeacon. She could easily have given her truthful testimony by now if she had wanted to. He has a lot of questions for her. "Yes," he replies to Xuthus.

"Why do you put so much faith in his judgement?"

"He uses Isaac Hawking as an alias to pass unnoticed by people. He is better known as Chief Compineer Dirk Schimmeratski."

A murmur rises from the audience. The other jurors and convenor suddenly sit up as if the tribunal had really got interesting. Diomedes glowers at Kylone. Xuthus looks stunned.

"Are you expecting us to believe that the Chief Compineer would go round Miranda as a workman electrician?" Xuthus asks.

"You wanted the truth. You got it."

Confusion flashes across Xuthus' face. "I think on this occasion I really do."

"That's ridiculous," Diomedes shouts.

Xuthus turns his head towards him. "It would help explain how Widow Alva Larsson became Assistant Alva Larsson."

Diomedes sits back as if he has been punched in the face.

"Why keep this fact from the Truth Tribunal until this late in the day?" Xuthus asks Kylone.

"You said it. Who would believe me?"

"Well, it certainly explains why you feel you could trust this man's judgement on what analysis results are significant or only tentative. It would also explain why you were loath to get him to be directed in his analysis by High Priest Diomedes. There is a coherency about what you are saying that points to you telling the truth. But this late, and relevant, admission leads me to wonder if we have heard the whole truth from you. Have we? I mean is there anything else you might wish to say that you now consider could be of relevance to this tribunal?"

A catch-all question, but unlike the others who asked earlier, he does not think Xuthus will accept his previous answers of it being up to the tribunal to judge what is relevant as sufficient. Nor can he find an ambiguous answer to avoid lying. Crunch time.

He could tell them about the tentative results of the rockborne being diverted by the type of rock on the plain. This alone would justify the analysis into the mining accidents. But that would give away Alva's role in the discovery, which would be as good as switching her talent off and more lives would be lost unnecessarily. He had found another way to warn the miners, through Meriel. His conscience was clear on that aspect. And then he made his mistake with Lenny. Having sorted out the issue, he then blundered totally unnecessarily. He is guilty of gross stupidity. He cannot forgive himself for that, at least not now. His shame feels too raw. Maybe in the future.

He could also tell them that someone else had identified Isaac Hawking as the Chief Compineer before the mining accident at Carbo Level 5. That someone had been the Archdeacon herself. But she had explicitly threatened to lie about that in a conversation with no other witnesses: his word against hers. He should have taken precautions against letting this situation continue. It would have shown someone else had good reason not to reveal his identity, someone responsible and respectable. He is guilty of at worst neglect, or at best naivety on dealing with the intrigues of power grabbing and using.

He could likewise tell them how the evidence Dirk had so far let him pass onto the Guardians of History pointed to the possibility of Chynoweth trying to mine out Miranda sooner rather than reinvesting in it. This was speculation, even if he believed it to be true. He could have, choosing his words carefully, voiced his concerns. But he had not, too overpowered by the people in authority and fearful of retribution. He is guilty of cowardice.

Guilty, guilty, guilty, of so many things – just not what he is accused of here. He wants to hide away from everyone here; ashamed he has not lived up to what was expected of him, both as a person and a priest. Especially as a priest: he should have had the faith to stand up to say and do the right things. His cheeks heat up with a flush. He is not fit to be a Mirandan.

He looks steadily at questioner. "There is nothing I want to add."

Xuthus narrows his eyes sharply. "Are you sure? Absolutely sure?"

"As sure as I can be."

He takes a few seconds to break off the eye-lock and turn to Convenor Skiron. "I have no further questions." He returns to his seat next to the other jurors.

"Do any of the jurors have further questions of anyone?" Skiron asks.

Each says no in their own their way.

"Do you have any testimony you want to add, Priest Kylone?"

"I do not."

"Does anyone have any questions or statements to make that they think will throw further insight into this tribunal?"

The chapel remains silent for many seconds.

"Then I will ask the jurors to adjourn to consider their verdicts and to let us know when they have reached their decision."

***

Kylone insists on standing while each of the jurors delivers their verdicts and their reasoning on each of the three charges. The first with outright anger, the second with great reluctance return guilty verdicts on each of the three charges as he expected. The final juror, High Priest Xuthus stands to deliver his verdicts.

"On the first charge of refusal to obey the High Priest Diomedes' direct order to leave Level 5 hub, guilty. Though there were some mitigating circumstances, Kylone could offer no direct defence. I advocate leniency on this charge.

"On the second charge of knowingly keeping the relevant data of Isaac Hawking's analysis from the Guardians of History, in particular Isaac Hawking's real identity which would have given more weight to the analysis, guilty. Whilst the motives of Kylone were well meant, there was an obvious lack of openness as required by the needs of our society.

"On the third charge of publicly contradicting the Guardian of History and thereby bringing its functioning into disrepute, guilty. Kylone gave no justification for his comments, which should have been first discussed in the privacy of priesthood, as required by our traditions."

Xuthus closes his eyes for a few moments before resuming his seat. This experience must have cost him some pain. There is nothing Kylone can do now to relieve him of that and must wait for the next part of this drama to unfold.

"Jurors," Skiron says. "Thank you for your considerations. Are you agreed that there was no evidence of malicious intent in committing his crimes?"

Each agrees in turn.

"It remains for me to pass sentence. Kylone, you have repeatedly brought the Priesthood into disrepute for no justification to society. You will no longer hold the office of priest, nor any other office in the Priesthood, even that of acolyte."

Kylone takes a deep breath while Skiron pauses. He had been expecting this as a minimum.

"Your actions have had a known impact on non-priesthood members. There has been much to commend in your actions, which were all part of what is considered normal priestly duties, such as counselling the trapped miners in the Carbo mine. This has to be balanced by detrimental impact you have had on people. You have given hope to various people that a cause for the mining accidents could be found, when there is none. You have caused the civilians to do work, when it was not needed, such as getting Coroner Sylvana to re-open the inquest into Hero Miner Raoul Larsson. This was a waste of precious resource. You have apparently, for no reason this tribunal can discern, earned the mistrust of at least one person, Miner Helena Tynsdale. Trust is the bedrock of society. It is what allows us to survive on Miranda."

The summary is damning. Kylone feels ashamed he has let so many Mirandans down, and bows his head slightly. He catches a glimpse of Patricianna in the audience. Her face is close to tears. She, like him, already knows which penalty he will have to pay.

"It is therefore with great sadness," Skiron continues, "that I have, according to our traditions and necessities, to give this tribunal's decree on your future. You are to be exiled from Miranda."

A couple of gasps escape the audience.

"Because there was no malicious intent in your actions, you are given a week's grace to get your affairs in order. This tribunal so rules. Do you, Kylone, have any final public statement to make?"

He stands up tall. This is his last chance to make any sort of good impression. "Yes please, very briefly."

"Go ahead."

"I wish to thank all who gave their time, support, statements and consideration to this tribunal. I can only hope that some good will come out of the result."

Silence.

"Is that all you have got to say?" Skiron finally asks.

"Yes, Convenor, it is."

"Unless an appeal is lodged under due procedures, this tribunal is closed."

Even if he spends all his waking hours in the gym building up his muscles, Kylone knows he will not be ready for the flight off Miranda. It will at best be very painful, and be followed by a life of poverty and struggle. He suspects his unusual anatomy may pull a nasty surprise on him and he will be crippled permanently. At worst, the flight acceleration will kill him.

Yet despite this grim future, he feels relieved. It is all over. He has no more worries and responsibilities. Even better, he finally has a real chance to get away from the reminders about Selma and how he lost her. He is heady with the euphoria of impending freedom, which brings with it its own dangers. He must control it, for now.

Kylone steps down from the platform and makes an effort to walk steadily down the aisle in the middle of the audience to the door at the back of the chapel. As he opens the door he catches some red and blue glints in his mosaic, the work he must now leave for someone else to finish. He smiles in appreciation of what he has achieved there, before leaving the chapel and closing the door behind him.

***

Kylone, wearing a new navy silk with cream edging, stands on the balcony to enjoy the Mirandan dawn like he has done these past eight years. The Priesthood has been generous. They are letting him stay in his condo until he leaves the moon of his birth. The Archdeacon pulled in a favour to let him join the dust and helium three mining crew orbiting Uranus. The gravity will be greater than he is used to, but Doc Acheson assured him he would survive.

Ghostly light streams are thrown over the surface's jagged horizon from the daylight creeping round onto the nightside of Uranus, the dark orb of the planet hanging above him.

In the four days since his tribunal had ended, Dirk has worked himself into a funk to try to find a provable reason for the increase in mining accidents, which would form a basis for an appeal. He has worked Alva and Meriel into exhaustion with extra tasking. Meriel had finally decided this could not go on and called a meeting of the four of them in her condo at Dunsinane that morning.

It is not something he is looking forward to. Dirk has gone into hyperdrive mentally coming out with sentences that are clearly important, but requires an understanding nobody else has. Meriel has increasingly become bad-tempered trying to slow him down. Alva has become withdrawn as if she has gone backwards in her grieving process. She is the reason he is going. He wants to help pull her out of her misery that is rapidly spiralling into despondency.

A glint from the five-eighths complete mosaic on the wall beyond the altar attracts his attention. The outline of lower parts of sheer ice cliffs at Verona Rupes can just be seen. He will never see the true Greening. He had missed the one time he was there because he was looking after Alva. Seeing it before he leaves will only give him another memory he would rather forget.

He has sold many of the possessions he cannot take with him and made just enough to pay for the one-way ticket to the mining hab and the necessary kit he needs to survive there, including a flexi lightweight spacesuit. He plans to take a walk on Dunsinane Plain after the meeting to start getting used to its different feel.

Despite all the turmoil, he has found a long-lost deep peace.

Another glint catches his eye; this time from the edge of the crater he took a sample from. He stares at the very spot trying to see the nick in the edge he left behind. The glint becomes a prolonged twinkle, then a continuous shimmer of dancing rainbow light. It is as if Miranda wants him to stay.

Rhythmic footsteps climb the stairs towards him. Their

gait is familiar, Priest Patricianna's. She comes to a stop beside him and places one hand on the bannister.

Without turning away from the light display, he says, "I'm sorry I've not turned out as well as you had hoped."

"No," she pauses, "you turned out better."

He smiles. "Nice of you to say so, but there's no need to soften reality."

"I'm not."

He snaps his head to look at her serious face. "What're you saying?"

"When you first came to me, I never expected you to ever be able to stand tall, psychologically speaking. Yet here you are, dealing with your impending exile in a calm, practical manner. I've no worries over your future. You'll be all right." Tears well up in her eyes. "Unlike me. I'm going to miss you."

"You mean you're going to miss my stubbornness?"

"That as well." She pauses. "The Archdeacon is asking for you."

"I'd rather not."

"She only wants to say goodbye. Surely you could do that?"

"I really don't want to."

"Why not?"

He bites his lip while trying to find the right words. In the end he opts for the truth. "Because she didn't come forward to testify on my behalf. It would've cleared me of one of the charges."

She mouths, "What?" Her eyes search his face. "You're serious, aren't you?"

"Regrettably, yes."

"But… that would make your exile null and void… why don't you say something? Put in an appeal?"

"To what end? It'll be my word against hers. The result will be the same. No, it's better, cleaner, this way."

"Oh damn it." She stamps her foot. "You'd have made one hell of damn good high priest."

"Me? Impossible."

"You really would have, Kylone."

He is thankful she has called him by his newly chosen name. He had surprised himself by realising how he has grown much spiritually since joining the Priesthood. So he had opted for the simple Kylone, more to identify what he had turned into rather than trying to be someone he could no longer be.

He glances at his wrist-pad. It is time. "I'd better go to meet my friends."

The sheen of welling tears in her eyes shows her compassion, but he also detects a glint of steel beneath liquid. Whatever she has in mind, he feels sorry for the person she is about to deal with. He hopes she is not going to tackle the Archdeacon on his behalf, as it will lead nowhere useful.

"Here, give me a hug," she says.

He squeezes her firmly, until she taps him on the back.

"Be off with you."

He smiles at her and glances out to the plain. The rainbow show has turned to greys. He turns and without looking back, makes his way down the stairs. A quiet sob from Patricianna whispers around the empty chapel.

He walks into reception, where Thyone sits at the desk concentrating on the screen. She wears the black with green edging silk of a priest. He must have missed her elevation. "Congratulations on achieving full priesthood."

She looks up, surprise etched into her face. After a moment's stillness, she fumbles her screen closed. "Sorry, I was concentrating. What can I do for you, Priest… what do I call you now?"

He recites his standard answer. "Just plain Kylone or Simon Redwood, whichever you feel comfortable with."

"Right. What can I do for you, Kylone?"

"Pass me my spacesuit and rucksack I placed under the desk for safekeeping please."

She scrabbles beneath the desk to retrieve a small well-filled rucksack that she immediately hands over, and a limp flexi-spacesuit attached to a belt with several pouches filled with air stacks, water, a computer, emergency medical supplies, back-up batteries and food.

A puzzled frown crosses her face. "This is the only one I could find."

He swings the rucksack onto his back. "I bought a new one. It's better for where I'm going than the heavy clunky Mirandan ones."

"Oh." She offers it to him as if it were something unpleasant she wanted rid of.

"Thank you." He droops the spacesuit over his arm.

"Kylone," she starts.

"Yes?"

"Those crystals you reported missing."

He had forgotten about those. "What of them?"

"Priest Theseus found them inside the lighting column."

This puzzles him. He never worked the mosaic with the lighting column out. His best guess is that Theseus found out who took them and to save their shame placed them in the column to be found. Whatever the truth, it makes no difference to him. "Thank you for letting me know."

"You're welcome."

Rather than taking the lift down, he walks down the staircase that curls round its shaft. The outer wall is etched with cameos of Miranda's history up to the opening of the chapel, which is depicted on the topmost etching. The next is the handover of the Pasture Star to the then Archdeacon. He tries to capture a memory of each etching as they go back through time. He stops at the last one, the clunky looking Voyager 2 probe flying past the first ever detailed picture of Miranda taken from space, with its mash of chevron scars and craters. The weight of history and tradition lifts from him. He is a man freed from his past and free to do what he wants with one glaring exception. Once he leaves, he must never return to the moon of his birth.

Kylone orders a mag-pod. It arrives promptly. Without looking back, he steps in and orders it to travel to the Dunsinane Transit Hall. Once the door closes, he slips off his rucksack and gets into his spacesuit. He might as well wear it to maximise the magnetic flux it travels through that will generate power to top up his batteries. The air gets stuffier. He sniffs in disgust, but knows he has to wait the ride out. He stares at the closed door.

The mag-pod slows as it rises, making him feel a little lighter. The door opens behind a rising column of plasma to indicate another pod is arriving. He has to step to one side to head towards the meeting zone.

Alva, Meriel and Dirk are waiting. Dirk has the dark bags under his eyes and a grey skin of having overdone things. Meriel has her stern crew captain's face on while talking. She is obviously in her sorting things out mood. Even with her back to him, Alva's hunched shoulders and head turned away from the others suggest she is withdrawn. Each in their way carries the burden of misery.

Kylone stops. He cannot face them like this. He has let each of them down: Alva in not finding the root cause of her husband's death; Meriel in not helping her and her friends out of the poverty they are struggling with; and Dirk in not being able to give him the friendship he clearly craves. A failure, this is what he is. He thumps his fist against the newly-risen wall, and his head drops to lean heavily on it. He cannot meet them.

He turns back to the pod he arrived in to find it is already descending and has to order a new one via his wristpad. The door for the one behind him immediately opens. He steps inside and closes the doors.

"What is your destination?" the lift's auto-voice asks.

"Get me out of here," Kylone growls.

"I require a place you wish to go to."

"Anywhere. Just leave."

The mag-pod sinks. He turns his back to the door, slides down to sit on the floor and drops his head into his hands. The mag-pod goes forward, making him momentarily lurch over his knees.

"We are heading for a randomly chosen parking bay. Chynoweth emergency services have been alerted to your severe distress and are on their way."

Kylone jerks his head to find his hands and cheeks are damp. "What?"

"We are heading for a randomly chosen parking bay."

"Where?"

"It is better for you not to know in case your tormentors contact you and you let slip where you are going. Chynoweth emergency services are–"

"Take me back to the Dunsinane Transit Hall."

"The Transit Hall is currently experiencing lockdown. You cannot go there."

Panic shakes his mind and body. "Take me to the nearest stop not in lockdown."

"This is not allowed when operating under emergency protocols in case your tormentors would think of this as your next logical step."

"But…" What the hell can he do? His breathing is rapid. This mag-pod holds him captive. His heart is thumping. He cannot use the escape hatch in the ceiling while it is moving. Sweat drips down his face. There is only one way to get out of this mess. "Where's the nearest stop you can drop me off at?"

"I am not allowed to tell you that in case your tormentors contact you and you let slip the information."

"But…" He glowers at the hostile control panel. Wait. This mag-pod's surfaces are slightly yellower than normal. This is one of the oldest in the pod fleet. Certainly old enough for its self-transit control unit to malfunction. But Dirk would never have allowed this to happen. As Chief Compineer he is meticulous in keeping equipment well maintained. He has to be on this harsh moon. "Have you recently been commissioned from storage?"

"Yes. Two days ago."

This mag-pod has not had a service since whenever. No wonder it is going wrong. "Put me through to the Chief Compineer."

"I cannot do that as he has been positively identified as one of your tormentors. Central comms has been alerted to this issue."

"Put me through to his…" Both Meriel and Alva had been with Dirk and would also be classed as 'his tormentors.'

The pod slows then turns left.

"Take me to the nearest stop you can. Can you comply with that order?"

"That is an acceptable order." The pod turns right.

He now has a plan. Get off at the nearest stop and order another pod to go back to the Transit Hall. He relaxes.

The pod sinks down, turns right then left, goes along a level path and sinks once more.

Kylone loses any idea of where on Miranda he might be. He is forced to wait as the seemingly random journey continues. The air gets noticeable stuffier. "I could do with some fresh air in here."

"I agree the oxygen ratio is less than desirable. I am stopping." The pod slows to a halt.

Kylone jumps through the opening door before the pod has a chance to lock him in again. He is in a wide tunnel with five personnel mag-pod plasma doors next to the one he has come out of. Further along are two wider plasma doors for bulk carrier mag-pods. The tech shows its age. The row of portholes opposite have a grey tinge, which warns that light from the outside can come into the tunnel, but none can escape. They hint at this being a farm centre.

While the pod's door closes, he steps over to peer through the nearest porthole. Being only half a metre wide, its metre length forms a short tunnel in its own right. A blaze of white from sunlit ice dazzles him. Once his eyes adjust he makes out that the porthole looks into a deep valley. The chasm wall opposite is sedimentary. Its embedded rubble of different overlapping colours, browns, greys and the occasional green, is the result of floating up through the solidifying ice the experts said. Its surface is riddled with pockmarks and gouged out channels from meteoroids, showing the great age of the surface. There is only one place on Miranda he can be, Argier Rupes, which is on the other side of the Inverness Coronae to Dunsinane. He is many kilometres from the Transit Hall.

He calls up a pod at the door next to the one he came out of, just in case the old pod is still there. The door opens within five seconds. As he steps in, he notices the yellow tinge on the wall and rapidly pulls himself back out. Of course it would be the same one, just moved one mini-block along in the lattice of tunnels with their magnetic guides along which the pods can travel. A central computer controls the whole transport system to minimise its total expended energy.

He needs another quick way out of here. There, the bulk carrier mag-pods will do. He rushes to call one.

The notice bar above the door lights up with the message: 'A Pod will arrive in 25 minutes.'

The delay seems excessive. He paces up and down in front of the door to burn off some edginess. Can he take another route out of here? This tunnel, from what he remembers goes to three hangars, large farms for main soil crops. In between them are tunnels that lead to farm rooms comprising of walk-around walls full of baskets with fruit and vegetable plants, places where Alva used to work as a farmhand, planting the small seedlings and picking the delicate produce.

The thought of Alva makes him stop. He never found the answer to her question about the rise in mining deaths. He is sure that given time, Dirk will. Kylone smiles. Maybe when the time is right, they will settle down together. Envy flashes through him, of their future quiet life together. That is not right. He is jealous of the life Dirk can have with her and forever denied him. An unknown time of stillness of confusing unfinished thoughts racing through his mind later, he realises Patricianna was right. He is fond of her himself, maybe more than that. Thankfully for her sake, it will never grow to anything more. He has been a wreck of a person ever since his accident, despite the vast improvements of finding that inner peace and confidence in the past week.

A personnel pod door opens to his right. Two men in their grey silks with red shoulders and wristbands step out. They wear red belts with pouches and a holster that contain a hand laser. They look him over and check their wrist-pads.

The silks are so rare that it takes a second for Kylone to register what they are, Chynoweth's guards.

The guards glance at each other. One moves his hand towards his holster.

Fear spikes. Kylone concentrates on finding a way out. He runs past the other bulk carrier pod doors and turns right through the plasma door into the back hangar.

The vast space has pillars placed regularly, far enough apart to allow farm machinery to operate between them. The crisscrossed lanes are planted golden wheat with its ears starting to curl downwards that is not far from being ready to harvest. Their leaves may be smaller than types found on Earth due to the difference in gravity, but thankfully the crop yield is the same. Wheel-tracks in the wheat give the ground a tartan pattern. The pillars have baskets of plants, some with speckles of small flowers that will turn into fruit. The light is natural, gathered from the surface outside and let in through strip lighting that form squares in the ceiling around each pillar. It reeks of damp and compost. The humidity drenches him in sweat. The varying buzz comes from bees and other insects, which he sees as dark moving splodges against the colour.

He turns left along the aisle against the wall that faces the Argier Rupes. The wheel-tracks form additional semi-circles round the pillars. This is the turning lane for the farm machinery. He runs along it keeping his feet as close to the ground as possible to maximise his speed and not disturbing the plants. Food is precious on Miranda, and nobody would forgive him for destroying any part of the harvest. Having been exercising in the gym these last few days, he knows his running speed has increased. It will not be enough. Chynoweth's guards are paid to keep fit week in, month out. Their muscles will be stronger and their footing for speed-running more precise. They will be more than a match for him. The realisation spurs him on faster, concentrating harder and sweating more. This cannot last. He has to use cunning if he is to get away from them.

As he runs, he searches the far wall between the rows of pillars for the familiar green of plasma doors. They lead to the emergency escape route through tunnels away from the hangars. There they are, ten aisles along. He continues running another three aisles along before turning right into one. He can hear the beat of the guards' running feet. He counts the pillars he passes. Once past the twelfth, he zigzags left than right three times.

The guards' running beats are no longer in unison. They have split up to search for him, probably one running down the turning aisle and the other at right angles running towards the far end. He cannot stop and hide. He zigzags right then left two times. He sprints past ten pillars.

"Got him," one guard shouts. "He's running for the back tunnel."

Kylone zigzags right then left twice and plunges through the plasma doors. The room lights up to reveal rails of hanging emergency spacesuits sorted by size. Opposite are three open personnel airlocks. He dashes for the middle one and hits the emergency exit button. He brings his hood over his head, seals his spacesuit, and turns just in time to see one of the guards come through the plasma door and aim his laser at him.

The airlock's pumping out the air takes too long. The guards will soon be able to take aim at him. How did they get here so quickly? Calling for the guards is not part of a pod malfunctioning procedure. Come to think of it, that pod should have been checked automatically before it went into service. Dirk would have made sure of that. A chill goes down his spine. This is a co-ordinated attempt to kill him. Its cold-bloodedness scares him.

Chynoweth is certainly involved. But they would have no motive. The Guardians of History do. Why could they not just let him leave in three days time? They must consider him a danger to their plans. But what triggered their reaction?

The meeting with Dirk, Alva and Meriel? It would certainly suggest to them he was still trying to dig up evidence against them. One thing he is sure about, there is a tie-in between High Priest Diomedes and Chynoweth. As to what they are working on together, he can only guess, but its criminal nature is now obvious.

The outer door starts to pull aside. He slips through the opening as soon as the gap is wide enough. Emergency lights switch on. He is in a tunnel heading away from the hangar, wide enough for four people to walk side by side. He sprints along the straight and only slows when he has to turn left.

The tunnel opens out into a narrow rock chasm. The path curves along the side with a guardrail to his right and enters another tunnel at the far end. He checks round for another route. The sheer wall has no climbing holds or ledges he can leap onto. Instead of the expected darkness below the guardrail, there is a carpet of orange, green, red and yellow twinkles, reflections and refractions of the emergency lights. He flinches. This is Snowdrift Chasm, where fine crystals have dropped to the bottom to form a white sand in a deep long narrow pit from which there is no exit. It is a favourite place for suicides to jump off from. He is unsure of how many bodies lie at the bottom covered by snow-sand, but hopes their last moments were more peaceful than what had brought them to their miserable fate.

He searches the chasm's walls below the snowline hoping to trigger his rockborne talent, and focuses on the one opposite. The twinkles merge to form a bright translucent sheet on the powdery surface.

His eyes are drawn deeper into the snow-sand to follow the penetrating light. The dimming is uneven, brighter sections forming misshapen cones or shallow basins that fade into the depth. Some split into smaller cones and basins. In the darker parts the colours switch between the reds, oranges, yellows and greens. Must be something to do with the snow-sand's changing density and material.

The light along the chasm's walls is brighter forming a kind of protective skin for the whole display. He guesses the rock is reflecting the light into snow-sand and concentrates on its texture: stripes of smooth, gravelly or crazed with lines, indicative of layers.

Their gradual slant downwards to his left steepens until, at the chasm's far end, they are nearly vertical. The bottom is very dark down, yet there is a grey shadow that looks like an opening.

A glint from the tunnel farther along the path interrupts his awe. His rockborne vision delving through the rock shows him standard spacesuit lights. Someone is coming through. He fears it may be another of Chynoweth's guard.

Kylone's nerves jitter. His mouth dries. His breathing becomes rapid and heavy. Sweat drenches him. His sight smudges. He desperately wants to be mistaken. These could be the last moments of his life. Terror rises in him.

His rockborne talent strengthens to see more detail. Unlike under the snow-sand, the dimming is uniform, which shows an even granularity in the rock surrounding the tunnel. He can clearly make out a space-suited man marching towards him.

His nerves flare up even more. He can barely stop the shaking rippling through his body. He sees through the protective layers of the spacesuit until he reaches the grey and red of a guard's uniform. He is trapped. They will kill him.

He grabs the guardrail to stop himself from falling. The shaking wobbles his sight. He tries to calm down, to think clearly about what he can do and regain some dignity in facing the inevitable. His sight slips to the grey shadow at the bottom of the chasm's end. It is the only possible escape route, if it really is one. He does not know. He has no other option.

He climbs over the guardrail and pushes off to dive into the snow-sand's mess of orange, red, yellow and green.

CHAPTER 7

Everything lingers. The twinkles dawdle as Kylone floats down. The snow-sand's cones and basins appear stationary. The speed at which he sinks past the chasm's wall seems so slow he could count the gravel stones protruding from its surface. He would, but his mind races on urgent issues. How close are the guards and do they have their lasers out ready to fire? When will they have line of sight to shoot at him? How can he drop faster?

The wall is close enough to touch with his outstretched hands and will come closer as he falls. Beneath the snow-sand's colourful top, the wall's bright surface bulges upwards to form a sharp-edged ridge. Other jumpers, being blind to it, would be injured by its sudden impact. It would be a mercy for them to fall fast enough to die instantaneously. These suicides do not bring climbing ropes to haul themselves up and invariably disable their comms before they take the plunge. They choose to die painfully by oxygen starvation, in the belief it is a gentle introduction to the reality of death.

Kylone squeezes these horrible thoughts to the back of his mind. He must concentrate on getting safely to that grey shadow.

His sight follows the ridgeline as it fades into the dimness to his left; it is dropping away. That is the direction he must go. He straightens his body and legs; this will give him a smoother entry into the snow-sand and reduce his inertia round his body axis to give him more manoeuvrability. His hands reach out to the wall to do what he can to pull himself diagonally downwards to the end of the ridge.

His body slowly turns to align with the direction he travels while speeding up downwards. He passes the gravel stones faster, but it is still too slow. The wall is closer. He is able to grab it more firmly. He pulls harder.

His hand slips. A red line of light flares beside him to hit the snow-sand. A guard has fired at him. His hands scrabble at the wall to pull harder and to the left.

He is damp all over and the stench of sweat confirms why. He is terrified, yet detached from this emotion. It is as if he is watching himself.

His helmet hits the snow-sand, slowing him down. Powdery particles are thrown up past his visor to sparkle in his spacesuit's lights. He ploughs his hands into the snow-sand. They scoop it up and throw it up behind him to blind the guards' aim. His actions pull him under faster. More scoops later, there is an extra tightness about his torso and then thighs. A backward kick lightens the pressure and will have thrown up a flurry. It also pushes him deeper into the cones and basins.

A quiet rasping is the particles rubbing against his helmet. His spacesuit is designed to withstand dusty mining environments in space, but will it be robust enough for this? Moving more slowly would help.

In his rockborne vision, a finger-size white plug falls past him, ice melted together by laser becoming dense enough to sink. He must change direction and twists left to dig towards the chasm wall. Deep memories come to the surface of a fascinating school lesson on swimming, a pastime enjoyed on Earth, Titan and in sub-surface oceans such as on Europa. A holograph explained how various actions propelled people through liquid. He concentrates on emulating what they called 'dog paddle' to head down towards the chasm's end. It works, much to his surprise.

He bumps into the wall and instinctively pushes away from it. Damn! He should check where he is going. He looks downward for the ridgeline; it curves into the chasm wall. Heading towards its far side will let him drop onto what looks like a dimly lit skin formed by the tops of boulders. That would mean walking across perhaps slippery and certainly tricky terrain. Continuing his dog paddle mid snow-sand is the safer option. His arm muscles grow painful, but he carries on as fast as he can. His survival demands his extra effort.

"We're got another jumper in Snowdrift Chasm," a female voice comes over his open comms. "Assistance required from anyone in the vicinity. Sec Con, can you get those specialist sensors here to check under the snow-sand?"

"Not again," a male voice replies. "O.K. Any idea who it is?"

"Didn't identify himself, but had a lightweight grey flexi-spacesuit on."

"Wait," a second female voice interrupts. "Did you say a flexi-spacesuit? Was he about a metre eighty tall?"

"Yeah, sounds about right," the original voice says.

"Seven hells of ice."

"What's wrong, boss?"

"That's probably Kylone. We've had a report that he's gone missing. Was expected at a meeting in Dunsinane Transit Hall, and he had his new spacesuit with him."

"Oh shit. Sounds like he lost it."

"I hate these suicides," the boss says.

Kylone is too busy swimming the snow-sand to let the shock of being called a suicide sink in. He checks ahead. The grey shadow is brighter and takes a common ragged triangular shape of slabs of rock locked into position after crushing against each other. It is still too dark for him to see inside it.

It has to be an escape route. He cannot go back. The guards will laser him, let him sink in the snow-sand and throw the offending laser after him to make it look like a quick suicide. He must go on. That triangle must be an entrance to somewhere. His throat tightens as his nerves make his stomach feel like a rattling dust pit.

The light extends into a tunnel, which carries on roughly level, its walls formed of angular slabs. It is wide enough for him to pass through. Where the hell does it lead? He has no idea, but it promises a way out. His nerves die back a little. With that the tunnel shortens in his rockborne vision, but its entrance beckons. He snow-swims hard into the light. Momentum keeps him going through the tunnel.

The snow-sand is heavier to shift. His muscles are tiring so he tries harder. Moving the particles from ahead of him seems easier than shifting it away from his sides. No time to work out why. He reacts by hauling the snow-sand from in front to behind him as close as possible to him.

The stench of sweat in his spacesuit is sickening and he does his best to ignore it. He is into a rhythm of strokes. He relaxes a little and concentrates on his surroundings. Where is the grey light coming from? Some of it is from his spacesuit lights. Could the rest come from another man-lit area? He hopes so. Where from? He cannot think of anywhere suitable. He gets more anxious. He focuses ahead in the tunnel. It continues level. About twenty metres ahead, it abruptly starts to rise and its cross-section changes to a circular shape.

That surely must be man-made, probably a long-abandoned mine. It continues up until it reaches a level where it suddenly darkens. Have they backfilled the tunnel with mining debris? That is what happens to most disused mines. It would mean digging his way through, and that would take precious oxygen he might not have.

His nerves flare, making his rockborne talent intensify. He sees into the edges of the circular tunnel, a uniform beige rock. The circular tunnel's darkening turns into a very dimly lit passage; clear of any colouring or haziness. It must be vacuum, empty of debris. Even better, once he breaks into the tunnel's vacuum, he will be able to walk forward with ease. He has a route that could lead to safety.

Wait. What has he got wrong? That circular tunnel is too perfect. No mine goes that straight for that long. Another long ago lesson edges its way into his mind: a volcanic vent for hot treacly magmas. No way it could be here on his home moon… unless in pre-human times an asteroid had broken off a warmer world to travel into the outer reaches of the Solar System and embed here. It is the only plausible explanation, unlikely though it is. That tunnel is here, so it must have happened. And it is snow-sand all the way to the vacuum.

Surely such a large asteroid must have shown up in the surveys? It is probably of no interest to anyone, especially if there are no signs of mineral deposits. So it never got talked about. This explanation does not sit right with Kylone. It feels really strange. Could his rockborne ability have got thoroughly trashed to perceive nonsense; or is he in a coma or hallucinating, or a dead man swimming through a posthuman existence?

He must stop these wild thoughts. Of course he is alive and experiencing this on Miranda. Stick to the basics. He needs to keep watching his oxygen supply until he can guarantee to reach some fresh air. It is good at the moment. Check. His spacesuit is functioning correctly? Check. His only option and hope is to go forward. This is what he must concentrate on. He forces his breathing and movements into a slow steady tempo while focusing breaking through the snowline. One, and two, and three, and four, and…

He nears the joint between the triangular and circular tunnels. He feels the pull of reaching a milestone. His swimming is more vigorous. Yet the snow-sand seems to have thickened. He is into the vent. There is a pull at him to return down the tunnel. He cannot return. More struggling strokes follow. The swimming becomes easier. He is back into his natural rhythm. One, and two, and three…

His hands suddenly feel less pressure. They are in clear vacuum. He pulls himself out of the snow-sand into the two metre high tunnel. The spacesuit's lights automatically brighten. The tunnel has a circular cross-section with smooth walls of beige, just as his rockborne vision had indicated. That his talent is working correctly eases his worry. His sight returns to normal.

He checks his oxygen. There is still plenty for now, but he needs a plan of how to get back into the Mirandan ventilated areas before it runs out.

The tunnel continues on an upward slope for about twenty metres and opens onto a patch of starlit sky. It is too small to distinguish any of the better-known constellations.

As he walks up the vent, it cuts through angled downward slopes of alternating layers of beige rock and accumulated dust. This would be typical of volcanoes erupting and depositing dust, to be followed by the pouring down of magma that then cooled into a solid.

He steps out of the vent onto a gentle iced slope. His spacesuit lights do not allow him to see that far into the darkness so he switches them off and lets his eyes adjust. The horizon line between total darkness densely packed stars and nebulae comprises gentle peaks with their tops cut off. Volcanoes. He checks the stars. The familiar constellations are gone, replaced by what? This is nothing like Miranda. Where in the scratching dusts is he?

He must be hallucinating or dead, yet there is a steadiness and consistency unlike any dreams or fantasies. This is weird, unknown and absolutely crazy. It is also peaceful, beautiful and soul satisfying. He takes a few moments to absorb the wonder of this strange place. Serene euphoria descends on him like a spirit taking over his life. Time slows. It is as if he sees everything while he is both part of this world and absent from it. Everything is so wonderfully in balance and coherent, like a true vision.

This has to be fleeting and insubstantial. Miranda's reality pulls at his psyche, but is not enough to drag him from this ethereal place. How did he get here? On balance he prefers being dead to hallucinating, because it means his troubles will be over shortly when his brain finally shuts down.

There will be no more struggle, must-dos or expectations placed on him. He is free to do what he likes. All his burdens of responsibility and obligation are gone, letting him feel as if he is floating in the comfort of vacuum. He stands and stares in awe at this incredible world of stars and volcanoes.

He switches his suit lights to very dim and pivots slowly to enjoy more of the view. About five metres to the side of the vent's entrance a man in a spacesuit lies on his back. The stillness, the black shading of the helmet's visor and lack of any suit electronic activity indicates the man is dead and his spacesuit has run out of battery power. The man's left arm lies on the ice pointing towards the vent and his right lies on his chest holding what looks like an independent clunky comms stylus, the type Kylone's parents had for emergency use in case of suit failure. Something else is off about the brown spacesuit, though he is not sure what. He focuses on its details. The gloves are of a thickened material that would make moving his fingers limiting. A single rill circles each of the wrists means the gloves are detachable. He has not seen that type of spacesuit since childhood. This design was last produced thirty, thirty-five years ago. Whoever this man was, he has been lying here for many years.

As he walks over to him, Kylone notices the slope rises to its own cut-off peak. He is on the slope of a volcano, which explains the vent. He gently removes the stylus from the stiffened fingers, and waves it over his wristpad until it kick-starts into lit-life from the energy transfer. A 3-D holograph rises from it without a request for unlocking as expected. It has been deliberately open for all to access. He hits the ident tab. A picture of a man in his late fifties with a shaven head, blue eyes, dark brown eyebrows, bulbous nose and toothy smile shines up at him. The name underneath is 'Kieran McCloud.'

Kylone blinks hard. He was three when the news spread about Kieran; the best rockborne Miranda had ever known, gone missing. Search parties had been organised in and around the Maze where he was last seen. The last likely sighting of him was exiting into Verona Rupes, but there was no video recording to confirm it. He had vanished without a trace leaving everyone puzzled.

The face staring at him from the screen looks familiar. He puts it down to remembering the pictures from the news stories at the time. Yet, that feels wrong as if he has seen it more recently.

A red bar flashes above the holograph: a message waits to be opened. He hits it. The holograph reverts to old-fashioned white writing on a black screen, which makes the words jump out at him.

'If you read this, then you've found me dead. Please do me a favour. There is a small box in my right front belt pouch. Make sure my brother, Lachlan McCloud, gets it. It contains a keepsake from Earth precious to our family.'

This man has a family, which after his own mother died Kylone did not. His mining crew became his family until that fateful day of his accident, and then the Priesthood. That is now truly behind him.

He pulls out the small brown box with a tarnished gold clasp from the pouch and opens it. Inside is small garland of carved black flowers and leaves attached to a silver chain. He has never seen such a stone before, but guesses it is jet, a form of pressurised dead trees that had long been in the making. No wonder it is a precious heirloom. He closes the box and packs it and Kieran's turned-off stylus into his own pouch.

He stands and signs a priestly blessing. "May you rest in peace, rockborne."

How can he get the box back to Lachlan? Finding him on Miranda would be a few seconds work for Dirk. Getting back there is the issue. This thought raises the question of how Kieran got here from the Maze.

He catches a glint coming off the top of Kieran's belt underneath where his phone had been. He kneels down to take a closer look. There are a few grains of snow-sand lodged between the belt and his spacesuit. He has been into the stuff down the Snowdrift Chasm. Did he arrive here by that route? No way, he would have been spotted en route from the Maze to the chasm. That means he travelled here from Verona Rupes in this volcano world and was going into Snowdrift Chasm to call for help. Something must have stopped him. Kylone has no idea what. It puzzles him.

There is another mystery. How did Kieran find his way from the Maze to here? The distance alone would have made this vent hole a tiny pinpoint on any view, actual or rockborne. How did he know?

He checks the stylus's navigation system and calls up the last known read place: Verona Rupes close to the bottom of the narrowest cliff opposite the Aerial Gallery. This proves Kieran travelled in this volcano world to here.

Thoughts click together. The Verona Rupes cliffs must have been Kieran's entry into this world, and he already knew about this exit in the Snowdrift Chasm. For some reason he could not return via Verona Rupes. As he had come from there to here, he had a navigation method, which means he superimposed a map of Miranda on this world. His strong rockborne talent might have been able to do that.

He looks in the direction he thinks Verona Rupes might be. There is no sign of it. His nervousness rises. His own talent intensifies. Faint shadows superimpose on the volcanoes, but they are too hazy to form a discernible picture. Panic sets in. His breathing and heartbeat quicken. He squeezes his eyes shut and counts stones in an imaginary gravel pile. He calms enough for him to feel safe to open his eyes.

The dim volcanoes are still real and substantial. But there is a ghostly overlay of a better-lit long valley with stepped cliff ice walls along both sides and random craters from meteorite impacts. Their layout is both familiar and wrong. He looks down the volcano slope, only to discover his feet in the ghost world are standing on nothing about twenty metres above an ice ledge. He suddenly recognises the ghost image for what it is, above a ledge of the Inverness Coronae looking along the valley of Argier Rupes. The wrongness is the height he is viewing it from. He should be falling, but does not move. His feet are firmly on the ground in the volcano world. He can see but not touch Miranda, so near and yet so far. How in the trillion hells of ice is he going to get back there?

Panic threatens again. With it comes sharper details and more solid colouring of the Rupes. Two worlds overlay each other. It is too much to take in in its broadness. His focus narrows onto individual features, a crater on Miranda, a frozen rivulet in the volcano world, a crack in an ice wall on Miranda, a fuzz of dust and snowflakes in the volcano. His eyes move further and further up the Rupes on Miranda and simultaneously along the valley in the volcano range.

A crater's cragged rim coincides with the top of a hummock down the real slope to one side of him. He shakes his head at seeing the merged surfaces to try to separate them. They remain stubbornly one. It is a place where the worlds coincide, at least view-wise. He mentally marks hummock and relaxes to slip out of his rockborne vision back into that of the world of volcanoes.

A steady walk gets him there in fifteen minutes. He steps on the hummock and uses his other foot to feel round the surface. It remains smooth, none of the crater rim's cragginess. There is no exit to Miranda here. He must go all the way to Verona Rupes to find that other way back to his home moon, which means relying on his talent to find his way there on Miranda while walking through the volcanoes. The sooner he gets to it the better. Urgency boosts his rockborne talent and he starts looking for his next waypoint.

***

Kylone checks his oxygen; about three hours left at the current rate of use. Like the rest of the walk, it has been depleting faster than expected. He checks his suit's integrity yet again via readouts on his visor, no leakage or holes. This may be normal for this type of suit, which is new to him. He doubts that very much. His heavy use of his talent might explain it, though he has never noticed this in the past. But then he had only ever used it for very brief periods of time – certainly not long enough to make a dent in air supply. He cannot stop now.

A glance at the volcanoes he has come from points to the direction he should look next. He turns his back to them to face the random rising steps of pale grey hexagonal blocks, height differences varying from a smidgen to twenty-odd metres. He plants his feet firmly on the ice, lets his fear of his impending death swell up, hoping his rockborne talent will come alive again.

It does. The straight cliffs of Verona Rupes solidify to loom darkly above him, their sheer faces diving deep into the ground. They confirm he is close to the position of the last GPS reading on Kieran's stylus, except on Miranda he would be in solid ice ten metres below valley's floor. There is a thin veil of darkening on the surface above him where feet have trodden in the fallen space dust into the ice.

His eyes are drawn up to the chaos of flat surfaces, level, angled, vertical, interlocking and intersecting of the combination of the Mirandan cliffs and hexagonal blocks. It is both fascinating and frightening. Extra surfaces break those he already sees into smaller shapes, crazy three-dimensional paving gone mad. He takes a slow breath. Some of the surfaces disappear to make the remaining shapes larger. That scares him even more. More surfaces form turning the whole view into an intricate mosaic. It is too much for him. He snaps his eyes shut into calming darkness.

Controlling his nerves is turning out to be a reliable mechanism to induce his talent, and even better he can control the extent it works at. It is a gift of understanding he rejoices in. If only he can return to Miranda to tell other strong rockborne like Alva.

She must have seen the kaleidoscope of flickering surfaces from the Aerial Gallery, which was what made her faint. He being the weaker talent can perhaps never see as much as she did. He forces his fear to the back of his mind and relaxes.

He is back on the ice facing just the hexagonal steps strewn with an occasional meteorite. He focuses on roughly where the floor of Verona Rupes, if extended, would cut through the hexagons because that is the level he must come out on Miranda. Ever so slowly, he lets his tension build up to bring back his rockborne vision.

Hints of cliffs strengthen to shadows until they are as real as the hexagons. He holds his tension at that level. Now where is that link between this volcano world and Miranda? It will probably look something like the one in the tunnel from Snowdrift Chasm, a mismatch of shapes lying next to each other.

No route is identifiable, not even a convoluted one. There has to be a way. Kieran found and used it to come here.

The dim light in the volcano world is not helping. Maybe there is a niche he has missed. Kylone switches on his handheld torch and waves its light over the hexagons. A momentary upward column of light appears. He inches his torch back until he sees a steady light column rise from above a hexagon some way up one of their spurs. About thirty metres up the fading column splits into two, two-thirds continue up and the other third bends to his left along a horizontal tunnel that then curves slowly round and down towards a small triangular facet in the Verona cliff. This is Kieran's entrance route to the hexagon world. He could not return this way. The jump up the column is too high to land in the tunnel and Kieran had not brought any climbing gear with him. Why he did not is a puzzle that must be left for later.

Kylone is trapped here too. He does not have the luxury of oxygen to return to Snowdrift Chasm, or of having a panic attack. His only hope is to find a way to reach that horizontal tunnel's entrance. He is running out of time and life, and therefore must do this logically and methodically

The first thing is to explore the bottom of that shaft from the hexagon that rises towards the tunnel. He notices the shaft's hexagon floor is unusually at an angle as if its front has been pushed down. That would explain the beam's change in direction. His eyes trace out a route from it down the hexagons he can climb in easy steps until it reaches the ice plain he stands on. After noting a couple of waypoints, he rushes towards the lowest hexagon and steps up along the zigzag route.

Three hexagons from the bottom of the shaft he feels a gentle pull towards it. He stops. Between him and it are normal scratches of meteoroid impacts, but only a single stone, no gravel or ice-balls. The vertical surfaces rising up the shaft are flat and glassy, in fact far too smooth. Something scarily weird is going on here. He picks up the stone and throws it up the shaft.

Its trajectory stays abnormally high and eventually hits the wall at what would be the back of the shaft. The stone sticks there, not bouncing off or sliding down. It slowly shrinks into the wall until it completely disappears and the wall is again smooth.

The strange attraction reminds him of the pull he experienced as he swam from Snowdrift Chasm towards the vent's entrance. This must be a feature of passing from one world to another.

If he touches that spot where the stone was absorbed, he will undergo the same fate. He has to pass through that shaft dead centre, like he accidentally did from chasm to vent. Kieran would have realised the danger and turned back, not knowing how to swim the snow-sand. Fear threatens. He cannot afford to let it trigger his rockborne vision too much and waste oxygen. He forces himself to be somewhat calmer, but with enough of his talent to see the lower part of the shaft.

He has only one data point for this attractor. He needs to understand how it varies throughout the shaft. He goes back down a few hexagons to pick up a couple of handfuls of gravel that accumulated in a niche, returns and throws up one handful. The gravel spreads out like a rising arch of a water fountain. The stones and dust do not follow the expected gravity-only trajectories, but are pulled towards and hit the walls. Their landing pattern forms a thick ring round the inside of the shaft, the distribution either side gradually thinning. He watches the dust and gravel converge and be absorbed into the ring until it is all gone.

Whatever force is in that ring it is powerful. His nerves flare. His rockborne talent ramps up, to extend the shaft and beyond. There is that opening high up of the tunnel that leads to the triangular face in Verona Rupes on Miranda.

He carefully steps onto the hexagon at the shaft's bottom, making sure he does not slip down its slope, and aims his other handful of gravel and dust at the tunnel's entrance. The heavier gravel falls back to the attractor ring in the hexagonal shaft. The dust, twinkling as it goes, rises until it forms a separate ring round the tunnel entrance.

"Nine hells of ice and dust," Kylone mutters as he closes his eyes. He has at least two such rings to pass through. There may be others. One is likely to be between the tunnel and the triangular face in the cliff of Verona Rupes.

An impossible task, yet he must go on, somehow. There still are too many unknowns. He has no time for more experiments. He has to get through that cliff face at the end of the tunnel, or he will die. One problem at a time. First he has to get through the attractor rings in the shaft and at tunnel entrance above him. He can see no way to climb up there. He is a dead man standing.

A strange calm descends on him. He has done all he can to return to Miranda and now there is nothing more he can do, just enjoy what he can of the time he has left.

Kieran must have felt similar in his last hours, which is why he left that message on the stylus that is in his pouch, along with the family heirloom. His own heirlooms are also packed in there, a few tools from his mining days that he thought might have come in useful as a dust and helium miner in orbit around Uranus. He pulls them out: his fine chisel for separating slivers off rock that he used to dig that Moebius gem carefully out; his distance measuring laser which he used for the first time to help Selma with estimating how deep a narrow niche went; and his laser knife for slicing through the ice that he had used to help cut his way out of the rubble of his accident. If only he could cut steps into that wall in time for him to climb up. This is impossible.

Panic hits again, and with it comes his rockborne vision. The walls are almost clear of the gravel and dust. He could jump up there, but would end up glued and sucked slowly into the shaft's wall. He frowns as he looks from the shaft's ghost gravel ring up to tunnel entrance and back again. The distance between the two also looks jumpable. He uses his laser distance measurer to find the heights of the two attractors: seventeen and twenty-nine metres respectively. A double jump is feasible if he can get a foothold at lower attractor and not get caught by it. An idea pops into his mind. It is a crazy one that will require precision timing and movements.

He scans the hexagons for one of the right size and with at least three edges free at its top; over there, down by the tip of a spur. He quickly steps down to it, cuts a half-hexagon slab off its top with his laser knife. He hefts it to get a sense of its weight and balance. The ice is uniform, no hidden changes in density and the cut is clean and even; just what is needed.

He has an hour of oxygen left. There is only one chance to execute his plan to stay alive. This is better than none.

He carries the slab back to a few steps short of the shaft and hefts it one last time to check its weight. He places his hands underneath it, takes a short run up the shaft's bottom and throws the slab up, aiming it at where the gravel ring had once been. At first, it rises normally under gravity and then is caught by the attractor. It hits the walls, briefly bounces out and returns to stay touching them while continuing to accelerate upwards.

Kylone returns to do a run up to the shaft. By the time he leaps up the half hexagon slab has locked into the ring and is slowly being absorbed by it. He grabs the slab's free edge to push upwards and as his legs pass it he bends them to jump off the shrinking surface to aim at the wall opposite the tunnel entrance. The shaft's walls now fully surround him. He has entered another world, but has only time to concentrate on getting his trajectory right.

His hands and a microsecond later his feet touch the wall. He twists as he pushes off and upward towards the tunnel. He takes a dive position and aims for the centre of its entrance. As soon as his hands are through he flips back his legs so they cannot touch the edges of the entrance. The ice switches from grey to blue-white.

He touches the tunnel roof well beyond the entrance to push himself down and ends up doing a forward roll to break his fall; thankful his spacesuit has individual pockets for the oxygen tablets instead of the rigid oxygen tablet stacks. He slides to a stop. His oxygen is very low. He gets up to half-run and half-skate down the tunnel round the bend.

The triangular face comes into view and he slows to a stop five metres short of it. He does not need to throw dust or gravel to know there is an attractor ring there, which will trap him if touched. The symmetric triangle is three metres tall and one and a half metres wide at its base. It is going to be a tight squeeze. He takes a few steps back. He runs up to the triangle, jumps up, aims his dive and twists sideways to fly through the narrow gap left side down.

He hits the dark ground but this time cannot roll to break his fall. He bumps and slides over the uneven surface to a stop. After a deep breath he looks up. Above him are the tall cliffs of Verona Rupes, the spur from which priests spray holy water and the dimly lit Aerial Gallery. He is back home on Miranda where he really belongs. Tears of joy well up in his eyes.

A red light blinks on his visor. His stacks have no more oxygen. He is living on the small amount left in his suit.

He gets up and skates as fast as he can across the chasm to the nearest airlock, regardless of the danger of the ice cracking beneath his feet. His air becomes stuffy. His face is warming from flushing due to carbon dioxide poisoning. He has to hurry. He sprints.

He gasps for air and is hot as he hits the open switch of the airlock. The outer door stays shut. It must be pumping out the air inside. He is woozy. His legs want to collapse. His chest is tight.

The door opens. He collapses onto the floor inside, just

managing to hit the button to close the outer door. He tries to open his helmet. It will not budge. His hand drops beside him. He blacks out.

He wakes gasping for breath. His helmet has automatically been opened for him. He lies there taking in deep breaths, letting the chest pain diminish, his face cool and the fuzziness in his mind disappear. One minute longer outside of the airlock and they would have found his corpse. He is thankful to be alive.

He carefully stands up and hits the inner door button. It opens onto a dimly lit corridor. Where now? The airlock will have automatically recorded his entrance, though it will not be flagged for security's attention because they will not be expecting him here. At least he assumes not. He had better get away from here quickly.

He is very tired, too tired to yawn. He needs somewhere to sleep. The nearest place he can hide in is the Maze. He takes sure steps there, through its door and on through the tunnelling into a far room with a bench made for two to sit on, one to lie on. He closes the room off from the rest of the Maze and collapses on the bench straight into a deep sleep.

Noises becoming recognisable as footsteps and people talking disturb him. Nobody enters his cubicle; must be congregants gathering for a Greening ceremony. He falls back into a dreamless sleep.

He wakes still tired but aware enough to think. While eating from emergency supplies from his backpack, he tries to work out where he can go. He glances at his wrist-pad. He has been asleep for over thirty-six hours. Everyone will know he has run out oxygen by now and think he must be lying dead at the bottom of Snowdrift Chasm. They will not be searching for him. This is one point in his favour.

The Priesthood will definitely not welcome him back. Dirk is too close to the Corp to be safe enough. He does not want to involve Alva as she has already been through too much. His mining friends have their own problems to deal with.

Only one person is sure to give him safe sanctuary; Meriel at Dunsinane. It is too dangerous for him to travel the mag-pods to get there and too risky to contact her, so it will be a long trek through the maintenance tunnels at night.

***

Five long arduous days of dodging people, sneaking into farms during dark hours to find something to eat, backtracking away from dead ends and endless walking leaves Kylone exhausted. He steps through the blue plasma door onto the walkway round the Rotunda. Made it at last. He no longer needs to keep his guard up. The people here are like him; society's rejects who will sympathise with his predicament. They will not betray his presence to Chynoweth or the Priesthood.

He is drawn to the window to look up and switches off his suit lights. Uranus is dark with only a thin navy halo round its edge. Stars twinkle and smudge as their light passes through the dome and air currents from the Rotunda's ventilation system. Although he has heard about it, he has never seen the like. It is beautifully strange. Silence and the smell of thyme mixed in with freshly mown grass and decaying compost penetrates his consciousness. The bees are not flying. A wisp of air accompanies a feathery touch on his cheek. His hand brushes the feeling away and ends flicking a soft lump into the plain.

"Always does that the first time," a man's voice says.

Kylone whirls round and switches on his spacesuit lights.

The old man he met the first time he came here stands at the next window along staring upwards. He turns to face Kylone with a smile. "Good to see you, Priest."

"I'm no longer a..." The face is familiar. Except for ageing, the ears would be the same, and the skull and jaw were definitely similar. The real giveaway is the bulbous nose. "Are you Lachlan McCloud by any chance?"

The old man straightens and looks him in the eye. “How did you know?”

“I have something that belongs to you.” He pulls out the wooden box and Kieran’s stylus from his pouch, and offers them to him.

Lachlan stares at the objects. “Never thought I’d see that again. Where did you find it?”

“I’m sorry to say I found it on your brother’s dead body. He left a message asking that this be delivered to you. You can see the message for yourself on his stylus.”

He tentatively takes the box and caresses it. “I’m not surprised. Where did you find him?”

Kylone does not know how to explain this.

“In his other world?” Lachlan asks.

“Is that what he called it?”

“He tried to explain it, but it never made sense to me. Sounded like a child’s fantasy. Guess it wasn’t.” He takes the stylus, moves his finger to the on switch and stops. “Might be better if I listened to this on my own.” He places both stylus and box in his pocket. “Now what about you, Priest?”

“I’m no longer a—”

“You’ll always be a priest to me. Having avoided death in Snowdrift, aye, I’ve heard all about that, you’re on the run, aren’t you? By the unkempt look of you, you are.”

The directness takes him by surprise. “I’ve nowhere else I can go. Meriel did say she’d help”

“Aye and she will. She’s on a scavie shift at the moment. Might be some while. Had that gleam in her eye if you know what I mean.”

Kylone did not know. “Where can I stay in the meantime?”

He chuckles. “She didn’t tell you? Well, her door is always open. Just push it and it will give. Her strays’ bunk room is the last door on the right down her corridor.”

“Should’ve guessed. Thank you.” He gives Lachlan the priestly blessing.

“You know your way there?”

“Yes. Aren’t you going to join me?”

"Nah. My job is to guard this place from unfriendlies. Or at least act as a warning system. Nobody thinks an old man loitering around is a threat."

"Oh." He is lost for words about how Lachlan takes everything in his calm stride, even his unsung bravery.

"Don't you worry about me. Get on with you. Mind you keep to the middle of the path."

"Thank you."

Lachlan draws back into the shadows.

Kylone makes his way to the strays' room. Nobody is in there. He is at his long journey's end and can relax. His tiredness is too much. He closes the door, rolls onto the bottom bunk and falls into the oblivion of long-needed sleep.

He opens his eyes fully alert and alive. Pains like a crick in his neck of having lain too long in his spacesuit encourage him to stand and push his helmet fully back to form a loose hood behind him. He listens carefully for noises; the usual whirr of fans and a faint whine of a drill followed by rhythmic thumping of metal on stone. He focuses on bringing up his rockborne vision enough to see beyond the door.

Meriel sits on the settee in the front room hammering a small chisel to work a groove into a slab of silicate lying on the table. Beside her are the makings of cubist mosaic picture in greens, browns and pale blues. The style is familiar: the necklace of Uranus she wore in the Transit Hall had a hint of it. He knows that style. Where from? That's it: pictures on the newscasts. His jaw drops. Meriel is Jacommo the anonymous artist whose sculptures sell for too much money to the off-moon super rich. He knows where all that profit has been spent, keeping Dunsinane Rotunda in a good condition. He grins as he approves of what she has secretly been doing. No wonder people are loyal to her.

He reverts to normal sight, very quietly opens the door, takes a few steps along the corridor, leans against the wall beside the kitchen away from the pushed-aside door of the chains, and folds his arms.

The chiselling of the groove to form a segmented spiral continues as he watches. On reaching the centre an awl is used to form an inverted tetrahedron shape. She puts her tool down, blows and wipes the dust off the slab, and sits back to eye her work. Her head slowly rises to meet Kylone's eyes.

"Hello, Meriel."

Her face pales as she sits and stares at him.

"Didn't Lachlan tell you I was here?"

She sits absolutely still.

He has to get some response out of her. "Seems I'm not the only one that has a secret, Jacommo."

Her mouth moves to form silent words and then a few croaks. "You bastard." Her voice strengthens. "How dare you let me and your friends think you're dead. Where in the nine hells of dust and ice have you been?" Her face is red with anger.

Shock at her reaction hits him. He had expected relieve and welcome, not this. He puts his hands up. "I was hiding from Chynoweth's guards who were out to murder me." This is only a small part of the truth, but the rest will take some careful telling to be believed.

"What?" she shouts as she stands. "Why the hell didn't you call me? Or someone? Even if it was just you shouting Dirk's name into the comms system. You know he keeps a tag on you. Still does."

"They were too close on my heels and I had to hide."

"All this time?"

Her face is less red than before, but the anger is still there under the surface ready to erupt. "It's not what you think."

"What am I supposed to think?"

"The guards had their own comms network, which they can link into the public network at will and very likely spy on people using it there. I'm pretty sure Dirk doesn't know about it. I'm not that tech-wise. But it's the only way I can think of that would explain how they could co-ordinate their attack. I had to be careful."

Her eyes dart around as if she is thinking in her world

until they again lock on his. "Then how the hell did you get out of Snowdrift Chasm? You couldn't do that without contacting someone."

"I walked, no kind of swam through the snow-sand like people swim through water to the other end of the chasm." He is reluctant to continue onto the part she will find incredible.

"And?"

"You're not going to believe this."

"You're already alive when you should be dead. So any story you come up with is going to sound impossible. Out with it. What happened next?"

"I found a small tunnel at the end of the chasm."

"There isn't any."

"That's why I need to talk to Dirk. How could the sensors have missed it? But I can't contact him direct as he works at Chynoweth HQ and his condo is too close to there for comfort."

"You won't get much out of him. He's been totally drunk these four days blaming himself for your death."

"Oh hell!" His hand rubs his forehead as he lets the latest shock news sink in. His friends have been wrecked by the grief of losing him. Meriel is venting her anger, Dirk is drowning his sorrows and starlight knows how Alva is reacting. He catches his breath. "Is Alva all right?"

"No. She's too busy covering for Dirk, though how much longer she can hold it together is another matter."

He is so alarmed his rockborne vision is back seeing shadows of valleys, cliffs and volcanoes behind Meriel. He snaps his eyes shuts and counts stones in a heap of gravel.

"I see you're beginning to realise the havoc you've caused," Meriel says.

He still counts stones.

"Kylone, are you well?"

He carefully opens his eyes a little bit. On seeing only Meriel in this front room, he fully opens them. "Sorry, Meriel. I know I've made a mess of things, but I really need to talk to Dirk, sober or drunk, without Chynoweth knowing."

"What for?"

"I know what's causing the extra mining accidents and he can help predict when and where the next ones are coming."

"Why in a zillion hells of ice didn't you say so in the first place?"

***

Kylone stands in the entrance to Meriel's condo and hears Dirk talking loudly long before Meriel and Vince finish dragging him by the shorter route from the Transit Hall across the plain.

"Whatz these bitz the air sl… slapz my face?" Dirk slurs.

Kylone cannot make out the words of Meriel's quiet reply above the buzz of insects.

"Beez? Sil… Silly… No flies in this gravity."

"They're genetically modified," Vince answers.

"Can't be."

"Come on, just through this archway and we'll be away from the insects," Meriel says.

"A mystery tour." Dirk hiccups.

Meriel with her shoulder under his arm pulls the drunk slowly into the walkway.

Dirk lolls his head as he blinks. His hair has loose strands pulled out from being tied back and there are blots of stains on his light grey silk. He stands still and moves his head forward with his bloodshot eyes looking directly at Kylone. "This is a good dream."

Meriel looks from Dirk along his line of sight to Kylone. "It's not a dream."

"Course it is. He's dead. Must have more of that wine." He turns back to the plain.

"This way, Chief Compineer." Vince steps into the walkway to turn Dirk back round.

"To dream, perchance to sleep."

Meriel and Vince nudge him forward.

The shock of how far Dirk has sunk finally wears off from Kylone. The only thing he can do is humour him. "I could give you one of my priestly lectures about misbehaving."

"Aw! Ol' timez. Your red fuzz doesn't suit you."

Kylone had decided not shave off his hair and beard after coming here; once it has grown more, it will disguise his appearance well enough for strangers not to recognise him as the supposedly dead ex-priest. He does not like this subterfuge, but it is the lesser of two evils. "I agree. But I don't want some people recognising me."

"I do."

"Why?"

"To be formal candi…date for Archdeacon. Stop you exile."

Dirk must have really lost it. "Nice try. Let me get you some of that wine you want."

"Rulez. You can never beat them."

He shakes his head and goes inside the front room to make some spice tea, while Meriel and Vince struggle getting Dirk inside and sitting on the settee. He places the steaming mug in front of Dirk. "Get that down you."

Dirk looks at the offering before slowly lowering his head to sniff it. He looks up at Kylone. "This not wine. What is it?"

"Ginger tea. Helps reduce the effects of the hangover you're about to have."

"Ew."

"I want to see you drink it all up. Consider it my revenge for making me drink all the camomile and lemon balm tea."

"Must I?"

"Yes."

Meriel holds up the mug. Dirk takes it and one sip later pulls such a scrunched up face that the lines make him look like a wizened old man. "Yuck."

"You need to drink it all," Meriel says.

"Nag."

"Every last drop."

Dirk looks at Meriel. "Only if I has a story. How," he waves the mug at Kylone, "he made it here from Snow… Drift Chasm. Let him tell it."

"You're not the only one that'd like to know."

"Can you cope without me?" Vince interrupts. "I'm due on shift."

"You get off and thanks," Meriel replies. She watches her son disappear out of the condo before turning back to the room.

"I'll tell you my story when you've sobered up a bit," Kylone says.

"Being drunk doez not stop my brain working. Damned thing never leaves me in peace."

"No."

"Yes. Or I walk." Dirk rises from the settee.

Meriel gently pushes him back down. "I need to know, even if it doesn't get through to him."

The tone of her voice is reminiscent of when she was a crew captain having to sort things out quickly. There is no stopping her from getting what she wants. Kylone knows Meriel will at best not believe him and at worst think him insane. Despite everything he has been through he still believes in the power of truth. He pours camomile tea for both himself and her, and sits beside Dirk and takes a sip while Meriel sits to hem Dirk into the settee.

"Where do I begin?" Kylone says. "I suppose that I had better start before Snowdrift Chasm, at the point my mag-pod's doors opened at Dunsinane Transit Hall and I saw you two with Alva waiting for me."

Meriel's eyes widen. "You were there?"

"Oh yes. The way you three looked so miserable, I realised I needed a few seconds to prepare myself. Things went wrong from the moment I decided I couldn't face you and ordered another mag-pod. So do me a favour, listen to what I have to say all the way through. You can ask questions afterwards. I'm sure there'll be plenty."

"You have my whole attention." Dirk takes another sip of ginger tea.

Kylone eventually gets to the point in his story where he rolls onto the bunk in Meriel's cabin. She has gone pale, and looks shocked and scared. Dirk looks bemused as if he is on a genteel cloud nine.

"That tunnel swim," Dirk breaks the silence. "Describe it again."

Of all the things Dirk wants to focus on, this makes the least sense to Kylone. Nevertheless he humours Dirk and retells his swim until he steps out of the snow-sand onto solid ice.

Dirk offers his empty mug to Meriel. "More ginger tea."

"I'm not—"

"Please."

Her jaw drops for a few seconds. "You seriously don't believe him?"

"Have to. It all makes… makes sense."

"Volcanoes? Here on this moon? Have you gone as mad as he has?"

"Yes. No. We see only part of true Miranda."

"What makes you think that?" Kylone interjects.

Dirk leans his head back against the top of the settee's back as if it is too heavy for him to hold up any longer. He slowly raises it and utters his words slowly. "Miranda is in four spatial dimensions. We exist in three. Kylone moved from one set of three to another through these rings."

Kylone is glad to see Dirk starting to have more lateral thinking even if it is nonsense. "Really?"

"No other explanation."

"Come on."

"Mean it. You had the extra pull from the ring where material from one three-dimensional world kind of mixed with material of another three-dimensional world. Fits in with the laws of physics."

"That's not any physics I know of."

"You were only taught what you needed to know to be able to change things to get the results you needed."

It takes a few seconds of probing that statement for

Kylone to accept Dirk is right. "You sure it's four-dimensional?"

"At the minimum. Absolutely."

"You two can't be serious?" Meriel croaks.

"I'm afraid he's right," Kylone says. "Rockborne are effectively starting to see through four dimensions."

"Come off it. That's just good extrapolation." She looks from one man to the other. "Isn't it?"

"Eyes," Dirk says.

"You what?"

"Eyes." Kylone points to his own. "Doc Acheson detected physical anomalies in mine and Alva's, and we're both strong rockborne. She hinted her instruments weren't good enough to detect similar anomalies in weaker ones, but she's working on trying to find a way to do so."

Meriel pales. "Seven hells of ice."

In the silence that follows, Kylone notices the bright Uranian light of when they had arrived has almost faded into night. He cannot believe it has been three hours and checks his wristpad. It has. On cue, the condo lights switch on. "We need to work out what to do next."

"Easy. Work out where rings are."

"How?" Meriel asks.

"Dig out dismissed analysez. Now have reason why centres of accident clusters exist."

Kylone catches on immediately. "You provide the where and I can physically check them out to see if we're getting volcanic ice flows through them, either way."

Dirk slowly shakes his head. "Not you. Other rockborne."

A smile creeps across Kylone's face. "Like it. Get Doc Acheson to verify who the truly strong ones are so we have a scientific basis for our assertions and I tell them the kinds of things to look for."

"That might work," Meriel agrees.

An angelic smile of satisfaction lights up Dirk's face.

CHAPTER 8

Vince's spacesuit makes Kylone sore in so many places that he feels raw and on fire. Its cooling mechanisms do little to help. With the visor darkened, he hopes he will not be recognised by any of Chynoweth's guards or security systems as he travels through the tunnels and in the mag-pods. He is on the final part of his journey to Doc Acheson's surgery. He walks as quickly as he can, but is hampered by having to drag a lurching and stumbling Dirk along under his shoulder. The Chief Compineer is acting drunk to give an excuse for his double appointment with the Doc.

Dirk swerves abruptly backwards.

Kylone curses in swearwords not used since his mining days, which die into silence on his locked-down visor. Nobody hears him. All his outgoing comms are switched off to avoid any comms system voice recognition apps homing in on his identity.

The pretend-drunk plunges towards the wall, slurring his words into nonsense burble.

He yanks the actor back sharply.

Dirk freezes with a look of pure astonishment on his face. A moment later he clutches his stomach as if he is starting to feel sick.

They resume their erratic walk, with less exaggerated movements from Dirk.

Kylone squeezes his burden into Doc Acheson's waiting alcove, plonks him down on a bench and registers Dirk's arrived for his double appointment. Dirk still holding his stomach sways back and forth while rhythmically mumbling the words of the old Queen classic *We Will Rock You*.

The door opens and a middle-aged woman leaves the surgery. One glance at Dirk makes her hasten without even noticing Kylone.

"Get your butt in here, Chief Compineer," Doc Acheson yells through the door.

"It is my love calling," Dirk slurs. He tries to stand and slumps back onto the bench.

Kylone's annoyance at such familiarity wants to escape into words, but he turns it into a silent stare through his darkened visor for a second longer than normal. He hauls Dirk up and drags him into the surgery without taking care whether he is knocked against walls or not and drops him onto the chair next to the Doc's desk.

"Ow!" Dirk's hand brushes over his wristpad ever so casually.

The surgery door closes.

"You can stop that playacting," Doc says to Dirk. She points a finger at Kylone and swings to point at the door. "You, out."

Dirk sits up straight and alert. "How did you know? And he stays and off your record."

"Your iris's reactions were normal. And he goes. Now!"

"Need a sobering up prescription," Dirk continues regardless. "To cover my tracks."

"No, no and no. Whatever game you're playing this time, I'm not giving you such a prescription for you to get drunk at leisure."

Dirk points at Kylone. "I don't want his would-be killers coming after me as well. So please, let's make it look good."

"Please?" She glances at Kylone. "Would-be killers? Don't be absurd. You're obviously here for a full psych-eval."

Kylone pushes his helmet back into a loose hood hanging behind him. "He's sane. It's the situation I'm in that isn't."

Acheson's eyes widen slightly.

"Don't worry," Dirk says. "I'm not used to people coming back from the dead either."

"You know if they find you in hiding like this, they're likely to execute you for not accepting your exile." Acheson turns to type into her console.

"I'm aware. My execution would make my whole life easier, believe me," Kylone says.

"Told you the answer. Get nominated for Archdeacon. Then you'd be too much in the public eye," Dirk says.

Kylone glares at him for his ridiculous suggestion.

"I'm serious," Dirk continues. "A bye-law suspends such things during the election and while you're Archdeacon. It gives you a chance to get off-moon. But your almighty stubbornness won't listen to me."

Acheson glances from one man to the other until she ends up staring at Dirk. "This is the first time I've ever seen you be really sincere. I never thought you had it in you."

"Playing the obnoxious fool keeps me from losing my temper with idiots. Of course you're one of the few exceptions around here."

"But I still don't meet your standards for you to be truly civil to me?"

A flash of pain crosses Dirk's face. "Oh hell." He puts his head in his hands for a few seconds before lifting it again. "You actually do. I just couldn't have you treating me with respect. Others might have got suspicious and wondered what was going on between us, and come to the wrong conclusions."

"That's no excuse."

"You're right. It isn't. I'm sorry. I really am, but I have no choice."

Acheson's jaw drops a little and her eyes widen.

"Can we discuss this during another appointment?" Dirk nods to Kylone. "Without him around."

"Might be wise," Kylone says sensing there is more to their relationship than he is witnessing here. His presence would only inhibit what they have to say to each other.

"Book an appointment at your convenience," Dirk adds. "I'll be here. Right now, his needs are urgent. We're not sure who's actually behind his would-be killers, but I'm monitoring their official comms in the hope they'll slip up. All I've got so far from that is they were worried about Kylone cutting off their flow of money. The only thing he's been involved in that could affect those kind of cash amounts is his analysis of the mine accidents, but that annoyed the Guardians of History. As yet I haven't even got a hint of how they tie in to his would-be killers."

"What do you mean you haven't found out who ordered my assassination?" Kylone asks.

"They're talking among themselves. No public or system access, but it won't be all that long before I work out what their internal comms system is."

"Tell me another fairy-tale." Acheson steps over to the dispenser to pick up a phial that has just dropped to the bottom of a shoot. She holds it aloft in Dirk's direction. "This is your medicine for getting sober. I've given it a bitter taste so you won't want to take it unless you really must."

"Oh give me a break. I'm going to have to stay sober for a very long time thanks to him." He jerks his thumb in Kylone's direction.

She hands over the phial, which Dirk pockets in his pouch. "That's the first sensible thing you've said in years." She turns to Kylone while sitting back down. "While you're here, I've got some more tests I want to do on you."

The matter-of-fact manner catches Kylone by surprise. "Haven't you got loads of questions?"

"Yes, of the medical kind and I'd rather do those tests before you get murdered."

Dirk sniggers.

She snaps her head round so fast that her red hair in its hair net flies almost horizontally. "When I've finished with Kylone here, I want answers from you about why my appointment slots have mysteriously filled with people who're not on my patient list. You've got ten minutes to think up some crazy excuses."

"That's my fault," Kylone interjects.

She turns back to him. "Explain."

"We need your help to identify reliable strong rockborne. They'll be crucial in finding out what's causing so many mining accidents."

"Surely they've tried that before?"

"Not in the way we will. I'd do it myself if I weren't public dead enemy number one."

"That still doesn't—"

"Doc," Dirk interposes. "It took him three hours to explain it to me and that was the short version. Do you have the time to spare?"

Acheson narrows her green eyes on him so they shine like miniature versions of the Pasture Star. "You only call me Doc when you have a real problem. Spill it."

Dirk scrunches up his face. "We need the rockborne to produce the necessary proof first. Only then would you think I've not gone insane."

"He's right," Kylone confirms. "I can help focus their talent. I've learnt to control the strength of mine. They might be able to do so as well, but they need to have that extra layer at the back of their eyes you discovered in mine and Alva's."

"You've just upped your tests to three hours minimum," Acheson says. "More like a whole day. We're talking full head to toe scans to search for any other anomalies and a psyche eval."

"I'd be happy to help out under less awkward circumstances."

"I need time to prep some of the tests anyway. For now, I'll stick to my original set. Swap places with the Chief Compineer. Want to check if there have been any changes in your eyes since your last scan."

Dirk gives her a sad scowl. Kylone wonders why, but this is not a time to ask. They do as they are told.

She controls the retinal scan instrument over Kylone's left eye, does some scans and reaction tests and then pulls the instrument away ready to move over his right eye. A light flashes on her console. "Do you want Assistant Alva Larsson to join us?"

Kylone eyes the closed door. "Alva. Is she outside?" He turns to Dirk. "You timed this deliberately didn't you?"

"Yes, we need her as part of the testing programme to

compare the results against," Dirk says. His face clouds with anger. "What gets me is your current reluctance to let others help you. I'm damned sure Alva would if asked."

"I don't want her, or others, involved in my mess if I can help it. It'll keep them away from becoming targets for my would-be killers. I'm risking enough people as it is."

"The Chief Compineer is right," Acheson intervenes. "I need Alva's results so I can compare the others against hers, and yours. It'll give a more accurate assessment."

"Thank you," Dirk says.

The two of them are against him on this, a unified team that is extremely unusual for Dirk. What is going on between them? Whatever it is, he does not like it. But this is not his most important worry at the moment. A few seconds more thought and he realises they are right about Alva. "Let me put my helmet on first."

"She can wait until I've tested your right eye."

He is annoyed at the Doc at leaving her waiting outside, even if she is being practical. His heart rate speeds up a little and his skin warms a little.

"Only a couple more minutes," Acheson says. "There is something specific I want to check."

He turns to let Acheson to put the scanner in place. His free eye focuses on her face; she has a kindly smile. Her reaction puzzles him until he checks her console. His vital statistics are on display. His heart rate and a couple of his sweat indicators have recently increased. Whoever invented remote medical sensors using sound and smells produced a blessing, but demanded a price; the doctors could work out some emotional reactions. He had just let the Doc know he actually liked Alva a lot.

Maybe more than liked, but this is all he can admit to in his current circumstances. "Just like being polite. That's all."

Dirk bursts out laughing and cannot stop for quite a while. "That's priceless. Absolutely priceless." He wipes away a couple of escaping tears from the corners of his eyes.

Kylone grits his teeth against his anger getting the better of him. This is a time to get things done, not to talk, argue or speculate about them. He becomes irritated by his own foolishness. As soon as the instrument pulls away he is out of the chair and yanking his helmet over his head.

"As I thought," Acheson says.

"What?" Dirk and Kylone say in unison.

She looks at Kylone. "The best I can explain it as in simple terms—"

"I know my biology well enough. Explain away."

"I will, at our appointment. Make it double appointment, it would take too long. For now, let's just say your extra thickness allows you to resolve distance within the retina. This comes on top of the normal 3-D distance resolution that comes from comparing images between both eyes. Basically you're resolving distance twice over by different mechanisms, which allows you to compare different distances yet again. It's a pseudo-seeing in four dimensions, if you would like to call it that."

"What?" Dirk says.

Kylone is puzzled by the man's surprise. He understands the geometry behind the explanation well enough.

"You need to add in superposition considerations as well."

"That's really interesting." Dirk rubs his hands together. "Damned interesting. For now, we need Alva in here." He slumps into his playacting drunk stance and rolls his eyes upwards in zombie mode.

Acheson opens the door. "Come and join us, Assistant Larsson."

She steps on the door's threshold and her eyes immediately land on Dirk. "Chief Compineer, are you all right? Do you need help returning to your condo?"

"No. Half left."

"Oh dear. How long before he sobers up, doctor?"

"With what he's drunk, I can't be sure," Acheson lies.

"That much?" Alva says. "Dirk, how many times have I told you to leave off the whisky? Where have you been hiding the bottles this time?"

Dirk rolls his head round and half-heartedly waves his hand to beckon her inside. "Come in and I'll tell yer."

"Oh really." She steps inside to let the door close behind her. "I'm awfully sorry about the Chief Compineer, doctor." She notices Kylone in his suit. "And whoever you are."

Dirk sits up straight and rubs the back of his neck. "Seven hells of ice that my neck muscles ache like hell. How do drunks do it?"

Alva stares at him, her mouth open.

Kylone drops his helmet to his back. "I apologise for this, but if I'm caught…."

Alva whirls round and throws her arms round his neck and gives him a tight hug.

Surprised, he has his arms round her in a gentle embrace before he knows it. He cannot feel the familiar warmth of a body this close through the spacesuit, but her scent of rosemary and lavender is welcoming and he relaxes into her. This feels so right.

Time is against him and the pull of urgency to stop more accidents brings him back to why he is here. He gently pushes Alva away. A hint of a smile on her face makes him feel warmer. Dirk's calculating stare turns him cold again. "It's good to have such a welcome."

"Is that how you do it?" Dirk asks.

"Do what?" Alva turns to him.

"The welcome bit."

"How would you do it?"

"He thought I was a dream, but to be fair to him, he'd had way too much to drink," Kylone says.

"Going to hold that against me? All of you?" Dirk looks at each one in the room in turn.

Acheson shakes her head while disappointment spreads across Alva's face.

"Of course not," Kylone says, "unless you become drunk again."

"Damn it, it was the only way to escape from the facts of life."

"Is it that bad?"

"I live by facts," Dirk snarls. "They are hard and cold. You can't change them. They are my prison and I've learnt to live as comfortably as I can within it. It's why I'm good at what I do."

"So you become drunk to live your dreams?"

"How…" Dirk frowns, his eyes taking on distant look. "I did until you came along and started teaching me how to turn fantasy into reality."

Kylone opens his mouth to discourage him from becoming addicted to escapism, and stops short. He had wanted to hide from reality after his own accident, and to a certain extent had done so by joining the Priesthood. Though he cannot pinpoint why, he is sure Dirk is trying to escape from something other than his prison of facts. This is a front to stop people from delving deeper. This issue can wait for a calmer time.

There are more urgent problems.

"I'm sorry I've had to reveal I'm alive like this, but I really do need your help to finish finding the cause of the extra mining accidents. If even a hint of me having escaped Snowdrift Chasm gets out, the Priesthood and Chynoweth security will be after you as well as me."

"Don't worry about me, I'm bound by doctor-patient confidentiality."

"I like having an excuse to be totally outrageous," Dirk says.

"And you, Alva?"

"I'll keep a low profile. I'm used to doing that, remember?"

This tears at Kylone wanting to protect her from harm. She stands as tall as her petite figure allows, daring anyone to defy her. It reinforces his belief that she gives as good as she gets. And yet, she may end up in the front line, the first to have awkward questions asked of her or worse. He has to allow her the freedom to choose her way. "I do. You'll be the most exposed of all of us if we follow the plan Dirk and I have come up with. If you want out at any time, say so. That goes for any of you. Is that understood?"

"You make it sound dangerous," Alva says.

"It is. Some of Chynoweth's guards already tried to kill me."

Alva and Acheson both gasp. Dirk turns on one of his rare looks of seriousness.

"You really meant what you said earlier," Acheson mumbles.

"What do you need?" Alva asks.

"Could you help train three others to improve their beyond sight? Even if it's just explaining to them what they should be seeing? Dirk and the Doc here will identify them and send them to you. I've learnt to control mine by varying the amount of tension I'm under. It's difficult, but I can do it. You may find these people have other factors that drive their ability. Do you think you can do that?"

"Is that all?"

"No," Dirk interrupts. "We need you to help them identify what they are seeing correctly because we'll be searching for cold lava and water-slush flows that will cause future mining accidents. That'll put us up against the Guardians of History as well as parts of Chynoweth."

Kylone could have punched him for being so blunt. He breathes deeply to calm down and realises Dirk is right. The prison of facts is best dealt with when all the relevant facts are known. Alva needs to be aware what she could be up against; it will make her safer.

She bites her lips in a long silence. "I may not have loved Raoul as much as he did me, but he accepted me as I was, took me in and protected me from those who… let's say, took a dislike to me. I owe it to him to find the truth of why he died. Count me in."

***

Kylone deliberately arrives late for the Greening so he

can join the tag end of congregants entering the airlock. As hoped for, nobody questions him about having his helmet up and his face hidden under a darkened visor. They are too eager to get out into the Verona Rupes and mingle with those already out there. He stays at the back of the crowd.

As the outer airlock door opens, they rush out and turn right. He lingers a little longer before stepping onto the ice and switching his spacesuit lights to power conservation mode. This will give just enough light to safely walk. The extra padding and plasters in the right places makes his walk in Vince's spacesuit less sore than his previous experience, for which he is thankful. There is still some discomfort, but he can cope with it. He turns left and hugs the cliff as close as he dares to avoid any fissures and piles of fallen ice chunks.

After about two hundred metres he glances back. Nobody is in sight. He can relax a little and takes the easier to follow path a little way out from the cliffs towards the tip of the Inverness Coronae. He would not be out here if he had any choice; this is the only way he can map the entrances to the volcano world without attracting attention.

At the tip he turns right to follow the low path in the long base sulcus at the bottom of the coronae. The light is dimmer in the little long valley and his suit lights automatically brighten to compensate, a price he is happy to pay to not be visible from the open plains of Dunsinane and Silicia. The only activity he notices is the navigation lights and faint green plasma plume of a rare spaceship arcing its way off-moon from the port next to the Rotunda.

He finally reaches the head of the Argier Rupes.

His leg muscles ache and a break from all the walking will be welcome. He finds a small outcrop and sits down to study the view. Unlike Verona Rupes, Argier is a deep valley of sloping sides, gentle hills and hummocks. This is a place of curves and ripples that contrast with the straight lines and plane surfaces of the coronae above him. He is puzzled by its uniqueness on Miranda. A chill runs through him. Is the ice here from the volcano world? Was the vent he walked out of a source of this ice?

Even with his extensive understanding of Mirandan rock and ice structures, he does not know where to start answering these questions. He goes over the various ideas, anything from Argier being the result of melting after a large asteroid strike to a heat ray cutting across this part of Miranda. He dismisses every single one for good reasons. There must be an explanation, something unique to Miranda's low gravity or materials. It would not be the first time. Chynoweth's early miners who became settlers had missed the full implications of the Mirandan temperature: trapped silane gas when mixed with evaporating liquid oxygen can spontaneously combust. It took two fires and five miners' deaths before Mirandans pinpointed the cause.

A memory of Patricianna floats into his mind, one that has stuck with him these past nine years.

"I'm going to be factual with you as this seems the only way to get through to you at the moment," she said. "You're grieving and depressed, as is to be expected. But you've got to understand that in your present state of mind, your view is blinkered, narrowed, focussed on the immediate future. You don't have the capacity to think broad picture, long term or away from the accepted norm. Your instinct is to follow the main herd. It's best you accept that for now, while we work on loosening your mind little by little back to what it was."

"I'll never be what I was," he had replied.

"I agree. By the time I'm finished with you, you'll be much better."

He had almost laughed at her ridiculous comment, but not now it has turned out to be true.

How can he broaden his perspective of Miranda to find out the causes behind Argier Rupes? Pray? No, this will not work here, certainly not in time.

There is a way, one that Patricianna taught him during his grief counselling. The first step is to gently push into the unknown, and the next to snatch at the confidence to believe what he is thinking is the right way forward, no matter what. Then it was climbing out of his emotional mess; now it will be to expand into the strangeness of the real universe and let go of what he had learnt as unchangeable as granite.

His mind accepts he must observe without the hindrance of assumptions. Next he has to see via his rockborne talent. He recalls the list of memories of his journey through the volcano world, put in the order of rising tension. He goes through them one by one to slowly increase his tension, bringing the volcano world into sight.

He looks over to where he expects the vent to Snowdrift Chasm will appear and is drawn instead deep under Miranda's surface. There are lit spaces for rooms from small cabins to large farm chambers, line segments of tunnels and shafts and layers of ice where light can penetrate from Uranus and the Sun. Occasionally some of the manmade features drop into darkness and others are suddenly lit, as if lights there were being switched on or off. The whole scene would look like an unreal abstract form of art if he could not label what the lit places were. Over there are the farm rooms and hangars of Argier; here is a mag-pod moving down a shaft; there the Snowdrift Chasm lit because someone must be in there, though they are too small to make out.

He recalls the time he needed to find a way to Verona Rupes through the volcano world. His nervousness rises, and along with it his rockborne talent intensifies to extend his view. Very dark rooms adjoin lit spaces, and darker lines and tubes link up between the lit tubes to build into one complex three-dimensional system of walkable tunnels, wiring conduits, water supply systems and waste piping. It sprawls out into a mess of clusters of entangled lines and lumps, too much for him to work out which is what. His focus naturally diverts to clearer areas. It falls on a set of almost black lines that form a ragged almost horizontal tassel deep into a layer of rock that is broken by an upward intrusion of ice. It is the kind of 3-D map that he has seen on holographs of mine plans where there is a lot of exploratory tunnels close together. Their shape is familiar and recently seen. He pauses in the hope of identifying where. Nothing comes to mind.

He goes over events ever since Alva first came to see him. There, that is it, the holograph of blue pipework with green nodules of Carbo mine, but seen from a different angle. What he is seeing under the ice is the real mine in darkness as nobody is working there. He shudders at the whole memory of the rescue and his nervousness worsens. His rockborne talent strengthens even more.

The volcanoes' world overlays his view of Miranda. Emptied flow tubes rise from the tops of frosted ice plugs sitting at the depths and branch out to vents towards the volcanoes' sides, through the layers of ice interlayered with sheets of accumulated space dust. The thing that strikes him the most about the surface is its clean smoothness, very few craters, no sharp edges, and the paleness. This volcano moon constantly reinvents itself; a live one as opposed to the near dead one he has been brought up on, his own Miranda.

He directs his gaze to Snowdrift Chasm and the tunnel turned vent he escaped through.

The volcano stands out from the others by its beige colouring of rock. His guess of long ago had been right. That one had arrived onto the other world from somewhere else. Somewhere in that universe is a broken-up planet that had once been warm. Life could have existed there, and may still exist. But the ice world he walked through shows all the signs of total barrenness.

He can do the speculation about this later. He came here for a different purpose.

There, underneath the snow-sand emitting its own light is a perfect circle at the place the tunnel becomes the vent. This circle must act as a transit mechanism from one world to the other. A circle he had not realised was there when he swam through it, a thing of nature in its raw powerful elegance. He feels privileged and humbled to be one of the first, if not the first to perceive this phenomenon, and takes a moment to savour its supreme beauty.

Much as he would love to stay in this moment of communion with the two worlds, he has a limited time if he is to keep his identity secret and must make the most of this discovery while he can.

He scans both worlds for similar loops. There is one, another circle, in another vent of the same volcano, but deeper into the darkened ice blocks of Inverness Coronae. A third exists close to it embedded within one of the volcano's dimly lit ice layers and inside the ice a few metres in from a cliff of the same coronae. Now he knows what to look for, he recognises a whole scattering of circular transit points. By the inclination and positioning of them, they exist on an invisible gently curving sheet that cuts through both worlds. His best guess as to why they have formed in the places is that is where the sheet allows flat circles to exist, an idea best discussed with Dirk when they get a chance.

His sight returns to the Carbo mine to find its nearest transit circle. There are two. One is beneath the Level 5 next to the intrusion on one side and a blocked off vent in the ice. This could explain the cause of that mining accident. The second is a short distance from the farthest out mine face of Level 7 and intersects with an oozing cold lava reservoir beneath the same volcano. It is too close for comfort.

He runs his forefinger along a black seam on the spacesuit's left sleeve. A blank holograph rises half a metre in front of him. He pulls out a stylus from his pouch and proceeds to draw an outline of the superimposed world and the portals onto the holograph. It is not the most accurate of drawings, but he hopes it will be good enough for analysis purposes.

The sketch is almost finished when a red square in the top right corner of his visor blinks a warning. It is time to head back to Verona Rupes if he is to sneak back into tunnels with the congregants who will attend the next Greening ceremony.

He will have to leave the sketch unfinished and hits a tab on a line of controls at the bottom of the holograph to take a photo of Argier Rupes to superimpose on his drawing and pulls the holograph down into the seam. He breathes out and tries to relax as quickly as possible. The volcanoes fade and he once again senses only his native Miranda.

He smiles. That picture is bound to keep Dirk out of mischief for quite a while. He starts the long walk back to Verona.

***

Kylone runs his finger over the surfaces of the centimetre cube green crystal he has been polishing for the last fifteen minutes. They are smoother than the finest silk and its corners pinprick sharp. Meriel will appreciate it and probably use it in one of her sculptures. He wishes he could do more for her after all her unstinting help. He places the cube on a tray lined with a silk rag and searches for another stone among the selection on the table that might polish up into something interesting.

The room lightens up with the front door opening.

Kylone freezes into position, hoping it is someone who already knows he is alive – or if not, his all too short hair and beard might prevent him from being recognised.

"Meriel, you here?" a man's voice asks. It is vaguely familiar.

A man in a miner's brown silk walks into the hallway to peer through the door of chains down the hallway. "Meriel, we need to talk."

Kylone finally places him, Miner Torvald who gave such an athletic display at the Kober Balyow.

Torvald turns to look at him. "Any idea where she is?"

Kylone silently points to the chains through which she emerges in a dressing gown, her head glistening with dampness having just come out of a spray-shower cubicle. He picks a deep blue scratched stone with a cream S-curve running through one face. In the right place it could enhance a mosaic.

Torvald turns. "Ah, good I've caught you. I'm looking for a scavie to join my new crew. It's only piecework, but it's better than sitting round doing nothing. Want to join us?"

"Possibly. I must admit I'm running low on stones for my jewellery," Meriel replies. "Got a rockborne or iceborne yet?"

"Rockborne yes, Charlie Summers. Iceborne, not yet."

Kylone knows Charlie to be a weak rockborne, but he gets on well with people. He starts polishing the least damaged part of his stone.

"Have you tried Oona McDonald?" Meriel asks.

"I'm working on her."

"That's unusual."

Torvald chuckles. "She feels she is off her ice-song. I think it's more to do with her self-confidence. I'll get her, don't you worry. You in or not?"

"Where?"

"Carbo Level 7, extending that exploratory mine face they abandoned a couple years back."

Kylone drops his stone, which lands with one soft click. This is exactly where the volcano's cold lava is too close to Carbo mine. If the mining goes ahead, there will be another accident, no ifs or buts.

Meriel stares at him.

Kylone shakes his head slightly

Torvald twists his head to follow her line of sight. "What do you know about it?"

"Don't accept the work, Torvald," Meriel says. "There'll be an accident."

"The Guardians of History and Chynoweth have assured us not."

Meriel's face turns stern. "They have their own agenda."

"Of course they do, but we need to open up new mines or we'll starve."

"Don't go there," Kylone says quietly.

"What do you know about it? You're not a miner."

Kylone is about to say he was, when he should be saying *is*. If it were not for growing his hair and beard he would look like one. He tries to work out a way of convincing Torvald not to mine there while staying anonymous.

"He's rockborne," Meriel snaps, looking angry.

Torvald studies him. "I know every rockborne on Miranda, but I don't recognise him. And anyway, what has that got to do with saying that Carbo 7 is too dangerous to mine. He's not been down there."

Kylone hears the dismissal in his voice, but cannot let him go ahead with the mining. "I am indeed rockborne. Let's just say I have sensed enough of what is down there to know it's far too risky."

Torvald's face turns from anger and irritation via a blank stun to bewilderment. "It can't be." He rubs his eyes. "Without the hair and beard… Priest Kylone?"

"I'm no longer a priest. Plain Kylone will do. I wouldn't be giving this advice unless I was certain of the consequences."

Torvald nods understanding. "But the Guardians of History and Chynoweth…"

"Are desperately wrong. I tried to tell them and look where it got me." Kylone does not add any of the detail about the volcano world. It would overload his credulity.

Silence.

Meriel after a few seconds makes them all camomile tea. Kylone is fed up after having so much of it and leaves his on the table to get cold. He gives Torvald time to absorb and accept the information, and let his pale face gather a little colour.

"I've a lot of questions," Torvald finally says. "My immediate concern is how to stop them mining there. Even if I got word out through my network of contacts to not take the work, others will come forward, like those desperately needing the money to feed their families."

"Have to agree with that," Meriel says.

Worry lines deepen on Torvald's face. "Only Chynoweth or a declaration from the Guardians of History will stop them. If what you say is true, that won't happen."

More silence.

"Seven hells of ice," Torvald says. "Can you not show another rockborne what you saw, so they can give the warning? I know it would mean you breaking cover with another person, but it would save lives."

Kylone strokes his stubbly beard. It is sensible plan from Torvald's point of view. "If only it were that simple. My rockborne talent has developed well beyond my previous capability, in fact beyond what anybody will be able to believe."

"That's impossible. Nobody's ever developed after they're twenty-five."

"I would've once agreed with you, but it doesn't turn out to be that simple."

"Then explain it to me."

"You wouldn't believe me if I told you the truth."

"His talent is as good as Kieran MaCleod's was," Meriel intervenes. "Nobody alive today has that kind of talented experience. How can he explain to others who are blind to what he senses?"

Kylone realises Meriel is being circumspect with the truth to protect Alva who can do much better than he can. Like him, she will not be listened to. There is no point in mentioning her.

Torvald shakes his head and slouches over the table looking glum. Meriel standing beside the kitchen bench with her arms folded reflects his misery.

Meriel straightens up. "I have an idea, but it's risky," She looks every bit the mining crew captain he used to know.

"Let's hear it," Torvald says.

"Kylone, can you identify a marker up to which it is safe to mine along Carbo 7?"

He visualises the picture he drew for Dirk. Nothing is obvious. There is one thing he can do, assess the safe mineable ratio of the distance between the mine face and the lava flow in the volcano world. Dirk can change that ratio into measurable numbers. "I can with someone else's help give you safe distance to mine up to."

"So we can mine up to that point without hindrance?"

"Yes, but it's not that far."

"When we reach that point, a few of us make a small accident happen without loss of life to act as a warning to stop mining. Can it be done?" Meriel looks to Kylone for an answer.

Kylone frowns while he works through what is feasible. "The pressure would be too high. Maybe a good iceborne can give a warning instead?"

"An iceborne?" Torvald's voice ups an octave. "What in the devil's heat are we dealing with here?"

"Water slush or the colder cryo-lava made from other substances." Meriel whispers with a look of terror on her face.

"No way. There's none around there… You're serious, aren't you? … How can a rockborne differentiate between rock and liquid?"

Kylone feels trapped. "I told you, you wouldn't believe me. It came with the increase in rockborne ability."

"Seven hells of dust, we need you down the… you can't go down the mines. How could you know about the stuff?"

At last, a question he can easily answer. "From wandering round on the surface and looking down."

Torvald gawps. "That strong." He turns to Meriel. "Do you believe him?"

Kylone feels hurt, but can understand his incredulity. Hell, he would not accept himself if he had not lived through it all.

"One, he's alive when he shouldn't be." She raises her fingers to count. "Two, all the scenery he has described to me matches up with known facts. Three, let's just say be brought back evidence of where he had been with him."

Kylone is thankful she is not heaping another hard-to-believe fact of Kieran's keepsakes on all the others

Torvald is coping with. The man is clearly under a lot of strain.

"Still, where is that cryo-lava or water-slush coming from?"

"It only takes one vent to travel the distance…" Kylone lets him come to his own conclusions about the rest.

Torvald wipes the developing sheen from his baldhead. "Let me get this straight. We're going to work up to safe point and then get an iceborne to look where Kylone directs them, so they can give the warning to get everyone out. And then let this cryo-lava or water-slush in to stop any more mining."

"Yes, but we need to make sure he," she nods in Kylone's direction, "is not arrested, and that may take some doing."

***

Despite the padding in Vince's mining spacesuit, Kylone is as uncomfortable as ever. He walks behind Meriel down the Carbo 7 to the debris-dumping cavity a hundred metres short of the mine-face, officially to help her sort out and pick up some debris for her jewellery work. He hopes the cavity will be close enough to identify when and where on the face the pressurised water-slush or cryo-lava will break through. If not, it can be sorted out. Other potential problems are more difficult to deal with.

He has no idea how to translate what he will see to how the iceborne, Oona, would feel for the reverberations of the ice movement and collapse. Suggesting the direction or area to concentrate on would be a start. What they recognise by touch has been learnt through experience and known rhythm patterns of the vibrations, and does not easily correlate to the equivalent visualisation. Better people than him have tried, and failed. Understanding how her talent works is an unknown he will have to work around.

That is bad enough. He is betting the water-slush, for that is the most likely, will transfer vibrations via its surrounding ice to the rock-face. How mangled they become in that handover is an all too real unknown.

The closer he gets to the debris cavity, the more his tension increases and the farther into the distance his three-dimensional rockborne vision through the rock and ice extends.

By the time he reaches it he has a clear view all the way down to the mine face and studies what is going on. There is the full complement of ten miners. He recognises one, Alva. What is she doing here? She helps to move the carts together to form a train, a job normally given to apprentice miners. His anger and fear for her safety explodes. The volcano world becomes visible. The treacly liquid eight metres behind the face has the crinkliness of water-slush. That is better than dealing with the colder cryo-lava.

It is far too close for comfort. How dare they put her in danger!

His visor shows a tag to indicate Meriel has opened a comms link to all the mining crew. He checks his own transmission is still on mute via his wristpad. It is.

"Hi all. I just need to show my sidekick what to do here in the debris cavity and then I'll join you. Be a few minutes."

"Sidekick?" Alva asks.

"Vince. He'll be scavenging stones for my jewellery."

"We could do with a clean-up here, so let's call it a shift," Torvald says. "Might as well let the rockborne and iceborne do their assessments and start afresh tomorrow."

Kylone is thankful subsurface mining on Miranda has been restricted for centuries to mechanical drilling with only very limited use of laser torches and explosives. The use of plasma ice-melters would have ruined some of the precious crystals and were more likely to cause mine-face collapses. The use of distantly controlled drones was found to be impracticable for several reasons: the controllers were so busy concentrating on where the drone was heading they regularly forgot the engine plumes could eat into the ice behind them; the command loop time-lapse because of normal comms delays was enough to slow down the mining of delicate ores and crystals to an unacceptable level; and most importantly, the rockborne and iceborne had to be at mine face to sense what the ices were doing and what lay behind the rock, capabilities that even the best neural and quantum computers could not emulate accurately enough.

All this slowness means he can react in sufficient time.

He sees the drill-head slow to a stop and the man on the driver's platform at the drill's controls look round. Everyone else stands beside the walls, waiting and looking at the drill. The driver fingers the steering holograph that rises out of the plate to move the drill back by three metres, shuts the drill off except for the holograph and steps down. A man and a woman rush over to the mine face while the others move carts around, check the drill and safety equipment, clean and tidy hand-tools away into storage units. This normal activity for a shift's end thankfully means there are no extra problems to sort out. This good news calms him enough to let his rockborne vision drop out of the volcano world.

He turns his attention to the mine face. Detail cannot be made out at this distance, but the spiral drill marks on the brown rock look far too normal. Complacency is a danger every miner is repeatedly warned about. They will be on their guard for the unexpected.

It is years since he looked round a mine with its equipment in place. He has learnt to cope with images, been in tunnels that were built as passages from one place to another, but not until now has he actually faced the real thing. Is he treating this view as an image, which stops him from feeling the fear and claustrophobia he had expected?

It takes a few more seconds to sink in he is back in a mine. The debris pile, a miner and the cavity walls are all familiar sights he thought he would never see again. Now he is here it is as if he has never been away. He is back home, his true one.

"I had forgotten what these places really feel like," Kylone says on a private link to Meriel.

"That's a good sign."

"So you brought Alva here as a backup to me."

"We really didn't have any choice. If you couldn't cope with coming into this mine, who else could we get to warn us when the cryo-lava or water-slush would break through?"

He takes a few seconds to consider her words. "It's water-slush. Next time, let me know so her presence doesn't come as a shock."

"A shock? You 'saw' her with your rockborne talent?" Meriel slowly shakes her head. "Nine hells of ice, your power has really grown."

Of course, this is the first time she has caught his empowered talent in action.

"Grown yes," he says, "but not by as much as you think. It's my newfound ability to control it that makes the vast difference. But, as Alva has learnt, it is best not talked about unless it acts to help someone else, and even then it is better to minimise the capability."

"I get the implied message. You want me to keep quiet about just how really good you are."

Kylone smiles. "Not much ever got past you."

He turns his rockborne vision back to the mine face. Two miners stand idly, looking round, probably wanting to find jobs to do. Charlie runs his fingers across a spiral drill mark, a typical guiding technique for a rockborne searching for clues. Alva comes to stand beside him, and glances and nods in Kylone's direction.

He returns the nod to indicate he can see her as well.

"Looks like Charlie and Oona are going to be some while," Torvald announces over the comms. "Those of you with nothing left to do might as well head back up."

"Thanks, boss," a woman says.

"I'll save you a beer at the Kober," one man says.

The two idlers are already making their way back. He quickly turns to do a fingertip search through the debris to keep up his cover.

"That goes for you too, Alva," Torvald says.

"I was just finding the patterning fascinating."

A small chorus of laughter ripples over the comms.

"Newbies!" Torvald says. "I'll give you three more months before you find you're as bored as the rest of us with the scenery. Now scarper."

"Can't I stay, boss?"

"Let her," Charlie says. "She'll get over her enthusiasm faster that way."

A woman pushes a cart tidily behind a row of others beside a wall, looks round and gives a salute and heads up the tunnel. That leaves seven miners showing all the signs of staying, more than Kylone hoped for.

Meriel gathers up a small cleaner from beside the debris and walks out of the cavity towards the mine face. "I'm bringing my pet fine dust sweeper down with me. Might as well have a thorough clean up."

A group groan reverberates on the comms.

"Dust only needs to know you're around to melt its way into the ice," a man says followed by laughter.

"Hey, maybe she could push it the dust miners' way?" a woman adds.

"That's an idea," the man replies. "How about it, Meriel? You'd earn a fortune with the dust miners in the rings."

"You're forgetting the expense and trouble of getting the dust up there."

Kylone twists his head round towards those leaving the mine. All three are well past the cavity. It is safe for him to look towards the mine face again without provoking any questions.

He ups his tension to bring back the volcano world into his vision and concentrates on the water-slush nearest the mine. It looks like a straight line heading for the edge of the mine face. He concentrates on its leading edge. It looks fuzzy as if some of it is escaping into the rock, or it could be just the effects of the slush cooling down to a solid. He really does need to know which it is and cannot find out from here. Time to set his backup plan in motion.

He checks on the people still down there. Meriel has just arrived and is setting her fine dust cleaner to work.

Charlie, Oona and Alva are still studying the mine face. The other four are working on standard drill maintenance tasks. Nobody is coming up the tunnel, which is what he wants.

He opens his link to the crew, clunks his wristpad to his visor then runs it along to produce a screeching sound over the link. He promptly switches it off. He climbs and digs his way into the upper part of the gravel layer of the debris until he is sure it covers him completely and a bit more, and switches off his spacesuit lights.

"Who was that?" Torvald asks. "Check in call, now."

The miners look round each other and call off their names one by one.

"Vince?" Torvald asks. "Can you hear me?"

Kylone does not reply.

"Emiko, Sasha, go up and look for him."

Kylone watches them stride up the tunnel, checking any niches of darkness to make sure they would not miss him on the way up. They arrive at the cavity and have a good look round, including shifting the top dust layer of the debris in case he had fallen in.

"Not in the cavity or along the way up to here, boss," Sasha says over the comms. "What do you want us to do?"

"Check all the way back to the hub. He's probably realised his comms are out and gone back there," Torvald replies.

"Will do," Emiko replies.

Kylone views them making their way towards the hub. As soon as he is sure they will not notice him, he emerges from the debris and quickly heads down the tunnel. There is just enough light coming up from the mine to see by. He keeps a careful lookout on the six miners down there. He is not worried about Meriel, Alva or Torvald noticing him and concentrates on the other three. Charlie and Oona are still at the rock-face. Oona keeps on touching it and yanking her hands away. Charlie is watching her rather than examining the rock. The third person, a man, is on the drill platform switching off its remaining live systems. The steering holograph blinks out.

That fuzziness at the end of the vent is extending. The slush is on the move, and judging by the speed it is edging nearer the mine face, it will not stop before it breaks through.

Kylone links into the crew's comms. "Get the hell out of that mine."

"Who's that?" Charlie asks.

"It doesn't matter," Meriel says. "Move."

"You heard what she said," Torvald adds. "Get out of here. Run."

The drill driver heads for the tunnel. Oona, hands splayed out on the rock face screams, starts shaking and collapses onto the floor. Alva faints to fall beside her. Charlie stands frozen looking down at the two women while Torvald and Meriel rush towards all three.

The man rushing up the tunnel on seeing Kylone stops and spreads his arms out to block him from going further down. "Vince, go back."

"Get out of my way."

"It's too dangerous."

"I know." He yanks the man out of his way. "Get back to the hub. Now!" He rushes on and concentrates on what is ahead.

Torvald pushes Charlie towards the tunnel. He takes a few tentative steps and then turns to look back at the others. Meriel kneels over Alva checking the readout that glows from her chest on her spacesuit. The slush's front is only a couple of metres behind the face.

"Hubmaster," Torvald calls over the comms.

"Go ahead, Torvald," the Hubmaster replies.

"Our iceborne and rockborne are down. Charlie's in shock. Oona's a shaking mess. Something's up. The new crewmember has fainted by the looks of her. We're bringing everyone back to the hub." He glances over to the tunnel as Kylone enters. "There are six of us down here."

"Do you need any help?"

"Not yet."

"I'm putting the hub on standby for possible rescue."

Kylone reaches Charlie and turns him round.

Charlie gawps. “You? It can’t be.”

Kylone forces him to walk a few steps alongside the drill. “You need to get out of here.”

“I don’t understand.”

“No time to explain. Just go. Run!”

Charlie suddenly looks alert and after a second makes a dash for the exit.

Kylone dashes past Torvald whose arm is under Oona’s shoulder and pulling her towards the tunnel and to Meriel tapping away at the medic screen on Alva’s chest. Her face looks exactly like when she fainted in the Aerial Gallery. Another glance at the approaching front.

It is only a metre away from breakthrough with a mass of convoluted thin trails already snaking through the rock’s pores towards them. The sight of those difficult-to-trace threads could easily have been too much for her. She would not cope with seeing them a second time.

“Meriel,” Kylone says on a private link. “We need to carry her away from here.”

“It would be easier if we didn’t.”

“No choice. She can’t cope with what her rockborne talent is showing her.”

“And you can?”

“She can’t control hers like I do.” He returns to grab a stretcher pole from the side of the drill.

Meriel eyes him as he lays the pole alongside Alva and twists its end knob clockwise at his end one notch. It unlocks a thinner pole that unrolls to pull out a flat sheet, big enough to carry a large person in a mining spacesuit. Both poles relax into a flexible cord with knobs at either end. She gets behind Alva’s shoulders ready to move her. “Roll or lift?”

Kylone grabs Alva’s ankles. “No time. Lift. One, two and three.”

Alva is heavier than he expects; he puts it down to the deadweight effect he has heard about. Once she is centred on the sheet, he twists the knob another notch to activate its memory configuration. It curls up to form a semi-cocoon round Alva to tuck her arms by her side and place her legs together, but leaves her visor and chest with its medic screen uncovered. Strips of material separate from edges at the top and bottom of the sheets but remain attached at the knobs, forming loops big enough for either to be slung over a person's body. One person can drag the stretcher along the floor; two people can carry it.

He picks up his loop and looks at Meriel. "Ready…" A cream spot glows at him from the rock face. It is getting larger. He drops his loop. "Get Alva out of here. I'll hold the slush back as long as I can. Move."

Meriel is off pulling Alva behind her, no questions asked or countermands.

Kylone is thankful for this as he rushes to the drill to pick up another pole and twists its knob in a counter-clockwise direction. A sheet unfurls as before, but this time the poles stay rigid. Another counter-clockwise twist and the sheet becomes a rigid board. He pushes the board against the growing cream spot in the hope it will reduce the flow into the mine long enough for Meriel to get a clear stretch out of here.

The pressure builds up on the board. Kylone pushes back as much as he can. The cream glow starts to creep past the board's edges. It will be a few seconds at the most before they turn into a flood. He glances back. Meriel is only just past the drill.

"Move it. I can't hold this much longer."

No reply. A good sign she is concentrating on what she needs to do.

He turns the board a little clockwise to cover as much of the cream as he can. The force against him strengthens. His arms start to ache with the effort. Another look back. Torvald without Oona heads towards Meriel. He has obviously left Oona somewhere safe and returned to help the women. They will get out of here more quickly.

His board sinks into the mine face at the bottom corner. A small stream of slush is jetting out onto the floor. A crack vibrates through the board to bring his attention back to the main flow. The mine face is breaking up and there are rocks being moved along the edges of the flood in the new vent, which is wider further back. The slush is eating sideways as well as ahead into the rock.

He is thrown onto his back and slides along the floor by gushing sticky liquid. He feels knocks on the board above him and against his legs. Those rocks could be dangerous. He does his best to hold the board in front of him to prevent rocks hitting his spacesuit.

His back hits a solid and he comes to a stop. His rockborne vision shows he is up against the drill. It will take effort to push his way through the pressuring slush and avoid the rocks to reach the tunnel exit. Ahead, the slush becomes more translucent and warmer the deeper into the volcano it is. It is at its coldest around him, and he in Vince's spacesuit can already withstand that. It would be safer to swim into the flow and the volcano world, and return through Snowdrift Chasm. He is thankful he brought some rope with him to climb out of the chasm. Forwards or backwards? He must make the decision now. Thoughts flash through his mind.

Back to Meriel and the others on Miranda? Too many new people have just learnt he is alive. It only takes one careless slip by one person in the wrong place at the wrong time for him to be caught and officially executed, if he is not immediately murdered. This fate is so close to certainty that it is a question of when, not if.

Swim forwards through the water-slush and portal into the volcano world? Let Meriel and the others think he died in the water down here, either through being frozen in when it solidifies or through running out of oxygen like he did before. Dirk will surely keep a lookout for him at Verona Rupes, but he does not plan to return that way.

What about the loose ends? Meriel is more than capable of persuading Charlie that in his panic he imagined Vince as Kylone. Dirk can easily falsify the records to show Vince exited the mine and slip him a replacement spacesuit without it being traceable. That side of his disappearance can be taken care of and he knows his friends would do so to protect themselves from being investigated by Chynoweth and the Guardians.

On the other hand, he would have to survive swimming against the flow. It would get easier the farther in he went because the liquid would not be so stiff, but he would be more tired.

It all comes down to how much confidence he has in himself. Confidence he has lacked this last decade. True it had grown bit by slow bit under Patricianna's care, but does he have enough now? It is nothing like his decision for calling the Truth Tribunal when he had the time to weigh up the pros and cons. This choice is full of unknowns. Does he have the confidence to deal with unexpected problems?

Ice chunks knock against the board. The water-slush has started slowing and cooling.

Decision time.

CHAPTER 9

He pulls the rocks aside from the solidifying surface in front of him and pushes his way into the water-slush. He swims into the newly made vent, stroke after stroke.

The stiffness of Vince's miner's spacesuit makes progress even harder.

There is no turning back.

Kylone keeps going and concentrates so much on his next stroke that he does not take any notice of the overlaid view of the volcano world on Miranda. Pull, kick, avoid a rock, pull, breathe deep, kick, pull, kick. He slows to carefully guide his way through the centre of the ring between worlds and turn upwards at the lava junction. Then it is back to kick and pull at maximum effort.

His hand pushes out and up into nothing. He yanks it back, clawing at vacuum then slush. Elation spurs his efforts, overcomes his pain and calms him down enough to reduce his sight back to the normal three dimensions of the volcano world. He scrambles to crawl onto the vent's floor and wipes the slush from his visor. A glance at it starting to freeze onto his arm means he must keep moving, no matter how agonising his muscles are. Otherwise the ice will lock him into position. He walks, almost runs up the vent's slope, rubbing what liquid and frozen ice he can from his suit.

He emerges out of the vent onto the volcano's dim slope and comes to a stop. He frantically continues scraping his suit until he is satisfied its joints, visor, external sensors and readouts are cleared. The suit has sufficient redundancy to cope with a few failures, but his in-built caution for safety drives him. It does not matter if there are solidified ice slivers on the stiff shields of his suit. It will mean carrying a little extra weight and moving with a bit of extra inertia, but not that much.

Pivoting, he takes a few moments to look around. In front of him are the familiar distinctive cut-off mountaintops of the volcano range against the star-field, the first thing he saw of this world's icescape, but turned a little round. He looks over to his left. One volcano along he just about discerns the darkened silhouette of a body lying on the ice next to the vent's entrance, which will lead to Snowdrift Chasm. Kylone smiles, so far so good.

He walks over to Kieran, checks his oxygen supply, switches off his suit's lights to conserve energy, sets an alarm for when it is time to move on and sits down to give his muscles a well-earned rest. Unfamiliar constellations are set against a background field of dimmer stars that form a translucent veil over the blackness. He just about sees the nearby ice hollows and hummocks. This is a world where shadows do not exist. There is no moon, planet or Sun to throw them, merely a hint of extra grey surrounding their high points. He tries to draw mental pictures of what groups of the bright stars could be; immediately above him is a fountain, beside it a drill, below both a not quite perfect circle of nine stars.

The alarm beeps. He stands and stares at Kieran. The rockborne does not deserve to stay in this lonely grave any longer. It is long past time to put him to a final rest. Kylone owes him for pointing the way out on his first visit here. Thankful for taking the precaution of packing the basic space-safety kit of a dust miner, he unpacks the rope and a telescopic rod from his backpack. He extends the rod to its full two-metre length and locks it into position.

"Sorry this is going to be undignified," he whispers to the dead man. "This is the only way to get you home."

It is ridiculous to talk like this, but a modicum of respect is maintained. The important thing is the return of the body to his family so they can finally have some closure.

Once Kieran is tied to the rod so that not even his feet and hands can flop loosely, Kylone gives him a priestly blessing. This instinct surprises him. It seems the old saying of 'Once a priest, always a priest,' is far too true.

Has he changed that much since he joined the Priesthood? He is unsure. True he has become more accepting of what is and cannot be changed, better appreciative of the spartan beauty of Miranda and abler to help both individuals and society to improve their lives. These aspects all manifest outwardly. What about his inner self? He is more comfortable and at peace with himself, but that would not be difficult given the mess he was in after his own accident. It is more than that. He is attuned with this volcano world, Miranda and all the other worlds he has glimpsed, and with himself and his future whatever it may be. He wonders if learning to control his rockborne talent had been the final fulfilling step of that journey. Probably was, but being personal to him, he cannot use it to help others in the future. This thought calls him back to the present.

He ties the free end in a loop round his wrist, gathers in the rope's slack in both hands and pulls Kieran towards the vent leading to Snowdrift Chasm. The smooth rock lets the body slide easily, but is too slippery for sure footholds. The care needed to move forward makes for slow progress.

A few steps into the vent and the body tips over the entrance's edge to make his hauling lighter. Another step and pull. Strain abruptly leaves his hands. A bump against the back of his shins tosses him upwards. The rope drops out of his hands leaving just the loop to keep him attached to the dead man. His rising is slow enough to allow him to look downwards. The body is sliding head first down the vent ahead of him, stretching the rope out.

A crazy idea develops. It might just work. He touches the approaching ceiling with his free hand to stop crashing into it and slow his progress down the vent. He swings his torso round to be upright. The dead man is now well in front shrouded in the vent's darkness.

His feet touch the floor. He wobbles, but manages to stay upright.

The body swings from side to side on the floor. He concentrates on trying to keep it in the centre but has limited control. A swerve to the right means a pull to the left, and vice versa. The rock beneath his feet is super smooth. He has time to wonder why he did not slip coming up the other way: Kieran's extra weight and the lack of snow-sand frozen to his shoes to form a rough enough contact surface to grip into the ice.

A small ellipse of brightness appears ahead. Must be reflections of his spacesuit lights from the surface of the snow-sand. Time to slow down. He yanks the rope violently to turn Kieran sideways so his helmet and boots act like brakes. He drops down to sit and then lie on the ice to place as much of his spacesuit as practicable in contact with the vent's surface. The ellipse grows.

His free hand digs out his laser knife from his pouch, switches on the blade and digs it into the rock. His hand is pulled up behind him, but he resolutely holds the blade as deeply into the rock as he can. The white ellipse ahead reflects enough light to envelop him in a weak aura.

Kieran ploughs into the snow-sand throwing up a shower of glints and sparkles. The rope goes slack. Kylone crashes feet first into the body, pushing him further into the snow-sand and throwing up a second bigger shower. They slow to a stop.

He sits up. All except the body's feet are submerged beneath the snowline. His own legs lying alongside are thigh deep. He checks his suit's integrity on his visor, all green. His wristpad indicates there is still enough time to get back to the air of the Argier hangars.

It sinks in he has not felt one iota of emotional panic. He has not reacted this decisively and positively in ten years. It feels good, really good. His former confidence has returned with a vengeance. He laughs into the echoless everywhere.

Best to get a move on.

He pushes Kieran farther in until his feet are buried a metre deep. He is damp all over with the sweat of exertion. The snow-sand repels his efforts with such inertia that this is going to be harder than anticipated. It would be so easy to make his way back without Kieran, but euphoric bravado eggs him on. He walks deeper into the snow-sand alongside the body pulling the drift out of the way to his sides until he is fully submerged and ahead of the dead man. Then it is step forward, heave on the rope, another step and heave repeatedly for an aching eternity.

The extra pull forwards warns of the ring's closeness between the volcano world and Miranda. He stops to check through his rockborne vision; three metres ahead. Only one person can pass through it at a time and even then they have to keep to the hole's centre as much as possible.

The plan was simple, but now looks impossible. If Kieran gets stuck in that ring there will be no way home for him. He gulps and sweat plasters his skin. His sight extends to a third world of translucent cloud bulges and veils with colours ranging from purple through blues to yellows and white. Stars twinkle through the cloud's thinner parts to give an impression of vastness. His chest tightens and his breathing is rapid and shallow, forcing him to stay still. The pounding in his ears sounds like a chorus of monotonic doom.

His overwhelmed, tiny and useless feeling turns into an acceptance of his insignificance. A surreal peace descends where he seems to extend his ability to touch and connect beyond the limits of his body. The pounding fades into whirr of his suit's systems. The suit dries off his sweat.

His rockborne vision is scaled back to Miranda and the volcano world with their transit ring. He is calm enough to take the next and most dangerous part of his journey.

He pulls Kieran alongside to be in front of him. While holding the dead man's feet, he adjusts the length of the rope to move his head until Kieran is in position to go straight through the ring. All he needs to do is to keep the body aligned properly. He tentatively pushes it forward to check his levering system can take the drag and strain of the snow-sand. It works. Kylone decides that going through by similar small increments is the way to do it. Another couple of centimetres move forward, and another, and again. The work is slow, tedious and requires concentration. Steadily the head, torso and thighs make it into the ring. His arms ache, his forehead is stuck in a permanent crease and his legs are a little shaky.

The ring's pull on Kylone is stronger now, almost irresistible. He has come as close to it as he dares with his feet on the floor. It is time for the next phase. Making sure Kieran stays in the aligned position, he kicks his feet off the floor and starts moving his legs up and down in a crawl swim-stroke. He moves gradually forward pushing the rest of Kieran through the ring. His legs' ache turns to pain as his head passes through. He keeps going; if he stops now he will be sucked to the edge and get stuck. The pain in his limbs becomes agony. He cannot stop. His mind tries to focus on carrying on, but his tortured muscles pull him back, nagging him to stop and rest.

He refuses to give in.

He must see this through.

Abruptly he realises Kieran's feet are well clear of the ring. He is through. He glances back. His hips are in the ring's centre. The pain is excruciating. He pushes Kieran, tipping his feet to push him downward out of the way, but keeps hold of the rope. Kylone pulls with his arms as well as kicking with his legs. The pain is almost unbearable. He wants to move or be still in any way that alleviates it, but dare not. He sees the dead man's head to his side in his rockborne vision. He must be through. He checks behind him. He is well through. He slowly sinks to his knees beside Kieran, tears from the pain blurring his vision.

A memory surfaces. He was beside Selma's mangled body weeping uncontrollably. Meriel had her arms round his shoulders trying to pull him away. He wanted to stay with his fiancée, never leave her, not like this. But Meriel and someone else's arms locked hold of his and dragged him away, shouting hysterically.

He is not like that any more. Some of that peace he felt earlier is still with him. He calmly stands and checks his oxygen level. More has been used than expected. He is running out of time and must ignore his protesting body.

He walks as fast as he can through the snow-sand into Snowdrift Chasm dragging his burden behind him. An amber long light warning bar switches on at the side of his visor. He has an hour of clean oxygen left. Heave, step, heave, step. Forty-five minutes left. He quickly glances up. His rockborne vison places him under a stanchion of the railing protecting the chasm's pathway to the Argier farm hangars above him. It has exactly what he needs, a knob on top around which a loop of rope can be secured. With the loose coil of rope held in his hand, he swims upward as fast as possible. Thirty minutes left. His head breaks the surface of the snow-sand. His spacesuit lights are swallowed in the gloom above and the stanchion immediately above is hidden from direct view by a slight overhang.

The first stanchion he can see in his ordinary sight is two along. His rope may not be long enough to reach from here. He swims towards it with one hand and legs while pulling out a grappling loop from his pouch. Once close enough, he makes the rope's end into the loop and fastens it with a bowline knot, and then switches on the fibre-optics down the rope's middle. He widens the loop and holds it up to let it take a snapshot of the aimed-at stanchion. With most of the rope free of the snow-sand he aims, and throws.

The loop rises fast, but is not lighting any of its micro-thrusters to adjust its direction. His aim was not close enough. He yanks the rope back and has another throw. This time spurts of outgassing can be seen in his lights. He waits as it rises above the stanchion, floats slowly down, opens and then locks itself round the knob. He has done it.

Ten minutes oxygen left. Change of plan. He leaves Kieran attached to the rope and pulls himself up it while walking the wall. He finds strength he does not know he has. He is concentrating so much on surviving that his body has no time for nerves or rising tension. He reaches the stanchion and jumps over the railing. Amber changes to red on his visor. Zero oxygen left. He is living on fumes, and given the tight fit of the spacesuit, there is not that much.

He takes a deep breath and runs along the pathway. His lips are warming. Agony grips his limbs' muscles in tight vices. He is into the tunnel. His chest hurts. He wants to take another breath, but dare not immediately. Hold on. Run. Open airlock. Breath.

He is inside the airlock. He collapses to the floor. His heart is rapidly pounding hell out of his ears. A band of tightness squeezes his chest. The door is closing. Do not open the helmet, not until the light is green. The door clicks shut. He feels faint, woozy, confused. The light is amber. He opens his visor. He gasps in the thin air. He gasps again and again.

His breathing slows. His pain lessens. He feels sensible enough to be coherent. He puts in a private voice call on his spacesuit's comms.

"What do you mean by disturbing an old man late at night like this?" a raspy male voice replies.

"Lachlan?"

"Who is this?"

"Are you alone?"

"What kind of question is that… Priest? You don't sound in too good a shape."

"Getting my air back. I need your help, but nobody else must know."

"What do you need, Priest?"

"I need you to come to Argier Rupes to collect your brother's body. Don't ask. It's a long story."

"I'll get a couple of people to help."

"No."

There is a pause. "We can talk later. I'll bring a trolley along."

"There's a rope tied to a railing in Snowdrift Chasm. Your brother is tied to the bottom of it. I need to hide for now."

"Why, Priest?"

"Too many people know I'm alive. Or I should say was. It's better for them to believe I'm really dead this time."

There is clunk at the other end of the comms of something being crashed. "On my way. Where're you going to hide?"

"Haven't figured that part out yet."

A few stroking sounds. "You're coming back to my condo, Priest."

"But–"

"I'm bringing a motorised trolley with two enclosed boxes, one for Kieran and one for you. We can argue when you get back here. Nobody's going to stop this stubborn old man, trust me."

There is confidence in the old man's voice. The pain Kylone had ignored takes its revenge.

The inner door opens. It is dark, which means nobody is there. He staggers to get up and after ordering the lights in the hangar to stay off he locates a medical box latched into a blister next to the airlock controls. He searches through it to find a painkiller injector pen and gives himself the maximum dose through the neck.

As the pain starts to disappear, he tries to remember where he can hide around here; inside a garage for one of the harvesters. "Seven hells of ice," he mutters as he struggles to get there.

***

Kylone lies on a bunk in Lachlan's condo on the top floor of the Dunsinane Rotunda. All he can think about is how to explore other parts of the moon for more rings to help stop more deaths. Strong rockborne are too few, and without any control they can only produce results randomly – even Alva, the strongest. He wants to pace up and down, whittle and worry, but must lie still. Lachlan has asked a priest to visit the condo to arrange Kieran's funeral.

Footsteps and muffled voices entering the condo make him more anxious. Restlessness and curiosity will not let him stay still. He is drawn to the sounds outside his cabin. The only way to get some peace is to listen in.

As quietly as he can, he steps over to the cabin's door to put his ear against it. He catches the odd word or phrase. The priest's voice is familiar, but he cannot attach a name to it. They move past him to the cabin at the back of the condo where Kieran's body lies still locked in his spacesuit.

More footsteps sound coming through the front door. Kylone turns his head sharply at their unexpectedness. His tension flares up and his rockborne talent comes alive. Through the walls he sees Alva, arms akimbo, staring straight at him. Their eyes lock. There is deep anger in hers. This must one of the times her beyond sight is functioning well enough for her to interpret what she sees. She might do something reckless. He puts his finger to his mouth and shakes his head to plead not to give him away.

She marches up to his cabin, yanks the door open to push him aside and slaps his face. "How dare you pull a stunt like that," she growls.

His cheek stings and he holds up a hand to it to try to soften the pain. "I had no real choice. Too many people knew about me. Sooner or later…"

Priest Xuthus walks up behind Alva, with Lachlan close at his shoulder. Hints of astonishment and confusion slip out of Xuthus' practised calm face.

"Couldn't you trust your friends?" Alva continues ignoring the men behind her. "We kept your secret from the authorities so they wouldn't arrest you. We were working to find a way off this moon for you. And how do you repay us? Another disappearing trick. Do you know how upsetting that is?"

"Look I…" His eyes meet Xuthus'. "You've let a priest know I'm alive."

"Him?" she tosses her head backwards. "He's one of the good guys. Thanks to you telling us about those

Chynoweth goons, Dirk has this past day been tracing those involved. Xuthus been mentioned by them as not being one of them. Dirk also found out a whole lot more about their nastiness."

He wants to say so much, but only comes up with a few words. "Hacking of any network, let alone a private comms one doesn't stand up in a court."

"Damn you! Can't you get it through your thick skull?" She grabs his face with both hands, pulls it towards her and kisses him.

He breaks off, but her lips are too warm and inviting. His mouth finds its way back and lingers long, enjoying the comfort. His arms curl round her back and pull her gently closer. She responds fitting herself snuggly into his body, encouraging him for an even closer embrace. He closes his eyes, enjoys her scent of citrus, her soft skin and the taste of her tongue. He cannot help himself.

His mind's warning finally pushes its way into his consciousness. He has no choice and opens his eyes to find he has reverted to his normal sight. He gently breaks off and takes a step back to put a little distance between them. There is no sign of Xuthus or Lachlan. He must have embraced her for longer than he thought. Yet it seems only a moment.

"I'm sorry, I shouldn't have kissed you," he says.

"Why not?"

"If I'm not a dead man walking, I'll be an exile and we both know what that means."

"So? Don't I have a say in this matter?" The darkness of anger clouds her face.

"I don't want to hurt you and you've already had more than enough of it." He looks deeply into her glowing brown ones. They start watering.

"It's not fair."

"I agree. I have no choice."

She looks away, biting and chewing her lips and a few tears escape her eyes.

He wants to take her back into his arms and say it will be all right, but knows this would be deceit.

She steps aside to let him out of the cabin. "Do what you must."

He nods a thank you, reluctantly steps into the corridor and on into the living room with a kitchenette opposite.

Xuthus stands with one arm across his stomach supporting the other at the elbow. His free hand is cupped around his chin. On noticing Kylone, he breaks off his conversation with Lachlan sitting on the bench. "There you are. I've just got a couple of questions about what Alva said earlier."

Alva stops beside Kylone, wiping away another tear.

"Go ahead," Kylone replies.

"Am I correct in thinking your so-called suicide in Snowdrift Chasm was in fact a murder attempt by these 'Chynoweth goons'?"

"Yes."

"So you went into hiding to avoid them?"

"Yes."

"Why didn't you take the first opportunity to contact the Priesthood to explain this? We could've helped."

Kylone bites his lips. "I don't know how to say this. I wasn't sure at the time, but I'm starting to have my suspicions that priests might have been in league with my would-be killers."

"Make that definitely," Alva intervenes. "Once we identified his would-be murderers, we could follow a trail of evidence to discover more illegal activities and…" she pauses, "that some priests *are* involved. It took time to get this far and we're not finished yet."

Kylone groans at the thought of Dirk doing more hacking. "Illegally I presume?"

Lachlan smiles while Xuthus' look of confusion changes to indignation.

"Hell no. Under license from Coroner Sylvana, with witnesses."

"Why haven't I heard about any of this?" Xuthus asks beating Kylone to it.

"To protect Dirk and anyone else involved in searching out Kylone's would-be assassins and the people – more like the organisation – behind them. The fewer who know, the better, until we identify and arrest *all* concerned. That's why it's under lock and key. I'm not allowed to say more."

Kylone almost chokes. "You're putting your lives at risk for me–"

"We know," she says. "None of us would want it otherwise."

"But–"

"You're not alone in this fight anymore. Accept our help. Call it a repayment for what you've done for us if you must. But it's not. We would do this because we want to."

Her words tug at Kylone. He is humbled, grateful and proud all at once, a mixture he has never experienced before and has no idea how he is expected to react.

"I… I don't know what to say. Thank you." Kylone takes a deep breath, straightens his shoulders and looks the priest in the eye. "I suppose you being a High Priest you're going to have to arrest me."

Xuthus rubs his chin. "No, I don't think so."

"What?"

"You, between you," he points to Kylone and Alva, "have given me sufficient reason to believe that your life might be in more danger from criminals if I did. You're better off hiding here for now. It also gives me the chance to find a way of nominating you for Archdeacon before someone else arrests you."

Alva laughs dismissively. "Sounds like the Chief Compineer has been giving you mad ideas."

"Interesting. And no. But it's nice to hear someone else thinking along the same lines. While Kylone's a nominated candidate for Archdeacon, he cannot be arrested for Priesthood infringements. It would allow him to openly leave Miranda."

"This is for real?"

"Yes."

The implications of what is being said finally sink in for Kylone. "Why are you helping me?"

"I was never satisfied with your testimony at your Truth Tribunal. You were hiding something. You still are. In return for my help I would like to know what it is."

Kylone stares through the grimed window and can barely make out the outline of the walkway's window opposite. He reviews his tribunal with all the secrets he kept then. There are a laughably small number compared to what he knows now. It would take a very long talk to bring Xuthus fully up to speed, but would he understand? If not, would he accept his words? The core of this issue is whether he can trust Xuthus.

He decides. "The truth comes with its own price."

"If you mean my silence until you're off Miranda, I can live with that."

"That's the easy price. No, it comes with total incredulity on top of disgust and a strong sense of betrayal."

Xuthus raises his head. "That bad?"

"Worse than you can possibly imagine."

Alva shuffles her feet. "Um… the last issue. The betrayal bit. We're not there yet."

Kylone gets the hint. The Archdeacon's failure to come forward to defend him is still not part of the Coroner's investigation. Dirk must be putting in some private hacking time. "Is it time Dirk had another of my priestly lectures?"

"Nooo. He's been rather busy to be other than well behaved. This one line of enquiry was the exception and it's given some, shall we say interesting results."

Kylone eyes her gorgeous brown eyes and wishes he could lose himself in them. "Now you've given me due warning, what did he find out?"

"She was and still is being blackmailed."

Kylone whistles towards the ceiling.

"Who?" Xuthus intervenes.

Silence.

"Is this the part of the conversation where I really will not believe you?" Xuthus says at last.

"Yes. It will be painful for you to hear."

"I think I'm already there, but continue. It'll sink in eventually. Who's being blackmailed and for what?"

"A witness who could have exonerated Kylone of at least one of the charges at his Truth Tribunal."

"Who?"

"The Archdeacon," Kylone says quietly.

"The..." Xuthus slumps onto the settee. "That would explain it."

It is Kylone's turn to ask. "What?"

"The Archdeacon has not been herself since... since you dropped into Snowdrift Chasm. She's announcing her retirement in two days time, immediately after she's taken the Greening ceremony."

"What! She's one of those unfortunates who can't see the Greening without fainting. It's not safe for her to go out there on the promontory. She'll fall to her death."

"She says she's been cured," Xuthus replies. "We have to take her word for it."

"No way," Alva says.

"It can happen as people grow older."

She slowly shakes her head, punctuating it with nos.

Kylone narrows his eyes on her. "More hacking?"

Alva nods.

"Enough is enough," Xuthus snaps.

"I agree," Kylone replies. "I'll leave you the pleasure of giving the Chief Compineer a priestly lecture. He does appreciate eloquence and imagination, and is more likely to react, as we would wish. Even so..." He bites his lips afraid of his new conclusion.

They wait in silence.

"From what you've said," Kylone nods to Xuthus, "I think she wants to kill herself and not make it look like suicide."

Alva has a sharp intake of breath.

Xuthus drops his head into his hands.

"You got to stop it, Priest," Lachlan says.

"How?" Xuthus replies. "If I can do so this time, she'll find another way."

"You're not the priest I'm talking to here. He is," Lachlan points to Kylone. "He's got more Priesthood in his little finger than most priests have in their souls."

Kylone stares at Lachlan, trying to work out why he is asking the impossible of a man in hiding.

"From the quiet of the observant," Xuthus whispers.

Kylone focuses on the priest who stares back at him.

"He's right," Alva says.

His eyes snap onto hers. The previous glow of her eyes has been doused to leave a dull earthen colour.

"You need to become the Archdeacon," she adds.

"I agree," Xuthus says.

"I'm no leader—" Panic chokes off any more words as his rockborne talent lets him see through the solidity around him.

"You may feel that way because you've been struggling, but it's not true. You're still standing despite horrendous circumstances. That alone gives you respect from both the good and the bad. You see something wrong and rather than get other people to sort it out, you do it. It's called leading by example, which is far better than organising and ordering. But above all, you care about people and it shows. People like you for that. They feel you're their friend."

It is quite a speech, enough to make him realise Kylone has more support that he thought possible. He is humbled at being so highly thought of. His panic, and with it his rockborne vision, dies.

"But I can't come up with speeches like you do," he says when he finally finds his voice.

Xuthus laughs. "Speeches? Mostly they're a form of mild hypnotism and no substitute for speaking genuinely from the heart, which is what you do. That's far rarer than most people think."

"But—"

"No buts, you're going to be the next Archdeacon and stop the current one from committing suicide."

Kylone strokes his embryonic goatee, working through what has been said. He cannot fault the reasoning or the good intentions. It sinks in he is the only person that can genuinely link into the Priesthood, the miners and their rockborne, the data controllers and – through Alva and the Rotunda's farm, the Greenhouse – the farming community; the four main pillars of the Mirandan society.

"Well?" Alva asks.

He makes his decision. "Xuthus, get hold of Priest Patricianna and ask her to counsel Archdeacon Ariadne about her feeling guilty about my, let's call it pseudo-death. Meanwhile you can suggest to her that without a body to prove I'm dead, I might still be alive. I know it's a weak rope to climb, but it's better than nothing. Alva here has had similar experiences with not being able to see the Greening. She can give you fact-based details that your sharp legal brain may be able to use on the Archdeacon. Let me know tomorrow morning whether you think these steps will be sufficient."

"Consider it done. How will I contact you?"

"Through Lachlan here."

"Aye, you'll make a good Archdeacon," Lachlan replies.

"Talking of which we need to plan my nomination carefully so that it isn't thrown out on the grounds that I'm 'dead'. Who can nominate someone for Archdeacon?"

"Any priest, though it is preferable a High Priest leads the nomination process."

The reason is obvious: it gives the candidate more credibility. "Are you willing to be the lead nominator, Xuthus?"

"I'd be honoured, but you'll need a second and a third."

"I have some thoughts on that. Let's talk this through."

***

The facemask Alva made him wear over his forehead and nose is sticky with sweat. The wig of loose-hanging blond hair with a fringe is itchy. His beard has been dyed to match the wig, leaving the skin underneath sore. Kylone just wants to scratch and scratch and scratch, but dare not for fear of loosening his disguise. This deception is an anathema to him. There was no other easy way of getting him into the High Chapel for the Archdeacon's Nomination Assembly without causing a commotion. He curls up his nose at his own stench as he approaches the reception desk at the chapel.

Priest Thyone looks up from her screen, her brow creased in annoyance and crow's feet showing at the corners of her eyes. "What do you want?"

He coughs to take preparation time to speak a few notes higher than normal. "To see High Priest Xuthus. I'm booked in. Roger Thorpe's the name."

"Oh really. At a time like this." Her eyes and fingers move along the screen. "What is that idiot thinking of?"

He had forgotten how irritatingly offhand she had become because of her father's protection. "It was the only time I could make it."

"There you are." She glances at the corner of the screen. "You're ten minutes early. Go and wait over there." She waves her hand in the direction of a settee. "I've called him."

"Thank you."

"And you be out within the hour or else. We've got an important Assembly meeting in the chapel after that. Stay away. Understood?"

"Yes." He wants to say a lot more, about her downright rudeness and how if he were in charge she would be off reception duties until she had had a full training course in basic manners. In fact, if truth were known, he would sack her as a priest and demote her back to acolyte, and maybe not even that. He grips the top of his shoulder bag hard as if trying to squeeze his anger and stares at the long tapestry of the Solar System behind Thyone. His rockborne talent flares up to see behind the material. The stitches are all neatly done, the loose ends having been tucked in. The whole tapestry is stretched over a black matt board with its edges turned round the back and tied into place. Behind that is another board that he assumes is insulation and then a thin layer of all too familiar pink veneer to seal the air in. The last is a reminder of how fragile their existence on Miranda is.

He focuses on Uranus hanging behind Thyone, blues and white shimmering out of the threads. The big vortices are there, but not the smaller ones to break up the larger patches of colour. The planet looks lost, forlorn of its glory. Strangely its sadness calms him down enough to revert to normal sight.

"Over there." Thyone points to the settee.

He nods and shuffles over to the seat, but decides to stand to study the rest of the tapestry, or to be more precise, work out what it lacks. His view reaches egg-shaped Haumea with its two moons and ring when Xuthus rushes through the door leading from the warren of tunnels behind the chapel.

"Welcome." Xuthus gives him the priestly blessing.

Kylone feels a lump in his throat: he cannot remember the last time he received one. He has finally come home to the familiar, and yet realising much needs doing. There will be no rest for him. "Thank you."

Thyone looks up sharply with a puzzlement written over her face.

He has slipped into his normal voice, gulps and stares at her waiting to see if she can penetrate his disguise.

Her frown worsens. She shakes her head and turns her attention back to her screen.

Panic over.

Xuthus walks to the corridor leading to the chapel. "Please follow me."

They make their way in silence up the stairs onto the balcony. Kylone glances at the mosaic. It is as he left it, unfinished, with crystals reaching only five-eighths up the wall. The work looks good, clean and neat, his lasting legacy, the only one so far he really feels proud of. He had never expected to see it again and this time may actually be the last. He relishes its beauty while he can.

Their plan is risky.

The only alternative was to stay in hiding until he was caught and dragged to exile, though more probably his execution like a cowardly rat. This way, if things go wrong he would feel no shame.

He follows Xuthus into counselling room one, a luxurious space with four armchairs round a table. A waiting priest puts down his steaming mug of coffee and stands to greet them: Priest Theseus, the one who had offered to help him before his Truth Tribunal.

Theseus waits until Xuthus has firmly closes the door. "Who is this?"

"You didn't tell him?" Kylone asks.

"I thought it was perhaps wiser," Xuthus replies. "The fewer people knew, the less risk of our enemies finding out what is about to go down."

Kylone smiles at the use of 'our'. It makes Xuthus feel like a brother, one he never had. He cannot fault the reason, but now has to convince Theseus to co-nominate him for Archdeacon. He pulls off his wig and drops it into his shoulder bag, brushes his hands through his short hair to get rid of the itch of sweat and peels off his mask. Cool air brushing his face takes away the oppressiveness of the mask and lightens his mood. "Do you recognise me now, despite my hair and beard?"

Theseus' eyes widen while otherwise remaining still for a couple of seconds. A smile creeps onto his face. "And never has such a sight been more welcome. Good to have you back."

"Good to be here and see you well." He holds out his hand towards Theseus'.

Theseus pulls Kylone into a welcome hug before standing back. "I'm glad to see you alive. But why are you here?"

"To be nominated for Archdeacon," Xuthus replies. "Would you be willing to be second?"

"Hell yes, but…"

"They can't under our rules arrest him then."

"Then doubly hell yes."

"Thank you," Kylone says, relieved, "but it will be

better if you nominate me under my birth name, Simon Redman."

"Whichever." He turns to Xuthus. "I'm sorry I haven't been able to pry Priest Patricianna away from the Archdeacon to join us."

Kylone sucks in his breath: Patricianna would only be this stubborn if she really feared for the Archdeacon. "Does she know about me?"

"Sorry, again no," Xuthus replies.

"I thought we needed three nominations?"

"We do." Worry lines appear on Xuthus' face.

Patricianna's words from their last meeting before his escape through the Snowdrift Chasm echo in Kylone's mind: 'You would have made one hell of a damned good high priest' and 'I have no worries about your future. You'll be all right.' Although they may have disagreed, she has never let him down and he is certain she will not in the future.

"What is the protocol for asking for more nominations to be Archdeacon during Assembly meeting?" Kylone asks.

"You're not seriously considering going ahead are you?" Xuthus says. "They could arrest you if a third is not forthcoming."

"I know the stakes, but I am confident someone will step forward."

"But—"

Kylone holds up his hand to quieten him. "In the worst case scenario you can both claim that you were trying to save a man's life. There will be no comeback on either of you. This is my responsibility, not yours."

"My conscience will not allow me to send an innocent man to his likely execution," Xuthus says.

"Mine will, though I trust your judgement." Theseus nods towards Kylone.

They both stare at him.

"I'm a practical man in a society that has developed sound practical answers to our issues. The problem we have now is the Guardians of History. They are not doing their job properly. If they were, there would be fewer accidents. Nor are they willing to change. Worse, they want to expand their bad practice by getting High Priest Diomedes elected as Archdeacon. We can do better than this. We must. It will save lives in the longer term. No, I do not like the thought of Kylone facing the firing squad. In fact, I hate it. But if he is the only one willing to stand up to them, then I say we must give him every chance of succeeding."

The speech surprises Kylone. It also humbles and burdens him. The mixture of emotions leaves him without words.

"That's the longest speech I have ever heard you make," Xuthus says at last.

Theseus shrugs his shoulders. "I'm a practical man."

Xuthus turns to Kylone. "Are you sure you want to go through with this?"

"Yes." He has never felt so certain in his life.

"Then let's go over the timings and details once more."

***

The door closes on Theseus and Xuthus leaving the room. Kylone becomes strangely peaceful, as if this is the last real moment of being his true self. He checks the time on his wristpad. Fifteen minutes until the start of the Assembly.

He makes some camomile tea and hopes this will not become a habit in the fraught-pressured life of being an Archdeacon. A smile crosses his face at the thought of Xuthus giving Dirk an eloquent priestly lecture. It will have more impact than any words he can come up with. His smile turns upside down; the Chief Compineer still has not been told he is alive and will not witness the meeting. He will miss what he would call *all the fun*. If he had not pushed the investigation and digging – make that hacking – into the necessary data, Kylone would not be here now. He sighs before taking a sip of his tea.

The door abruptly opens and Thyone steps inside. "I

told you to leave by…" Her eyes widen and her skin pales even against her pearly hair.

With a surreal clarity he quickly and calmly stands to close the door behind her. "You have a choice to make. You can go back out there and fetch someone to take me into custody, in which case you will find yourself on a charge of conspiracy to murder me. Or you can sit here quietly and have some tea with me until I join the Assembly."

She turns to leave and stops short of opening the door. "What the hell do you mean conspiracy to murder? I've done no such thing."

He resumes his seat and starts to make a fresh cup of camomile tea. "On the contrary. You played your part in helping the Guardian of History bring a complaint about me to the Archdeacon's attention, which started a series of consequential actions that led to me being chased into Snowdrift Chasm. I would've died there in the snow-sand had I not discovered a new way out."

She absently takes the mug he offers while continuing to stare at him. "I could not have foreseen those consequences."

"True. But by getting me arrested now you'll be deemed to confirm your intent of those original actions. That alone makes you culpable, especially as you've just been made aware of the facts."

She slumps into the chair opposite. "This is one of Xuthus' silly legal ploys isn't it? It'll only delay the inevitable."

"On the contrary. This is all about you and where you stand in life. Do you want to side with your father and his play for power no matter what it costs other people? Or, do you want to see Mirandan society develop and grow successfully? Make no mistake about it. Your father is not open to the truth of what is going on, as you've seen for yourself with Isaac Hawking's graph. Your choice: continue to act as your father's pawn or become an integral part of helping our society to survive. You can't do both. Which is it to be?"

His speech is incredible even to his own ears. Maybe Xuthus had a point about talking from the heart.

"You want me to go against my father? You're crazy."

"I *hope* you'll stand for Mirandans." He pauses to watch her reaction, but she gives nothing away. "The door is there if you don't." He points to it and then sits back to drink the rest of his tea.

She looks at the door then back at him. "How can you sit there so calmly?"

"I haven't had enough of this tea to drug me into calmness if that's what you're asking." He lifts his mug in her direction before setting it down on the table. "I know I've done the best I can. Can you say the same of yourself?"

"Of course I can…" Her brow creases and she rubs her temple with her forefinger.

He checks his wristpad. "The Assembly should've started. If you'll excuse me, I need to attend it."

"What?"

He smiles at her on his way out into the noise of general chatter of the priests and behind them the acolytes echoing through the chapel. As expected, they fill the front rows of the main floor, the rest being left empty. They are too preoccupied to be looking up and behind, waiting for the Archdeacon. She is late. Not a good sign. Nevertheless, he stays sufficiently back from the balustrade to be in the shadows while still having a view of what is going on.

The altar has been removed and the Archdeacon's empty tea green chair has been placed against the wall. To one side are two rows of chairs facing the clear wall filled with green-edged black silks and the many white-haired and bald High Priests. Diomedes sits in the centre of the front row chatting to his neighbour, one he does not recognise who probably must have come from the other side of Miranda. Opposite are twelve chairs with civilians chosen by lottery invited to witness the proceedings. Sitting in the back row is the familiar tied back dark hair of Dirk.

Kylone looks towards the ceiling. He had not expected Dirk to hack his way to being here and wonders what he has planned; hopes it will not interfere with Xuthus' ploy. From the corner of his eye, he notices Thyone head towards the stairs. He is not sure why she has not had him arrested, but guesses she does not want to spoil her father's triumph.

A wave of quiet spreads from beneath him through the room. Heads are turned towards the main entrance beside the bottom of the stairs. The Archdeacon must have made her entrance.

She comes into his view as she walks down the central aisle towards her chair. Her shoulders are rounded as if she carries a great weight, stray strands of hair escape her chignon and her head is bowed – not the usual stance, held up high. She emanates such an aura of brokenness that the relief of leaving office will not cure whatever is bothering her.

Kylone knows her guilt at not being a witness at his tribunal is only a small contributor to her wretchedness. She would know her role was very minor leading up to his reputed death. He can only guess at what other things she has been made to do against her will by Diomedes.

Patricianna walks a few steps behind with all the dignity her age and grey can muster. If she were not in the black of the priest, anyone would think she were Archdeacon.

The Archdeacon slumps onto her chair, rests her elbow on the armrest and bows her head to hide her face behind her hand. Patricianna stands beside her and watches her intently. The whirr of the air fans echo through the room. There is a stifled cough from somewhere in the audience; a few seconds later the rustle of someone moving in their chair presumably to get more comfortable; the jolt of someone kicking something solid doubtless by accident. Unease mounts.

Patricianna bends down to nudge the Archdeacon's hand lying limp on the armrest.

The Archdeacon lifts her head and stares at her friend.

Even from this distance Kylone can see her silent message of anxious pleading and shame. She glances hatred at Diomedes before looking back at Patricianna for help.

That glance shows Diomedes is the cause for her abdication. She has lost her war of political infighting within the Priesthood to which she has dedicated her life. Dejected is the only word to describe her.

Patricianna nods to her.

The Archdeacon sits up straight as if making one final effort. "Priests." She pauses. "I find I am no longer able to lead you. You must choose another to take my place." She sags back down and stares at the floor in front of her.

High Priest Euphemios at the front corner of the High Priests section stands. Despite his white hair and heavy lines, he looks much more alive than either the Archdeacon or Patricianna. "As the most senior High Priest it falls to me to direct the election of a new Archdeacon. Does anyone here object if I fulfil this role?"

His dazzling blue eyes scan the room, leaving the balcony until last. His eyes light on Kylone and stop there for a moment before moving on.

Kylone lets out a breath. The darkness up here has kept his identity hidden.

Euphemios takes a moment to gaze at his spidery hands and then stands straight to look over the audience. He seems to want to avoid making fuss over a stranger who has sneaked in to silently watch the Assembly. "I call upon Convener High Priest Skiron to ensure the regulations and correct procedures of this election are followed. Please stand by my side to advise."

Diomedes looks sharply up at Euphemios while murmurs slither round the room. This is an unexpected move, but one nobody can object to. Kylone wonders if the old man has recognised him after all. There is nothing he can do about it except wait and see. A smile creeps across Diomedes' face. He must think this extra formality must play to his ambitions.

Skiron's face briefly looks puzzled, before taking on a

priestly demeanour of calmness. He steps out from among the High Priests to stand next to Euphemios. "I am honoured you have called upon me in my capacity as Convenor."

"I call for nominations to be the next Archdeacon," Euphemios says.

A dark-haired high priest behind Diomedes stands before the announcement is finished. "I nominate the Guardian of History, High Priest Diomedes."

A female priest in congregation adds: "I second High Priest Diomedes."

A third voice, male this time from the other side of congregation adds: "I third High Priest Diomedes."

Euphemios turns to Diomedes. "Do you accept this nomination?"

Diomedes stands. "I most humbly do."

Kylone is sure this has been choreographed to obtain maximum buy-in from the Priesthood and civil observers.

Euphemios turns to Skiron. "Is this nomination compliant with our rules."

"It is."

"The Guardian of History has been nominated for Archdeacon."

"He's a traditionalist," Dirk shouts out and stands. "Is that what you want? The same ways of doing business. What has happened to the Priesthood once renowned for improving life on Miranda? He'll lead you all, every single one of you to uselessness."

He is booed and shouted down.

Euphemios waves his hands to quieten the audience down. They eventually settle.

"Chief Compineer," Euphemios says.

A few gasps echo in the whirr of the air fans. Some people must still know him as Isaac Hawking. The worry as to what he might do could have made Euphemios call on Skiron.

"Chief Compineer, unless you have a specific point to make about why the Guardian of History cannot be the Archdeacon, then please just observe our proceedings."

Dirk glares at the man. “I am currently involved in an investigation under lock and key and cannot reveal my findings until I have permission to do so from the Coroner’s Office.”

Skiron takes a step forward. “Are you implying the Guardian of History is involved in something illegal?”

“I haven’t come to the end of my part in the investigation yet.”

“So you don’t know?”

“I’m not at liberty to say.”

“Have you any idea when this investigation will end?”

“That is up to the Coroner’s Office.”

“You do realise that by bringing your under lock and key investigation to the public attention of the Priesthood, you are breaking the terms of the lock and key.”

“I had special permission to say what I said, which was on condition that the Guardian of History was nominated. You can check this out with the Coroner’s Office.”

“I will, immediately after we have finished here. But for now the Guardian of History must be presumed innocent of any wrongdoing. Therefore his nomination stands.”

Dirk shakes his head. “I’m not stopping his nomination, just the election until I’m allowed to make my findings public.”

“No,” the Archdeacon groans.

“Can’t you see Archdeacon Ariadne is in no fit state to continue in office,” Patricianna intervenes.

“We do need an Archdeacon to function in office,” Skiron adds.

Euphemios nods to Skiron. “Thank you for your advice. We will proceed.”

“You’re making a big mistake. That’s my opinion, not my judgement.” Dirk drops down onto his chair and pulls his ponytail round to the front to stroke and play with its weight. He looks miserable.

This is the first time Kylone has seen his friend defeated without being able to resort to a remedy. Having to take ‘no’ for an answer is such a rare event for Dirk he has no idea what his response should be to get him out of his funk.

"Are there any other possible objections to the Guardian of History?" Euphemios asks.

Silence.

"Are there any other nominations for Archdeacon?"

Xuthus sitting in the far end of the back row of High Priests stands. "I nominate Simon Redman."

"What?" slips from the Archdeacon who sits up to stare at Xuthus.

Dirk sits up straight. Patricianna's jaw drops. Everyone else Kylone can see looks puzzled.

"We need someone familiar with the ways of the Priesthood," Skiron prompts.

"Many of you here would have known him as Priest Kylone."

"But he's dead," Skiron explodes.

"Not true," Kylone's voice rings out as he steps up to the balustrade.

All eyes turn on him. Being the focus of so many people makes him feel like he is under microscope. One wrong move will be far more than an embarrassment. He must not think of what could go wrong. He must do what is right. He walks as slowly as he can along the balcony, down the stairs and up the aisle to the front. He nods a thank you towards Xuthus who nods acknowledgement back to him. Of the people at the front: Diomedes has an aura of dark anger; Skiron is struggling to keep calm; Euphemios is rigid with shock written all over his face; Patricianna has a hint of a satisfied smirk; the Archdeacon's eyes exude joy and pleading for forgiveness; and Dirk has a hand over his mouth giggling.

Kylone glares at the Chief Compineer's undignified behaviour.

"I know, I know," Dirk says. "I'm due for one of your priestly lectures."

"No," Kylone replies. "I'm leaving that pleasure to High Priest Xuthus who is far more eloquent than I could ever be."

His laughter is chased away by shock. "Nine hells of ice."

Euphemios shakes himself to recover his composure. "Convenor, now that Kylone has proved himself to be alive, does he need to be a priest to be nominated as Archdeacon?"

"No. As I said earlier, he only needs to have significant experience of the Priesthood. Given that he was eight years a priest, nobody can deny he has had that experience."

The visibly deep breath Euphemios takes effectively says he does not believe what he is about to say. "Is there a second for Kylone?" He scans the room.

"He should be arrested," Diomedes yells.

"Not true," Skiron immediately replies. "The process of his nomination for Archdeacon has started and therefore he has immunity from arrest for purely priesthood infringements. The charges brought against him at his Truth Tribunal were of that nature. Please proceed, High Priest Euphemios."

Euphemios waits for the chatter and whispers to die down. "I repeat my question. Is there a second for Kylone, otherwise known as Simon Redman?"

"I second the nomination of Kylone," Theseus says from behind Kylone. "I have heard why he had to go in hiding. He still has his sentence of exile hanging over him, and should at least be given the opportunity to leave of his own volition. This is the only way I know of he can do so openly."

Kylone watches Diomedes closely. His darkness perceptibly pales, enough to indicate he knew about the assassination attempt. Theseus' life could now be in danger. "I have told a few others besides Priest Theseus."

"And yet they have not come forward?" Skiron intervenes.

"With good reason," Kylone replies.

"I can second that," Dirk adds.

Skiron glances from one man to the other before nudging Euphemios. "Proceed."

"Is there a third for the nomination of Kylone?"

Patricianna opens her mouth but is beaten to it.

"I third the nomination of Kylone for Archdeacon," Thyone says from the back of the room.

Diomedes rises from his seat. "What the hell are you doing?"

"What is right," Thyone replies. "If Theseus is right, then Kylone should be allowed to leave Miranda without hindrance. This is the least we can do. But I suspect there is more going on than we have been told. I want the truth, like every self-respecting priest here will do. We, as a community on this harsh moon, can only survive by telling the truth."

Her speech surprises Kylone. He turns to look at her. She is trembling. A female priest rushes over to give her a hug of comfort. Through the furore of people talking he mouths a clear 'thank you' to her.

"Quiet," Euphemios says loudly.

The clamour continues.

"Quiet," he shouts.

Those closest to him start to calm down, but it does not lessen the cacophony.

"Quiet," he booms above the noise.

People finally settle.

"Are there any other objections to Kylone?"

The unease and excitement magnify the quietest sounds of the ventilation system, breathing and people moving uncomfortably in their seats. Nobody speaks a word.

"The nomination of Simon Redman, otherwise known as Kylone, formerly Priest Kylone for Archdeacon is accepted. Are there any other nominations?"

Nobody stands or says anything.

"I declare the nominations closed," Euphemios says at last. "As there are two contenders, there will be a blind voting session at a time to be announced within a week after the ballot arrangements can be put in place. In the meantime Archdeacon Ariadne will continue in post. This session of the Assembly is now at an end."

Kylone closes his eyes and reclaims a calming peace.

He is glad that the stress of this meeting did not push him into his rockborne vision, which means he can control it even in publicly stressful situations. A smile creeps onto his face. This is not the end of sorting out the mess Diomedes and Chynoweth have made in a world they hardly understand – though the link between them still needs to be proven – but it is the end of the beginning.

The volume of indistinguishable words breaks through into his peace. It is time to start putting things right. First off he has a few apologies to make, to Dirk, Patricianna, Doc Acheson for a start. And then will come the thanks.

Only then can he concentrate on dealing with Diomedes, his cronies, Chynoweth and the mining accidents.

CHAPTER 10

Morning rush hour is at its height in the Arden town plaza. People crowd the tables for breakfast and jostle along packed pathways. The noise is loud with chatter, footsteps, the clinking of faux china and cutlery, and the clicks and beeps of payments and auto-acknowledgements of orders. The unaccustomed warmth and stale air gives Kylone the perception of being unnaturally hemmed in; the smell of coffee, teas and freshly cooked food encourages him onward.

He is thankful at experiencing life like this. With Theseus making it clear at his nomination that he can use this opportunity to voluntarily go into exile, there is no reason why the Chynoweth guards and the Guardians of History should try to kill him. He will be gone soon enough without putting them to the trouble of making him go.

That is what he likes to believe.

He actually suspects Dirk and Meriel between them have somehow put a discrete guarding service in place for him and let High Priest Diomedes know.

Early for his appointment with Coroner Sylvana, he shuffles round a miner, steps into a space left by a farmhand entering a café and is crowd-pressured to follow her. He searches for a bypass route through the Viennese's elegant tables. Dirk sits at one with three large cups, steam rising only from the one closest to him.

A huge grin snaps onto Dirk's face. His hand waves at Kylone and then taps the empty space on the settee next to him.

Kylone wants to get out of the chaos and into the quiet of Sylvana's office sooner rather than later.

Dirk puts his hands on the table as if he is about to push himself up.

With an inward groan, Kylone knows he is not going

escape his friend's attention. He quickly meanders his way through three tiers of tables and drops down to sit beside him. "Can't this wait?" he half-shouts.

"No." Dirk's blue eyes sparkle pure mischief.

"You're a caffeine junkie."

"Yes."

A waitress places a cup of lemon balm tea at his elbow. He stares at it, its message clear: he is not going to like what the Chief Compineer has to say.

"Thought you might need it," Dirk says.

He has a flash of rockborne talent showing the hollowness inside the table, but quickly brings his unease back under control. He pushes the tea away. "Get it over with."

"Sylvana's asked me, Doc Acheson and Alva to join you for the first part of your meeting. They're meeting me here so we can go in as a group."

"I guessed as much about you. Why the Doc and Alva?"

"How in the nine hells of ice should I know?"

"What?"

"I've been too busy making a list and connectivity map. And listening to your Priest Xuthus. He's really good at lectures, isn't he?"

Kylone blinks once and becomes very still. In contrast his mind is a furnace of speculation. Dirk is far from his normal self, being truly overstretched for the first time since he walked into his life in the chapel. This whole thing may have started with trying to answer why there had been so many mining accidents, but has spread into several major issues: mapping of the fourth spatial dimension from verbal description and photographs, and assessing its impact on Mirandan mining operations; investigating Chynoweth's running down of mining on the moon and their associated criminal activities to maximise profit; tracing the spread of the avarice disease into the Priesthood, particularly among the Guardians of History, and how it held back societal development here. He had coped with all this without having even a hint of being rockborne. It was a measure of the man that he accepted he was limited in some ways without complaint and just got on with the job. It is not surprising it finally got too much for him.

"Want me to stop Xuthus giving you his lectures?" Kylone asks.

"Hell no. It's the only time I get to relax. Lets me forget about me and my issues. He's very entertaining. How's your campaign to become Archdeacon going?"

"Give me a chance. I've only had one full day at it. And besides I have to sort other things out." He does not go on to say he feels he has been given a breathing space before at worst he goes into voluntary exile.

"Why should I? Diomedes won't. And you'd make a rather good, if annoying Archdeacon."

Dirk has a point.

It dawns on him he does not know how to campaign. Come to that, he does not do big organisation politics either. One basic quick step he can do is send out a priest-wide video to state his case. What he has to say will depend on what Coroner Sylvana will reveal and allow him to say publicly. He strokes his wispy beard, which has had the dye removed.

"What issues do you have?" Kylone asks, diverting the focus away from himself and his lack of campaign.

Dirk slowly shakes his head. "You don't want to know. I'm a mess, a ginormous one that even the best of your counselling Priesthood can't untangle."

"I guessed that much some time ago. So was I, but Patricianna taught me things can be unravelled given time and effort, step by single step."

"It'd take too long in my case."

"Even so, sorting out even one problem makes life easier. For instance what is up between you and Doc Acheson? There's something there judging by your reactions when we were last in her surgery together."

Dirk's lips press together while his eyes water a little.

Whatever is troubling his friend, it is painful; Kylone's counselling training kicks in; he waits quietly for an answer to be eased out.

"She's one of the few people I can talk to without getting irritated," Dirk finally says. "But it's best I keep my distance in her case."

Kylone frowns. This does not fully tie in with his memories of their meetings. The tetchiness between them seemed to be always there, as if the Doc were permanently annoyed by his friend, and yet… it was tolerated on his part, and hers. "Why don't you let yourselves become better friends?"

Dirk snorts and stares into his coffee.

"After all," Kylone continues, "it's not like family who you can't choose."

A spasm of pain flashes across Dirk's face. "That's digging deep."

"Yes. It took me a long time to really understand the old saying applied to more than blood relatives. It applies to those you fall in love with. You've got no choice about those either." Kylone wishes he has more time with Alva, but he does not think he can become Archdeacon. The vote will be the cut-off time for his freedom and he must leave Miranda by then. "You've just got to live with the love choices made for you."

"Live with?"

"Yes, live with. There's no other way. You can bet the love of your life will feel the same and unless there's some impossible obstacle you can't overcome, you'll inevitably get together." Kylone finally takes a sip of his tea to dampen his increasing sadness.

Dirk stands and waves his hand wildly to attract someone's attention. Doc Acheson in a green medic's silk breaks through the pathway crowd and works round the tables towards them. Behind her is Alva in the grey silk of a Chynoweth assistant. A bubble of quiet crowd attention encircles them as they pass. Alva stops and eyes Dirk and then Acheson, her jaw dropping slightly.

Kylone checks back on Dirk. His eyes are like twinkling blue diamonds and his face is a picture of pure happiness focussed on the Doc; Dirk hadn't been joking when he had called the Doc his love in her surgery. Their chat must have just triggered something in him to release his inhibitions.

Maybe one of the threads tying Dirk in knots has just unravelled.

Alva catches his eye. She is nodding for him to move away and head towards Sylvana's office.

He stands as Acheson comes to a halt at the other side of the table.

"Marry me?" Dirk asks her.

Surprise hits Kylone.

Darkness starts to cloud Acheson's face.

Something needs to be done fast to stop them having a bitter argument; Kylone says the first thing that comes into his mind. "Oh for goodness sake. You need to be more eloquent than that. Think of Xuthus' priestly lecture, do the same only praise instead of condemn. Tell her how you feel about her."

Both Dirk's and Acheson's eyes turn on him.

"He's not that bad an ogre," Kylone blurts to the Doc. "Err… I think I've said enough."

They continue to stare at Kylone making him feel uncomfortable, more like a complete stranger. He steps towards Alva and they both get past a couple of tables.

Her grin turns into giggling. "Well, that came as a pleasant surprise, though I'm not sure why he chose this moment."

Kylone has no wish to discuss Dirk's confidences with Alva, especially if the subject turns more personal. "Shall we get to the Coroner's office and not wait for them?"

Alva nods and leads the way, shouldering her way through tables, chairs and people. Just as they arrive at the entrance a distant cheer can be heard over the hubbub.

"I think that's a yes," Alva says.

Kylone closes his eyes. "He's never going to let me live my interference down."

"No, but it'll add to your priestly reputation."

"I'm not a priest, not anymore."

"Doesn't stop you having a reputation."

As if his life is not confusing enough. "I suppose I'm stuck with that."

He follows the tinkle of her laughter away from the noise and aromas of everyday life. Coroner Sylvana is waiting beside a ceiling-to-floor screen of a still pseudo-receptionist. She is in the Coroner's uniform of a dark charcoal silk with crimson bands. Her pendant adds to her red. This interview is already being recorded for evidence purposes.

"Sorry, we're late," Kylone says.

"You're not. I'm expecting two others."

"They're getting engaged, so they might be late," Alva says.

"Are they?" Sylvana pauses, her face remaining serious. "No matter. There are some issues I can deal with without their presence. Receptionist, please direct Doctor Acheson and Chief Compineer Schimmeratzski immediately to office three when they arrive."

The receptionist comes alive. "Duly noted. Are there any other instructions?"

"Yes, please block out my schedule for the rest of today as booked. Any emergency appointments should be referred to the standby Coroner."

"Understood, Coroner Sylvana."

"You're not expecting our interview to take all day, are you?" Kylone asks.

"Far from it," Sylvana says. "If my guesses are anywhere near their mark, I expect to be busy sorting out the consequences well into tomorrow." She leads the way to her office.

The damp freshness of the air hits Kylone as soon as he enters the office. The plants in the basket shelves look more mature than his last visit.

They take their seats, Sylvana in an armchair facing the settee on which Alva and Kylone sit. There is coffee and tea in flasks waiting to be served and beakers already filled with water on the table between them.

"First off, Kylone, would you be willing to make a formal statement on Chynoweth's guards trying to kill you?"

"Yes, but it feels like a lifetime ago. I may have forgotten some details."

"Just the basics will do for what I need."

He tells his story from when the mag-pod's door opened on the Transit Hall to the moment he was shot at in the Snowdrift Chasm, without mentioning how he used his rockborne talent. He is about to describe how he learnt to swim through the snow-sand when Sylvana put her hand up to silence him.

"Pendant," she says. "Does the work the Chief Compineer did for me identify beyond doubt who Kylone's assailants were in Snowdrift Chasm?"

"Yes."

"Would that evidence be legally valid in a court?"

"Yes."

"Are they on Miranda now?"

"Yes."

"Please issue their arrest warrants on a charge of attempted murder to Deputy Security Chief McCluskey and his team only. I want those three arrested simultaneously at noon today. Given the seriousness of this crime, please arrange a full three Coroner trial excluding myself as soon as the advocates for both sides have gathered their evidence and no later than four months hence."

The silence gives Kylone the chance to pour some coffee for them all.

"The arrest warrants have been issued and acknowledged as received by Deputy Security Chief McCluskey. I will follow-up on necessary procedures to set up the trial," the pendant finally reports.

"That's the easy bit done," Sylvana says.

"Won't their arrest alert their criminal bosses that we have started identifying who they are?"

"Absolutely. It's why I asked for the arrests to be done by McClusky and his team. I've been assured by the Chief Compineer they're definitely not part of the conspiracy, and believe me, he was more thorough on that point than I would've been. The arrests will be discrete and simultaneous. McClusky and I have already agreed on that."

"Even so, their bosses will be sure to find out soon."

"Agreed, but not before I'll persuade one of your would-be killers to give me their names in return for a sentence reduction. Facing the possibility of a firing squad does tend to concentrate the mind, so I've been told." Sylvana tilts her head slightly. "Is that true?"

Kylone has to take a moment to think back to his decision to face a Truth Tribunal, and then throwing it. "Not quite. It's more forcing you to understand yourself better, and therefore clarifying your true aims in life."

"Thank you for that insight. It'll help me to be more persuasive with your would-be killers."

"Wouldn't Dirk's evidence alone be sufficient?" Alva asks.

"I want the case against them to be beyond any possible doubt. That's best done with two completely separate bases of evidence. This is going to come as a shock to Mirandans, so the case has to be beyond solid."

"That makes sense," Kylone says.

"Of course, we will need you available for the trial for cross-examination purposes."

"That might be difficult."

"Setting up an off-moon vid-link can be arranged."

"That's not the problem."

Furrows form on Sylvana's forehead. "I thought you intended to leave before the Archdeacon vote is in? That's what Priest Theseus implied at the Assembly."

"Dirk's been trying to persuade me to become the Archdeacon, without exactly telling me why. Guess I have to do something about that."

"That might get you a few votes," Alva chips in with a look of worry on her face.

Sylvana eyes him as if waiting for further explanation.

Kylone resolutely says nothing.

"Pendant," Sylvana says, "the rest of this session is under lock and key until such time as I give permission for it to be made public."

"Understood," the pendant replies.

"Doctor Acheson has summarised the results of the

medical research you two instigated. Basically quite a few rockborne have not been performing to their full strength. When I got the Chief Compineer to map their under-performance it was limited to a few levels."

These words unlock a rapid cascade of cause-and-effects in Kylone's mind. His eyes widen as he comes to the final conclusions. "Are you telling me that the performance of the rockborne is so reliable that it can be used to warn of the presence of that damping crystal Alva and I first noticed out on the plain below the chapel?"

"Yes. Let me make this more personal for you. Do you remember your first find?"

"No rockborne forgets their first experience. Of course I do. The Moebius gem."

"And didn't you and your crew move mines shortly after that?"

"Yes to Xeno where…" He still could not easily talk about his mining accident. "Meriel found the crystal."

"There's no need to go into detail. But the point is you underperformed as a rockborne for most of your mining career without realising it."

Kylone accepts this as true, but finds he is grappling with the consequences of the miners – and hence, Chynoweth – not getting the best out of the rockborne finding valuable gems and ores. He only has to review his own past carrying the guilt for his fiancée's death – when it was not his fault – to know how devastating it will be for some.

"Wait," Alva intervenes. "What about Raoul, my dead husband? Did his death occur in one of those areas?"

Sylvana pauses. "Pendant, do you know the answer and if so what is it?"

"Yes and yes."

A sob escapes Alva.

Kylone wants to comfort her, but all he can do in this formal witness hearing is place a hand over hers and squeeze it gently. "We don't know if it was because the rockborne could not read properly."

"I know I'm jumping ahead of myself." She takes a deep breath. "I'm all right."

"There may be more to that damping crystal," Sylvana says. "The Chief Compineer has not yet given me his full results, but he looked into the crystal's distribution with respect to the entrance rings you mapped."

By the seriousness of her face, he guesses he is not going to like what comes next. "What does he suspect?"

"There are a high proportion of the rings you've mapped where that crystal is known to be close by, too high for him to be comfortable. So he looked into how that crystal could be produced and he was genuinely puzzled."

"Was?" Alva asks.

"The only way he can make it is in four-dimensional space."

"That would prove the fourth spatial dimension is real."

"Not so fast. Not finding a method in three-dimensional space doesn't mean it can't be done, just that he hasn't found out how."

"Seven hells of fire!" Kylone explodes. "You're telling us that the presence of that crystal could be an indicator of a ring nearby."

"Yes, *could* being the operative verb."

He understands her and Dirk's caution. Even so his mind probes the consequences of this tentative theory. His eyes widen at a surprise conclusion. "If that crystal has to be made in four spatial dimensions, then it will be found close to the rings. It doesn't give us rockborne much of a chance of finding them."

"Which would explain why it's taken such a long time to discover them," Alva says.

"It adds up to a coherent picture of what has happened," Kylone says. "Even so, the Guardians of History should've been looking into the correlation between rockborne performance and mineral distribution as routine."

"We don't know they didn't," Sylvana says. "It's one of the areas still under investigation."

"Though given what's happened to me…"

"Yes, it does suggest High Priest Diomedes knows of the correlation."

Kylone instinctively knows he does. He sits up straight. "Which areas are they mining now where the rockborne are underperforming?"

"Carbo Level 6, Xeno and Lantha. Do you want me to close them down with an emergency executive order pending Council discussion?"

This will affect a large number of miners. They will lose their income, be on the breadline and tensions could rise enough to cause riots and untold damage. Those mines must stay open. "Yes, but let's make this close down shorter. I'll go down to examine them and identify where they can work safely. Then it'll be up to you and the Council to follow my advice."

"I'll join you to act as confirmation," Alva volunteers.

"Thanks. I'll start with Carbo Six at two this afternoon and will keep you," he nods to Sylvana, "and Dirk informed of progress."

"Pendant, set emergency executive orders in progress to close the mines Carbo Level 6, Xeno and Lantha, immediately and call a General Council meeting."

"Closing down orders and council calling notices have been issued," the pendant replies.

"Be careful," Sylvana says. "Chynoweth will not thank any of us for this. You'll need some protection in the mines."

"You're right. Please have Miners Cris and Torvald join me. They're good in a fight if it comes to that."

"Pendant please send out civic service duty orders for Miners Cris and Torvald Polhem to come here for one o'clock."

"Civic service duty orders sent."

Dirk rushes in followed by the Doc. "What have I missed?"

"Congratulations to the both of you. We've the rest of the morning to get all our formal statements recorded," Kylone says.

"And this is the man who thinks he hasn't got it in him to be Archdeacon?" Dirk grins.

***

Kylone, leading Alva and the Polhem brothers, strides into the Carbo Level 6's hub and hits a wall of noise, heat, human sweat, kicked-up dust and miners. Their husky voices and clipped words reverberate tension round the room. Worries about when they can return to work and be able to feed their families are understandable. A hint of a red glow from his chest confirms the witness pendant he wears is active and he has the deputised authority of a Coroner. He waits to be noticed.

An outward ripple of people turns towards him and become quiet.

"So this closure is your damned fault," a mocking voice shouts from the other side of the hub.

Turning faces point to the source. Diomedes is a couple of steps up to control room. The darkness on his face makes even the black of his priest's silk look pale. A pathway opens between them as if to let the high priest through. It reveals two priests standing attentively at the bottom of the steps. The Hubmaster, bulking out her grey uniform, exits the control room to tower over the man. Her face is red with anger.

"I'm here to get as much of this level working as soon as possible." Kylone bites back any more comments about why because questions will only delay him. "Hubmaster, please allocate spacesuits for me and Assistant Alva."

"You heard him," the Hubmaster says into the control room. To Kylone she adds: "What else do you need?"

"You're not fit to go into the mine," Diomedes intervenes taking a step towards Kylone.

"He's been seen down on Level 7 doing all right," a woman shouts.

"That stupid story."

"I've been able to return to the mines," Kylone says, "ever since some of Chynoweth's guards tried to kill me at Snowdrift Chasm. Now can we get on with sorting out this level?"

An explosion of noise is far louder than when he entered. An overtone of a woman's voice saying, "Quiet, quiet!" becomes clearer as people turn their attention on her. Meriel stands on something to push her head and shoulders above the rest in front of the sickbay's green partition.

Kylone is surprised Meriel is here. Her practical common sense will help calm the crowd.

"I don't like this any more than you," Meriel continues. "We need to work to survive. We also need to survive to work. Kylone would not be involved in this shutdown unless he has a damned good reason. He's fighting for your survival." She points to one person, then one after another. "And yours and yours. He's trying to save your lives. All of them."

Alva joins her on the podium. "Friends, you know my husband, Miner Raoul Larsson died saving his crewmates and is buried in the Heroes Gallery."

A murmur of agreement passes through the crowd. Kylone is astonished at how confident she is. Need of some sort must be driving her.

"I asked the question nobody dared to ask," Alva continues. "Why are there more mining accidents now when mining is as easy as it was centuries ago? That's what Raoul had told me. Kylone took up that question. He took it to the Guardians of History, but was told it was not a top priority."

A growl riffs through the miners towards the priests.

"Kylone did what he could. It's been a long twisting tunnel to get here. It's too late for my Raoul, but this closedown is necessary to save your lives. Let's do what we can to get some of this level open. Kylone, what do you need?"

The spotlight is back on him. His nerves along with his rockborne vision flare and fade in a moment. Time is not his friend and he must move on. "The rockborne currently working this level, Meriel, the control room staff, Cris and Torvald Polhem behind me, and you, Assistant Alva." He emphasises her title so others would assume she is working for the Chief Compineer rather than give the real reason for her being here. "The rest of you, go home. Report for work as usual tomorrow unless you receive a message not to. Meriel, given your experience, could you organise shift rotas for tomorrow once we've found out where the mining is safe on this level?"

"That's Chynoweth's job," the Hubmaster says.

"Coroner Sylvana is, as I speak, arresting some of Chynoweth's admin staff on charges of conspiracy to murder and profiteering by planning for deaths, among many lesser crimes. This is the quickest way to guaranteeing your work continuity. Meriel, are you willing to organise shifts for tomorrow under these circumstances?"

"Sounds like it's better me than somebody else. Yes. Miners report to me here tomorrow morning unless I contact you to say otherwise."

A general murmur of assent passes through the miners.

Diomedes glares at Meriel. "You, you're the secret Union Leader. I invoke my rights as a High Priest. Arrest that woman for incitement to revolution."

The two priests step towards her to find their way blocked by a wall of miners. "Let us through," the female priest shouts.

"Stop," Kylone orders. "The Coroner's Office is recording this. This overrides the High Priest's authority, which can only be exerted in the absence of a Coroner or their deputy. If any charges are to be pressed, the Coroner will see to it in due course. We have more important things to do now."

"You? A deputy?" Diomedes glares at him. "You're a criminal and can't take such a position."

Cris and Torvald edge between the miners to stand nose to nose with the priests. "Leave," Cris says. "All three of you."

The two priests look at Diomedes. The male priest shakes his head slightly and walks slowly towards Kylone. "Come on," he says, "there's nothing we can do here."

The female priest follows him, making a show of dragging her feet. Once they are into the tunnel, the miners' determined faces turn to Diomedes.

"As Hubmaster, I'm ordering you to leave. Your presence is no longer welcome."

Diomedes twists his head round. "What?"

"Go," the Hubmaster says more loudly.

"You can't…" His face goes from dark to dull white. A slight tremble escapes his shoulders. He takes one slow step towards the tunnel, his eyes glancing left and right, then hurries through the gap in the miners to stop by Kylone. "You're finished Kylone. You and your diseased so-called rockborne mind. The priests won't vote for you after this."

"That is up to the priests."

"We'll see." Diomedes stomps off into the tunnel.

"He's really lost it," Torvald says unwinding his fists.

"All of you except those Kylone asked to stay, leave," the Hubmaster says.

Kylone makes his way against the flow of noisy people to the suiting area and pulls one off the rack that his name lit up against.

"Excuse me," a man says from behind.

Kylone turns to face a young woman and a notably older man already in mining suits except for the helmets. Their bone structures are similar enough to suggest they belong to the same family. "What can I do for you?"

"It's Miner Serena Vaughan here," the man points to his petite companion. "My daughter's one of the rockborne you asked to stay behind. Only…"

The worry in their faces warns him to be gentle and take time with them. "What's the issue?"

"She never goes into this mine without me," the father says. "She's prone to fainting fits and I…"

Kylone does not need to hear the rest; she is paying the price for being a strong rockborne. "Hubmaster," he yells across the emptying workspace, "Miner," he looks at the man.

"Richard."

"Richard Vaughan will be accompanying his daughter as usual."

"Good call," the Hubmaster replies from inside the control room.

Kylone notices their shoulders relax downward and relief on their faces. He is the one that is now worried. This could be dangerous for her. The question is by how much? "Pendant, where on the A-K-M scale I agreed with Coroner Sylvana is Miner Serena Vaughan?" They had named this experimental scale to avoid giving away it was a measure of the overall retina thickness a person has; A is for Alva, K for Kylone and M for Meriel who has no rockborne capability. If the thickness does not work as an indicator of the true strength of rockborne talent, then most people will not be any wiser.

"A third of the way down from A to K," the pendant replies.

She is stronger than he had thought; not as good as Alva but much better than him. He should have heard about her and bites his lips while figuring out what to do.

"What's wrong?" Richard asks.

Kylone needs more information. "What's your rockborne history?" he asks her.

"I started showing signs when I was fifteen on Level 2 and they immediately transferred me here to Level 6."

"When did you have your first fainting fit?"

Her eyes widen. She glances at her father. "Shortly after I arrived here at 6."

"Hells of ice and dust." He wonders how many more potentially very talented rockborne had been pushed to working too close to the damping crystal. They would have never had a chance to achieve their full potential. He places a hand on the wall to help support him and closes his eyes.

"What's wrong?" Richard asks again.

A thought snakes into his consciousness; if Chynoweth was wanting big profits they would have let the rockborne work in those areas they were more successful. The Guardians of History's work would certainly have picked up on this and told them. Why did Chynoweth then force Serena to work here on Level 6? It could have been a mistake.

"Did Chynoweth give you a reason for transferring to Level 6?"

Richard shakes his head.

"The assistant said it was on the advice of the Guardians of History," Serena says. "That's why I stuck with this level."

At last, a definite link between the Guardians of History and Chynoweth on directing the rockborne, one that can no longer be denied. "Can you remember who the assistant was?"

"Yuri? Sorry, can't really remember."

The name is so unusual that Kylone pinpoints the Assistant who took him to Dirk's office the first time he went there. "Could it be Jürgen?"

"Might be. You know him?"

"Only met him the once. Pendant, send this conversation that I have had with Miner Serena Vaughan to the Chief Compineer and Coroner Sylvana, marked as extremely urgent."

Father and daughter look at each other, puzzled, and then at him.

Kylone stares beyond them into nowhere as a cascade of conclusions fall into place. Strong rockborne were pushed to work in places where their performance was dampened. The Guardians of History would have identified those places through their analysis, but not known the cause; the damping crystal and the consequence of it being near the transit rings between different three-dimensional worlds.

Rockborne have a tendency to head for the nearest mineable prize, whether it be a precious gem or an ore deposit. But the nearest did not mean profitable. A lot of times the nearest prize was the lesser prize, and should have been ignored; the stronger the rockborne, the greater the monetary loss if they got it wrong. It made commercial sense to dampen the strongest rockborne away from pointing to the distant mining prizes. But that could have easily been done by asking them not to go drilling more than certain distances depending on the material they were working through.

So, why force them to move?

Of course – Chynoweth wanted them for precision close-to analysis to cut out as much of the valuable ores as possible. The rockborne are cheaper to use than the sophisticated instruments that would give similar results. Maximising profits was what this was all about.

High Priest Diomedes, the Guardian of History would have been party to the analysis and discussions with Chynoweth on using the rockborne like this. He must have known about the suffering it caused. Yet he did nothing to alleviate it, as he should have done.

Which can really only mean one thing.

There was something in it for Diomedes.

He shakes his head, wondering how he could he have missed the link between the power-grab and being seen to order things in the mines; all show, for a false profit. It would not surprise Kylone if Diomedes was also taking a cut of the profits from Chynoweth.

Profits that could have been so much more if they had done the right thing as Dirk had originally suggested: that had the rockborne been given their freedom to work where they wanted they could have slowed the rundown of mining on Miranda as they were doing up to ten years ago.

He cannot let a man putting his own greed ahead of others' welfare become Archdeacon. He, along with his co-conspirators, for that is what they are, must share their blame in Selma's death and others'.

His gaze focusses back onto Serena. She too has been cheated. Like all strong rockborne, she has never been given a chance to become sure of her talent and come to rely on it. They have missed out on sensing beautiful worlds beyond most people's reach. Anger rises up inside him for her and others' ability being stunted, and what the effects of that will turn out to be on them. Maybe their crippling may affect other parts of their lives in ways nobody can anticipate.

His talent flares up. The spacesuits around become translucent shapes of different types of intertwined tubing sandwiched between two thin layers. Bodies turn into compact interconnected organs packed in and around skeletons. The suit racks switch to being hollowed tubes with wiring and fully visualised supply reservoirs. His talent is definitely becoming stronger. He puts this down to practice and accepting what he can do. He snaps his eyes shut and puts a hand against the rack to steady himself.

A hand gently squeezes his shoulder. "Are you all right?" Meriel asks.

He forces his nervousness back down and takes a few moments to open his eyes. "I should've listened to you all those years ago. You're right. My accident wasn't my fault. We may end up bringing charges of mass manslaughter."

Their faces turn pale. Serena puts her hand over her mouth and runs off to the sickbay. Her father follows her. Kylone lets the remaining five people around him recover, their faces turning from shock to grim determination. The only one he does not know is a bald tall brown-eyed man. "You the other rockborne on this level?"

"Yes, Miner Connor Fraser."

He glances at his A-K-M scale. A C has appeared well below the K. Connor is a very weak rockborne and will not therefore suffer the fainting fits like Serena. "Good to have you with us. Let's finish suiting up. I want you to register where you get any rockborne talent flashes and where you feel access to your talent is deadened or out of your reach. Don't tell anyone here of your reactions until we get back, but put it on record and transmit your comments real-time to Coroner Sylvana's office."

"Understood."

By the time they enter the big airlock as a group, Serena has joined them, her face grimmer than the rest.

Her father is close beside her, his attention focussed solely on her.

***

Kylone, with Xuthus at his side, enters the Green Room. The Archdeacon sits on an ordinary chair with her head supported by a hand, her chair of status having been moved to the chapel ready for the election. She is thinner, her cheeks hollow and her eyes have dark rings. Patricianna stands beside her, looking older and more frail than usual. He guesses keeping the Archdeacon going even in her fractured way has taken its toll on his old counsellor.

"Why haven't you left Miranda?" Patricianna snaps.

"I wouldn't be a very good Archdeacon if I did," Kylone replies.

"Like hell you'll be. You haven't done one iota of canvassing amongst the priests."

"She's right," Xuthus adds.

"And shutting down sections in the mines hasn't helped your cause either," Patricianna continues.

"I'm aware, but that's not why I'm here," Kylone says. "Archdeacon, I need to know what hold High Priest Diomedes has over you. If you don't tell me now, it will come out in the public election debate."

"How in the nine hells of ice can it if you don't know?" Xuthus asks.

"Can't you see the poor woman is broken? Isn't it enough she's going blind?" Patricianna yells.

Kylone looks eye-to-eye at the Archdeacon. Beneath her eyes' layer of dullness is a glint of awareness, an intelligence briefly giving itself away. He ups his tension just enough to see deeper into them. Her retinas are milkier than he expected, almost totally opaque. He glances into Patricianna's eyes. They definitely are more translucent than the Archdeacon's. He checks Xuthus', same again. If he can see her eyes with his talent, she has probably seen the same in his own. Whether she can interpret what she views and deduce the consequences is another issue. He calms his nerves and drops back to his normal sight.

That glint of liveliness means her depression and illness has been an act. Why? If she pretends to be going blind then she can claim not to see, which would include beyond the surfaces. Nobody could then benefit from her talent. So what?

The only open use on Miranda is by the rockborne. The other use is uncovering secrets kept behind walls, in shut drawers and closed rooms. Diomedes must have caught her out. He could claim she was a liar and that would have been the end of her Archdeaconry.

"You slipped up with Diomedes. He could show you up as a liar couldn't he?" Kylone asks.

"Leave her alone," Patricianna says. "Go!" She points to the door.

"The Alva problem?" Xuthus whistles.

"What problem? Both of you go."

A slight smile creeps onto the Archdeacon's thin lips with all the hallmarks of cunning deviousness, sorrow and kindness rolled into one. She knows.

She must have deduced that priests unable to take the Greening ceremony were due to their thickened retinas. His own thickened retinas would have been obvious to her. From there so would have the consequence that the rockborne had the same 'capabilities' as herself and those priests. To her, he became an obvious conduit to getting closer ties between the Priesthood and the rockborne. Her motive? He is not sure, but making the Priesthood more useful to the miners is an obvious one. That is why she started pushing him to get reconnected, the first step being to take Miner Raoul Larsson's funeral.

That changed the day she discovered he was getting help from Dirk. She needed the Chief Compineer's help as well, to get to the bottom of what Diomedes was up to and to find a way of stopping him, and more personally, get her off the High Priest's blackmail.

He frowns. Sure it was all conniving manipulation, but he has never known the Archdeacon to do that for purely personal gain. If she could get these talented priests working with the rockborne... his eyes widen at the whole idea. Working together, they would make the mining industry better for society.

"Well played, Archdeacon," Kylone says.

"I don't understand," Xuthus says.

The Archdeacon sits up straight. "It's taken you long enough to get there, Kylone."

Patricianna looks wildly from one to the other. "Ariadne?"

"Now you know what being an Archdeacon is really like..." She keeps her eyes locked with Kylone's. She is subliminally asking him if he still wants to become head of the Priesthood.

Behind that question is the implication he will get his ordinary priest status returned to him regardless of whether he is elected Archdeacon. It certainly would give him a chance to finish the mosaic in the chapel, something that has become part of him.

However, following this path of comfortable existence would make him guilty of failing others. There is no choice. He is about to say yes when he realises there is another hidden dialogue: can he cope with the politics and the multiple layers of meaning? Politics yes: Xuthus had pointed out he spoke from the heart and that is all that is needed. Multi-layered meanings? He has come a long way from the naïve priest the Archdeacon approached to take his first Hero's funeral. "I can understand why you would wish to take a back seat."

"Good. I'm glad we're in agreement. Computer, switch to record formal session of Archdeacon's business and implement instructions."

"Recording and standing by," the computer's baritone voice echoes in the silence.

"Reinstate Simon Redman, formally known as Kylone, as a priest."

"You can't do that," Xuthus says.

"Send my witness statement that has been under lock and key to all the priests in this room. They are free to do what they wish with that statement." She turns to Xuthus. "I think you'll find that covers your point more than adequately as it exonerates Priest Kylone of one of the charges at his Truth Tribunal."

"Oh."

The Archdeacon grins. "It's been years since you've sounded so surprised. Nice to know I can still keep you on your toes. I suspect you'll find your new Archdeacon even more surprising than me."

"I don't understand."

The Archdeacon turns back to Kylone. She nods to the computer's box on the wall. "I presume I've given your pigtailed friend enough time to dig up dirt for a certain priest to be arrested in front of the whole council on criminal charges?"

"Yes." He is glad to see the Archdeacon back to her normal self. He would have called her a friend, but she has been more of a mentor and cannot ever really be trusted again. Her motives may be good, but her demonstrable deviousness will always make him question why she does things.

"Nine hells of ice," escapes Xuthus' lips.

"Ariadne," Patricianna croaks. "What's going on?"

"All will become clear shortly. I'm only sorry I had to dupe you as well as many others."

"You mean all this depression… was an act?"

"Yes. Computer. Please let it be known to the Priesthood that I of my own volition formally endorse Priest Kylone as my successor." She stands. "I think it's time for us to go to the chapel. Priest Patricianna, may I pretend to lean on your arm one last time?"

Shock is written all over Patricianna's face. "You want me to continue this falsehood?"

"Of necessity. We have a much bigger problem to root out."

"What're you talking about?"

"I've been told there's a rather long list of criminal charges," Kylone says.

"Who…" Patricianna's eyes widen. "You don't

mean..." She places her hand on the back of the chair to steady herself. "Good grief. How did I miss all that?"

"How much real contact have you had with him?" the Archdeacon asks.

"I... You mean he avoided me?"

The Archdeacon nods and holds out her arm for support. Colour slowly returns to Patricianna's face and after a few seconds takes up her position of supporting counsellor by taking hold of the proffered arm. Together they shuffle their way through the door.

"Any other surprises I ought to know about?" Xuthus asks.

"Not yet."

"What's that supposed to mean?"

Kylone walks over to the door and says over his shoulder: "They'll be waiting for us in the chapel."

He steps into the corridor and on hearing footsteps behind him, he follows the women. The chapel doors open. The blaze of light from the room turns the Archdeacon and Patricianna into darkened shapes. Beyond them towards the front of the chapel at either side are pale heads atop the darkness of Priesthood silks. The future waits for him to take centre stage.

As he approaches the door, he glances down the corridor towards reception. The glow of the red pendant in active witness mode catches his eye. Its wearer is Coroner Sylvana who waits with Meriel and a crowd of heads behind her – no doubt a mixture of trustworthy Chynoweth guards and Union miners. He nods a signal they should join the Assembly.

With Xuthus immediately behind him and fighting to keep his nerves under control, he follows the Archdeacon and Patricianna at a respectful distance through the empty rows of chairs and the standing priests, up the aisle, coming to a halt alongside Diomedes next to the Archdeacon's chair. Xuthus moves to the side to stand behind the seated High Priests facing the clear wall. The full blue light of Uranus shines through it to liven the place up, but is absorbed by all the black.

"I'm surprised you're still here," Diomedes says quietly enough to be not heard by others.

Kylone forces a smile. "I'm not leaving Miranda."

"You won't win this election. I've seen to that."

"That's for the Priesthood to decide."

"Exactly." It comes out as sneer. "You're finished."

The Archdeacon sits down on her chair and straightens her coat while Patricianna fusses over her. She nods over to High Priest Euphemios to start the proceedings.

He stands up from chair at the corner of the High Priests. "Close the doors."

"Wait," Sylvana shouts from the back of the chapel. She and four guards take their time to walk to the front of the aisle. The rest of the guards and the miners file in to take seats behind the priests. Two guards remain standing at the entrance.

Euphemios looks nervously at the new arrivals and then at Kylone. "Did you invite these people, Kylone?"

"It's Priest Kylone," the Archdeacon says. "I just reinstated him."

The atmosphere switches to intense anticipation as an excited murmur ripples through the crowd.

"Nice try," Diomedes whispers to Kylone. "It won't do you any good."

"This isn't about me," he replies. "It's about you."

Diomedes gives him a startled look.

Convener Skiron coughs and comes to stand beside Euphemios. "Kylone cannot be reinstated as priest given the result of his Truth Tribunal."

Xuthus joins Skiron while fingering his wristpad. "I have just sent you and the two other jurors a testimony which exonerates Priest Kylone of one of the charges. I therefore change my judgement from guilty to not guilty for that charge."

The Convener opens a window on the sleeve and reads a file. His eyebrows steadily rise until they reach a seemingly impossible height. He pulls his eyes away from his sleeve and looks to the Archdeacon.

She sits up straight. "The file is valid."

Skiron turns to face the High Priests. "Jurors, have you read the file?"

A man stands. "I have. Like High Priest Xuthus, I must change my verdict to not guilty."

"In the light of this new evidence, I also have to change my verdict to not guilty," a woman says as she rises.

"In that case, I have no other choice than to declare Priest Kylone innocent of the charge of knowingly keeping the relevant data of Isaac Hawking's real identity from the Guardians of History due to exonerating circumstances. This verdict means that the sentence of exile must be rescinded."

The exclamations, gasps and consequent chatter crescendo.

"There's still the other two charges," Diomedes says quietly enough for only Kylone to hear. "You won't get off them that easily once I'm Archdeacon."

"We'll see," Kylone replies.

The chatter dies down.

"Did you invite these people, Priest Kylone?" Euphemios repeats while pointing to Sylvana and the people she brought with her.

"No. I was told they would be here for a specific purpose."

"What is that purpose?"

Sylvana steps up to Diomedes with two Chynoweth's guards. "High Priest Diomedes, as a senior civil jurisdiction officer I am arresting you on the criminal charges of conspiracy to murder Priest Kylone as he is now known, neglect of duty that has led to various miners' deaths and conspiracy to break up Mirandan society by helping to extract mineral resources purely for personal gain. There are numerous other civil criminal charges that will be presented to you formally in due course."

"What the hell is this?" Diomedes yells, his white hair loosening from its normal neatness by his violent shaking. "How dare you."

Sylvana remains placidly calm. "It is my duty to arrest you given all the evidence I now have."

"You've got nothing against me."

"Pendant, please summarise the evidence on the charges already announced."

"Three independent Chynoweth witnesses who have turned in detailed voluntary statements in return for leniency. Independent analysis of data accounts corroborating their statements and identifying the accused's illegal activity. Judicial analysis of the evidence gathered to date indicates there is no plausible explanation High Priest Diomedes can give that would find him innocent of all three announced charges."

Silence of disbelief weighs the room down.

Kylone has seen enough of Dirk's evidence to know beyond a doubt that Diomedes is guilty. Still, hearing the pendant's judicial analysis verdict comes as a shock of sickening realisation. Those words are as good as finding him guilty – and with that will come the death penalty, unless he turns in voluntary evidence and shows remorse.

"I would suggest we postpone the election of the Archdeacon until such time as the judicial process has been completed," Kylone hears himself say.

"No," the male juror says from among the High Priests. "We need an effective Archdeacon in place. Though it pains me to say it, High Priest Diomedes will either be busy clearing his name or he is guilty of crimes outside the Priesthood code of conduct. Either way, he is not free to take up the high office now. With all respect to Archdeacon Ariadne, she has not been performing her duties effectively these last few weeks and has rightly asked to be replaced. That leaves only one option. We declare Priest Kylone Archdeacon on condition that the election is rerun if and when High Priest Diomedes proves his innocence."

"Is that within our rules?" Euphemios asks.

"It is not excluded by our rules," Skiron replies.

"No," Diomedes murmurs. "No, this can't be happening." Tears threaten and his lips tremble. "All I've ever worked for…" He stays very still his eyes seemingly looking into nothing, as if he has switched off.

A high priest vacates her chair and gently guides him back to it to sit down.

Kylone stands akimbo watching her get Diomedes to put his head down to his knees. "What a mess," he mumbles.

"And it's one you'll get to clean up," Euphemios whispers from his side.

Kylone jerks in surprise. "Sorry I didn't notice you there."

"Didn't mean to startle you. I need to formally hold the vote that you'll be our new Archdeacon."

"What about the other charges from my Truth Tribunal?"

Euphemios purses his lips. "Let's call becoming Archdeacon your punishment."

Kylone closes his eyes. The High Priest is right. He is not a natural leader. He does his best to concentrate on what needs to be done. He locks eyes with Euphemios. "Let's get this over with."

Euphemios gives a curt nod, resumes his position beside a questioning Skiron and holds up his hands to silence the chatter. "Please hold up your hand if you wish Priest Kylone to become Archdeacon subject to having a new election if and when High Priest Diomedes proves his innocence."

Xuthus' and Theseus' hands shoot up. A few more tentatively follow, then more and more until a final flurry makes it look like a thick dust patch of them.

"Priest Kylone is elected Archdeacon by a vast majority if not unanimously," Euphemios says. He ceremoniously bows to Kylone. "Do you want to say a few words?"

Kylone shakes his hand. "Yes." Out of the corner of his eye he notices the now ex-Archdeacon stand. "Please stay there for now, High Priest Ariadne."

"But…"

"Priests," Kylone yells to quieten the noise yet again. "I'll be brief. Thank you for electing me Archdeacon. For now, please continue with your duties as before. Things will change but I would like to see it done in a sensible and orderly manner. The one immediate appointment I wish to make is for a deputy in the event I cannot be contacted. I name High Priest Xuthus as my deputy. He can make any decision I would have to in my absence." He pauses for breath while a round of clapping takes place. "One other thing. Will all those who cannot take the Greening ceremony please arrange an appointment with Doc Acheson for medical tests. You will be needed to assist the rockborne in the mines whose workload has suddenly increased."

The audience needs to absorb what has already gone on and many will be too numb to take in the incredible truth about the fourth dimension and its entry rings.

"Wait," Skiron says. "Are you telling us that those who can't cope with the Greening are rockborne?"

"Very likely. Those medical tests are looking for physical characteristics that have recently been identified as unique to stronger rockborne. There are reasons why that connection was not made earlier." He did not need to go into the detail. "Had the Guardians of History not been diverted by High Priest Diomedes to other analyses for his benefit, they would have come to the same conclusion." There is much more the audience must want to know, but the chaos of having to do and explain so much at once nearly overwhelms him. "I know you will have a lot of questions. It's a long explanation that will be made public in due course. For now all I'm going to say is we have a lot to do to get Mirandan society back on its feet and thriving – but we will."

Nods and sounds of approval chorus round the audience.

"What about the Guardian of History appointment?" Skiron asks.

"For now I would like you to do it."

Shock registers on his face. "But I have no experience…"

"We need fresh management in there given they have been falling short."

"I see your point, in which case I accept, but please hurry with a new appointment."

Ideally Kylone would like to make Skiron's appointment permanent sooner rather than later, but must wait for him to realise that he, being trained in impartiality, is the best man for the job. "Now we have work to do. Meriel, a word please."

She snakes her way through the exiting priests towards him. Her thin lips warn him he is in trouble, being Archdeacon or no. "You could've warned me."

"The Archdeacon, sorry ex-Archdeacon's one. A rockborne I mean. A strong one too, given what she's demonstrated to me. Once she's recovered her appetite, which I'm pretty sure will be very soon, I'm going to appoint her in charge of the priests on loan to you."

"You knew this when?"

"I guessed a long time ago, but only became sure in our interview just now."

She chews her lips around. "All right you're forgiven this once."

"A couple of other things. Thanks for helping out with the miners. You know what I mean."

"That won't last without results… ah, now I understand why you're getting those rockborne priests to help. Since when did you become so devious?"

He is offended, but uses his priestly training to hide it. "I'm not. It's having more pieces to choose from, which can make it look like deviousness."

Another chew of the lips. "You're going to become devious if you're not now. It goes with the job."

"Meriel!"

She shrugs her shoulders. "What's the other thing?"

"Keep a watch on Diomedes."

Her face switches to one of grimness. "Wouldn't it be better to let him commit suicide?"

"If he really wants to while you're watching him, he'll find a way. Otherwise it'll be his depression doing the action for him."

"And you don't want that on your conscience. I get it."

She glances over to Diomedes who is being helped into a wheelchair by two Chynoweth guards with Sylvana looking on. "All right, I'll see to it." She wanders over to grab hold of the wheelchair's handles.

Kylone looks at his five-eighths-finished mosaic and wonders if he'll ever get the time to complete it. It has a way of soothing him that very few other things can. He makes a mental note to send out an order banning anyone from approaching him when he is on the balcony at dawn.

"Why me?" Xuthus says on approaching Kylone.

"You're better at seeing through politics than I am."

"That's blunt."

"You can't be bought or blackmailed."

"Ah!"

"You want to help Mirandans and you're the best man for the job."

Xuthus studies him. "Thank you for your confidence in me, Archdeacon—"

"Call me Kylone in private and that's an order." He knows Xuthus will get the implicit message; treat him no differently now that he's Archdeacon.

***

Kylone stares out of the Aerial Gallery above Verona Rupes. The sheer faceted cliffs opposite gleam grey-blue to silver, dimming as they descend into the shadows of the canyon. Keeping hold of the railing he looks down through the clear floor. Twenty kilometres below are the speckled edges of craters where the light sneaks in from the canyon's entrances and has been refracted upwards by ice crystals. There is a concentration of light from spacesuits immediately below him, where eager fervents have already started gathering. Otherwise it is total darkness down there. It will be another forty-five minutes before the Greening ceremony starts. He has chosen Priest Theseus to take it, as he does not want anyone to gossip about why he is here.

His fingers play on the rail. He is tense with anticipation, and keeps having to haul his sight back from the extra dimensions behind the cliff's facets: the hexagon ice columns of what he now thinks of as Kieran's rather than as the volcano world; the column he jumped up; the three entrance rings he had to pass through; the tunnel that slopes all the way back down to the triangular facet here in the cliffs.

It has been a long gruelling six months getting the mining into proper shape and the Priesthood back to prioritising the welfare of Mirandans. There had been trials to attend, witness statements to give and minor disciplinary sanctions to approve. What had both surprised and pleased him is Priest Thyone has lost her arrogance and is now acting like a priest should. He guesses the shock of losing the protection of her father has something to do with it. Chynoweth management back on Earth sacked the profiteering criminals and made what they called 'a fresh start' with a new team he had to educate in Mirandan ways. He helped Meriel, Cris, Lenny and Torvald keep the miners' frustrations in check through all the upheaval, so much so that Chynoweth recognises them as key motivators and listens to them.

He still keeps Dirk on the straight and narrow, keeping him busy with helping discover new entrance rings between the worlds and identifying the safe approach distance for Mirandans. It's enough to stop him thinking up new tricks to play on people who have really annoyed him. But he cannot take all the credit for Dirk's more amenable nature. Most of it goes to Doc Acheson, who has now moved into the condo next to his.

She has hauled him into her surgery for more tests trying to find out about how rockborne sight works. Progress has been painfully slow. Her latest theory is that a lot of the ability comes from the way the brain processes the signals from the extra retinal layering. Dirk has tried to help out where he can on how such signals might be processed, but so far there has been no match between his theories and brain neural signalling.

Other medics from around the Solar System have tried to find people with similar retinal development, and failed. Numerous theories have been suggested as to why the rockborne talent is unique to Miranda: ranging from the practical someone has to be the first and it happened to be the Mirandans; via the complicated there must be a right set of genes pushed to switch on in the Mirandan environment; to the crazy idea of the right type of Uranian light altered the composition of their eyes. Whatever is the truth, it will be up to the medics and scientists to work it out.

Likewise, Dirk and scientists from around the Solar System have made very little progress in understanding why the rings work.

Kylone is more puzzled by why other rings have not been discovered around the Solar System. There certainly has been more than enough time on Earth, Mars, the main Jovian and Saturnian moons. Why they should be unique to Miranda adds to their mystery, beauty and wondrousness. The rings are a miracle to be cherished, and every time he looks at one, he is simultaneously in awe and at one with their existence and himself.

He is finally glad to have a few precious hours to himself.

The door clicks open behind him. Familiar footsteps pad their way to beside him.

"It's as beautiful as I remember," Alva says.

He turns to look at her. "Absolutely."

She smiles at him. "Why did you ask me to come here of all places? Especially after last time…"

"I thought I'd help you navigate your rockborne vision around the structures opposite."

"We could have done that elsewhere in a less… imposing place. Wait. Won't you faint?"

"I know what I'm looking at. You haven't really had the chance to distinguish and recognise various features. I'm here to help you with that to fine-tune your beyond sight."

She takes a step back and waves her hands as if putting

up a barrier between them. "I don't want Dirk finding out I'm improving. He's already showing signs of being… let's call it more cautious around me, as if he's got something to hide. As if I would end up being in competition for his job."

Kylone pulls a couple of electrical fuses out of his belt's pocket to dangle in front of her. "It's useful having an electrician on your staff. Priest Theseus gave this place a thorough checkout for monitoring devices and removed all of them."

"Oh," she giggles, "Dirk will be so upset."

"I'd give him three days to put the itching powder in my condo. Better make it four if he and the Doc are on better than normal terms."

"He's more likely to have a go at you for being a prankster. And he'll do it in public."

"I look forward to it. But I didn't want him to overhear what I want to say."

"Archdeacon—"

"Kylone, please."

"Kylone. What's this really about?"

"You remember when you tore me off a strip in Lachlan's condo?"

"I do." She pauses. "Can we call that topic closed?"

"Not quite. I just wanted to thank you for keeping my feet on the ground. I needed that."

"Oh."

"I still need somebody to keep my feet on the ground. That's the trouble with being Archdeacon. You're always kept busy with approving this or that, talking to people to find out what's going on, getting half a story and generally going crazy piecing things together. And all it took you in Lachlan's condo was half an hour to get through to me how stupid and frightened I'd been. I need that occasional half an hour."

"Of course. What are friends for?"

Kylone realises a lot more of what he wanted to say has not been said. This is the first time in six months he has been tongue-tied. His tension rises. He sees another type of world waiting through a translucent veil of hexagons in Kieran's world. A pattern of small facets makes it look like polished rainbow rock, reminding him of all the crystals he saw on the way to see Dirk in his office.

This is the source of the gems they have been mining on Miranda. All this glinting and glittering is mesmerizingly beautiful. He takes a moment of eternity to relish the sight. This is what Alva must be seeing via her beyond sight, where the dazzle would confuse and disorientate her.

"Kylone, you all right?"

A distant voice calls him back to Miranda, to the place he wants to be. He calms down and ends up staring into her glowing green eyes, gems of far greater worth than the faceted mountain. "I love you. Will you marry me?"

She blinks, once, twice and a third time. "Is this real?"

"Very much so."

She squeals with delight, throws her arms around him and gives him a long kiss.

After a couple of minutes he breaks off. "I take it the answer is yes?"

"Of course."

Just before he wraps his arms around her he catches sight of Theseus walking out on the promontory. He is looking their way and nods in that spaceman's wink kind of way before continuing his walk, which says he will stop Dirk from being too inquisitive about what he and Alva are doing here.

Kylone pulls her very gently closer to start a caressing long kiss.

He has, finally, found his place in life.

ACKNOWLEDGEMENTS

So many people have helped me with *A Truth Beyond Full* that it is impossible to list all of them here. I am grateful to every single one of you for anything from a single insightful comment that made a difference to an intense critique following a full read through.

Special thanks go to Paul Evans for setting the exercise in our creative writing class that inspired *A Truth Beyond Full* and guiding me through the initial steps of its world-building. I owe a debt of gratitude for the patience of my fellow students who watched and constructively critiqued these struggles.

Pulling the novel together into a coherent whole was aided by the British Science Fiction Association's Orbits – work-shopping groups where we support each other to improve our fiction. Even at the end of this, I knew there were consistency issues. Gary Dalkin kindly stepped in to help identify them. All their help was much appreciated.

I can't end this without saying thank you to Peter and his team at Elsewhen Press for publishing *A Truth Beyond Full.*

ALSO FROM ELSEWHEN PRESS

The Sundering Chronicles by Mark Iles

I: Gardens of Earth

Imagine an alien life force that knows your deepest fear, and can use that against you.

Corporate greed supported by incompetent surveyors leads to the colonisation of a distant world, ominously dubbed 'Halloween', that turns out not to be uninhabited after all. The aliens, soon called Spooks by military units deployed to protect the colonists, can adopt the physical form of an opponent's deepest fear and then use it to kill them. The colony is massacred and as retaliation the orbiting human navy nuke the planet. In revenge, the Spooks invade Earth.

In a last-minute attempt to avert the war, Seethan Bodell, a marine combat pilot sent home from the front with PTSD, is given a top-secret research spacecraft, and a mission to travel into the past along with his co-pilot and secret lover Rose, to prevent the original landing on Halloween and stop the war from ever happening. But the mission goes wrong, causing a tragedy later known as The Sundering, decimating the world and tearing reality, while Seethan's ship is flung into the future. The Spooks win the war and claim ownership of Earth. He wakes, alone, in his ejector seat with no sign of either Rose or his vessel. When he realises that his technology no longer works, his desperation to find Rose becomes all the more urgent – her android body won't survive long in this new Earth.

ISBN: 9781911409953 (epub, kindle) / 9781911409854 (264pp paperback)

Visit bit.ly/GardensOfEarth

II: A Voice in the Darkness

A gateway and a changeling on a colony world, prompt a return to Earth to confront the aliens.

When children on the colony of Semillion go missing they return changed, the parents even claim they are not their offspring. Sherrif Andrews soon finds himself investigating the bizarre situation. What he discovers leads to him being recalled by the military and sent back to Earth, a place now quarantined and where colonial humans are forbidden to venture. The intention is to recruit ex-commando Seethan Bodell, who's living with the survivors of The Sundering and the mythological creatures that now inhabit the world.

Earth is still ruled with an iron fist by the alien Spooks, but there is something else going on behind the scenes, a new and deadly threat. To succeed, Andrews and Bodell need to call on that grand tapestry of inhabitants: the shapeshifters, elves, the ravening pack of werewolves that Seethan now belongs to, and even the dead; in the hope that it will be enough to prevent an escalating situation that could so easily lead to war.

ISBN: 9781915304575 (epub, kindle) / 9781915304476 (192pp paperback)

Visit bit.ly/AVoiceInTheDarkness

ABOUT ROSIE OLIVER

Rosie Oliver has been in love with science fiction ever since, as a teenager, she discovered a whole bookcase of yellow-covered Gollancz science fiction books in Chesterfield library in central England. It sent her on a world-spinning imaginary journey from the depths of Earth's oceans to multi-verses with varying time speeds, and beyond!

After obtaining a degree in mathematics at Oxford University and having a down to Earth career as an aeronautical engineer turned systems engineer, she can now devote her time to gardening, needlework, being a National Federation of Women's Institutes handicraft judge and writing science fiction.

She has had around forty of her short stories published (one ended up in the Best of British Science Fiction 2020 anthology) and been a Finalist in the Writers of the Future Contest. Her other varied science fictional activities included obtaining an MA in creative writing from Bath Spa University, being a co-editor of the *Distaff* anthology and blundering her way into being a minor contributor to a research paper on the northern lights. Recently, she has had her debut novel, *Edge of Existence, C.A.T. – the novel*, published by TWB Press. Yes, she loves cats, meat or robot AI, but especially the rascally ginger ones. Mrrooowwww!

Milton Keynes UK
Ingram Content Group UK Ltd.
UKHW032231021024
449145UK00001B/27

9 781915 304483